D1161387

WORKING

WITHDRAWN

3 1705 00166 8323

WORKING

MY LIFE AS A PROSTITUTE

DOLORES FRENCH

WITH LINDA LEE

STATE LIBRARY OF OHIO
SEO Regional Library
Caldwell, Ohio 43724

E. P. DUTTON   NEW YORK

Copyright © 1988 by Dolores French and Linda Lee
All rights reserved. Printed in the U.S.A.

No part of this publication may be reproduced or transmitted
in any form or by any means, electronic or mechanical, including
photocopy, recording, or any information storage and retrieval
system now known or to be invented, without permission in writing
from the publisher, except by a reviewer who wishes to quote
brief passages in connection with a review written for inclusion
in a magazine, newspaper, or broadcast.

Published in the United States by E. P. Dutton,
a division of NAL Penguin Inc.,
2 Park Avenue, New York, N.Y. 10016.

Published simultaneously in Canada
by Fitzhenry and Whiteside, Limited, Toronto.

Library of Congress Cataloging-in-Publication Data
French, Dolores.
Working: my life as a prostitute.
1. French, Dolores. 2. Prostitutes—United States—
Biography. I. Lee, Linda, 1947– . II. Title.
HQ144.F65 1988   306.7'42'0924   88-14953
ISBN: 0-525-24670-3

Designed by Nancy Etheredge

1 3 5 7 9 10 8 6 4 2

First Edition

Portions from the introduction and from
chapters 1, 2, 4, 7, 9, and 11 first appeared in
Cosmopolitan (August 1988).

A portion of chapter 5 first appeared in
Penthouse (August 1988).

*This book
is dedicated to
my parents
from whom
I inherited strength
and
learned courage.*

CONTENTS

ACKNOWLEDGMENTS

ix

AUTHOR'S NOTE

xi

INTRODUCTION

1

1

THIS LITTLE PIGGY WENT TO MARKET

3

2

THE FORTY-MINUTE HOUR

19

3

ALWAYS A BRIDE, NEVER A BRIDESMAID

47

4

GOOD GIRLS GO TO HEAVEN,
BAD GIRLS GO EVERYWHERE

65

5

PRIMERO NECESITO DINERO

78

6

IF THESE ARE TENS AND TWENTIES,
WE MUST STILL BE IN SAN JUAN

102

7

I'M FOR HIRE

135

8

THE MOST PUBLIC PROSTITUTE IN AMERICA

161

9

LADIES NEED NOT WEAR TIARAS

197

10

BETTER SAFE THAN SORRY

232

11

COPS AND ROBBERS

251

APPENDIX

281

ACKNOWLEDGMENTS

This book would not have been possible without the friendship, support, and encouragement of thousands of people in my life. Here I will thank just a few of them. If my parents had not tutored me after school every day, I might have never learned to read or write well enough even to keep notes, much less to write this book. Paul Krassner, who is the editor and publisher of the *Realist*, is also one of my closest friends. Without the encouragement of Sunny, there would be no adventures to write about. Every day that I worked on this book, I read at least a sentence, or a few paragraphs, written by my dear friend Rosemary Daniell; my copy of *Fatal Flowers* is ragged from being carried around the world. I am eternally grateful to Margo St. James, for pioneering prostitutes' rights in the United States. I appreciate the Honorable Andrew Young's appointing me to the Task Force on Prostitution and maintaining his support after my arrest. I appreciate John Preston's taking time from work on his own books to advise and console me throughout the writing of this book. Without the help of Berl Boykin and Becca Collins the final manuscript would never have gotten finished. I appreciate the enthusiasm, patience, and cooperation of Joyce Engelson, my editor at E. P. Dutton. I thank my agent, Wendy Lipkind, for holding this project together. Most of all I want to thank my husband, Michael Hauptman, for his patience, support, assistance, and love during the writing of *Working*.

I also want to thank: George Alexander, Marcie Alexander, Priscilla Alexander, Ursula Alexander, Yvonne Antoinette Huffman Alexander, Norma Jean Almodovar, Dr. Walter Anderson, Sydney Biddle Barrows, Buren Batson, René Beckloff, Perlie Biles, Renae Bishop, Jackie Boles, Julian Bond, Lizzie Borden, Candice Bottorff, Dr. David Bryant, Alex Kenagy Carson, Raines Carter, Robert Citronberg, Dr. Judith Cohen, Jay and Randy Cohen, Marvin and Sandy Cohen, Jerry Collins, Beth Coonan, Dolores Danska, Dr. Bill Darrow, Foy Devine, Diana, Maria Dolan, Lucy Draper, D. J. and Vickie, Kat Elliott, Ester, Louie Favorite, Brenda Fields, Larry Flynt, Rodger French, Lon Friend, Dr. Mark Gilson, Martha Wrens Gaines, Myha Hahn, Harold Halpern, Margie Pitts Hames, Lady Lynn Hampton, Jeffrey Hauptman, Rachel Hickerson, Al Horn, Tom Houck, Dr. Susan Hunker, Elizabeth Hunt, Geneva and Odas Huffman, Glenda Huffman, Jan, Jennette, Jennifer, Flo Kennedy, Melinda Langston, Carole Leigh aka Scarlet Harlot, Lori Martin, Bruce and Jackie Morris, Gale Mull, Michael Pattberg, Cassius Peak, Gail Pheterson, Mary Price, Sheila Rae, Eric Redd, Dr. Barbara Reighard, Rita, Robert, Gil Robison, Robert and Caren Rothstein, Margie Rushton, Toni Shifalo, Lake Sirmon, Barry Sonnenfeld, Mark Van Spix, Annie Sprinkle, Wendy Sylvester, Linda Thomas, Judge A. L. Thompson, Tita, Elaine Valentine, Veronica Vera, Rebecca Wackler, Judy Walkowitz, Andrew Wood, Major Vernon Worthy, Dr. Sharon Youngleson, Yvette, and all my working sisters and brothers.

AUTHOR'S NOTE

Many people suggested—and several customers, a couple of hookers, a cop, and a politician all asked—that my life story be cre-
atively reconstructed for publication. I've taken great pains to preserve the authenticity of my autobiography without endangering
or embarrassing anyone. All of the prostitutes' names, the mad-
ams' names, the agents' names, and the clients' names have been
changed, and all personal characteristics not relevant to the story
have been changed, with the following exceptions: Sunny, a prostitute, who asked that her real "work name" be used; Sydney Biddle Barrows, who has written about her own experiences, and Heuft,
who ran a whorehouse in Amsterdam. A few dates have been al-
tered and—for the protection of many people—the details of who
did what, where, and when have occasionally been adjusted. Even
so, in essence, my life and my account of The Life are intact.

—DOLORES FRENCH

WORKING

INTRODUCTION

Did it all start with I Love Lucy? *It was the summer of 1955; I was five years old, and on Mondays I got to stay up late. I sat on our scratchy sofa, snuggled against my mother, and waited, full of impatience, for the television event of the week:* I Love Lucy.

At five, I could identify with Lucy's tenacious attempts to take charge of her life. But I also knew I didn't want to grow up to be like her—to be a housewife, to be scolded and told what I could and couldn't do.

Ricky seemed to be a tyrant, an unreasonable nut always yelling, "Ai, yi, yi, yi, yi!" And Fred was a nincompoop. Yet, week after week, Lucy and Ethel had to trick those nitwits into something, like taking them along on a fishing trip or just giving them extra grocery money.

And I'll never forget the time that Ethel had to beg Fred to let her take driving lessons.

But now, one night, there was something unusual: a beautiful guest star, draped in a shimmering silver evening gown, stroking the tails of her fox stole over Fred's bald head. "She must have been poured into that dress," my mom muttered. She sounded impressed.

Even my child's eyes could see that there was a difference between this woman's lot in life and Ethel's and Lucy's. This glamorous lady radiated a sense of confidence and independence, as if she didn't have to scheme or to beg anyone to get what she wanted. And Ricky and Fred were falling all over her, lighting her cigarette, giving her a seat.

Lucy and Ethel, on the other hand, didn't seem to like her. "Why are they being so mean to her?" I asked my mom.

"Shhhh." She waved her hand to quiet me. Then she whispered, "They think she's a . . . call girl."

I kicked my Donald Duck slippers against the couch and watched the flickering black-and-white screen. Then I whispered back, "What's that?"

She looked at me and hesitated for a moment. "It's a woman who . . . entertains men for money," she said, choosing her words carefully.

"Oh."

From what I had seen in my short life, women were always trying to entertain men. This woman simply got paid for it. In my mind, she had picked a profession that should be admired, like becoming a doctor or a lawyer. She got to wear glamorous clothes that sparkled and swirled around her when she moved. And she didn't have to make excuses about what she was doing or where she was going or with whom, or why she wanted money. Lucy and Ethel could have picked up a few pointers from that woman.

"That's what I'm going to be when I grow up," I announced.

"Oh, hush!" my shocked mother said. "You don't even know what that means."

I insisted, "Yes, I do."

Of course my mother, a practicing Southern Baptist, tried to make it clear to me that night that proper little girls didn't aspire to become call girls. But in 1955, I already knew that proper young ladies didn't aspire to be doctors or lawyers either.

1

THIS LITTLE PIGGY WENT TO MARKET

Your whore is for every rascal, but your courtesan is for your courtier.
—ANONYMOUS ENGLISH WRITER,
   1607

It was twenty-two years, one sister, three dogs, five colleges, two husbands, three careers, and one hell of a good time later. It was 1978, and I was twenty-seven years old, when I finally got around to pursuing my chosen career.

To be perfectly honest, I had all but given up the idea of becoming a glamorous, self-confident, financially independent woman who entertained men for money. I had worked in telephone sales, as an art director, as a director of public relations, and as a census taker. I had marched for civil rights and the ERA and against the war in Southeast Asia. I had worked on political campaigns for dogcatchers and presidents. I was a feminist and concerned about the way people in the Midtown area of Atlanta, Georgia, were always trying to throw prostitutes out of the neighborhood. And I had written away for copies of Margo St. James's *Coyote Howls*, a publication by and about prostitutes, and for research by two academics, Jennifer James and Jackie Bowles, who had written about prostitution. That was as close as I'd gotten to the subject.

Except for *Coyote Howls*, my understanding of prostitution was based on either academic theory or Hollywood movies. I was soon to see that research projects by respectable Ph.D.s were based on studies so small their conclusions amounted to little more than lofty opinions. When I began working as a prostitute, I saw few of the Hollywood stereotypes of working women: emaciated models with surgically sculpted bodies, cast as high-class call girls and down-on-their-luck drug-addicted streetwalkers.

I had a job as an administrator and fund-raiser for a small radio station in Atlanta. My life wasn't a mess, but it wasn't that perfect either.

I loved working at the station, but after a few years my job had become pretty boring. Half of my time was spent hiring and firing personnel—both paid and unpaid. (A lot of people volunteered to work at the radio station, just to *be* there.) The other half of my time was spent developing and coordinating fund-raising activities, getting the station out of the red and into, if not the black, at least the gray.

The latter was a fairly unrewarding job. Few people thought that fund-raising was noble or even honorable. Their attitude was that it was a dirty job, and someone had to do it, but preferably not them. (Fund-raising was not on a par with, say, producing a documentary on migrant workers from Guatemala.) Part of me enjoyed the challenge of doing something that was inherently so uninteresting. On a purely professional level, I became a big fan of the right-wing Republican fund-raiser Richard Viguerie, who really knew how to turn out the bucks. Using some of his techniques, I turned the radio station around.

That, however, led to more fund-raising jobs. (Motto: Never do something well that you do not want to do at all; you may be asked to do it again.) I got to fly around the country, dropping in on one foundering or decrepit station after another and giving them advice. Because I was good at my job—and because I asked the people who worked in the stations for their ideas and involved them at every turn—by the time I left, I would hear rumblings of: That was easy! We didn't need her at all! Why, we did it ourselves!

It was, in other words, not very satisfying. It was not in any way related to painting or drawing or even graphic design, my real interests.

We had the usual mix of employees at our Atlanta station: gays, blacks, a lot of women, a few egocentric deejays—your usual middle-class straight guys—and one or two people who seemed to be working there by accident.

And then there was Stephanie, the station's general production manager. The two of us looked strikingly alike. Nearly everyone either mistook one of us for the other or was sure we were sisters. If Loni Anderson's body and mine had merged during a freak scientific experiment, à la *The Fly*, something like Stephanie might have been the result.

Her breasts were a little bigger than mine; her waist and hips were a little smaller. Stephanie's hair was longer than mine, thicker and prettier. But I had longer nails and smaller, prettier hands. Her eyes were definitely Liz Taylor blue; mine were indefinitely blue or green or gray.

But then there was the matter of style. Stephanie wore high heels and I wore cowboy boots. I wore Levi's jeans; she wore designer jeans. She wore stockings and I wore socks.

Since Stephanie had been hired a few weeks before me, I didn't know at first how someone wearing emerald earrings and a diamond engagement ring fit in at our small station. I heard she was working on her master's degree in political science. As I soon found out, she was also a prostitute.

Office gossip being what it is, I heard all about Stephanie and her mother. It seems they were in the same business—the business of selling Stephanie.

Stephanie was normally self-confident and worldly—except when she was on the phone with her mother, who was eager to see Stephanie married, as often as possible. Then it was "Yes, Mommy" and "No, Mommy," in a little girl's voice. Stephanie sometimes acquiesced to her mother's proposed marriages, but when she did, it was with all the cunning and compassion of a swampland real-estate agent. Her philosophy was "There's a lot of money to be made by marrying pathetically desperate men." She explained to me that she never actually lived with the guys she married. Her mom saw to it that an agreement was made with the prospective husbands that Stephanie would live at home—with her mother—until she was out of college. The husbands, of course, footed the bills for their rent and Stephanie's tuition.

When she told me that I blurted, "You are the greediest bitch I've ever met." She became a little, shall we say, insulted, and I tried to pretend I had meant it as a joke. She said, "But I'm only giving everyone exactly what they want and deserve."

Stephanie saw men not as people but as prey. And she was not at all shy about revealing this opinion to co-workers, which delighted our lesbian station manager.

One day, after work, she explained to me how she flushed out society's saddest souls. We were at happy hour in a dark, dingy, and depressing motel bar—the kind of place that serves tepid deep-fried hors d'oeuvres and Bloody Marys made with tomato soup. Stephanie looked around the room and declared: "Any man in here who can coordinate a shirt and suit is a candidate for marriage." Then, switching her tone suddenly, she announced, "It was right here that I met my fiancé."

I hadn't seen him coming, but she had. On cue, he slid in beside her on the vinyl bench. "Snuck up on ya, darlin', din't I?" he asked, before offering her a slobbery kiss. He was a homely, skinny, ignorant, sickly, neurotic man who had a nervous twitch.

I was amazed, amused, and horrified—I felt toward her about the same way I feel about TV evangelists: amazed that they can get away with it and horrified that they do. The way Stephanie led her life was comparable to melodrama. And here it was sitting right acrosss the Formica cocktail table from me.

Even as she sat drinking tomato-soup Bloody Marys with me and her fiancé that night, Stephanie was already married. Her mother, at the same time, was cooking up another marriage to a rich lawyer whose family belonged to their country club.

It had never occurred to me that anyone lived this way. I said as much to Stephanie, and she answered: "It isn't illegal, you know, to marry people for their money. I mean, I never even have to have sex with them."

"How can you not have sex with them?" I wondered.

"I don't stay married that long." Stephanie explained that her mother once scheduled a tonsillectomy for her on her wedding day. "Right after the reception, we loaded the presents into our station wagon, and then my mom announced that I was ill, and the next thing you know, I was in the hospital." By the time she was ready to come out of the hospital, her mother was busy getting that marriage annulled.

What Stephanie's mother did not know was that Stephanie, bored with simply marrying a bunch of pathetic losers, was also answering ads in the local newspapers and working as a prostitute. She told her mom that she needed a separate apartment, so she could study. In fact, she used the apartment as a staging area to work as a call girl. (Her mother controlled all the money she made from marrying men; Stephanie, in turn, felt she wanted to earn some money for herself.) She confided to me that she had banned her mother from her apartment. "I tell her it breaks my concentration to have her around, even to have her call me there."

So that was Stephanie: marrying men she didn't have sex with—for their money—and having sex with men she didn't marry—for *their* money. And Freud asked, "What do women want?"

One day, before she went home from work, Stephanie stopped by my office to tell me that she had made a "date" to see a guy the next day and that she wouldn't be able to keep it. She had a dentist's appointment. "You wouldn't like to go in my place, would you?" she asked. After all, she said, she had only spoken to the man on the telephone. She hadn't seen him in person and he hadn't seen her. All he knew about her was her height, her hair color, and her measurements.

"The money will be good. Seventy-five dollars for an hour, and he'll never know it's not me," she said, guilelessly. I was making $187.93 a week, after taxes.

I was not at all concerned about the idea that I might be breaking the law by committing an act of prostitution. People of my generation had learned a certain amount of contempt for laws, starting with those that made marijuana use illegal. As far as I was concerned there should have been laws forbidding poverty, or people wearing prints with plaids, but not laws forbidding a woman to accept money from a man for her company.

Instead I worried that it wouldn't be honorable to tell a man that I was Stephanie just because I looked like her. And, even though I had always been curious about what it would be like to get money for sex, I wasn't sure I was ready for it.

"Oh, I'd have to lose weight," was the first thing that came out of my mouth. I was carrying twenty extra pounds and, as far as I was concerned, that disqualified me from charging for sex.

"Don't be silly," Stephanie said. "You look great. Men really like women to have a little something to them."

So I told her I would think about it. But I said to her, "I'm not really sure I'd know what to do."

"No problem," she said. "I'll tell you everything you need to know tomorrow—if you decide to do it." And out the door she went.

That night I lay in bed, thinking about what it would be like to walk into a strange room the next day and have sex with a strange man, for money. I had already slept with a number of men I hadn't cared for, for the company or the pleasure or as a favor or just because we were both there. What was so different about this? I wondered. The money, of course, the "great equalizer," as someone called it.

My thoughts went back to when I was thirteen, and struggling with the idea of giving up my virginity. (And that was indeed the way I had been socialized to think about it.)

The message from my parents, my teachers, the church, was clear: Hold on to virginity, at all costs, until Prince Charming comes along. But when I looked around my neighborhood at the Cinderellas who had held on to their virginity, women who had waited for their Prince Charmings, who should have been wonderfully happy—like the women I saw on TV commercials—I saw instead women bulging with beer, burgers, and bawling babies, Cinderellas with tired faces and their hair cranked up in bobby pins or brush rollers for some exciting night at the bowling alley. The diamond solitaires were dingy with detergent residue; it didn't seem like much of a reward for waiting.

And the men these women had saved themselves for, well, let's just say there were a lot of frogs out there.

Since it didn't look too promising to wait, and since I was burning to find out what sex was like, and why people thought it was so important, at thirteen I gave up my virginity—threw it away, actually. (I was glad to be rid of it because I was sure I didn't want to marry a man who prized virginity.)

Of course later, in the eyes of society, I redeemed myself. I married: at nineteen to a man I loved but couldn't live with, then later to a man I could live with but didn't love. They were no Prince Charmings but they certainly were decent, honorable, and hardworking frogs.

A few months back I'd had a relatively boring brush with death.

During an emergency operation for appendicitis, the surgeon had discovered instead that a softball-sized ovarian cyst had ruptured. The couple of weeks I spent recuperating in the hospital and a few more at home gave me plenty of time to contemplate my life and my death. For the first time I felt regret. Not for anything I had done, rather for all the things I hadn't done. I regretted that I had never gone hang gliding. I regretted not doing more to contribute to the quality of other people's lives. I regretted never going to Europe, never seeing the Louvre, the ceiling of the Sistine Chapel, Gaudí's architecture in Spain, van Gogh's collected work in Amsterdam. I regretted never becoming that glamorous, self-confident, financially independent woman who entertained men for money.

Here I was at twenty-seven suddenly realizing how immediately life could end. Having a prestigious, low-paying job, working part-time on political campaigns, having wonderful parents and good friends, learning to parachute, developing my painting and drawing skills were fine. But all this didn't make up for what I hadn't done, experiences I hadn't had. Lying in that hospital bed, I decided to grab every appealing opportunity that came along and to experience as much about living as possible. Stephanie seemed to be offering one of those opportunities.

I thought: If I go see Stephanie's client tomorrow, then at least I'll know what it's like to be a prostitute. That seemed worthwhile. And I was eager to know what someone like Stephanie felt when she walked into that room. Was it shameful or degrading? Or would it be sexually exhilarating?

I was about to turn a corner. I was going to charge for sex, and I was already thinking about how I would spend the money.

After tomorrow, I thought, no one will ever be able to use the word *whore* against me. After tomorrow, it will no longer be the worst curse someone could throw at me, it will simply be a statement of fact. Maybe it would be worth doing, I thought, just to take the sting out of that word.

He had the smallest penis I have ever seen before or since. He was well over six feet tall. His cock in a full erection was about the size of my thumb from the knuckle down. I wondered, Is this the kind of man who hires prostitutes? There was so little there, why bother? While I undressed, he took his two fingers and masturbated, like someone playing with dollhouse furniture. Stephanie had told me a few things about what I should do when I got there, but she hadn't told me anything about this. She hadn't seen him before, so who would have dreamed that something like this would, so to speak, come up.

He made a comment about it being kind of small. And I said, "Yes, it is." There was no way I could pretend otherwise.

He wanted to have intercourse, if you could call it that. (I think there should be some regulation about what can be considered intercourse. This was more like bumping into someone in the elevator.) But he was my first client, and I didn't want to commit a faux pas by complaining. He was pleasant—I guessed anyone with a dick that small is going to be either very pleasant or an ax murderer. The way I figured it, it made sense to get paid to have sex with a man with a penis that small, because there was no possibility of a woman getting any sexual pleasure out of it.

It was over with quickly, and I got dressed. He was delighted to give me money—seventy-five dollars plus a ten-dollar tip, nearly half my weekly salary.

That man treated me with more respect than I had gotten in most other occupations, and he paid me a lot closer to what my time and my mind were worth. He paid me with a smile on his face . . . and I was proud to have been able to help him.

Fortunately for my career as a prostitute, there was a woman named Elaine working at the radio station. All I knew about Elaine, an elegant woman who looked a few years older than me, was that she had come from Chicago and, I heard, was living off of a trust fund. In any case, she had plenty of time to work on political campaigns and to work at the radio station part-time.

Elaine knew about my experience with the dickless wonder. (By now everyone in the office knew. Stephanie was hardly discreet.) Elaine came up to me and said, in her reserved but kindly way, "I hope you're not going to get involved with any more of Stephanie's 'boyfriends.' "

"Well, to tell you the truth, I thought maybe I could learn something from her," I said.

"Dolores," Elaine said, giving me a level look, "why don't you come over to my place tomorrow night? I think we should talk."

I expected that Elaine would deliver one of those older-but-wiser kind of talks: tell me how it was OK to sow my wild oats once, but that if I did it a second time, or made a habit out of it, I was going to get myself into trouble. But I had never been invited to her apartment before, I liked her, and I figured I might as well hear what she had to say.

When I arrived, there were logs burning in the fireplace and a bottle of wine chilling in a silver ice bucket. A couple of electric lights illuminated portraits of her grandparents and a Salvador Dalí lithograph. A freestanding candelabrum lit the foyer, and I could see more candles glowing in her bedroom. One room had a floral scent, the next herbal. There were huge satin and brocade pillows on the Oriental rug in the living room. I noticed her phone because it was so ostentatious—alabaster and brass. Next to it was, I swear, an ostrich-plume pen-and-paper set.

Central to the living room was an antique velvet fainting couch, and on it sat Elaine, dressed in ivory silk Japanese lounging pajamas and wearing a toe ring on the middle digit of her left foot.

This is . . . something, I thought. Probably class, but of a kind I had never seen before. Maybe this is the way people live up north, I thought. I was originally from Kentucky. What did I know about Chicago elegance?

Elaine said: "How do you like these things? I picked most of them up from yard sales. And I made the pillows myself, filled them with stuffing from my kids' sleeping bags."

"Big sleeping bags," I said.

"Lots of kids." She laughed.

I was surprised. "I didn't know you had any."

"Five, all grown, thank God."

"Five grown?" I asked. "How old are you?"

We went through the how-old-do-I-look routine, and then she admitted she was forty-nine.

Forty-nine? How was that possible? I thought she was—at most—thirty-two, and here she was telling me about being a divorced grandmother.

She handed me a glass of wine and settled herself on the couch: olive skin, off-white pajamas and black, black hair, vibrant red lipstick and nails—all set off against the berry-wine velvet. "Look," she said, "I have something to tell you. Nobody knows about this except my customers and a friend who's a cabdriver, but I'm a courtesan."

A courtesan. What the hell was that? I knew it had something to do with sex, but what?

She told me the history of the word. A courtesan had originally been a court mistress, she said, a companion to the royal. A courtesan conducted herself as a public lady, while the legal wife stayed in the royal apartments to bear and raise children. Elaine explained that, as the centuries rolled by, a courtesan's job became less formal and more of a paid affair. She told me that she was not a call girl, like Stephanie. "A call girl is available for one night, or by the hour," she said, making it clear she did not approve of Stephanie or her work habits. "I have an ongoing relationship with my clients."

A courtesan, she said, keeps up the fantasy that she and the man share a life together, albeit a secret one. A courtesan knows all about a man's family, his job, what kind of wine he drinks, what books he reads. "There are lots of women working as courtesans, right here in Atlanta," she said.

I was amazed. What she was describing was completely different from what Stephanie was doing, more sophisticated . . . and she wasn't trying to marry the men for their money.

I had a feeling that Elaine was the person I had been waiting for, someone who could teach me the fine points of prostitution. If anyone knew the upper-end scale of prostitution, it was Elaine. She was the picture of elegance. She took care of her hair and skin. She went jogging every day and had a body the envy of a twenty-seven-year-old: me. She had not lost her dignity, as some sociologists claimed was inevitable. Although she was discreet, she was proud of what she did.

"But how do you find . . . um . . ." I trailed off, not even sure what to call a man who pays for a courtesan.

"Referrals," she interjected, making it sound like she was running a doctor's office. "And I run ads in the newspaper."

"But isn't that dangerous? I mean, how do you know they're OK?"

"Oh, I screen everybody first, on the telephone. If they seem OK, I have them meet me somewhere for coffee or tennis."

This was all still something of a shock. I mean, it was one thing for me to consider being a prostitute. It was one thing to think of Stephanie as a call girl. But Elaine? I began to wonder how many "working" women there were.

She explained that she charged sixty dollars an hour for her time or made some other arrangement for compensation. One man bought a car for her, and in return she agreed to see him four times a month for three years.

I asked her how she'd gotten started, and she told me she had been a housewife in Lake Forest, Illinois. Her husband had been an executive in the city, and she had stayed home to raise their kids. She had wanted to leave for a long time, she said, but she had no marketable skills, except being a secretary, and that wouldn't support five children. One day, after years of marriage, she simply packed a small bag and left a note telling her husband where to find the car. (She said she didn't want to leave the marriage with anything more than she'd started with, nor did she want to give him an excuse to come after her, or a way to trace her.) Then she left the car at a rest area along the interstate and found a trucker who gave her a ride. She simply said to him, "I'll go wherever you're headed," and off she went. She was thirty-five.

The truck driver gave her a ride as far as Atlanta, and that's where she ended up. "I figured it was as good a place as any," she said. After the truck driver found out she didn't have any money with her or a job, he offered her cash in exchange for sex.

"I was pretty naive at the time," she said. "I never for a moment thought it was prostitution. That was my first job—or my millionth, depending on how you look at my marriage."

Elaine barely had enough money to get a room in a cheap motel. To support herself, she started working as a waitress. Since she was good-looking, and had a great body, someone at the restaurant suggested that, if she really wanted to make money, she get a job in a nearby strip club. By that time, Elaine felt she was too far into it to go back to her husband. "I was struggling to survive, but it was still better than living with him." On the other hand, she hated working in the strip club. It was too trashy for a woman from Lake Forest, Illinois, she said. A lot of guys offered her money to go to bed with them, but she was afraid of being arrested. She said she wanted to keep her record clean so she could get custody of her kids someday.

Still, she was sleeping around a lot and not getting any money for it. She finally figured out she would be better off financially if she sold sex directly and quit her job as a stripper. She went from a sleazy motel to a bad apartment and then to a better apartment. By using her clients as references, she got a job as a secretary and a lease on the apartment she was now living in.

Two of her younger kids moved down with her, and she supported them too. She saw clients when her kids were in school. As far as her kids knew, she was making a living working at the radio station.

When men see a courtesan, she said, it's because they want

an ongoing relationship. A lot of men didn't like to think of Elaine as seeing anyone else; she told each one of those guys that he was the only one. "But they're not stupid. They know that's not really the case. They just like to hear it. The truth is: They know it's a business and they know I'm the best. They're willing to share me."

As far as Elaine was concerned, it was comparable to having several paid, ongoing affairs.

When the shock wore off—not the shock of what she was doing, but the shock that someone like Elaine was doing it—I told her I thought it was great. I felt this was something I had been waiting for all my life. "Do you think I could learn to do it too?" I asked. "Would you train me?"

With my first client, I had felt so awkward. If I'm going to become a prostitute, I thought, I need to lose weight. I need to learn the trade. I need to learn how to handle the unexpected. What I needed was training and coaching. I decided that Elaine, who had her life so much together, was the one who could teach me.

She said she'd think it over.

A few days later, Elaine and I came to an agreement. She would teach me everything she knew about the business, and she would pass some clients on to me. In return, I would work out of her apartment and pay her fifteen dollars per person.

I mentioned what I was doing to a couple of close friends. They were amused more than shocked. One thought it was great. "It's a harebrained idea," another friend said. "A lark, like when you took up skydiving." This person figured that, if he just let me amuse myself, I would eventually settle down and take life seriously. He felt quite sincerely that prostitution was not something I would do forever, that at age twenty-seven I was nearly too old to begin.

Before she started training me, Elaine told me to read Xaviera Hollander's *The Happy Hooker*. She said that a lot of it was trash, but that some of it was very accurate: how Xaviera had set up her own business, how she looked at the job, how she enjoyed the work. Xaviera thought it was important for a prostitute not to be whorish. Her hands were to be nicely manicured. She was supposed to dress in the ways that men fantasize about but not look cheap or tacky. The idea was to attract better clients and not get arrested.

"Xaviera does a good job of describing what the business is like," Elaine said. "If you enjoy sex, it affords you the opportunity to have a lot of sex. And if you don't enjoy sex, at least you're being paid."

Elaine and I talked for six hours the first training session. We then met almost daily over a three-week period.

Part of the time was spent discussing our agreement, especially how we would handle Elaine's apartment. She was living there; I could use it during the days to entertain guests. If either of us needed to be alone in the apartment, we would let the other know a day in advance. If we both scheduled appointments for the same time, whoever scheduled the apartment first had first option to use it. The agreement was all written down, but I didn't keep a copy at her place or at home because I was afraid it could have been used against us in court.

The agreement covered things like forwarding calls on the telephone, what condition the bedrooms were supposed to be in, that Elaine was supposed to provide fresh sheets every morning. She had a closet full of beautiful sheets, some satin, a set of Porthault, an antique set from 1910, a few pairs of Irish linens, and some flannel sheets, which were sexy in their own way.

Elaine had a typical modern two-bedroom apartment, in a two-story complex. There were more hookers working there, she said, than anywhere else in Atlanta. The great advantage was that it was close to the moneyed North Side. Clients could stop by on their way home to the suburbs, yet it was close enough to Midtown for them to breeze by during lunch.

One theory Elaine had was that her premises should be nicer than her clients' homes. Her apartment was decorated in a way that, no matter how wealthy the clients were, this was better, with original art, expensive linens. "When you're serving anything," she said, "it needs to be served in the nicest possible way: linen, lace, crystal, silver." It was almost like geisha training. "If you can only afford two Waterford crystal glasses, have two," she said. "Have two bone china cups and saucers. Get a matching plate and a matching bowl, and a little salad plate. You don't have to have an entire set of the best silver, just two place settings and two spanking-white linen napkins." Her towels were very expensive. And she felt the apartment had to smell wonderful, so as soon as the client walked in the door, he felt as if he ought to be paying lots of money, just to be there. She had an assortment of men's colognes, and she encouraged men to have a shower after sex. She wanted to make sure they didn't go off smelling like they had just been in bed with someone, whether they were going home to their wives or just back to the office.

Elaine said, "You have to have the very best lingerie, nothing trashy. Nothing cheaper than Lily of France. It's got to be better than their wives' or their girlfriends'. You won't need any Frederick's of Hollywood, except for certain clients. There are some people who want you to get dressed up in cheap, tacky outfits," Elaine added, "but they need to understand it's just playing and that you normally wear better things. That you are worldly, sophisticated, full of charm."

She told me that we never asked for payment in advance, and she told me never to touch the money, just to have the client leave it on the bureau. She believed that if you didn't take money in the man's presence, you were safe. (This was based on the idea that a vice cop couldn't have sex with a prostitute and that hand-to-hand passing of money was what got prostitutes convicted—neither of which is true.) She felt that the atmosphere she had created was so genteel and gracious, no one would consider not paying—or not paying enough.

She also told me that we never called clients johns or tricks. Between the two of us, we called them clients, customers, jobs, or dates. To their faces we always referred to them as friends.

But Elaine warned me not to think of them as friends. "Don't ever forget that this is a business," she said. "These men are not lovers, they are not friends, they are clients. And don't even consider getting personally involved," she warned. "Then, after you do get personally involved with one or two, you can go back to remembering, 'Never get personally involved.'"

She was always very proper. As I worked and learned things, she drilled into my head that I had to maintain the right perspective.

"You have to feel honorable about the service you're providing," she said. "Most of these clients don't want to feel they're seeing a professional prostitute. They would like to think of you as a lover or girlfriend, but because they can't give you all the things a woman might honorably expect—like love, devotion, children—they are going to feel they have to compensate you with money."

Elaine was convinced that it was stupid and unenlightened for women to have affairs with married men and *not* get paid. Any woman who is not getting paid is being duped by middle-American morality, she said. In one way these women were flaunting middle-class morals by having the affair, but they were afraid of taking money for it.

If women were happy with the affair, fine, she said. "But a lot of single women feel rage and frustration over their situation. That's when women start making demands like 'Leave your wife, or at least spend Christmas, my birthday, or New Year's Eve with me.'

"That happens because the relationship is so unequal. What makes it equal is a woman getting paid. As long as you're getting paid, you're not looking for something more the next time to make up for what you didn't get this time. There comes a point in almost every sexual relationship where one person is obviously getting more out of the exchange than the other, and the one who's getting more is usually the man."

She went on to talk about the typical unpaid affair: The man, at first, brings presents—flowers, perfume, books, jewelry, clothes. He takes her out to movies and theater and restaurants. Then he starts dropping by on his lunch hour. After he feels he's established himself, his presents start being for himself: wine, lingerie, panties, lubricants, sex toys.

"It would be so much simpler if women just came right out and asked for money," Elaine said.

And as for the wives of these married men, Elaine thought they would much prefer that their husbands see a clean, expert prostitute than that they have an affair with a woman who would either be sexually indiscriminate or eventually demand they get a divorce.

Elaine told me that she charged sixty dollars for a one-hour session. Because the person I had seen before—Stephanie's client—had paid me seventy-five dollars, I asked her why we didn't raise our prices. She said the going price was sixty dollars, and she didn't want me to charge a different amount than she did. I said, "How about if I charge seventy-five dollars? And if they ask why, I'll tell the truth. That you take care of the sheets and the towels and so on and I pay you?" She thought about it and agreed.

Elaine got her clients by advertising in the personals column of a weekly publication, *Creative Loafing,* and in monthlies like *Singles Magazine.* She would run surrealist ads like "White roses, red wine, satin sheets, Lago Maggiore, Puccini, Monet, artichokes," and then a PO box number. They sounded like something written by Salvador Dalí: "I'm a clock that has never kept the right time."

Not very many clients actually believed these ads were placed by someone looking for a boyfriend. As simple as her ads were—without anything overtly sexy, without a mention of her measurements, even her hair color—men for the most part assumed she was offering paid sex. (That proved to me that it doesn't matter how you go about selling sex. Men expect sex almost everywhere and, often enough, they find it.)

Most prostitutes ran ads that were a little more obvious than Elaine's. They described themselves as models and actresses and requested that the gentleman be "generous." Eventually the magazines put a stop to personal ads using the word *generous*. Then all the prostitutes switched to *financially secure*. Pretty soon the magazines banned that too. Finally it got so that you couldn't say anything about the man's financial position. *Discreet* became the key word in the ads. Then *discreet* got eighty-sixed.

We got out a pad and pencil and wrote my first ad. "We've got to think of your best points, what makes you different," Elaine said. Since I never went out in the sun, I thought it was worth mentioning that I had white, white skin. Atlanta is warm and sunny; almost everyone has a tan. My white skin made me different. Everything in the world is appealing to someone, I figured. My ad was a pretty fair description of what I had to offer: "Redhead, green eyes, 27 years old, 38-28-39, light complexion, no bathing suit marks, no freckles, 5'5½". Seeks generous gentleman for ongoing relationship."

After I wrote my first ad and sent it off to the newspaper, a terrible thought occurred to me. "Elaine, what if I don't get any letters?"

She looked at me askance, as if I hadn't heard anything she had been teaching me. "Don't be ridiculous," she said.

THE FORTY-MINUTE HOUR

The prostitute appeals by her fresh and natural coarseness, her frank familiarity with the crudest facts of life; and so lifts her customer for a moment out of the withering atmosphere of artificial thought and unreal sentiment in which so many civilized persons are compelled to spend the greater part of their lives.
—HAVELOCK ELLIS,
The Psychology of Sex, 1910

Since it would be a few weeks before I started getting answers to my ad, Elaine suggested that I slip into the profession by seeing one of her regular clients. Tyler, she explained, "loves a little variety. He likes to see new women. He's a perfect gentleman," she said. "He's gracious. A very nice man. A nuclear power plant PR executive."

"He does public relations for nuclear power plants?" I asked. "What am I coming to?" After all my years of social consciousness, of picketing and fighting environmental polluters, now I was going to provide sexual services for someone who glorified nuclear power plants?

"Tyler understands he's not paying top dollar," Elaine said, "and he understands what top dollar is. He doesn't demand or desire any more than what he's paying for. He's very quick. The sexual part won't take more than four or five minutes."

So I saw Tyler. In retrospect, I realize why Elaine wanted me to see him early in my career. Tyler made me understand that I could get beyond personal bias, that as a prostitute I would have to deal with people as they were, and consider the possibility of mutual gain. Before I became a hooker, I wouldn't have given any pronuclear person the time of day. (I have to admit, some part of me still might not.) But if he was a client, I would be willing to get to know more about him and to accept him as a person.

Elaine helped me get ready. I still have the first piece of lingerie she gave me: a black silk teddy. I borrowed a sheer lace floor-length dressing gown from her. I was to meet Tyler at the door wearing that, and a pair of marabou high-heeled slippers I got on sale at a J. C. Penney outlet up the street from her apartment. She fluffed up my hair, took a close look at my makeup, and pronounced me ready.

"Tyler's just going to love you," she said, and left me to my own devices.

When the bell rang, I tried to arrange myself and not be nervous, but I was. I was lucky that Tyler knew the apartment as well as, or better than, I did. He came in the door, gave me a smile, and proceeded directly to the hall closet, where he hung up his suit coat. Then he suggested we have a glass of wine. Over our wine, Tyler told me that he had kids he loved dearly and was putting through college. "I can't spend a lot of money on women right now," he said, apologetically. "I've got to buy one of my kids a car. It's gotten so that I can't afford to pay for hotel rooms. What's best for me is if the young lady comes directly to my office. I've got a big private office and a sofa bed," he said. He confided that, if the young lady made an office call, he bought a new set of sheets for the sofa bed and gave them to her when she left—as a little memento of their afternoon together. "Even a forty-dollar pair of sheets is cheaper than a hotel room," he said. "And that way we're both ahead."

Tyler, as I discovered, wasn't corny or silly or creepy or out of touch with reality or awkward. He knew how to act. So I said to him, as he was undressing, "How could you do PR for nuclear energy?" He said, "Somebody has to do it. I try to take into consideration what the power plant wants versus what the impact will be. I think I can have some humanitarian influence. Probably more than if I—or you—stood outside carrying a picket sign."

Sex with Tyler was unremarkable in that it was exactly what you would expect, or at least what I had expected: that he was extremely normal. His penis wasn't particularly large or small and it was, typically, circumcised. All he was interested in was fellatio, and he was quick and businesslike. If I could have taken an orgasm out of a display case, given it to him in a paper bag, and said "Have a nice day," I think he would have been just as happy. He treated the whole encounter as if I had sold him a nice pair of gloves.

Elaine failed to mention to me that Tyler had a withered leg, but to tell the truth I didn't notice it until he was putting his pants back on.

He paid me, and I paid Elaine her fifteen dollars. We were in business.

A week later, on my way to work at the radio station, I went to the post office and hauled away about thirty letters. There were more letters waiting for me the next day and the day after that. For weeks the letters arrived: dignified business envelopes—some of them from out of town—odd stationery, cheap stationery, handwritten addresses; some in the shaky writing of old men.

I sat on my bed at home and pored over the letters, completely confused about what I was supposed to be looking for. Then I called Elaine and said, "How do I know which ones to answer?"

She suggested I bring the letters to her house, where we could go over them together. She went over them and *showed* me what to look for. If the man didn't use English appropriately, for instance, if he didn't come up to upper-middle-class standards, he was definitely out. Elaine said, "You're looking for people with money. If they can't write a decent sentence, they don't have enough money." She especially scrutinized people under thirty and forty, because they were not good bets as clients. There were more chances of something being wrong with them, including the fact they might be vice officers. Elaine's rule: Suspect everyone of being a vice officer, which I considered rather strange since she smoked dope with almost all her clients—she liked it, and she also thought it made them easier to deal with. Some of them were aging hippies who had become pretty straight businessmen, and for them this was a chance to return to their youth.

So when we read these letters, we were trying to weed out kooks and cops. Anyone who sent photographs of himself in the nude—and didn't have extraordinary justification—was automatically out. Anybody who would be so tasteless as to send a stranger nude Polaroids, anybody who would talk about what a great cock he had, or anyone who saw himself as God's gift to women was out. Elaine explained all these things to me looking over the top of her reading glasses, like she was my mother or grandmother and best friend rolled into one. She felt that she was passing on this lore to someone who could use it and who would someday pass it on again.

Spelling wasn't as important as good grammar, she informed me. "John Kennedy couldn't spell, and he would have been a good client." The ideal letters were from people who explained where they worked or were retired and who gave a phone number and, preferably, an address. We wanted to hear from people who told us about their jobs, themselves, their lives and who explained what they were looking for in a polite, discreet manner. Saying they were married was good. Working downtown was good. Living in the suburbs and working downtown was even better.

After she showed me what to look for in the letters—and before I interviewed my first respondent—Elaine had me listen in while she screened people on the telephone. She impressed upon me that the most important thing in the initial call was to give as little information as possible while getting as much as possible. "Never forget," she said, "that we are the only vulnerable parties here."

Usually, she said, if a man wanted her to call his office, he would use a code in the letter. He'd write, "Say you're Nancy Huntington" or "John Hopkins's secretary" or "Say you're Mrs. Klemmer from Delta Airlines." "If I'm not there, tell my secretary you'll call back." Elaine said that any man using a code showed lucidity. If he gave no code, she simply announced to the secretary that she was a personal friend.

When Elaine made those calls, she was seductive and alluring. She purred, "I got your letter." Then she went into some kind of wonderfulness: "You have the most beautiful, exciting handwriting I've ever seen." If she'd had the letter laying around for two months, she might have said, "I just got back in town this morning and stopped by the post office. As soon as I saw the yellow pansies on the envelope, I had to call you. I haven't even unpacked."

She tried to pick up on something he had said in the letter, if, for instance, he asked her to call herself Loretta.

"I had to call you first," she might say. "I love the name Loretta. As a child I thought Loretta Young was the most beautiful woman in the world. If I dress up like Loretta Young, will you call me Loretta?"

As hokey as that sounded, she made it seem sincere. The men ate it up.

After listening to her make several calls, I said, "I'll sound ridiculous doing this." Elaine had a kind of mature sensuality that seemed impossible for someone under thirty to pull off. She laughed, looked at me over the top of those glasses again, and said, "When you've practiced a few times, you'll get the hang of it."

She reminded me that the main purpose of the telephone call was to screen out cops and lunatics while selling yourself. And, she explained, "This conversation will set up the way you relate to this person as long as he's a client. Don't give him so much that he doesn't need to come see you. Get as much information as you can, as quickly as possible." She said her seductive bullshit was one way of not giving any real information.

"They're trying to find out if you're charging money and they're trying to make sure you won't cause problems in their lives," she said. "Sometimes they worry that you might be a police officer, or that you're an extortionist and not a prostitute. Sometimes a guy will even worry that his wife put you up to this. But mostly they're not paranoid. No matter what affects our lives—like the fear of being arrested—the men don't think it affects their lives. And when it does affect them—when johns get picked up by the cops—they treat it like it's a big misunderstanding."

If a man starts talking about sexual activities on the first call, you know you're in trouble, she said. "I sound real offended and say, 'I don't think you know where you are. This is the South, and in the South men don't talk that way.'" (I later found it amusing to use that line with cops, because, as a rule, vice cops are crude and obscene. They'll use language no normal person would use with a stranger, like "Do you do blow jobs?" or even "How about ass fucking?" Normal men in America have better manners than that, or at least are afraid to talk that way.)

"Throughout my whole career," Elaine said, "not more than four or five percent of the straight jobs I've done have alluded to sex at all on the phone."

One of the things Elaine taught me is that a man who will talk dirty on the phone is not likely to be as good a client as someone who is polite and gentlemanly. We used a tone of femininity and discretion as our way of maintaining control over the situation. She said, "To every client you are his mother. You are the teacher he first had an erection over and you are his first girlfriend or the girl in high school who never went out with him. Remember that.

"You've got to treat his history with women as a delicate thing. Maybe his mother didn't love him. The teacher might have flunked him. The girl could have humiliated him. You may be the one who's going to pay for all that." Elaine warned me not to bring up a man's parents unless he did. Why? Because a man's relationship with his parents is not sexy. She said, "Watch out for people who talk about their parents, because it isn't normal. And look out for a man who washes his hands more than once when he comes in. He's full of guilt and he could be dangerous. If nothing else, he might not pay."

What she was telling me were commonsense things. She was smart, and she made it clear to me that I had to be smart too. She trained me to bring deeply buried thoughts, perceptions, suspicions to the front of my mind: You're alone. A mistake could mean anything from simple unpleasantness to jail or death. She said, "If women looked for husbands this carefully, they would be a lot happier. If there's anything wrong with the person, if he's the least bit suspicious, this is no time to be open-minded."

So I said, "Doesn't that mean that most of the clients you see are boring?" She nodded, and then said, "After a while you learn to be grateful for boring. Boring men are easier."

The most important item of apparel I would own was a watch, she said. I needed to make sure that one client was out the door before the next client arrived. "Always figure on a forty-minute hour," she said. "That will leave you enough time to get ready for the next."

When I brought a client to the bedroom, she told me, I should wash him and myself. For this purpose she would supply me with fresh hand towels, small washcloths, and little, individually molded pieces of soap. (As I later discovered, very few men objected to being washed. About the only time they had ever had their genitals washed while they were horizontal was when they were babies or if they were in a hospital. I usually washed myself first, and I made quite an erotic show of it, so they could hardly object when it was their turn.) Elaine told me that, if a client didn't seem clean, I should suggest he take a shower. If he said he didn't need to, I was to coax him into the shower by promising him something sexy and wonderful. It was great advice, but I never had to use it until I got to Europe. The men who came to Elaine's apartment were always well-groomed and bathed.

Elaine told me we didn't need to use prophylactics to protect ourselves against venereal disease. (I used an IUD and Elaine had had a hysterectomy—so we didn't need them for birth control either.) We were looking for the kind of person who had a monogamous relationship. Who was going through a midlife crisis. Who was no longer getting what he wanted from his wife. As she said, "Why should he be? It's too much work."

What we were creating at Elaine's apartment was a situation that was virtually impossible for a woman in a close personal relationship to sustain. A few married women are able to do it. They have kids, a job, and they still find time to plan a romantic and exciting weekend with their husbands. They'll pick up on which pictures their husbands look at in *Playboy*, and they'll buy clothes and a wig to look the same way. If they notice their husbands staring at pictures of twins, they'll call an escort service and find someone who looks like them. They'll put a whole scenario together. And when it works out, the husbands enjoy it and believe it.

But there aren't very many wives who want to do that.

Elaine would not give a man her address until just before he was supposed to come for their first session. Most often she would first arrange to meet him somewhere public, usually a restaurant or a bar or a health club. And she always talked to him twice on the phone before that. She explained to me that it was important to come up with some reason for a delay until after the second phone call. "Oh, I have to go," she'd say on the first phone call. "Oh, I didn't realize how late it was. I have to go to my French lesson—"

or her masseuse, or her calligraphy class. She warned me never to use excuses like "I've got to go get the laundry" or "I've got to check the mousetraps."

Elaine did this so she could ask the same questions again and see if he gave the same answers as before. What kind of car did he drive? How many kids did he have? How old were they? Had he been divorced? How long had he been at this job? Where did he go to college? What kind of odd jobs did he do to put himself through college? Had he changed careers? Why did he decide to answer a personal ad? What did he have in mind?

It was amazing to watch Elaine take notes while she was on the phone. She took shorthand and then transcribed her notes onto neat, legible five-by-seven-inch cards. She had everything she needed to be a successful courtesan: this seductive voice and great efficiency. And I was impressed with how much understanding she had of my need to listen to her screen calls. I was afraid she was going to say, "You listen to a couple, and then it's your turn." But for three days she let me listen to her screen calls, and then she hung up the phone, finished making her notes, and turned to me to analyze what each man had said and what it meant.

In the first conversation, Elaine explained, it was important to plant the idea that some money or some kind of compensation would be expected. And she didn't mean dinner.

This was a tricky part to handle; she suggested I ask, "Why did you write? What did you like about my ad?"

If he said, "It just sounded like the kind of situation I was looking for," he knew. I was to listen to the tone of his voice. Did he sound sympathetic or sly? Innocent or knowing? Did he give hints throughout the conversation that this whole thing needed to be kept on the quiet side?

Screening clients was a hell of a long process, as I found out when I started calling the men who had answered my ad. I picked eleven to start with—almost all of them middle-aged businessmen. I immediately learned that when I called men who sounded interesting and who were my age, I was wasting my time. Some men were totally innocent. They were really just looking for a girlfriend. They thought I wanted a guy to take me to dinner, a guy who just happened to appreciate my kind of looks. ("You're not looking for a boyfriend," Elaine reminded me. "You're looking for a man who wants to pay.")

I sat there, making call after call, and Elaine gave me advice after each one. "Your tone is good," she said, "but you've got to ask more questions. Take more control of the interview." And, she advised me, it was good policy to be sensitive to the naive ones. They were never to be treated like they were stupid. If I understood that they were looking for a girlfriend and I was already on the phone, I should simply come up with a polite reason for not seeing them: I'd already arranged to meet someone else, or I was looking for someone older, or younger.

I think Elaine was so careful with these innocents because she had so much integrity. She made it clear to me that no matter how much money I would make, I still had to deal with how society thinks of prostitution. So I had to maintain integrity with myself. No matter how centered I would be able to stay with my own feelings, I would still have to deflect criticism. Even if I knew in my heart that what I was doing was OK, I might start to feel sorry for myself and believe I was a bad person. I might start believing that I really did have a lower standard of morality. So, Elaine said, it was important for us never to think of ourselves as bad people, never to act like bad people.

She taught me to explain to all my clients that I was not a prostitute. (She also made sure I understood that we were.) She said the clients wanted to believe they were just helping out financially. I was supposed to say that I did something else for a living. (That's where working at the radio station came in.) If I couldn't tell a client that he was the only man I was seeing, I was supposed to explain why I needed "extra" money. Getting ready for a trip to Europe was more glamorous than needing a new transmission for the car. I started planning a trip to Europe right away.

Then Elaine taught me how to keep a file and code it. I was going to be putting this person's whole life on a card, anything he told me about himself: career, wife, kids, colleges, hobbies, interests, and friends. It was a dossier, far more than anyone wanted some strange woman to know about him. Then, even if he called six months later, even if he had a common name, I could look him up and, by asking him a couple of questions, determine which one he was, or if he was the person he said he was.

This system was also helpful, if I was going to be seeing a lot of clients each week, in keeping people straight. Elaine said, "It's always good to ask, 'How are the kids doing? Did your daughter make the gymnastics team?' and to pretend you are deeply interested in his life."

Elaine recommended I read *How to Win Friends and Influence People*. "All the things Dale Carnegie talks about make a good courtesan," she said. "You need to appear to be truly, deeply interested in a stranger."

She told me also to make notes of where to send Christmas cards and birthday cards. "Always find out when his birthday is, and send a discreet, expensive card." The first time I saw a client, she said, I should write him a little note on expensive stationery saying how much I'd enjoyed meeting him. I could bring up one or two personal things, but I was never to mention anything about sex.

Of course all these file cards, with names and addresses and personal information, especially about sex, could have been used against us in court if we were ever arrested. But Elaine had a system for making the cards refer to something other than prostitution. She had a set of abbreviations that made it look like she was doing magazine sales, or a marketing survey. There was a code for what kind of sexual activities a man liked. "Interested in brass quintets" meant a blow job. "Classical" or "jazz" indicated whether it was straight sex or something kinky.

Elaine did give me a few pointers about sex, but they were minor in comparison with the information she gave about keeping records and house. She told me I should never have an idle hand. She said that men were coming to us for things they didn't get at home, which for some meant a lot of oral sex, for others having a woman on top. Another thing men didn't get much at home or from hookers either was kissing. (A lot of wives reach a point in the relationship where they are too mad or preoccupied to kiss their husbands. I was amazed that men wanted as much kissing from me as genital contact.)

But more than sex, Elaine talked about money and gifts. "People always ask, 'What can I bring?' " she said. "If they're really into flowers let them bring flowers, but fuck flowers. Flowers wilt and die. Find out what they can afford. Find out if there's some kind of wine or liquor they like, and ask them to bring it. Tell them what kind of perfume you like. It's amazing how many of these guys want to bring you something fancy."

Prostitution, the way Elaine described it, seemed pretty straightforward, much safer and nicer and more pleasant than I had expected. One thing she told me impressed me more than the information on how to get gifts out of clients and set up file cards. It was the idea that prostitution is a valuable service that goes beyond sex. "People always think that prostitutes use sex and hate men. And when you talk to friends about your work, you're going to end up talking about the weird clients and the mean clients and the bad clients, because they make hilarious stories. But even weird clients are usually nice people. You're providing a valuable service to these people—all of them. You're helping someone with a crippled sense of self-esteem."

Part of the art of prostitution is using sex to create a feeling of trust and intimacy, to bring people in touch with their own self-worth, she said. Regulars are sometimes hard to do, she said, because each time you see them you have to go deeper, you have to give more. Men might not even understand why they keep coming back to us. They think it's for the sex. But they're coming back because we touch them emotionally, because we're real people. The way she described it, prostitution is a noble profession, right up there with nursing and teaching.

As I started working, I found out that many of my clients were isolated and lonely. They would read an ad and answer it because they didn't have anyone else. If I could make that client walk out the door feeling happy, feeling good about himself, feeling he might actually be interesting and fun to be with, I had performed a great service. To do that a person has to love men and enjoy being with them, which I did.

Elaine mentioned that we were going to see another client, a person who looked just like Harrison Ford as Han Solo in *Star Wars*. "He's a cross dresser," she said, "and he's lots of fun."

She was quite tickled as she told me this. She waited for me to react, to ask what a cross dresser was. (I had learned as a small child that, when you want people to teach you something, the best way is to be excited and titillated to the degree they expect. One of the interesting things about prostitution is that it *is* surprising and shocking because it goes against almost everything most of us have been socialized to believe, so it was quite easy to act surprised and titillated.)

I sat there with a polite smile on my face and put the word *cross dresser* through my mental word checker. I asked myself, Is this a word in my vocabulary? and decided that it wasn't.

"What's that, a cross dresser?" I asked.

Elaine gave me a pleased and mischievous smile.

"It's a straight guy," she said, "who likes to dress up in women's clothes."

"What *kind* of women's clothes?" I asked.

"Oh, he wears lingerie and panties and high heels, silk stockings, women's shoes . . ."

At that point in my career I had seen two clients, one with a micropenis and one who was a perfectly boring nuclear PR executive. I felt I had already pretty much seen everything, and what I hadn't seen, Elaine had told me about. I knew about transvestites because when I had reviewed rock concerts for the *Great Speckled Bird*, while I was in college, I went to drag clubs and saw slim and effeminate gay men dressed up in women's clothes. And I had to admit that transvestites looked darned good. There was something kind of exciting about seeing a homosexual man who was better-looking than most women. But there was something very weird to me about a straight man dressing up. I wasn't sure I had ever heard of such a thing, and I was amazed to think that this big, hulking, straight man was going to come over and do something I hadn't even heard of in front of me.

"Women's shoes?" I said. "Didn't you say he was built like Harrison Ford? What size women's shoe?"

"I think they're 14B."

"Well, where do you get women's shoes size 14B?" There was some part of me that thought she was making this up; there was another part of me that knew it must be true.

"He orders them out of special catalogs that have big shoes and lingerie for men."

Elaine explained that she was going to set us up as a double. It would be a hundred dollars for the two of us for an hour. It all sounded pretty weird to me.

When he arrived he had a pink shopping bag from Frederick's of Hollywood and eight shoe boxes. Elaine acted just thrilled to see him. I was sitting on the sofa when she brought him in. She sat down on the chair. He sat on another chair and started opening boxes. He had seven pairs of shoes for Elaine, and they were not cheap shoes. She started examining each and every pair—very high heels, ankle straps, red patent leather, a pair of white suede shoes— shoes with the highest heels I had ever seen, what I later learned were called fetish shoes and had to be ordered specially. He got down on his hands and knees and started putting them on her feet and kissing her toes. She had very nice feet but, except in *Cinderella*, I had never seen anyone come close to kissing a foot.

Then he took out this big pair of black pumps, the biggest shoes I had ever seen, high heeled, for himself. These shoes were so big they looked like display shoes. They looked too big for anyone ever to wear. Elaine oohed and ahed over those and told him she couldn't wait to see him in them.

Then he took out a pair of stockings for her—panty hose that were cut out on the cheeks and the crotch so they looked similar to stockings and a garter belt. (I had seen those things in the backs of some magazines and had always thought they looked ugly.) Elaine went into the bedroom and came out wearing the stockings, a pair of the new shoes, and a see-through negligee. And I thought, Well, even a beautiful woman can look terrible in those things. He started oohing and ahing over her, and I just nodded agreeably, almost enthusiastically, like you do at a church picnic when you're asked if you'd like another helping of the minister's wife's coleslaw. When he went into the kitchen for a minute, I leaned over to her and said, "Do you really like those?" and she said, in a breathy voice, "Oh, yes!" Then he went back into the bedroom to change.

She whispered, "If he likes them, then I like them. That's part of his fantasy. It isn't even a question of whether I like them or not."

He called out, "Ready, mistress," which I thought was very strange too. I asked her, "Why does he call you mistress?" And she said, "These kind of men just are like that." I thought, There's got to be more explanation than that.

When we got into the bedroom this person had made the kind of change Superman made, but not in the same direction. As I stood there looking at him, I was intrigued that something could be so shocking to me and yet be quite innocent in the great scheme of things. After all, this guy wasn't napalming babies. He was just a man wearing women's clothing. And he was not attractive doing it; those stockings were covering big, hairy legs, the lace panties looked ridiculous stretched over his erect penis. Elaine, meanwhile, was telling him how great he looked. (I was busy trying to figure out whether she really thought he looked OK, and whether *he* thought he looked OK, and why he was calling her mistress, and why he did this in the first place.)

I had done a lot of things in life. I had had sex with five guys on a plastic sheet covered with Mazola oil while doing acid and drinking champagne, I had been teargassed in civil rights demonstrations, I had seen *Deep Throat,* I had even parachuted out of a perfectly good moving airplane. And here I was, shocked and stunned, paralyzed by the sight of a big, hairy man in stockings.

Elaine started telling him what a bad boy he had been. And he said, "Yes, mistress." Right away I wondered what he had done, either recently or cosmically, to seem so in need of scolding. Now she went to the dresser in those five-inch heels and those silly stockings and picked up a wooden hairbrush. Then she told him to stand up and bend over the bed. And he did. She pulled down the top of his panties, to expose the cheeks, and smacked each cheek a few times. And in between the smackings she kept telling him what a bad boy he had been.

Considering that torturing someone into a confession was the kind of thing that I had picketed about, this made me feel a little uncomfortable. Clearly she wasn't hitting him hard enough to hurt him—they were little pats—but still it seemed a bit like torture.

I was standing there with my mouth open, observing all this the way someone might observe a traffic accident, and at the same time trying to appear as if this was the sort of thing I saw every day. I didn't want to interfere. I wanted to disappear. I was thinking: This is the kind of experience I used to have to take drugs to have.

She walked over and started explaining to me the use of this brush, while Han Solo waited—within hearing and still bent over. She said, "Use a brush instead of your hand when you spank someone, because the brush keeps you from bruising your hand. And besides," she said, leading me to him, "it has bristles on the other side and that gives you another texture to work with."

She stood on one side and I was on the other. And she was showing me where to hit with the brush, the same way the manager of a donut shop would show a new employee how to warm up muffins in the microwave. She had switched from her sultry, sexy role into a teacher, and that was comforting to me. I thought, I'm really learning something now.

This person's ass was now a learning aid, an anatomically correct model for my instruction. It had no more erotic fascination than a model of a light bulb. At the same time, it didn't make me cringe either, as the model of a brain or an eyeball might have.

While Elaine was explaining the fine points of spanking to

me, Han Solo started stroking his cock, which by now had popped out of the panties altogether. Eight or nine thick, hard inches of throbbing cock were now projecting like a wind chime between his legs. As soon as Elaine noticed what he was doing, she swatted him several times, hard, on the ass while screaming, "Stop that, you disgusting, pathetic worm. I told you never to touch yourself there unless I gave you permission!"

"I'm sorry, mistress. Please forgive me. May I please touch myself there, mistress?" he pleaded.

"No!" she screeched. Swack.

Each time she smacked the brush against his butt, his erection got bigger and bigger, like Pinocchio's nose. This was pretty thrilling, I thought. Then she handed me the brush.

She explained that using a flat, wide brush would not leave marks. She told me to try doing it the way she did. So I did, a little pat on one side and a little pat on the other. And she showed me how you got the ass to a rosy glow by hitting it several times. You didn't try to do it with just one blow. It was fascinating to see there was actually a right way to do all this.

Then she walked over to a dresser and pulled out a Ping-Pong paddle. She said, "I like these too, because they have texture to them. They are broader and flatter, so they have a kind of sting that neither the brush nor your hand is going to give, and, because they're so big and wide, there is even less danger of leaving marks." (I remember thinking to myself that someone interested in child abuse might appreciate that information. I also remember thinking that it was information I couldn't imagine using.)

After I had these instructions, I certainly felt quite proficient in using the brush and the paddle. Elaine told me that, unless a client requested a belt, I shouldn't use it because it might leave marks.

Then she ordered him to go to the corner. She came over to me, led me to the bed, and said, in a very gentle, motherly voice, "Here, dear, lay down like this." She bent over and kissed me and then brought him to me. She spread my legs apart and told him to get on his knees between my legs and to bend over. Then she instructed him in the art of cunnilingus. She asked me, "Is he doing what I'm telling him to do?" And she asked me to give a critique.

That was pretty hard for me to do. My only previous experience with cunnilingus had been either to enjoy it or to hide the fact that I didn't. My usual way of coping with disappointment in bed was simply not to see the person again. But I found it was fun to be in the position of telling someone how to perform. It had never occurred to me before that people could be instructed in these things.

At some point, however, Elaine came up to me and whispered in my ear: "Act like you're enjoying it."

I didn't find that as hard to do as giving a critique, I just had forgotten to do it.

He never gave any sign of having had an orgasm, and he didn't want to have intercourse. Elaine explained that he wanted to go home and have intercourse with his wife, who had no idea how much foreplay he'd already had.

I spent weeks at Elaine's apartment wearing nothing but lingerie, and I started making tremendous amounts of money. I saw five people who had answered my ad—a high school principal and four boring business executives. Three of them repeated the next week, plus I saw five new clients. The next week I saw ten and the week after that fourteen. Elaine was thrilled that I was so successful—after all, she did make fifteen dollars for each client—but I began to see a strange shift in sentiment between us. She was a pro, and she was good. Elaine looked about as good as a forty-nine-year-old woman can look, but she knew that some of her clients, when they saw me, decided that a newcomer, someone fresh and innocent, might be interesting too.

I kept working at the radio station—inertia mixed with a sense of obligation, I guess—but the schedule was killing me: up in the morning, go to the station, hit Elaine's at lunchtime, back to the station, back to Elaine's, and then home to bed.

Some people at the station knew I was now "working" in addition to working. The ones who knew thought it was interesting and exciting; the ones who didn't know weren't told. And no one asked who I was working with, so Elaine remained one of those elegant, slightly aloof people who seemed so out of place at the station.

Meanwhile, my entire life *except* for the radio station became satin and marabou. I found that I loved traipsing around in lingerie with soft music playing in the background. The pace was languid and, when Elaine was around, almost collegial. We would sit in her living room sipping warm Grand Marnier after seeing the last clients, and we would rehash what had happened, the way college girls might talk about the night's dates. The only difference was that we would have three "dates" to talk about instead of one.

I set my own schedule, I set my own limits and made my own rules, and I didn't have to answer to anyone—which was fine with me. When the doorbell rang, I knew I was about to have a new experience, whatever it was. There was always something different, usually pleasant, to deal with: what a client wanted, what a client was willing to pay for what he wanted, what I was willing to do for the amount the client was paying me. I learned a lot about myself: what I would and wouldn't do for money, and I learned what I was willing to do for the right amount of money.

Best of all, I was in control. I didn't have to sit by the phone and wait for Ralph to call, I didn't have to wonder what Bob thought of me or when Tim and I were going to get serious. If Ralph didn't call, or Bob or Tim, I would certainly hear from Glen and Robin and Haywood and Charlie and Tom and Dick, not to mention Harry. And if none of those guys called, I could open a letter, call someone, and, within a short period of time, that man would be paying to have sex with me. I didn't have to see anyone I didn't want to see. If a man was too boring, or too rough or too crude, if he took too much time, I didn't have to see him again. I loved it.

I found that, generally speaking, the men who came to me didn't get anything they couldn't get at home, unless their wives were ill or for some other reason had stopped having sex with them. Most wives knew that their men enjoyed oral sex. Most wives wanted to please their husbands. They just didn't want to, or didn't have time to, please their husbands as often as the husbands wanted to be pleased.

Then, too, men occasionally wanted to have sex without having to talk about what was wrong with the garbage disposal, or the car, or the roof, or their kids. Sometimes men were in town on business, away from their wives for weeks at a time. And often men were simply curious about what it would be like to have sex with a new partner. For them, going to a prostitute instead of having sex with their wives was comparable to going to a restaurant instead of eating at home every night. The food is often better at home, but that doesn't stop a man from wanting to eat out—at places ranging from fast-food joints (massage parlors and street prostitutes) to four-star restaurants (which is what Elaine and I felt we were offering).

Our four-star restaurant offered ambience, clean linens, attentive service, quite a wine and liquor list, and a complete deluxe menu. Men being men, most of them wanted at least two choices from the menu. Almost all men wanted to see and kiss my breasts. (Clients often asked us to describe our breasts over the telephone. Elaine had perfect, firm breasts—a credit, she said, to nursing five children. I had breasts most men considered beautiful, but I hated to describe them over the phone, since what I thought was beautiful and what a man might expect were quite different. But my breasts *were* beautiful; what was surprising about them were the large aureoles and the firm nipples. "You'll just have to see them when you come by," I would say.)

After breasts, most men would opt for oral sex and then intercourse, or intercourse and then oral sex. I could have brought most men to orgasm with oral sex alone—if they'd let me—but almost all men wanted to have intercourse too.

And so, within the context of another day, another new client, some verities began to emerge: breast worship, oral sex, intercourse, orgasm. After orgasm almost every man said the same thing: "Boy, am I going to sleep well tonight!"

It seemed kind of strange to me—and expensive—that, in order to sleep well, these guys needed to have sex with a prostitute.

I soon found that being a courtesan is a lot like acting. If I had the flu, or a cold, it didn't matter. Once I had my makeup on and was in my lingerie and high-heeled slippers, I became a different person. I was doing my job. The client was paying me to be not just pleasant but delightful. If he wanted to be with someone who wanted to discuss problems, he could be home with his wife.

I found, however, that most men thought I was acting when I had an orgasm. I had as many orgasms as I could. Sometimes I had to work hard at it, but being a prostitute gave me the opportunity to learn how to make myself come. I had a lot of practice with guys who were inadequate in bed.

There were times when I would psyche myself up, when I would be at the point of having an orgasm, and the guy would look at me and say, "You don't have to do that."

I didn't *have to* do that? It seemed to me that, as long as we were both there, doing what we were doing, I should enjoy myself as much as possible.

In order to convince our clients that we were seeing them exclusively, we had to change our ads every few issues of the magazine—and hope the respondents didn't notice the same post office box number. Since I still had ten or fifteen pounds to lose, my new ad said: "Female artist, 27, former artist's model, red hair, Rubenesque body, white skin. Needs patron. To see portfolio, write to: ————." It was interesting how few men made any kind of pretense that I was serious about showing them my portfolio or being an artist. But I made every one of them look at my drawings. I guess I wanted them to know that I *was* a wonderful artist. And I also enjoyed pretending that I was shocked when they had something else in mind. It was fun seeing how many times I could act shocked.

I never brought up the subject of sex. Instead, I let the men offer me money as an artist's patron and then imply that—of course—I should offer in return a token of gratitude, in the form of sexual services.

That seemed to me pretty much how life worked. What amazed me was that women were arrested for providing sexual services, while it was the men who almost invariably proposed it.

One of the things Elaine taught me was about body care—manicures and pedicures. "Every time I take a bath this is what I do," she said. "Oil treatments, pumice stone, depilatory. And, since we spend so much time with our shoes off, I give myself a pedicure every week." She said Sunday was best because most of our business was on weekdays, and we needed to go shopping on Saturdays. On Sunday she would do a facial and her hair and feet and nails. "Every bit of hair on your legs has to be removed," she said. "And if you're going to dye your pubic hair, this is the time to do it."

I bleached my pubic hair to a light reddish blond, and men adored it. They would say, "You really are a redhead, aren't you?" (It apparently never occurred to any man that I bleached it.) I started getting hot-oil treatments on my hands and feet. I got professional facials. I had my hair dyed and permed. I had it conditioned. I paid for fancy haircuts, body oil massage, health spas. I steamed my makeup off every evening. I used one of the most expensive lines of skin-care products. I felt that, if I used Elizabeth Arden's Millennium Cell Renewal Program religiously at twenty-seven, I would be able to look as good as Elaine when I got to be fifty.

When I spent that much attention and money on my body I discovered something else: If you take care of your body, and if men are constantly telling you how beautiful and desirable you are, you begin to love yourself deeply, even if you didn't to start with. Being a courtesan, for me, brought about a whole new feeling of self-esteem and self-worth.

Elaine and I did two other doubles, where we both saw one guy. Then she mentioned that something special was coming up. A regular client of hers, Chuck, was in town; he owned an airplane leasing company. He rented planes to corporations and liked to use Elaine to entertain corporate executives. Elaine set this one up for nine o'clock in the evening, which was unusual because we mostly saw daytime clients sneaking away from their jobs or stopping by on their way home from work.

Elaine told me in advance that this client always had cocaine and pot with him. And she explained the logistics of this kind of double, with two men. Unless the men paid extra, we would be paired up and stay with the man we had started with.

It turned out that they were in their early thirties. Chuck told Elaine right away that he wanted the man he was trying to impress to see her, since he knew how good she was, and that he would try out the new girl, me.

They were dressed up in suits, so it looked strange to see them handling hash pipes and big joints. (The only people I had known who did drugs were hippies and beatniks and rock musicians and, occasionally, record executives.)

We smoked some dope and did some cocaine. I didn't know enough about cocaine to know if it was good or not, but I knew it was good pot. I noticed that the cocaine and the pot together made it more like a party than a job, and that bothered me. I had been working long enough to know that it was important for me to keep business separate from social situations. And the drugs definitely made me feel social.

We started out in our lingerie in front of the fireplace. The guys wanted us to give them blow jobs, and we did. But I found out that men who are doing cocaine have a hard time getting and keeping an erection, and a hard time getting off. Elaine and I were working hard, but to no avail.

This was the first time I had seen Elaine operate in a business-like manner when clients were present. When neither Chuck nor his friend got off, they said they wanted to stay longer and switch partners. Elaine said that to do that they would have to pay more money—the full rate for a second hour.

They stayed for another hour. I took the new client into the bedroom, washed him up and, after about a half an hour, got him off. My jaws were really sore, like I had just had dental surgery. Chuck, I later found out, spent his time with Elaine just talking. He did ask her, however, to pretend that he had come, for the benefit of the client he was trying to impress.

Chuck paid Elaine the full amount for two men for two hours: $300. My share of this night's fee, $150, was the most I had made on one job, and it seemed phenomenal. It was amazing to me that people would spend that much money to get off, or even not to get off.

The first freebie I ever gave started with an obscene phone call.

I had been working all day and half the night at Elaine's, during which time I happened to have seen three or four clients who were really into cunnilingus. My pussy had been licked for two—possibly three—hours, and it was suffering from tongue drag. I had just gotten into bed and was about to fall asleep when, at about 2:30 A.M., the phone rang. I picked it up, and there was this guy with a deep voice saying, very slowly and lasciviously, in a fake black accent, "I want to lick your pussy."

Jesus Christ, I thought, this weirdo is going to call me all night long. Late-night callers usually are people who work at boring jobs—night security, hotel desk clerk—that leave them feeling lonely, like they're the only people on earth. Or they are horny clients who don't want to pay for their thrills, but who hope to get off by masturbating at home while talking dirty.

Confrontation is the best answer to phone freaks. Besides, I had to leave my phone connected because I was expecting an important call in the morning. So I had to deal with this character head-on.

I said, "No, no, no. My pussy has been licked enough for one day. However, if you give me your name and your telephone number, I'll call you back tomorrow and we can make an appointment for the two of us to get together. I'll charge you seventy-five dollars for a half an hour or so. Does that sound like what you had in mind?"

This guy, who had just said in a deep black voice, "I want to lick your pussy," suddenly switched to a high voice like Mickey Mouse's and said, "Gee, really?" (Isn't it interesting that, when scared white boys make obscene phone calls and want to sound sexy, they affect a black man's voice? I don't know if they have fantasies about black men or if they just pick a voice that's the furthest thing from what they really are.)

I said to this kid, "Now, the deal is that you can't call me back tonight. You understand? What's your name?" And he said, "Phillip." "OK, Phillip, what's your phone number?"

He was mystified into cooperating with me. Once he dropped the fake black accent, I could tell he was just a kid. "You *are* eighteen, right?" I asked. He assured me he was.

"And why are you making obscene phone calls at two-thirty in the morning?"

"Because I'm horny," he said. "The girls at school just want to play games. Most of them don't even want to go out with me."

"Why's that?" I asked.

"Oh, they're all real snobs. And I don't have much money." His voice was sweet, rather endearing, I thought. I impressed the idea on him that, if he called me back that night, he would never get to see me, which would mean that he would be missing the experience of his life. He agreed not to call me back, and not to call anyone else that night either. That way not only could I enjoy a good night's sleep but the rest of Atlanta could rest easy as well.

I did try to call him the next day, but he had given me a false phone number. Before the afternoon was over, however, he called back. We made a date to meet at Elaine's apartment.

Elaine thought it was funny that I had made a date with some kind of maniac who made obscene phone calls. Then she started to get nervous. She made sure she was there when he arrived, just in case something was fishy about him. I assured her that he sounded fine, only a little young and foolish. Besides, I wanted to meet someone face to face who spent his evenings calling strangers on the phone and saying, "I want to lick your pussy."

I jumped when the doorbell rang. But when I went to answer the door I found a beautiful little baby-faced kid who appeared to be about twelve or thirteen. He was so short I had trouble seeing him through the peephole. Once I saw him, I told Elaine she could go on out to dinner. I thought I could handle this one on my own.

When he came in I made him show me his driver's license, to make sure he was eighteen. His height, five foot two, and his scrawny frame combined with his big hands and feet, made him look like a young pup. His brown hair was pulled back into a ponytail. He was wearing blue jeans and a T-shirt, which made him look like he was on his way to play in a Little League game.

Phillip was as nervous as any clichéd kid about to have his first sexual experience with a hooker. I offered him a drink, but all he wanted was a Coke. He asked, hesitantly and politely, as if he were in some dying aunt's hospital room, if it would be OK for him to smoke a joint. Maybe the music is a problem, I thought. Elaine and I usually kept the radio tuned to a classical station, on the theory that our place should sound like some Neiman-Marcus department store. That was supposed to keep the clients humbled and less likely to act up. What this boy needed was a little confidence and all the comforting I could muster.

I suggested he try to find some better station, and he tuned in Z93 FM, "the rock of Atlanta." Then he sat down and smoked his joint. I asked him if he knew he frightened women by calling them in the middle of the night, and he said he didn't mean to. Actually, it seemed to me that his thrill was more in pissing women off than it was in either frightening them or turning them on—a sort of sadistic streak. "And besides," he sort of squeaked, "how else can I get off?"

So I invited him into the bedroom. I explained to him where to put his clothes, and then I busied myself pulling back the lace coverlet on the bed and turning down the sheets. When he got down to his underpants I stopped and turned in amazement. There was one of the biggest, most beautifully formed cocks I had ever seen. It was so disproportionately large, he looked like a big dick with a little kid attached to it, like some kind of fake photo of a jackalope. I gasped, and then tried to act like a professional.

I invited him to lie down between those nice, crisp sheets, all the while restraining myself from jumping on top of him. By now he was feeling a little more comfortable with me, so it was a moment of ecstasy for both of us when my lips finally touched the tip of his humongous penis. I could have licked and caressed and sucked that cock for a long time—it was sweet tasting, like wheat or fresh-cut hay—but I was afraid that if I spent too long with my mouth on him he would come before I got a chance to feel that magnificent structure inside me. So I kissed it good-bye, positioned my knees alongside his tiny hips, and lowered myself onto him. His penis was throbbing so hard I could feel palpitations inside me. The look on his face was of someone thrilled and excited beyond his wildest dreams—like a kid who has just tasted candy for the first time in his life. I, in turn, had never been so turned on in my life. After coming I don't know how many times, I asked him if he would like to get on top.

Sure, he said, and we changed places. He didn't really know what to do. After about a hundred confused and misguided strokes, I decided this boy needed some pointers. I showed him where to put his knees, how to support his weight. I spoke with him about the importance of rhythm, and how to control his thrust, and suggested that thinking of a pattern, any pattern, might help him. Long, short, long, long, long, short. Anything would do. In the course of these lessons I managed to come many more times. After a while I began to realize that his time was long over and we hadn't even gotten around to his licking my pussy. I got him to come in one, long, glorious series of moves, and then I told him, "You've got to pay me now and go."

As he was getting dressed I did ask him where he had gotten his money. He said he had an after-school job and had been saving up to buy a car. It seemed clear to him, however, that this was better.

He called me again a week later, and we made another appointment. When we got together he showed me how closely he had listened to my lessons. He was wonderful. What a treat for me. He paid me again, but I knew that he wouldn't be able to pay to have sex with me as often as I wanted to have sex with him. Since I didn't have a boyfriend at the time, I offered him a mutually satisfying deal: If he could see me whenever it was convenient for me, I wouldn't charge him.

I saw him for quite a while after that, usually on Friday nights, my nights off. The day he graduated from high school he spent the night with me. I thought he would eventually meet some teenage girl who would be more suitable for him, someone who would enjoy beer, drag racing, and drive-in movies. And what a surprise this boy would have for her.

He, in turn, is no doubt responsible for a few of those stories you've heard about the hooker with a heart of gold.

Three or four months after I started working as a prostitute, I quit the radio station. By now I was making an average of $500 a week at Elaine's, for very little work. At the radio station all I got was headaches. Besides, I hated getting up early in the morning, which is to say before noon.

It was summer when Elaine expanded my horizons by teaching me about shopping mall hooking. Going to the mall was a multipurpose event, she said. First, we had to go shopping for our clients. That is part of being a courtesan in an ongoing relationship, and it put us in a position of importance. We did their Christmas shopping; we did their wives' birthdays. We asked to see pictures of their wives and asked how tall they were, what their favorite colors were. We told the men, "Sneak a look at her driver's license to get her height," because we knew she would be thrilled if he would buy her something that fit.

But we weren't just in the malls to buy presents for our clients' wives. We had a lot of money. We needed to shop for ourselves and for the apartment. And then there was a third purpose—picking up new men. Elaine told me that I would find more customers in the shopping malls than I ever would through the personal ads. ("Think of all the letters you automatically throw out," she said.)

Because we were working, Elaine said, it was always important to look our best when we hit the malls. "Wear expensive jewelry," she said. "You can never have too many diamonds." It was also OK to wear conservative costume jewelry, as long as it was clearly worn as an accent and not as true jewelry. And of course we didn't wear wedding rings or anything that even looked like a wedding ring. Our nails were always beautiful. Our nails looked better than anyone else's possibly could. They had to be perfect. I found that if I had long nails and high heels, a man wouldn't notice that I was wearing a gunnysack. But of course I never wore a gunnysack. I wore something that would fit in with suburban standards of dress but would still stand out: a low-cut black velvet jacket and pants.

Men in shopping malls in the afternoon are invariably on the stroll, Elaine said. I was to think of the mall as a town square. We were looking for someone who was in no hurry, someone who had no place to go or didn't want to get there. Someone who looked as if he would like something interesting to happen. Some men looked as if they were on a mission, all business. Obviously, I was to leave them alone. And it was always a good sign, Elaine said, if the man looked at me first.

"This is suburban streetwalking," Elaine said, and headed off toward the chic shops on the second level.

And where did she suggest I start looking for shopping mall clients? In expensive lingerie shops. Men were not going to be doing utilitarian shopping there. Elaine said, "You can't pick up someone who's trying to buy a lawn mower." I was to look for someone who was uncomfortable buying lingerie and then offer to help him. Elaine explained that this was especially safe, since we could be pretty certain the guy was not a police officer trying to catch someone advertising in the personals.

On the other hand, we still found out, right away, what he did for a living. If he turned out to be a cop, it was, "Well, have a nice day."

I soon learned to stand outside men's shops—tobacco shops, pipe shops, clothing stores—as though I was looking for a present. And because I was so striking, every man who had an opportunity to talk to me did.

After I had convinced them that I was totally sophisticated, someone they would never imagine to be a prostitute, I would let them know I was. Men were fascinated.

When I would say I was a prostitute, the man rarely believed me. This is where the fine art of shopping mall prostitution comes in. This was the closing of the sale. Either he was going to ask how soon he could see me, or he was going to accuse me of lying, or he was going to think I was nuts, or he was going to be deeply disappointed and feel I'd tricked him into believing I was a nice person.

This last kind of person seemed to feel that I had jeopardized his integrity. (After all, someone may have seen him talking with *a prostitute*.) He might turn arrogant and angry and self-righteous. This person, who just a moment ago had thought I was charming, was now ready to have me arrested—if it didn't mean that there would be a commotion and he would be embarrassed.

It only took me a few weeks to perfect my act. It was so successful I could almost script it:

I would pick the man out long before he saw me. I would pose myself in front of the store window so he would have the most striking view. (Granted, I needed confidence to do this. I spent a lot of time first practicing in front of a mirror, the way I had when I was a teenager.) I would arrange my body language to look approachable—even by this self-conscious, insecure stranger. I would look inviting, so that he thought, Why, I could go up and talk to her. I had to give him some kind of opportunity: For example, I always wore a beautiful and obvious watch, so he could ask me the time.

Now he sees me and he's thinking about trying to talk to me. He gets close enough so I can look at him pointedly. I give him one good solid moment of eye-to-eye contact. (People are frightened by eye-to-eye contact, I found, because it means something is going to happen.) When my eyes meet his, in just a split second, I have to let him know that it's OK and that I don't see or care about his glasses or his paunch, his buckteeth or his bald spot. I don't want him to get distracted with his own self-consciousness. I have to be welcoming—kind, warm, and serene.

Then he gets closer. He's trying to get a good look at me, but I don't want him to know that I'm aware he's looking at me yet. I love doing this. There's so much art to this next part. I let him know not only that it's all right that he's looking at me but that I am surprised and flattered and would like to know him better, but I'm shy. I would like it, however, if he would just come a little closer. By now he realizes that we're looking at each other. But I can't let this become too sappy. There's not going to be a swell in the music. But then again, I have to implant the idea that there might be music . . . soon.

I look into the store window. And because there are men's things in there, he looks too. The bigger the window, the better. If the window is too small, he probably will feel threatened.

Now that he's near me, I look at him as if I want him to be with me. Here's where judgment comes in. I have to decide if I'm going to initiate contact or if I'm going to let him. I may drop something or start to walk away, reluctantly, coyly.

(I love walking away in Latin countries. That's one of the sexiest things you can do to a Latin man. But some of them will call you on it. "I saw you looking at me," they'll say. "And now you act like you're not interested. But I know you are. Who are you fooling?" American men either don't think this or they would never say it.)

This process doesn't take very long. Pretty soon I'm talking to him and finding out if he has any money to spend. By the time we are two department stores away I know if he's a reasonable candidate. I find out why he's there and what his problems are and where he's willing to go with this encounter. The most important thing I need to find out about, right away, is if he's in the throes of a divorce, and just wandering through a shopping mall trying to pick up the pieces of his life.

Newly divorced men are terrible clients. They demand a lot of attention. If I'm going to deal with them on any real level—the way I prefer to deal with them—it means I have to spend a lot of time making them feel OK about what's happening. That doesn't mean I say, "It's all your rotten wife's fault." But I do try to help them reach some comfort with the choices they've made. I know that I will have to go into all this, right at the beginning, with a newly divorced man if I am ever going to get past it and see him as a steady client.

Either that or I will hear, week after week, what a heartless, bloodsucking bitch his wife is. "She even took the pencil after she wrote the note," they'll wail. "The next thing I knew, she'd sold the house." If I let them keep it up, eventually they'll either start crying or something worse. Luckily, I know how to say, "How do you feel about that?"

I hate it when divorced men start crying and pleading for me to stay with them, no matter how long I've already been there. I tell them, "Look, this is what I do for a living. If you want me to stay for another hour of counseling, I need to be paid." These men really don't want a prostitute; they want their wives or what they think their wives should have been. They certainly don't want to be reminded that they have to pay me to be there. They'll say, "If you had any heart at all, you wouldn't leave."

This is not the time for me to remind them, "At least I'm taking only seventy-five dollars and not everything you've earned in the last four years—or forty." This is the time that recently divorced men can get bitter and scream, "You're just like her. All women are alike." This is the time to have my car keys in my hand and to excuse myself abruptly.

Some divorcing men make good clients, but only after they've come to realize the advantages. Few of them ever understand, however, why their wives have left them. And that's why we picked up men in lingerie departments or jewelry stores or men's clothing stores. Elaine said that a man looking over dinette sets is likely to be a man whose wife has just thrown him out.

We didn't want to deal with him either.

3

ALWAYS A BRIDE, NEVER A BRIDESMAID

Good families are generally worse than any others.
—ANTHONY HOPE
The Prisoner of Zenda, 1894

I was brought up in a middle-class family in Louisville, Kentucky, but of course it wasn't quite as simple, or as boring, as that. Until I was three, I had no understanding of who my parents were because I grew up in a houseful of adults, not all of them related to me.

My mother and father had both grown up poor. My father's side ran a tobacco farm near Shelbyville, Kentucky. During the Depression my dad, his seven brothers and two sisters all skipped a lot of school days to work the farm. My father was fifteen years old when his family moved to Louisville to tend a truck farm.

Daddy was sixteen when he went to work in a town on the

outskirts of Louisville helping an old man who ran a gas station. He got paid eleven dollars a week and the man let him sleep in a corner on a pile of oil rags. My dad would eventually own that gas station.

When he and Mom met for the first time, she was buying a Coke from the machine in front of the station. They had everything in common. And poverty was at the root of it all. They both borrowed the clothes and the shoes they got married in. They spent their first six months together living in a corncrib in back of a barn. Mother got a job packing gunpowder into bullets in a war weapons factory and Daddy got drafted.

By the time he returned from Europe, she had saved enough money to make a down payment on the gas station. From that one gas station, the two of them built a little business empire: an auto body shop, a used car dealership, a wrecker service, a grocery store, and real estate. And my dad invented things, he had race cars, and he bred and trained hunting dogs. My parents had worked their way into the upper middle class—by postwar Louisville standards—by the time I was born in 1951.

As was common in the housing shortage after World War II, my parents shared their home with Mary and Melvin, a couple also trying to get on their feet, and their ten-year-old daughter, Margie. Melvin was my father's deputy and best friend; Mary was my mother's age and best friend. When I was born, the baby-birthing-and-child-rearing business must have seemed like a relative breeze to my mother. She had a built-in friend and co-parent in Mary, and the services of a baby-sitter in Margie. According to my baby book I didn't cry, and why should I? I had ten hands reaching for me, petting me, feeding me, soothing me.

Because these four adults—and Margie—raised me communally, the odds were in their favor. Five people all concentrated together on one small child, rewarding her for every successful step, every word pronounced.

No wonder I was speaking full sentences by the time I was a year and a half old. When you have five people working on you, each one trying to show off to the others, there's a lot of forced learning. They kept immaculate records too, as if they were running their own Yerkes Research Center for the training of chimps. Ah, the fifties.

*   *   *

Everybody in town knew my dad. As his oldest daughter, I was paraded around. At the age of three I had been dressed up in a stiff blue dress and voted Little Miss Ferncreek. I always felt I had an obligation to live up to my father's reputation and expectations. He was a wonderful person: taciturn, decent, honest, and with his own standards. He was a country person. He knew about farming and all the things necessary for life. And, like many farmers, he was at heart a practical man. People respected him and trusted him, but they also thought he was a son of a bitch. He was somebody who did not put up with bullshit. If he told somebody to be at work at eight o'clock, and the man dragged in at nine, he'd likely fire him. And he had an eagle eye—he knew exactly how many cases of oil or antifreeze, how many tires an employee was stealing.

Once when he fired somebody I heard him say, "If you come back, if I see you on this property, I'll shoot you." And he meant it. More than once I saw him go get his gun; I only heard him fire it once, though. His threats were as good as his word, and so were his promises. He was reasonable. It wasn't like he'd ambush anybody.

On the other hand, if people followed his rules, he'd bail them out of jail, make sure their kids were taken care of and, of course, pay everyone on time. It wasn't unusual for my dad to lend a new employee his first week's salary on his first day of work.

One Christmas Eve my dad got a call from a woman who couldn't get her car started. It turned out the car had been sitting for months, next to their shack. It was just her and the kids, her husband having left some time before. They didn't have any Christmas decorations or presents, so my dad picked up a big box of candy, some toys, and a little artificial tree with some ornaments and lights for her. Mom filled a shopping bag with a smoked ham, some cookies and cranberry sauce and candied yams, plus green beans and stewed tomatoes from her own garden. My dad took all that stuff over to those people's house that night.

Before I was born, Dad had decided what was right and what was not right on very basic levels. One of the things I remember most clearly from my childhood was his attitude about war. He was against it. In the fifties you didn't hear anyone talking about being anything less than a willing soldier. But Daddy told us that, when he was being shipped overseas in World War II, he didn't want to go. That was the first I had ever heard of such a thing. Before being sent to Europe to join the Fifth Armored Division, he went AWOL, but the MPs found him. He said he was crying and kicking and screaming, and it took four MPs to throw him on the boat. I asked, "You cried? Weren't you afraid they'd do something awful to you, Daddy, for fighting them?" And he said, "What worse could they do to me? They were sending me off to get shot." And he was, too, at St. Lo. But not before he was captured by the Germans and put in a prison camp, from which he escaped just in time to storm Normandy Beach. Maybe it was experiences like this that gave my dad the perspective he had, and the confidence to become the kind of man he was. He was a great influence on me.

Years after I'd become an adult, he denied he'd ever told the story about going AWOL. I still don't know what the truth is about that, but I know that the basic truth of what he told me about being afraid and choosing what seemed right to him then, seemed right to me as a child. It does to me now. I probably got from my dad the idea that you say whatever is on your mind, you do what is in your heart, no matter what the rest of the world thinks.

As he got older, I think Dad became disappointed to find that good and right don't always work. He had cared deeply about his gas station, but at some point the oil company wanted it. One afternoon two men in dark suits came up our drive carrying black briefcases. Yvonne and I were shooed off into our rooms, but I could hear their voices through my door. The men said they represented the oil company, and they seemed confident that they had an offer Daddy just couldn't refuse. But he did. He told them to leave, and I heard him explain quite calmly that there was no need for them ever to come back. One of the men said, "But, sir, our oil company wants your corner. And we'll get it, whether you take this money or not."

The future proved that man right, and it crushed my daddy. He wanted to keep working—he probably wanted to die working at his gas station—and the oil company took his work away from him. A lot of his friends got old and died. Everything seemed to be changing, and he changed too. No doubt several years of operations and treatment for cancer had taken their toll. He went from lucid and thoughtful and generous to sad and resentful and more cantankerous than ever. A couple of years ago, Mother said he claimed he was voting for a Republican. (After the election he assured her he hadn't.) He adopted a lot of popular ideas instead of sticking with his own. Not only am I not exactly the same Daddy's little girl, but Daddy's little girl's Daddy isn't the same anymore either.

As a child, I thought that, as long as my parents were supporting me, it was only reasonable to try to make them proud of me. It was a good way to grow up.

I was a good kid and, as I saw it, there were certain advantages to being a good kid, among them the fact that you rarely got lectured or spanked. I saw that children in general were not very powerful and that it was not a good idea to go against people who were bigger than you were and who controlled the economy, because you'd lose. My sister saw things differently. She believed in confrontation. She felt her parents were obligated to feed her and take care of her, but she wasn't obligated in return to do anything she didn't want to do.

The 1950s being what they were, my sister and I weren't taught to grow up to earn a living. To prepare us for our role as Southern Ladies, our mother's dearest wish was that we take music lessons, go to dancing school, take art classes, make good grades, dress nicely, be polite, and be forever grateful that we had so much. In my mother's mind, all this was preparing us for a southern fantasy world: crinolines and lace and beaux and cotillions or at least designer clothes, new cars, palatial homes, good husbands, and social status. In her mind dancing lessons and comportment were crucial to a properly raised southern girl's social and economic future. Somehow, she felt, being "nice" and genteel and educated would make money come to me; I guess the idea was that I could at worst fall back on giving music lessons or teaching art in school. More important, my mother had never had a chance to take music lessons or dance lessons—in fact she had dropped out of school in the eighth grade—so for her these things were the key to a better life. I understood and, as much as I hated dancing lessons, I didn't resent her very much for making me take them. Childbirth was a lot for her to go through. The least I could do was take ballet.

I was in awe of my mother. She ate and never gained weight. She was beautiful. She could get more done in a given amount of time than any other person on earth. And she never started a thing she didn't finish. When Yvonne and I were growing up, she managed her own grocery store and her own gas station. She cooked our meals, sewed our clothes, was up before anyone else, dressed like Donna Reed, and drove us to school every morning. After she dropped us off at school, she would pick up the maid and then come home and do the dishes.

My mother's life revolved around cleanliness. There was no part of her house, not the closet, not the basement, where you couldn't serve a four-course meal off the floor.

After Mother did the breakfast dishes, she helped the maid clean, including windows and ceilings. Dust on the ceiling might fall into our food. After the house had been cleaned to her standards, my mother would go to the grocery store and gas station, to pick up receipts. Then she would work at the store or bring her bookkeeping back to the house. Dad's gas station was less than a block from our house, so every day at around noon my father would come home and my mother would prepare a meat and potatoes lunch, with three vegetables, fresh-baked biscuits, and a homemade dessert. Then she would go to the bank and back to work at the store until it was time for my sister and me to come home from school.

The first thing we did when we got home was change clothes. We changed clothes at least twice a day. My mother believed that school was dirty and that there was "no telling what germs those kids were passing around." She didn't like me playing with somebody who had a sister who was sick, because, she said, the sister might have cancer, and "who really knew if it was contagious or not." I was not allowed to go to a public park or playground or play with any other children before I went to school for fear of catching polio. I was allowed to play with cousins, but that was it. I could go to dancing school, but I couldn't drink from the water fountain or sit on the toilet seat.

By six o'clock my mother would fix a big southern dinner, serve it, and afterward clear the dishes and wash them. Then my sister and I would dry the dishes and put them away. And then my mother would sit down to help us with our homework. On Sundays and Wednesdays, our mother made us go to church, which often included missionary lectures and sermons about the less fortunate. Our mother made it clear to us that we were more fortunate than most, and that it was our moral duty to help others—something I reminded her of when I began working for prostitutes' rights.

Looking back on her life, I can see why I didn't want to be a mother and housewife—like my mother or Ethel or Lucy. What they did was fine for them, but it would have completely overwhelmed me. When I go home for Christmas dinner, even now, my mother will have made eleven pies. She will have cooked a turkey *and* a ham. There will be green beans she grew in her own garden, and of course her house will be spotless. In comparison I feel domestically incompetent. There was no way I could compete with my mother on the home front, or even live up to her.

I entered first grade already knowing the alphabet and my numbers to a hundred. I knew how to do simple addition—$2 + 2$, $5 + 1$—and how to spell a few words: *cat, rat, horse,* and *house* among them. But first grade proceeded as if children knew nothing.

I sat at my little desk and cried—quietly sniffling and wiping away tears and snot with tissues from the purse pack of Kleenex my mother had put in my handbag. I desperately believed I should be someplace else. School wasn't what I had expected. I had been told, for instance, that I was supposed to learn something.

On the desk in front of me was a mimeographed sheet with a picture of a house, a horse, a cat, and a rat. On another mimeographed sheet were the words *horse, house, cat,* and *rat*—framed inside little boxes made with dotted lines. I was supposed to cut out the words and paste them under the right pictures, but my paste and my safety scissors lay untouched. "Why are we supposed to do this?" I asked my teacher, Mrs. Hutchinson. And she replied, "Why, that's to help you learn the words."

"But I already know the words," I informed her.

"Then it should be easy for you to paste them in the right place," Mrs. Hutchinson said. "Why don't you show me that you can do it?"

Show her? I had just *told* her.

It was a horrifying moment for me. For the first time I was aware of, my integrity was in question. When I said something to my dad, he believed it. I had been raised to think that lying was the worst of all possible crimes. To do something wrong was bad, but to lie about it was much worse. I myself had never knowingly seen anyone lie, except on television.

Only a short time earlier, I had arrived for the first day of school with my mother. Each first grader's name was written on a three-by-five-inch index card with a felt-tipped marker and taped to the upper-right-hand corner of a desktop. My confidence in what I thought of as the infallibility of education was crushed when I saw that my card was embellished with the name DELORES.

"Look," I complained to my mother. "They can't even spell my name."

"We'll have your teacher fix it," Mother promised.

But when the teacher fixed it, she didn't bring a fresh, new card. She didn't even bring the same colored pen—red—but simply wrote over the first red *E* with a blue *O*. Now my name card looked ugly; it didn't look like any of the other kids' name cards. And it stayed on my desk the entire year. For one year I faced that nasty reminder that my teacher might not know what she was doing, and that I should always check things with my mom. Through my whole first year of school, I suspected some terrible mistake had been made.

By the time I started school, Dad was no longer the local sheriff. Mom made him give the job up because it was too dangerous. But he had all the police vehicle repair and service contracts and police towing contracts. So he worked with the police daily.

Cops congregated around my dad's twenty-four-hour gas station every night. So did everybody else who wanted to be out past midnight on a weeknight in our suburban town. Dad's corner gas station was quite a hot spot.

Every night the summer before my sister Yvonne was born, my mom and I went down to Dad's station. An elderly black man everyone called Rivers would always be there, rocking on a couple of wooden soft drink crates and leaning back against the Coke machine. Rivers played the harmonica and whittled and told me stories about exotic places, five-headed cats and web-footed women. We sang songs and I danced on some crates pushed together to form a stage. And sometimes people dropped spare change on us after the show—the money went straight into the Coke machine. I liked 7-Up, and Rivers preferred root beer.

The summer after my sister was born, my dad took me to the station with him. While he checked out the cash register, I caught the crickets that hopped around the bases of the giant metal poles underneath the station's lighted sign.

One such night, when I was catching crickets, my dad yelled for me to get in the car, a new brown-and-beige Buick. "Hurry up," he said. "I think the police are going to chase a car right through here." Sure enough, a car came flying between the two pump islands and down the road. Two police cars came roaring right after, and Daddy went tearing off behind them.

When the car they were chasing turned onto a dirt road past Floyd's Fork, Daddy said, "They got him now. He probably figured he'd lose them up here in the hills."

My dad stopped behind the police cars and said, "Look yonder. You see what's going on up there?" Some policemen had a teenage boy up against a tree, and they were beating him. My father then gave me this advice. Although I didn't know what he had in mind when he gave it to me, it has served me well: "Don't ever let the police or anybody else chase you to where there's no one else to watch what happens," he said. "You want the most people around to see you if you get caught." And then he said, almost to himself, "They shouldn't be beating him like that."

He yelled out, "Hey, Roy," to one of the policemen. "Roy," he said, "you know you shouldn't be doin' that."

Roy stopped. He seemed surprised to see us.

Twenty some years later my sister, Yvonne, told me of Daddy taking her on an almost identical outing at about the same age. We agreed that these field trips had served us well.

It was important to my father that I be initiated in a respectful way into politics, doing genteel things like prancing around in a paper dress as a Humphrey girl. Politics was central to my dad's businesses. As he explained to me, he was granted the city towing contract based on who was elected. "If the Democrats are elected, I make money," he said. "If the Republicans are elected, Tommy Johnson's daddy makes money."

This feast or famine aspect of politics bothered me. "Why don't you and Tommy Johnson's daddy just get together and share," I said, "so you both make some money all the time?" My father answered me, gently, "It ain't right but this is the way we do it. Maybe when you're grown, you can come up with a better way."

At age eleven I had my first "sexual" experience. The son of a family friend asked, when we were walking together on Halloween, if he could touch my breast.

"Why do you want to touch it?" I asked.

"I never felt one before," he said. I decided that, since he didn't have a sister at home, this was probably true.

"OK," I said.

"OK?" He could hardly believe his ears. Then he looked nervous, as if he had planned everything up until the point I said yes. "OK," he said finally, "this is how we'll do it. I'll walk ahead of you and I'll reach back and touch it. OK?"

"Sure, I guess," I said, but I thought: Pretty weird.

He walked a step ahead of me, reached back, and touched my breast so quickly—through my coat, sweater, and bra—about the only thing he could tell was that it was soft. Then he snatched his hand back as if it had been burned and walked on ahead. Very peculiar behavior, I thought.

I didn't see him again for a year. Then he and his mother came to visit. He waltzed into my room and asked if he could touch my breast again. "No," I said.

"But you said yes before!"

"If I could say yes before, I can say no now," I countered.

He reached for me anyway, and I smacked his hand away. He was in my house, in my room, and his mother was in the kitchen with my mother. I was amazed that he thought he could get away with this. "Get out of my room," I said.

At this stage of my life knowledge was coming fast and furious. I had picked up on the fact that boys were not supposed to touch girls, except maybe on the arms and shoulders, and girls weren't supposed to touch boys, except on the same places. Any other kind of touching, we were told, could lead to dire things. Apparently the whole world operated around a complicated set of rules about who could touch whom, when, where, why, how, and with what; who couldn't, and what the consequences might be. I realized that duels had been fought, wars waged, people killed, friendships made and broken, and reputations established and lost— all over who touched whom. It made no sense to me then, nor does it today, but then neither does the gold standard or the price of bell peppers.

I heard a little bit about sex at school, most of it claims about how to prevent pregnancy that sounded more like superstition than fact. So in seventh grade, when I read in a magazine that *Human Sexual Response*, a book by Masters and Johnson, was coming out, I thought I would be performing a desperately needed public service if I did a book report on it. When I stood up to give my report, however, the teacher said, "That's not the kind of thing a twelve-year-old should be doing a report on. You can't get the facts straight!" And I insisted, "Yes, I can." It seemed logical to me that if I was able to read a book and could look up words I didn't understand, I could do a book report on it. The teacher answered, "This isn't a matter children should be discussing." And I said, "But they are."

It was obvious to me that we were reaching a point in our lives where we needed to know about birth control, and a few other things too. But the teacher thought I was being insolent and sent me to the principal's office.

My parents were a little bit more understanding. My dad, being practical, said, "If you can read it, I guess you can read it." My mom, when I started telling her about the book, first laughed and then acted a little embarrassed. She eventually said, "Well, why don't you let the kids read it for themselves?"

Between Masters and Johnson and the details I had heard in school, by the age of thirteen I had a pretty good idea of what sex was supposed to be like. I was outraged that society conspired to keep kids from knowing about sex, as if adults owned the subject. I thought everyone had a right to knowledge about sex.

It was more than a right. It was a matter of taking control of my life. I was a complete adult at the age of thirteen—as tall as I am now, and with a much better shape. I was often mistaken for an adult. I wasn't carded once after I was thirteen or fourteen. I went to a high school of 3,000 people and was often mistaken for a teacher.

I wasn't interested in having any serious boyfriends because I didn't want to end up a housewife, without the kind of education that the boys had. At that point in my life I knew I wanted to be an artist. I was considered artistically gifted, and had already received some advanced art education scholarships and had even had a painting in a children's exhibit at the Museum of Modern Art in New York. So I concentrated on academics and art.

Diane Sawyer and I attended the same high school. Even though she graduated years ahead of me, she was an inspiration. She was so sophisticated—Miss Teenage America, you know. She carried herself in a way that demanded respect, like that lady on the *I Love Lucy* show I told you about. Diane Sawyer did not always get respect, however. People seemed to resent that she was so damned good at everything she did. Not only did she get good grades, she was a calendar girl, and the homecoming queen and she was voted "most likely to succeed." Still, people would say hateful things in front of her, or gossip behind her back if she wasn't right there.

Diane behaved as if she already had developed that sympathetic and yet reserved mien that works so well on *60 Minutes*. Many years hence, when I found myself having to deflect criticism while working in a Caribbean brothel, I thought of Diane often and tried to respond to it as graciously as she had.

Realizing the significance society put on virginity was like discovering that brontosaurus bones had been found in my backyard. There was social pressure to do something with these bones, like preserve them in a museum, but I thought it would be a lot more expedient to just dig them up and get them out of the way. When at thirteen I decided to dispose of my virginity, I needed a partner, of course. I found a decent candidate. He was a basketball player at an expensive private school. Even though he was an athlete he didn't have a stereotypical jock mentality. He was tall, of course, but he wasn't big and dumb. I didn't want to feel embarrassed later to think that I'd had my first sexual experience with a nitwit. It was important to me that it be with a boy who was intelligent and well thought of.

He was a few years older than I was. My mother had never known that I had gone out with him. She thought I was with my girlfriends. He was old enough to drive and—an important point— he had a car, a Volkswagen. On the one hand, I wanted to have my first sexual encounter on the backseat of a car at the drive-in. It was so classic. But on the other hand, I didn't want to. According to society, this was one of the single most important events in my life, besides baptism. At the time I suspected that the first time was a story to be remembered because I would someday be called upon to retell it. (And sure enough I was.)

I also considered that, years later, it might become more important to me than it felt at the time. So I wanted to leave myself the sentimental option. We did it at night, in a park preserve, under a big tree, which is still there.

We didn't use any birth control. I timed it carefully, so I knew I wasn't going to get pregnant. The basketball player had no sexual experience. He was nervous; I was nervous too, though not about my performance. I was nervous that somebody might come around, ask what we were doing, and turn us in to the police or, worse, our parents. I've never had much fear of being caught, but I hate the idea of having to explain what I'm doing, and I hate having things turn out differently than I've planned.

It was in the fall, and I remember that the ground was cold, hard, and bumpy. And I was on the bottom.

I remember how it felt when his penis slid inside me. It was very hard, and I was surprised that a part of a person's body could get to be that hard without there being a bone in there. I wondered about that while we had sex. I wondered, Why *isn't* there a bone there? I mean, there are 206 bones in the human body, why not one there, where you really need it?

I also remember thinking that people who were in love wouldn't be thinking, Why isn't there a bone in there? They would be too busy feeling in love and worrying that their lives might be ruined.

Afterward, I thought that, if the basketball player were any better at this, sex could be terrific. I thought, This is amazing data. I could see the potential in sex, but I could also see that high school boys weren't likely to have realized much of their potential. So I didn't have sex again for three years.

Shortly after this, my best friend, a girl I'll call Susan, got pregnant and was expelled from school. Her parents wanted Barry, the boy who had gotten her pregnant, to help pay for her hospital care. Things went as far as a paternity suit in court. But I heard that Barry's father paid several boys to testify that they had all had sex with Susan. I knew her well, and I knew she had only had sex with Barry. Those other guys were all virgins as far as I, or anyone else, knew.

After the trial, the guys walked around school bragging and acting like studs. They were proud of themselves, because they not only got paid but brought glory on themselves by saying that they'd had sex with a girl.

Susan meanwhile was sent to a home for unwed mothers. Out of sight, but of course not out of mind. Because of Susan, I suddenly understood how the system was rigged against girls. These guys went on through high school with big reputations and she was ruined. By the time she was sixteen, she was working as a prostitute on the streets of Saint Louis. (Susan, by the way, eventually put herself through college and became a public relations expert.)

She left school when I was fourteen. For the rest of my school years I carried the burden of having been the friend of someone who appeared to have slept with more than one boy. Because I was her friend, I was, by association, considered a slut too. There were people who would not allow their kids to go to a movie with me because of my "bad reputation."

I hadn't done anything—or at least anything anyone knew about—but still people talked. My reputation was quite effectively ruined. On the other hand, if I hadn't been saddled with that bad reputation, I would by default have been associating with the kind of bigoted and petty people who were condemning her and me. The people who did befriend me, who were willing to take me as I was—mostly people in the art department—were much more kind and sophisticated, and in the end much more interesting than the people in high moral dudgeon over Susan's fall from grace.

It made me appreciate the power of hypocrisy. I had to deal with it for the next three years—until I graduated—because, you understand, those high school kids didn't have much else to gossip about.

I was eager to graduate from high school and start college. Since I was interested in art, my parents agreed that I should go to art school. I was accepted at John Herron School of Art in Indianapolis, my first and only choice. It was not so far away that my parents would feel I was deserting them, and yet it was not so close that I would have to live at home.

Herron had a relatively modest museum but offered all the art courses I could want. I arranged to visit the campus during a student and faculty exhibit. One hallway was papered with the day's figure drawings. Almost all of them were better than my drawings, and none of them was less than something I would have been proud to do. In another hall, freshmen had hung huge, magnificent, meticulously detailed pencil drawings of insects. Whatever these students did to develop the skills to so powerfully portray a lowly water bug, I wanted to learn too. I could no longer be satisfied with whatever mysteriously ended up on my easel; now I knew there was a way to be better.

My dad had hung my drawings and paintings in his gas stations. And a part of me felt it was sort of sinful to want anything more than that, but I did.

I threw myself on the mercy of the admission committee. I just wanted a chance to be in the starting class. (I knew that Herron accepted fewer than ninety students, and that places in the freshman class were coveted.) They looked at my portfolio, gave me a take-home exam, and let me in.

I now look back on John Herron as the Parris Island of art institutions. Sheer strength and stamina were our first priorities. We were advised to bring mats to stand on while we did our life drawing class. Hour after hour we stood in the unair-conditioned studio at our bigger-than-life-sized easels, drawing bigger-than-life-sized nudes at the pace of low-impact aerobics. The instructor played loud music to spur us on and then shouted out instructions over the music: "Left hand only! Now, right hand only! Both hands standing on your left foot! On your right! Faster, faster!" Our professor walked back and forth, tyrannical, frantic, pacing around and slapping his yardstick rhythmically. My feet and legs ached and felt cramped. My arms throbbed, trembled, and then went numb.

Anyone caught resting would have Professor Sergeant Bilko in his face, bellowing criticism. Our attention would be drawn to the "lazy, arrogant student who thinks he deserves a break."

"Do these look like the drawings of someone who doesn't need this class?" the professor would scream, the veins standing out on his neck.

Two or three warnings of this nature were allowed before the instructor would order the student out of the class for the day. Three days of being barred meant automatic expulsion from the class with a failing grade.

Art history, English composition, color theory, design problems, and technical drawing filled out my week. Hot summer days drifted into pleasant fall breezes, T-shirts became sweaters, socks slipped under sandals, which were soon traded in for boots, and so the semester went. In no time we were layering on clothes to avoid freezing to death in the drafty studio. And I drew, and drew and drew.

By 1970 nearly all college students were smoking pot and experimenting with drugs. *Monty Python's Flying Circus,* the Grateful Dead, and psychedelic art—that was my freshman year of art school. Nearly every day at school I would hear about a new drug someone had tried the night before.

The weekend after midterms, one of the older students invited me to a party at his house. A friend turned up to take me to the party and announced that he was tripping on acid. I asked him several questions: How do you take it? What does it do? How long does it last? Will you have flashbacks for the rest of your life?

Even though he was tripping, he sounded very coherent. I was impressed. My high school health teacher had told us that people on acid were raving lunatics, and Art Linkletter had said taking acid made his daughter jump out the window. But here stood my friend, indicating that taking acid could actually be pleasant.

Staying in control had always been important to me. Perhaps it was possible with acid to stay in control and to be out of control at the same time. What a trip.

My friend said that he had a tab of acid he was saving for later, but that, if I wanted it, I could have it. It was only half a hit—a tiny eighth-of-an-inch-by-a-quarter-of-an-inch piece of paper with a purple spot on it, cut on three sides, torn on one.

"This is it?" I asked, sure he was putting me on. He said he had ripped it in half, but that it was "blotter" and pretty good and that half a hit would be plenty for my first time. I swallowed it with some milk. If that itsy-bitsy piece of paper had any effect on me, I was going to be impressed.

We went to the party and I felt nothing. The host played folk songs on an acoustic guitar; people passed joints around and drank jug wine. Since I didn't want to smoke or drink for fear it would interfere with my trip, I thought the party was pretty boring. The one thing I remember clearly was how the host's cats kept trying to climb on my lap and rub up against me. My eyes swelled in allergic reaction to all the cats, and I began to sneeze.

The host came over to ask if I was all right.

"I'm fine," I said. "I'm just allergic to all your cats."

"I don't know what kind of drugs you're doing," he said, "but I have only one cat."

So my acid trip had begun. Everything began to look weird, and I didn't feel so good. I wandered off to a bedroom, found a phone, and called someone whose number was on a scrap of paper in my purse. I hardly knew the guy, but I blurted out to him what was happening and how I felt and he talked me down. It was a little bit like someone giving skiing lessons, or teaching you to ride a bike, by telephone. But in no time I felt perfectly balanced. My allergies cleared up and, for the rest of the night, I had a wonderful time. To my amazement I discovered that the world on acid did indeed look like a psychedelic poster.

My mother hadn't wanted either me or my sister to date in high school—not because she was afraid it would lead to sex but because she was afraid it would lead to marriage. She said she had been very lucky to have found our father, but that he was unique and we might not be so lucky. My mother was—and is—a very strong woman. A lot of men, she felt, might not take kindly to strong women. My father was often exasperated by my mother's independence. If she wanted to go to a movie, and he didn't want to go, she would go by herself, which was almost unheard of. He would say, "I don't know what I'm going to do with you. You think you can do what you want to do." But he didn't try to stop her.

In general, she felt that marriage was a trap for women. She felt that women didn't come up to their potential when there were men around. I wonder how much of what I've done with men is just a way of following my mother's instructions: Get what you can from men, enjoy them, but don't let them get in your way.

When, in my senior year of high school, I got engaged to Rodger French, a music major at the University of Kentucky who I had met in accordion orchestra, my mother was disappointed. But since I went on to art school, and my fiancé went into the navy, she seemed mollified. At Christmas, however, Rodger called from his navy base in Boston to say that he was being sent overseas. He suggested that, if I took time off from school and married him, I could get a free trip to Europe, compliments of the U.S. government.

Two weeks later we were married and I became Dolores French. Since the wedding was such a rush, family members and friends gossiped that I might be pregnant. My mother was relieved to hear that I was not. I was simply ready to take a break from art school and see the world. Her parting words to me, as I set out on my new married life, were "Don't ever depend on a man for anything."

So, amateur psychologists, there you have it. What in that history "made" me become a prostitute? Was it my too-perfect mother and her fear of germs? My temperamental father? My experience as a Humphrey girl? The fact that my first-grade teacher couldn't spell my name right? The cavalier way I got rid of my virginity? Reading Masters and Johnson? The boy who felt my breast at the age of eleven? My tough introduction to fine arts as aerobics? My marriage at age nineteen?

Or was it the introduction my father gave me to the rights and wrongs of this world? His sense of honor and fair play? Or was it the hypocrisy with which the entire school, and most especially the boys of the school, treated my pregnant friend Susan?

And while you are at it, amateur psychologists everywhere, what do you make of this? My sister, Yvonne, grew up to be a self-sacrificing nurse, who today deals magnificiently with dying patients, is happily married, and has one child.

4

GOOD GIRLS GO TO HEAVEN, BAD GIRLS GO EVERYWHERE

The work is relatively well paid, demands a minimum of training, and can be seen as performing a socially beneficial function. Yet only in very restricted sections of society is it regarded as a viable career option to become a prostitute.
—HILARY EVANS
  Harlots, Whores and Hookers, 1979

I worked at Elaine's apartment through the spring and summer and saw an increasing number of regular clients. As time passed, I realized what a blessing regular customers were, whether I saw them once a month, once every six months, or once a year. Repeat business made me feel like I could be a success in my chosen profession. Regular customers were, however, a mixed blessing. I usually knew what they wanted, and they knew what to anticipate, but they often expected more time or more involvement each time they saw me. Some would drop their best behavior and feel more free to be themselves; sometimes they started acting like I was their employee. And, worst of all, once a guy had established himself as a customer, I could never raise his price. To this day I see a couple of old clients for seventy-five dollars.

After only eight months I had a few thousand dollars saved, so I told Elaine that I was going to take two months off to see Europe. I never did get there with my first husband, Rodger—his orders from the navy were changed and I was stranded in Boston, taking art classes at the School of the Musuem of Fine Arts while his ship wove around the coast of South America. Now, however, I had enough money to go to Europe without the help of the United States Navy. I wanted Elaine to go with me, but she couldn't. She had too many responsibilities: the business to run, her apartment to keep up, her children, college tuition for one, dental work for another, and Christmas wasn't far off when you consider that she had to shop for five kids, one daughter-in-law, and three grand-children. In some ways I think she was jealous of my freedom to pack up and leave.

I was in the process of buying the big twelve-room Victorian house I lived in, in the Midtown section of Altanta. (Despite its location, most of Midtown is residential, with houses set in leafy yards.) I rented out my extra bedrooms to friends, who were happy to keep up the house for me. They could handle my mail, monitor my answering machine. I could call them at any time for an up-date on my life. I was absolutely free to see the world, so I went.

I got an airline ticket for Rome and set my itinerary to include Italy, Switzerland, Holland, France, and Spain—your basic Great Art tour of the Continent. I didn't plan to work as a prostitute; in fact, quite the contrary. I wore clothes that would make me totally unappealing to men. (I had heard that pesky Italian men con-stantly bother women. Having been an art history major, I was determined to see a vast amount of fine art in eight short weeks, and I was not going to be able to keep to my schedule, I thought, if Latin men were constantly propositioning me.)

A pair of men's jeans I bought from Goodwill became the cor-nerstone of my European look. The jeans must have been from the shortest, fattest man ever; they had a fifty-four-inch waist and still barely came to my ankles. I roped this vast waistline in with a belt, and topped the outfit with an equally huge thrift-shop shirt that had giant red and white checks. I looked like a Ralston-Purina nightmare. I took three pairs of shoes: plastic high-heeled mules (to keep my feet in shape for heels), Earth shoes, and a pair of running shoes. I was hideous looking, but somehow Italian men could see right through this disguise to the pretty, young American underneath.

At first I tried to shoo them away. They'd back off with sad eyes, like a pack of puppies being ordered home, and then they'd be right back. I decided to put them off by telling them, "*No, no. Prego.* No touch. You must spend money—*lire*—to touch me there." They were delighted to find out that only money stood between them and what they wanted. After two or three weeks in Italy, I gave in and used all the tips Elaine had given me about shopping mall hooking to pick up men at the feet of Michelangelo's David, in the Uffizi in Florence, at Saint Mark's Square in Venice, even walking the Park Guell in Barcelona. I found clients underneath the Eiffel Tower, in the Louvre cafeteria, and on a tram en route to the Rijks Museum in Amsterdam.

I didn't know what the going rate was in Europe, so I just told the men any price that popped into my head, and then raised the price every time a man agreed.

The night I came back by train from Barcelona to Rome, traipsing around in a cold Roman rain, in my Ralston-Purina outfit and my Earth shoes, I noticed that a man was following me. I was desperately looking for a hotel room, cold, tired, thirsty and hungry, and in no mood for an amorous Italian. I just wanted him to get away from me. I was actually kicking stuff at him and telling him to leave me alone, but he just kept telling me how beautiful I was. And he kept following me into the hotels, which meant that none of the clerks would give me a room. They all thought I was working as a prostitute, and here I was, trying my darndest not to.

The only hotel that would even allow that they might have a room had one that was suitable only for a soccer team, a room with seven beds that cost a hundred dollars for the night. This was at a time when the kind of room I was looking for rented for sixteen dollars a night. I turned to the man, who with my limited Italian I had learned was a doctor, and screamed, like a raving bitch, "OK, fine. If you'll pay for this room, you can come up for one hour."

When we got upstairs, we found this vast room with beds lined up like a barracks. I was soaking wet and cold, so I suggested a bath, together. He started washing me and, without even touching himself, certainly without me touching him, he had an orgasm.

He said that I was so beautiful, he couldn't help himself. Twenty minutes after we entered the room, he bid me a gracious good night and left.

I spent most of my days in Europe going to museums. I'm the fastest museum viewer in the world—the sort of person who can do the Louvre in forty-five minutes. I knew exactly what I wanted to see. I found it. I saw it. And I got out. In between bouts of museum going, I hung out with my ex-husband, Rodger French, and his girlfriend, Toni, who were also on a grand tour of Europe. I loved Rodger and I was great friends with Toni. She and I had a lot in common: Rodger, for instance. We knew a lot of things about him. I could understand what she saw in him and why she was with him. She could see why I'd left him. We were great buddies. Toni was traveling with her whole family, arguing and brawling their way through Europe.

I saw Rodger, Toni, and Toni's mother the day after I had spent the night in the soccer-team hotel room. We were all trading travel stories and I told mine, how I had despaired of finding a hotel room until this doctor had offered to rent this huge room for me, and then had left after twenty minutes. Toni's mother thought this was hysterical and said, "Good for you. If more women dealt with men that way, they would be a lot better off." After I went on my way, she asked Toni about me. Had something happened in my life? I suddenly seemed much happier and healthier, she said, and I seemed to have lots of money. That was how she found out that I had become a prostitute. And she announced to Toni that it couldn't be a bad thing if it had done so much good for me.

In between touring museums and visiting with Rodger, Toni, and Toni's parents, I worked whenever a man bothered me. I worked in Spain and France, Switzerland, Amsterdam. The Italians were arrogant, yet so charming, and so good in bed, that I eventually gave in to having fun with a few of them, no charge. Italians are by far the best lovers in the world. Even American-born Italians have a sexual flair. I don't know if it's hereditary, cultural, instructional, or instinctive; maybe it's eating Italian food.

I don't know where people get the idea that French men are so romantic. I discovered after having sex with a few of them that they were generally out for themselves. They could pour on the romantic savoir faire, but that all seemed to me to be a con, in order to get me to do whatever it was they wanted. If a French guy said, "I want you to have my children," I was supposed to be impressed and grateful. When I responded, "Couldn't you just run over me with your car?" he was offended. Spanish men, on the other hand, were almost as good as the Italians. I don't know how Spanish and Italian men can have such a gift for lovemaking, can be so reverent about women, and then have the self-involved French wedged geographically in between.

Swiss men were sort of boring. In fact, the farther north I went, the less fun the men were in bed. I met British men in lots of different countries, and I thought they were all strange. They acted guilty about the very idea of sex. Sex to them wasn't something natural. It was a fetish.

For the Dutch, however, sex was ordinary. Dutchmen were very reasonable about sex. They didn't get worked up about it. Instead they thought it was something wonderful, something everyone deserved to enjoy every day—like a good hearty cup of well-brewed coffee.

After two months in Europe, I returned to the States. Going back to Elaine's, I entered the best period of my life. By living off the money men gave me for sex, I was able to achieve the independence from men my mother had always wanted me to have.

As I worked with Elaine, I started buying the things I had denied myself all those years I had been a politically correct hippie. I paid all my bills and got a good credit rating. I bought a new TV, a new stereo. I discontinued my subscription to *New Woman*, where women whined constantly about not having money, and began buying *Cosmo* and *Vogue*. I started thinking about what people could buy when they had money, because I finally had some of it myself. I bought beautiful clothes: $400 skirts, $200 sweaters, $150 shoes. My goal, however, was not to make a lot of money but to enjoy life.

I paid for the house I lived in. I put carpeting in my house and bought myself a new bed. And I put up the kind of curtains I had always wanted—made with very expensive, fine Dutch lace that I'd picked up in Europe.

I never lived beyond my means, but I was living right up to the edge of them. One day I decided that I could afford to have some especially nice things that would enhance my life, such as fine sheets and pillowcases. I went to stores that I thought would have the very best; I tried Macy's, Rich's, Saks, but they didn't have anything special. I thought of myself as so sophisticated, going out to buy the very best pillowcases. How much could the best pillowcase cost? I figured. Maybe ten times the price of a normal pillowcase. That would mean eighty-five dollars, a hundred dollars, which was expensive, but I could afford it and I wanted it and I deserved it.

Finally I went to Neiman-Marcus. And they had the goods. The saleswoman brought out a gorgeous silk pillowcase with handmade lace. It was beautifully designed. It was also $600. For one.

It was a struggle not to gasp. I was really honest with her, and I said, "Gee, I thought it would cost no more than a hundred dollars." I said, "I guess I'm going to have to reevaluate my income." And I told her I would be back. A whole set of those sheets would have cost $3,000. It never occurred to me that I would never have these sheets. As long as I stayed healthy, I knew I could afford anything. The minute I saw those sheets, I decided to raise my prices. I mean, I wasn't going to do without anything to get them. I had the attitude that no matter how much anything cost, by some divine appointment, it was within the price that any prostitute could afford, and her clients would be glad to pay for it.

I also learned something from that clerk. She wasn't embarrassed to come right out and say how much the pillowcase cost. It was $600. She acted as if I might well have the money to pay that, and if I didn't she still admired my taste and expected to see me back in there someday when I could afford it. There probably are a lot of eccentrics who shop at Neiman-Marcus, people who look like winos, who come in and ask for the best something or other and then pull a couple of thousand dollars out of a paper bag, pay for it, and leave. From then on, when I stated my price to a client, I tried to remember that salesclerk and to think, This is what I'm charging, this is what I'm worth. If you don't have the money now, perhaps you'll have the money sometime in the future. She was certainly an inspiration in how to tell customers that something they wanted was about to cost six times what they expected.

While things were going well for me, Elaine was running into trouble. During the time I had been in Europe, she had made an exception to her rule of not befriending the clients and had let one of her dates sleep over. When she woke up the next morning, her TV, typewriter, and stereo were gone. When she reported the thief to the police, the man, in his own defense, said that she was only a prostitute. (And therefore, in his mind, apparently not worthy of keeping her TV, typewriter, and stereo.) The police, of course, were quite interested in this accusation, but Elaine acted surprised: "He says that a fifty-year-old *grandmother* is a *prostitute*?" The police apparently thought that was a reasonable answer and let it go. The man returned her stuff, and they both dropped their charges. The next month, however, when Elaine went to her landlord to pay the rent, the landlord told her the police had been around to inquire about her apartment being the center of a prostitution ring.

I went to my lawyer for advice, and he suggested I go down to the courts and watch a few proceedings against call girls and prostitutes. He also suggested that I start saving some money, perhaps $10,000, which is what he thought would be required if I ever had to defend myself through a jury trial and appeals. I went to court and got worried. I saw women being treated by judges and police and even their own attorneys as if they were not there, as if their crime was a joke, something for boys to be making cracks about. Many of the women who didn't have attorneys took advice from their arresting officers on what plea to enter. There seemed to be a locker room attitude in the courtroom. And while these whole incidents were really amusing to everyone else, these women were being sentenced to prison, convicted of a sex crime the same as any rapist. And during all of this, the courtroom personnel acted as if these women's lives weren't important or serious, nor were their children's lives ever considered.

Not only was I mad about the way the system treated prostitutes but I felt it as a direct threat to me. I thought that time and ideas were going to have to change a lot before a prostitution case could be tried under the same legal ethics as other cases. Let alone that prostitution should not be a crime to start with. At that time I didn't have the money, the political clout, or the experience to deal with it all.

My friends knew I was a prostitute. They thought it was exciting and interesting. But being arrested, and battered by a hypocritical judicial process, was not an experience that would appeal to me. For one thing, my parents were bound to find out what I was doing for a living. (They thought that I was doing quite well selling my artwork.) For another, it would cost me money, more money than I had. And for a third, I might end up in jail.

Elaine and I agreed that we should cool things at her apartment for a while. I didn't have the money to set up another apartment for myself, one that I could use exclusively for seeing clients. And I didn't want to have anyone come to my home. (My attitude was that home is home and work is work. My house was a sanctuary. I didn't want strangers coming in, looking through my things, looking through my roommates' things.) For the moment, doing out-call work appeared to be my only option. I would meet clients in their own apartments or at a hotel. And, since it was getting close to Christmas, and a slow season for prostitution, I knew I was going to see clients I didn't think were particularly fun or pleasant if I was going to make a living. I went back to the piles of answers to my ads and began calling guys I had previously rejected.

One client made me an offer I couldn't refuse. His fantasy was to trim my pubic hair. "I'll be careful," he said. "It won't hurt, and I'll make it pretty."

I had seen this guy, Frank, quite a few times before. He was seventy-two, and he liked to have me to play house, maybe cook something for him—while wearing a camisole, high heels, and an apron—before we had sex. (A lot of women didn't want to see old-old clients, but I felt the old-old need sex the most and can afford it the least.)

He had already discreetly brought up the idea of trimming my pubic hair. This day I figured, He seems fairly sane, and he isn't so old he can't handle a pair of scissors. He's offering me twice the usual rate. Why not?

"All right," I told him. "You can trim it, but you've got to be careful."

He seemed so grateful. I lay back on the bed, undid my teddy, spread my legs, and thought about what Christmas presents I needed to buy and how many Frank was paying for.

Every once in a while I felt a tickling sensation. I could see the top of his head bobbing up and down as he peered through his bifocals at his work. The whole thing was quite soothing, like having someone give you a shampoo. I lost track of time. But then it started to feel a little breezy down there. Oh-oh. I knew, even before I looked, that I was in trouble.

He had destroyed my pubic hair. What had previously been a beautiful golden bush now looked like one of those sculptured, patterned rugs, which had been hacked up with a Weed Eater. It was down to the skin in some places; the rest was stubble, sprigs, and clumps. I flew into a rage.

"Look what you've done!" I shrieked, leaping up to the mirror to examine the damage. "I won't be able to work for a month. What am I going to do now?"

My wailing apparently scared the wits out of Frank. After some negotiation, he paid me $400 on the spot and wrote out a check for another $1,000.

Frank was, therefore, my first client who paid me lots of money. In retrospect, the ruination of my pubic hair was almost worth it, because it showed me there was more money to be made in prostitution than I had imagined.

Things got busy and Elaine changed her mind about "cooling" things, though we agreed to schedule our appointments elsewhere and to use her apartment as a rest stop. I saw some middle-class executives who didn't normally go to prostitutes and who were relieved to find a nice clean girl like myself willing to have sex with them for money. I saw clients so old that a walk from the living room to the front door was a big trip. I saw a man with a crippled wife. He was looking, with his wife's permission, for someone to satisfy his sexual urges. (I "saw" him in their specially equipped Winnebago.) One fellow owned a garage where they did body and mechanical work. (And where I got great service on my car.) Several men owned their own businesses. Almost all of them were married. Some of them had trouble getting erections; some of them had erections that never went away. But most of them were normal married men, bored with their lives and looking for entertainment. I began asking Elaine if "Han Solo" was ever going to come back, just for a change of pace.

Some clients were in themselves a change of pace. One client, another cross dresser, didn't seem to know how to explain what he wanted from me. And since he didn't want to be spanked with a hairbrush or to put high-heeled shoes on me, I didn't know what he wanted either. Every time I went to see him, it was a fiasco. He was a real-estate appraiser and very soft spoken. His place was almost empty of furniture, and it was very, very clean—too clean, if you know what I mean. About the only items in his apartment were a stereo, a conductor's podium, and a bed. He would stand at his podium, read sheet music, and listen to records while I stood and watched.

He did this dressed up like an old woman. Instead of sexy underthings, like a normal cross dresser, he wore garments a church lady would wear: a girdle or a very utilitarian garter belt, the kind elderly women get from Sears; Red Cross shoes; a dumpy dress; and heavy makeup but no wig. He sort of reminded me of Tony Perkins in *Psycho*.

Originally he had been one of Elaine's clients, and Elaine hadn't known what to do with him either. He said he wanted to be treated like a girl. But what did that mean? That I should tell him not to get his dress dirty when he went out to play? That I should warn him about little boys? Put a barrette in his hair? Spit on a hankie and clean his face?

One day I told him how weird I thought he was. I asked him how he chose his outfit, and he said he had an aunt who dressed this way. I asked if he'd had sex with her or if he wanted to have sex with her, and he said no. He couldn't, or wouldn't, tell me any more about it, so I have no idea what the particular bent in his psyche meant.

I felt so awkward, week after week, trying to pick up clues as to what he wanted from me. Eventually I worked out a routine where I stood in front of him while he lay on the bed. In his "aunt's" voice he would say things like, "Do you want to see what I have under my dress? Well, if you lift it up, you can see."

I would say, "Why don't you show me?" Then he would pull his dress up, pull his girdle down, pull down his plain white rayon panties and masturbate. But he paid me $100, and it usually took less than thirty mintues, which meant that, despite the fact that he was the strangest person I'd ever met, it was an easy session. I saw him every week or two, and I'd probably still be seeing him if he hadn't eventually bounced a check on me.

Then I met Moishe, who lived in an apartment complex that catered to elderly Jewish people. Moishe, who was sixty-eight, answered one of my ads.

When I got there, he said he didn't want to pay until afterward. I told him it was seventy-five dollars, and he said he wanted to pay only fifty dollars. (Not only was he decrepit, he was argumentative.) I knew that he had retired with a bundle of money, and that he was just being stingy. I said, "Fifty dollars will get you a half hour," and I agreed not to be paid until we were finished. When a half hour rolled around, however, he wasn't finished. (Something more I was learning: old men take longer.) I was there for an hour and a half, doing oral sex until my cheeks were concave, and when I was ready to leave, Moishe tried to tell me that he never paid on the first date. "Next time I'll pay you twice," he said. I said, "No, you won't, you're paying me now." Then he handed me an out-of-state check for fifty dollars. He said, "It's good." (What a cantankerous old buzzard.)

I said, "Look here, I'm not taking an out-of-state check. I want cash or a check on a local bank. And it had better be good, or you won't have the equipment you need to call another hooker." I was getting tired and cantankerous myself.

He told me to come back the next day, and he would have a local check for me. When I returned the next morning, he was shocked to see me so soon, shocked enough to get out his check-book and write me a check on a local bank. Then he said there was someone else in the building he wanted me to meet. So he gave me the apartment number, and that was how I met Herman.

Herman was the oldest-looking man I had ever seen. He was seventy-four and wrinkled from head to toe. Later I heard there wasn't a hooker in Atlanta who hadn't seen him. He was a wealthy man, a retired stockbroker, who saw three or four hookers a night and who always gave them a hard time about money. Not only was he wrinkled and tight with his money but he was bigoted, racist, and a pain in the butt. After Moishe I knew how much trouble older men could be, so I told Herman that I wanted a hundred dollars.

"You're the most beautiful woman I've ever seen," he said.

"Yes I am," I said. "And well worth a hundred dollars."

He said, "You'll make more money from me than you will from anyone else. I'll see you maybe one, two, three nights a week."

"That's fine," I said. "This hundred dollars will get us off to a good start."

Herman said "all" he wanted was oral sex because he had had a prostate operation and couldn't maintain an erection. Some-times, he said, he couldn't even come. Herman offered to see a couple of other women first, so they could kind of warm him up and get him ready for me. (Whatta guy!) After a lot of negotiation he talked me down to sixty-five dollars cash. I said OK, but in advance.

Herman lived close to my house, and as he promised I saw him once or twice a week from then on. But somehow, every week, he only had sixty dollars. Every week he'd say, "I'll pay you the five dollars next week," and the next week he would have only sixty dollars. And on top of that, my one hour always turned into an hour and a half.

During that hour and a half I got to know a lot about him. He told me, for instance, that he liked to go to the bus station and find some young woman wandering around, someone with a child, maybe. He would take the woman and her child out to a meal, and then he would ask them to come back to his apartment. Once they were there, he would say to the woman, who was usually running away from home or from a bad marriage, "If you have sex with me, I'll pay you."

These were innocent women—young, poor, and desperate. They weren't prostitutes. (He showed me photographs of some of them, to prove that he had actually done this.) Then, after they had had sex, Herman would pull the old I-don't-have-any-cash routine. Oops, and no check. Sometimes they would steal things from him. ("You just can't trust anyone," he said.) Eventually, if they gave him a hard enough time, he would pay them. I told him, "That's so dangerous. You're dealing with desperate people, and you're taking advantage of them. And besides that it's not nice."

He laughed and said, "OK, I won't do it anymore."

Herman was no thrill as a client, and he wasn't paying much, but he lived just blocks from me and he was regular. He wasn't a cop, and he wasn't dangerous to anyone but himself. And besides, I needed the money.

Eventually he owed me sixty dollars. So the next time I went to see him, I said, "You owe me sixty dollars. If you want me to stay, you'll have to get another sixty dollars."

He said, "I don't have it. Stay now, and I'll pay you tomorrow." I said no, and I left. The next week he paid me, and then we started in all over again.

Something happened at this point that sent my life off in a new direction: When I went to Elaine's to tell her I had finally gotten the money out of old Herman, I found that my key didn't work in the lock. When I realized that the lock had been changed—and not that my key was bent—my whole body sighed.

I should have expected it. Since the police had questioned Elaine, she had been seeing fewer and fewer clients. While I was in Europe, she had taken up with a new client, Nelson, who had recently offered to move in and support her. And she seemed a little jealous of me.

I had hoped to keep working with Elaine for a long, long time. And I considered her my best friend.

I went home and called Elaine to ask her what had happened. She told me that Nelson had suggested it, in fact, had insisted on it. "It's not you," she said. "Nelson and I are getting married."

While I was reeling from that one, Elaine said, "Hey, look. I got a call from Sunny." (Sunny was another working woman who lived nearby.) "She says there's lots of money to be made in the Caribbean, and there's almost no chance of getting arrested. A guy named Buddy had called looking for two girls to go down to Saint Croix and work at some luxury hotel. She says he'll take care of airfare both ways, rooms, meals, drinks, transportation, medical care, and armed escorts to the nude beaches, if you need them. Three weeks on your back, and then you get a week back here. All expenses paid. Why don't you call Sunny and ask her about it? I'd go myself," she said, "but . . ." But the fact was that, at the age of fifty, Elaine was getting out of the business.

As suspicious as this deal sounded, it didn't take me long to decide. It was wintertime in Atlanta, and I had never liked cold weather. The cops seemed to be closing in. Christmas had wiped me out financially. I desperately needed money. Maybe I was a little bored with doing the same thing over and over again, and I knew there was more to prostitution than what I had seen so far. Maybe moving to the Caribbean was part of the Big Plan.

5

PRIMERO NECESITO DINERO

There are three wants which can never be satisfied: that of the rich, who want something more; that of the sick, who want something different; and that of the traveler, who says, "Anywhere but here."
—RALPH WALDO EMERSON,
 "Considerations by the Way," 1860

Sunny was in her thirties, square-jawed, honest, straightforward, and I liked her. She had been a nurse until her son's health-care costs dictated a career change. For the last five years she had been working as a hooker to pay medical bills. In order to go to Saint Croix, she had to make arrangements for her son to receive extensive medical care while she was away.

Buddy called Sunny almost every night to make sure we were still coming down. It sounded to me like the man was either dumb or desperate, and that made me skeptical about the whole deal. I asked Sunny several times to get some information out of Buddy: the name of the hotel we were going to, what kind of clientele it had, if there was any possibility that we would get heated water beds, things like that. But Sunny never quite asked Buddy any of those questions. Despite their nightly conversations, I got almost no information about what we were walking into. She finally admitted that the two of them spent their time on the phone talking dirty to each other and masturbating, though they intended to talk business. "But, hey, what can I say, I'm in love," Sunny explained. "Don't worry, Buddy will meet us at the airport in Saint Croix and take us straight to the hotel. There's nothing to worry about."

As Buddy had promised, the prepaid round-trip tickets were waiting for us at the Atlanta airport. I tried to prepare myself for what was to come by buying a guidebook on the Caribbean. It mentioned that Saint Croix was famous because five American golfers had been killed there by rampaging Rastafarians. Swell.

Buddy had requested that we look like classy, trashy high-priced call girls when we arrived. So I was wearing black velvet pants, a multicolored sequined tube top, a feather boa, my highest black heels, two gold necklaces, and the diamond earrings my mother had given me as a high school graduation present. Sunny had dressed down a bit but still looked like a well-kept suburban lady: brown pants, a beige print top, platform shoes, and big gold earrings. On the baked chicken flight from Atlanta to San Juan—where we were to board a commuter plane for the Virgin Islands—Sunny and I figured we could have made a couple of hundred dollars if only Eastern Airlines had given us exclusive use of one of the washrooms.

We got off the air-conditioned plane at San Juan and were immediately greeted by a blast of hot humid air and a lot of attention. Puerto Rico apparently was unprepared for the sight of two dishy, fair-skinned women traveling alone. A large portion of the men in the terminal—both crew and passengers—turned around to stare.

"Do you have a good grip on your purse?" I asked Sunny. From where I stood, these guys looked like a mass gathering of muggers. It was only fair to warn Sunny, who was as blind as a bat without her glasses, that we were in treacherous territory. "I believe they want our money, our jewelry, our clothes, and then perhaps our bodies," I said.

"Why us?" she croaked.

"Because we're fair haired, white women—and I mean *white*. Whiter than any women these people have ever seen. I can't be in the sun for more than a few minutes. I wear number 15 sun block and haven't been out of the house in daylight for years," I said.

Purses gripped under our arms, we headed for the exit to our commuter plane, where even more men rushed to see us. "My God, what's going on?" Sunny asked.

"Remember how I said we were real white—amazingly white—to these people? Well, apparently the guys inside went to tell their friends, and now everyone's coming over to look at us. Like we're a couple of floats in the Macy's parade." I was glad these men had lechery instead of larceny in their hearts. Some of them started winking and waving.

"Look," I said, "why don't we just do what they're doing? Let's wave, you know, like the Pope, and throw in a wink and blow a kiss every once in a while, like Miss America." We went vamping and sashaying through the terminal like two fools.

Then one teenage boy broke from the crowd and came over to ask Sunny, who was carrying my bag: "Is *she*"—he indicated me—"a movie star?" Sunny figured the right answer was "Yes, she is! Now get out of her way."

We thought that, when we got on board the twin-engine four-teen-seat Prinair for the island hop, our troubles were over, but it turned out a whole new category of troubles was just beginning. Sharing the ride with us were a bunch of islanders and a champion fighting cock. When we took off, the cabin pressure made the windows pop open and the bird start flapping. Turbulence was making that little airplane skip up and down like something in a Hanna-Barbera cartoon. The other passengers seemed unfazed. The prize fighting cock didn't even have his feathers ruffled. But I was becoming a shade of whitish green. Aviation exhaust poured into the passenger compartment, just to add to the deluxe ambience. I asked Sunny if she would be embarrassed if I asked for a parachute. (I was ever so grateful my first husband had given me skydiving lessons for my twenty-first birthday.)

But a crew member overheard me and said, "No. No. Not yet. I'll tell you when to put on parachutes." Then he smiled and said, "We fly this plane fifteen years and we never haf to use dem. Dey prob'ly don't even open no more!" And he smiled some more. Caribbean charm school, I guess.

Somehow the plane made it to Saint Croix, and Buddy met us at the airport. He was a tall, thin gangster in training—all six feet four inches of him tropically suntanned. He was wearing jeans and a T-shirt that read ARMADILLO CAFÉ. With that he had tastefully coordinated about $10,000 worth of jewelry—rings, chains, bracelets, and a watch.

The swank luxury resort turned out to be a twenty-four-unit motel with broken black-and-white TVs in every seedy room. Buddy took us on the grand tour: a tacky patio and the lounge where the reggae, salsa, and calypso never stopped. Darkly tanned Caucasian men sat on rattan bar stools drinking rum concoctions under a slow-moving ceiling fan, like extras in *The Treasure of the Sierra Madre*. Buddy told us the men were pipeline workers, taking a break.

Buddy took us to his room, then, for the pièce de résistance. "Here's my pistol," he said. "It's small enough so I can keep it pretty well hidden, yet it'll do some damage when you pull the trigger. Tomorrow you girls come back and I'll give each one of you yours. They won't be traceable. If you have to kill someone who's getting out of control, there's a man we can call—you'll meet him tomorrow—and he can dispose of the body and the gun. That's all there is to it. The same guy can erase any police records you two might run up."

When I indicated that I wouldn't count on me to use a gun, Buddy said to me, "You mean if I picked up this gun right now and threatened you with it, you wouldn't try to stop me?"

After a few seconds' thought I said, "No. I don't think so. I believe in self-preservation, but my background has done nothing to prepare me for a threat of violence, until it actually happens."

Buddy gave me a look of deep disbelief.

All the furniture in the room Sunny and I shared was cheaply made and then covered with a thin wood veneer. To remind us that we were in the tropics, there were lamps with burlap shades and bamboo bases. And the room had the worst Sheetrock job I had ever seen. Someone had had the good taste not to put any pictures up, so it wasn't all bad, but after working at Elaine's place, it was a definite comedown to be at this motel.

I unpacked my clothes and the two wigs I'd brought. Wigs have never been out of fashion in the South, where women always complain about what the heat and humidity do to their hair. I figured that wigs would be indispensable in the Virgin Islands, which were even more humid than Atlanta. My Gibson girl wig, something every prostitute should have, was too formal for the islands.

My Orphan Annie wig was perfect, however. I took a shower, reapplied my makeup, slapped Little Orphan Annie on my head, and waltzed myself down to the bar to see what was happening.

Picking up men in a bar couldn't be too different than picking up men in shopping malls, I figured. As it turned out, picking up men at Buddy's lounge was like trying to sell water in the desert, since all of the men knew exactly why we were there and that was why they were there. On the other hand, the pay was crummy: Sixty-five dollars was about the top, and a lot of men wanted to argue me down to forty-five. And I found out that wigs, and the rest of me, got pretty rough treatment from oil refinery workers.

After five trips from the bar to the room, looking quite a bit more disheveled each time, I realized the Caribbean was no place to wear a wig. Then I noticed that Sunny had been sitting in the same place all night, drinking with the bar crowd and making cow eyes at Buddy. Buddy, meanwhile, had made it quite clear to everyone including Sunny that (a) he was married; (b) his wife also had one of those little guns he had offered us; and (c) she had no compunctions about using it on another woman.

The next day a woman named Tammy showed Sunny and me the nude beach. Tammy was the mistress of a millionaire who ran a numbers operation all over the South. This guy paid Tammy $2,000 a week, basically to park herself in Saint Croix and be available to him, which didn't sound any too bad to me or to Sunny. But he wasn't there very often, and Tammy had become bored. So to amuse herself she started hooking on the side for a hundred dollars an hour.

Sunny was particularly impressed with the life Tammy described. This was how she had envisioned life with Buddy: all suntan lotion and tropical beaches, $2,000 a week, and a little free enterprise on the side. Buddy seemed to be swimming in money, and it wasn't from the little motel. He was constantly getting phone calls from foreign countries, and he was always on and off the island. He might have done anything from laundering money to being a hit man for the mob. Whatever he did for a living, Sunny was impressed with him.

When we got to the beach—with me all covered up in hats and caftans and sun block—Tammy asked us if we had our guns with us, since she had forgotten hers. When she found out we had never picked up our guns, she hustled us back to the motel.

*   *   *

After meeting Tammy, Sunny was even more determined to nail down her relationship with Buddy. After three days he couldn't take it anymore. He made up some story about how the pipeline was threatening to declare his motel off-limits to its employees if we "working girls" didn't leave. (This didn't make any sense, of course, but Buddy offered to pay us for the next two weeks and find us a nice room at the best hotel in Christiansted. I thought any place had to be better than the place we were.) Sunny and I were chauffeured to a ritzy hotel at the other end of the island. Sunny immediately went out and got a straight job as a bartender at a place called Susie's.

What I like about Sunny is that she just doesn't quit. Her notion about getting a bartender's job was that Buddy had rejected her because she was a prostitute. If she got a "good" job—that is, one that paid five dollars an hour—she thought Buddy would respect her more than if she was making fifty dollars an hour as a prostitute. What she didn't understand was that with Buddy money not only talked, it stood on its hind legs and jumped through hoops. He had no objection to any woman making good money.

While Sunny went off to Susie's to learn her new trade, I lay around the hotel room. Ever since the flight I had felt strange—tired, achy, seasick, sweaty. I had been denying the signs for days. It wasn't until I woke up in the hotel room with aching breasts, however, that I realized that—despite my IUD—I was pregnant. I even knew who the father was. For the last six months, the only man I had not used a condom with was the little high school boy. It didn't make sense to me to ask a kid who was trying to adjust to the most mundane aspects of adult life to hold the hand of a twenty-eight-year-old woman while she had an abortion of a baby she very much wanted to keep. I felt that, as far as a baby was concerned, it was now or never. But with my life-style, I didn't see how a baby would fit in. On the other hand . . . I didn't have the money for an abortion. But then, if I couldn't afford an abortion, I certainly couldn't afford a baby.

About then Sunny burst into the room with great news. There was this *darling* little room at Susie's, and Bonita, the happy-faced Santo Domingan who owned the bar, said it had been used as a trick room. Sunny said, "If you want to work out of there, it's yours. Come see it."

On the way to Susie's I bought some saltines that I hoped would soothe my raging morning sickness, though it was now late afternoon. Susie's was a dark, grimy little place with fifteen stools, six tables and a jukebox offering Latin, reggae, and country-western music. The customers, more pipeline workers, seemed exceptionally glad to see me, but what a grungy group. With a lot of apprehension I whispered, "These are the men you want me to see?"

"Yeah, they're a great bunch of guys. They're in love with you already. I've told 'em all about you. A couple of them have been waiting all afternoon."

"Oh, really?" I thought: They aren't any dirtier than the men who worked at my father's garage.

Sunny took me back past the kitchen and into a filthy little hole she called the "trick room."

"It needs a little fixing up," she said. We looked around the room, at the never-been-washed sheet on the bed, the never-been-mopped concrete floor, the ragged fiberglass curtains with the square hole cut out where the air conditioner went, the bare light bulb dangling from the ceiling, then we looked at each other and laughed. In unison, we said, "This is another fine mess you've gotten us into." We both stared at the room for a moment while the enormity of the disaster crept into our consciousness. Here we were, two nice middle-American call girls who had been lured to a luxury resort hotel on Saint Croix but had ended up in what was very close to the Black Hole of Calcutta: a trashy trick room at a sleazy bar called Susie's.

A lot of thoughts went through my mind as I stood at the doorway of that room: "I can't do this" was foremost. But I also heard my mother's voice saying, "I don't want you girls to ever be too proud, or think you're too good to do what you have to do to survive. Why a little soap and water will clean this place right up." I was near-broke; I knew I couldn't make as much money as I needed back in Atlanta. And I was pregnant.

My mother, after all, had started married life in the corncrib of a barn; who did I think I was, anyway? I felt as if I were Alice facing the looking glass. My solution, perhaps a great adventure, was right through that doorway. I walked into that room and decided things weren't so bad after all.

When I returned to the barroom I began bargaining with the customers. It was hard not to be insulted by the kind of money they were offering. Forty dollars. Thirty dollars. I had never heard of such prices. Finally one particularly flush or horny fellow put in a bid for sixty dollars, and I found it was quite possible to maneuver a client so that either he was on the bottom or we both were standing up. There was no way I was going to touch that sheet or that bed, even fully clothed.

Sunny and I went out the next day with thirty dollars of the money I had earned and bought a set of sheets and pillowcases and some inexpensive fabric to make curtains and a bed ruffle. We also bought a mop—Susie's bar didn't have one—some Janitor in a Drum, Lysol, bug spray, a lampshade, and scented candles. After about ten hours of work, the room didn't look bad at all. As a matter of fact it looked kind of cute.

Business was brisk, so brisk that Sunny and I could afford to rent an efficiency apartment near the bay. I saw mostly oil workers and merchant seamen and the ever-present Latinos. I would have been making really good money if I hadn't had to spend half my time with my head in the toilet. (Pregnancy just didn't agree with me.) By the time the return date on the round-trip ticket Buddy had paid for had rolled around, I had enough money to fly home to Atlanta, get my abortion, and spend some time recuperating before I returned to Saint Croix to finish the adventure I had started. Buddy, by the way, was now long-forgotten history, as far as Sunny was concerned.

The month I worked at Susie's seemed like a year. Sunny had brought her family down, not just her son but also her ex-husband, and installed them in our apartment. There we were, three adults and a kid, living in one room. And, I decided, the situation at Susie's left a bit to be desired.

So I tried out other trick bars in the red-light district.

El Echo, run by Yolanda, was next door to Susie's. The other prostitutes I was meeting said El Echo was too restrictive. They had rules about starting at 8:00 P.M., working until closing, living on the premises. If you left the premises you had to give Yolanda ten dollars. No drugs, no boyfriends; a lot of rules. But it was nicer and cleaner, it had better security than Susie's, and cabdrivers would bring sailors there when they asked for a whorehouse. But for someone like me, who hated rules, El Echo didn't seem the answer. I never, and I mean never, went to homeroom during my entire high school career. I just didn't see the point of homeroom and I refused to go. The school threatened to expel me, and I told them, "Go right ahead." But they never did. So the idea of working as a prostitute and having to follow rules as nonsensical as homeroom didn't appeal to me in the least.

Raphaelo's, the other whorehouse in town, was loud and raucous, had no rules, and also allowed me to live on the premises. I said good-bye to Sunny and moved bag and baggage to Raphaelo's. I also made a deal to start sending money to a friend in California, who promised to keep my cash in a nice American bank for me until I decided to move back home. (I didn't trust the banks in Saint Croix. My ambition was to pile up at least $10,000 from my stay in the Caribbean, and the best way to do that, I figured, was to put the money where neither I nor anyone else could get their hands on it. And every time I sent $200 or $500 to my friend, I wrote a letter, telling him about everything I was seeing. He saved those letters, which is why I have a record of all this.)

It was at Raphaelo's that I met Patty, a blonde California girl and archeologist. She had a wonderful attitude about prostitution: she had decided to travel around the world where she had access to good "digs" and to pay her way by working in the local whorehouses.

Patty was in her midtwenties, and she was full of exuberance. Raphaelo's, you have to understand, was one of the sleaziest places in the world. It was the sort of place where, if your family accidentally stumbled in, your mother would say, "Don't touch anything." There were people at Raphaelo's who were killers, people who didn't kill out of fear, mind you, or in self-defense, but who killed as a primitive form of communication. And yet, in the midst of this chaos, ignorance, and squalor, Patty and I were making fistfuls of money.

We made money not just because we were young and collegiate looking, but because we understood psychology. One night I watched Patty deal with this drunk who could have been a problem. Like a violent problem. The man may have been not only drunk but crazy. Patty and I were leaning on the bar, both of us in mule pumps and Danskins, and she was talking to this guy as if he were in therapy. He was trying to give her a hard time—telling her "You look just like my wife, that bitch, I ought to smack you both"—and she was talking to him like a social worker. "When did you first notice you felt like you wanted to hit someone?" In other words, whatever the guy said was not simply the beginning and end of it. And finally she got the guy to go home and talk to his wife, settle things peaceably. This guy had been a problem ever since he walked in the door, and now he was saying to her, "You're OK, let's go upstairs, you're OK." And she was saying, "Why don't you go get a good night's sleep?" And she did this not because she was scared of him but because she thought it was really the best thing for him to go home and talk to his wife, now that he had calmed down. She had a realization that you had to maintain humanness in the business.

Patty was a wonder at dealing with people who were terribly upset. She said these people would be good clients once they got over being drunk and angry. In other words, there was a tinge of altruism in her social-worker approach, but it was altruism based, ultimately, on profit. There was always a payoff, and the payoff was that business was light anyhow at the bar, and the guy might remember her and come back on a better night. She said Psych 101, 102, and 103 ought to be required education for anyone wanting to be a hooker. Oh yes, Abnormal Psych wasn't a bad idea either, she said.

After a series of bad incidents, Raphaelo's liquor license was suspended and most of us women moved to El Echo. Yolanda still had all those rules, but her place seemed a little safer. As soon as we moved in, the hookers who were working there warned us about the water.

"We shouldn't drink it?" I asked.

"No, you've got to get some gallon jugs and fill them with water. Yolanda turns the water off an hour after the customers leave. She thinks we use too much. Especially hot water."

Now this was something as unimaginable to me as needing a gun. What kind of place was the Caribbean, where people shot at you and turned off the water?

It was at El Echo that I accidentally rolled a client who wanted to marry me. He was a little man from India who worked on a Panamanian merchant ship, and he promised me his whole paycheck every month if I married him. That came to $640 a month, which really wouldn't quite have covered things.

He had been a perfectly ordinary client, though he was terribly drunk and had fucked forever. It was taking him a very long time to put his clothes back on, and now he thought we were in love and he was planning the wedding. "Thanks for asking," I said, "but I don't think it's suitable." He was so sincere, in his very drunk way, but I was trying to get him out of the room so I could go back to the bar and get another customer. And he was talking and buttoning one button, talking and buttoning another button. I saw a little wadded-up bill drop out of his pants. I thought, If I give this dollar back to this man, it'll take him another fifteen minutes just to put it in his pocket. Since he's already paid me sixty dollars, I thought, what's another buck? He's wasting more than a buck of my time getting dressed. So I reached under the bed, grabbed the bill, and tucked it into my bag.

I didn't know how much I had taken until I was sitting with Patty, on the bed, counting my money the way hookers count money. Only kids playing Monopoly and hookers count money this way—sitting on the floor or on the bed, in a circle, making little piles of tens and twenties, counting out loud, because it's really a kind of competition, in a friendly sort of way. I was straightening my money out, counting it, and I ran across one bill, all wadded up. "I got this from that Indian guy, the one who wanted to marry me," I said. It made us both laugh that I could remember which dollar came from which client. But I could, just because of the way different nationalities handle money. It was so typically Indian to wad money up this way.

When I pulled out this wad and held up this bill, I saw it wasn't a one but a hundred. I felt very guilty that I had done that, and I told Patty, "If you see that guy in here tomorrow, would you tell him that he dropped this?" I didn't even send the hundred dollars to my friend in California but kept it at El Echo, in case the Indian guy came back, but he never did. If you are reading this now, sir, and you were making $640 a month on a ship of Panamanian registry in 1980 and you remember proposing to a redhead at El Echo on Saint Croix, I owe you a hundred dollars.

It was Patty who told me about the Black Angus back in San Juan. I had told her that I hated living on Saint Croix. It was too small, too sunny, had no telephones, or at least too few. There was no TV or radio worth listening to. We didn't get the Sunday *New York Times* until Wednesday. There was never a movie playing that hadn't played in the United States three years before. And Yolanda cut the water off, on a regular basis.

"If you want something more exciting and closer to home," Patty said, "you ought to try the Black Angus in San Juan. It's a huge place. The biggest whorehouse on the island. You ought to at least stop by and visit. It's quite an experience, like a Fellini movie."

Since Patty had once told me that the thing she liked about

being a hooker was the freedom—"I can have no money at all, arrive in any strange town, and start earning a living"—I decided to do an experiment. Even though I had some money saved up, I went to San Juan with only my plane ticket and enough money for a hotel room for two nights. (I did have a fallback, of course. I left some money with a friend and asked her to send it to me if I needed it. I never did. Being a hooker, I found, is like minting money. From then on, whenever I traveled, I started out with nothing, confident that I could get any amount of money I needed by working.)

I got off the plane in San Juan and found a hotel room for sixty dollars a week. The air conditioner at least drowned out the sound of traffic, since it had no effect on the room temperature. There was, however, hot water. Then I caught a cab and said, "The Black Angus, six twenty-seven"

"—Fernando Juncos," the cab driver finished for me. Obviously it was a well-known place, and I was not the first woman to get in the cab and ask to go there.

I found the man Patty had recommended and said, "Patty sent me." Those were the magic words. The fellow, Carlos, told me all I needed was a medical card and I could start working. (I soon found out this was nonsense. None of the women there had a medical card. "Just tell Carlos you're waiting for it," they said. I actually went to the address he gave me, just to see how a bureaucracy for hookers works, and I found an abandoned building, which somehow figured. Carlos was required by the police to tell us hookers to get a medical card. We were required by law to have a medical card. But there was no way to get one.)

When I saw the bar at the Black Angus, I said, "This is the place for me." John Waters had obviously been here. The Black Angus Bar-Hotel had been set up in World War II, supposedly by the U.S. government, when there were a lot of troopships stopping in Puerto Rico. The furnishings in the hotel rooms appeared to be old army surplus: functional, sturdy, made of heavy wood. All the army-issue furniture was appropriate to the place. The Black Angus was like a boot camp for prostitution. It prepared you for battle, it made you physically fit, and it was a darned good place to meet other foot soldiers.

Forty women from all over the world worked there every night. The bar looked like a world tour of what people thought looked sexy: grass skirts, leis, sarongs, saris, native costumes from Iceland,

Poland, Sweden, and one local woman who dressed like she was at a church social. This woman was fat in a housewife-who's-had-too-many-children sort of way. She wore a white eyelet short-sleeved housedress with a full skirt and buttons right up to her chin. She carried a white handbag and wore low-heeled white pumps. The only jewelry she wore was a gold cross, a watch—which no whore would be without—and a wedding ring. I saw her go upstairs as often as anyone else. One woman had been working there for thirty years, wearing the same sort of outfit—a black wig and a sarong—year after year.

An employee's wife worked there as a hooker, and I'm sure Divine was modeled after this woman. I wanted to find out where she had her hair done—it was styled like something from a 1950s outer-space movie, bleached white and swept up into a kind of double pompadour. Every hair was in place, and she said it cost fifty dollars to get it done that way. She wore makeup as heavy as that of a circus aerialist: thick white makeup under dark, heavily painted eyebrows, bright red blush, seven shades of eyeshadow, some of them metallic, thick false eyelashes, and meticulously applied lipstick. All of this was on a very dark complexion. Her clothes were very expensive and ran to beaded cocktail dresses. Many nights she just sat there, motionless as a statue. This woman charged fifty dollars, when she got a client. Most of the women charged twenty or thirty dollars.

Since what I was selling was Anglo-American good looks, I decided to charge thirty dollars for the "short-time." (OK, I know Puerto Rico is part of the United States, and I know that all the Americas are considered American, but even in Puerto Rico people asked me, "Are you American?" That's the way they referred to it, and that's the way I'm referring to it here.) I was one of the few hookers at the Angus who didn't wear a wig. My hair was short and curly, and it looked cute in an all-American way. I wore mostly tube tops and wraparound skirts, high-heeled sandals, and L'Oréal Sea Pearl nail polish, the ladylike polish I had learned to favor at Elaine's. You could put on lots of layers of it without it looking like a mess, and if you missed and painted your finger too, no one could tell. I thought I was the only hooker on earth, besides Elaine, who wore Sea Pearl until I got to the Black Angus. When I discovered that nearly all hookers wore it, I switched to red. One of the things I learned at the Angus is that all women are selling basically the same thing. All of our bodies looked more or less the same underneath our clothes. In order to make money, you had to find some way to stand out.

No matter how much you earned at the Black Angus, you earned every cent of it. If someone gave you a hundred dollars, he was so rough or so demanding, you'd wish he'd paid only thirty dollars for a quickie.

For thirty dollars they got seven minutes with a woman—they were told it was twenty minutes—plus they had to pay six dollars upstairs for the use of the room. The sheets at the Black Angus were simply thrown over the bed for each encounter. They had a big HOTEL 627 inside a circle stamped on them, like a brand, and they were so clean you could get detergent burns from lying on them. Young Puerto Rican men ran into the room and replaced the sheets the minute we were done. The gray marbled linoleum floors were never mopped, so I quickly learned not to take my shoes off.

Like most women who worked there, I used only breakaway clothes, usually I didn't wear any underwear, and I never wore stockings. I could undress in ten seconds and dress in fifteen. I would hang up my Danskin in such a way that all I had to do was stand up, fling it on, and pull the strings and I was dressed. If a guy was a big spender, I would say, in the fifteen seconds it took me to get dressed, "That was wonderful" *(Tú eres muy superbo, muy grande)* and hope I'd see him again. With regular, seven-minute clients, I could do up to nine jobs a night. If things were going well, and I found clients who wanted to pay for something extra, I'd do two or three a night. I never tried to shave a minute off here or there, the way some women did. I was always polite and gave the guys their full seven-minutes' worth. As a result, I often had regular clients who were waiting for me when I got back downstairs, and I could go straight back up. I earned a pretty steady $100 to $500 a night, working from 8:30 to 4:00 in the morning.

Most places you can get used to in a few days, but no middle-class American girl could have gotten used to working at the Black Angus, ever. I had time every day to really think about what went on. If I had any doubts or questions about what I was doing, I could do a reality test the very next day. What was the best approach? Where was the best place to stand? What were the best clothes to wear? The Black Angus was a little laboratory for prostitution. Most experiences are unique, but at the Angus, I could repeat things again and again, to find out what worked best for me. If something didn't work out, it didn't mean my career was over. It just meant that I earned a hundred dollars less that night. I could always make it back later, the next night or the next week. It was all process. I could try wearing a wig, put on a new shade of lipstick, a new nail color. Sometimes I wore an outfit all the other women said was great, and I didn't make a cent. I even had the luxury of wearing it again, to see if it was the outfit, or if it was just one bad night. I kept notes on how much money I made under what circumstances—what were the realities and what was the mythology.

One of my most successful outfits looked a lot like the dress that glamorous guest star wore on *I Love Lucy*—a very tight-fitting dress with draped gathers and spaghetti straps. I had it in two fabrics, one black and the other leopard print. I liked the leopard print, but the solid black one made me more money. People said they loved the leopard print, but the men spent their money on solid black. I learned that if I wore two outfits exactly the same, one red and one black, the red didn't make as much money as the black. And I don't think it was because the black made me look thinner. I think it was because men find black sexier and more formal. Maybe there is something cheap and trashy about red.

At the Black Angus, the most aggressive prostitutes stationed themselves near the door. Some of them would have their hands in a man's pants before he reached the bar. The more expensive women were farther in and toward the left, near a grand piano that no one ever played. A jukebox blared constantly, mostly songs in Spanish but that year Dolly Parton's "Nine to Five" was on too. The bar itself was lit with red lights, which meant that women had to wear extreme makeup—like black eyeliner around their mouths— so their lips wouldn't disappear. The red lights in the bar made everything and everyone look good for the country boys coming in to San Juan for the night of their lives. Then, when we'd walk these boys up the stairs into the normal light on the second floor, to stand in line at the booth where they bought their room tickets, it looked like a freak show.

It was like a scene from some county fair, with simple country boys lined up alongside sequined, feathered, and painted women from the sideshow, all waiting to buy tickets for a ride on the Ferris wheel. Some of the country boys would get a good look at these women for the first time under the white lights and suddenly change their minds.

The women in line taught me all the Spanish I needed to know. *"Yo mamo y chucho buena."* If there was a wait for a room, I didn't want the guy to walk out on me, since I had already spent ten minutes in the bar picking him up. So I entertained myself and the country boys by having them teach me the rudiments of Puerto Rican Spanish.

But sometimes the wait for the room just got too long. The guy was only contracting for what he thought was twenty minutes of sex. After a twenty- or thirty-minute wait, he sometimes bolted. Then I would have to go down to the bar and start all over again. Most guys, however, stuck with it because they were so eager to get into those rooms.

We would march down the long hallways to, say, room number 19. We would dash inside, he would hand me thirty dollars— usually in fives and tens—then close the door and ten seconds later I would be undressed and at the sink, washing myself. I would make a gesture at undressing him—like unbuttoning the top button on his shirt—and then I would suggest he get his pants unzipped. Every room had a bathroom with a hand towel and a complimentary bar of soap with some other hotel's name on it; it was my job to get the guy into the bathroom and wash him up. Some of those Puerto Rican country boys considered themselves clean if they had bathed in the last month, if they had been swimming in the ocean any time in the last week. Each bathroom at the Angus was different. My favorite had a turquoise bathtub and pink ceramic wall tiles. I washed the customers' cocks at the sink, just above a shallow little plastic trash receptacle that, by the end of the night, would be filled with discarded tampons and rubbers, cigarette butts, soap wrappers, and little slivers of used soap. Then I would lead my client back to the bed and slip a rubber on him. Two minutes into it, I was either sucking or fucking.

Five minutes later, just as the guy was about to come, the sheet boys would start pounding on the door and yelling, *"Pronto, pronto. No más tiempo!"* After that, we'd have maybe one more minute, and then it would be *"Pronto, pronto"* time again. If I had a client who was willing to give me more money, and if I didn't want the sheet boy hassling us for another six dollars every seven minutes, I could hand the sheet boy five or ten dollars and tell him to come back later. I found that if I was courteous and polite to the sheet boys, if I didn't treat them like low-class servants but instead dealt with them as co-workers, they could be a lot of help.

There were signals to use, for instance, that would get you out of there for sure in seven minutes. If the guy was a pain in the ass, the sheet boy would say, *"No más tiempo,"* then stand there until the guy left. It was a far cry from working at Elaine's place, but I found there was something compelling about it. Every day I thought, This day is going to be my last. And every night I was back at the Black Angus.

Some of the prostitutes used to sit around and make shoptalk: fingernail polish and fellatio were the big two. A hooker wanted to find fingernail polish that would never wear off, and she wanted to find a way to suck a guy off in the least time possible. Every woman there thought that she had the superior method. I was eager to learn, so I asked them their secrets. Some of them thought the whole idea was just to suck hard. Some thought tongue flicks could bring a guy off the fastest. Some thought deep throat was the answer. Others believed it was up-and-down speed, some thought if you stuck a finger up a guy's ass, and one thought it was all in the moaning-and-slurping sound effects she made.

I tried each of their methods—after all, I was there every night, and every night I saw at least three clients—and I decided that none worked especially well for me. That is, none of their methods worked well for me in isolation. But when I put them all together and found my own rhythm, the men found it pretty darned exciting.

I think I learned the idea of patterns from Japanese clients. When a Japanese man fucked, he didn't just go in, out, in, out. That wasn't the Asian way. The Asian way was in, farther in, a little out, way in, a little out, a little out, a little out, way in, in, in. You could get lost in those patterns and rhythms. I always wanted to ask one of my Japanese clients if there was some kind of traditional musical pattern he was following, maybe something composed especially for intercourse. But none of them ever spoke enough English to tell me.

I was fascinated by these Japanese fucking rhythms, and I figured men might like a blow job done the same way. That meant giving it in an artful way, and not just going suck, suck, suck. There was a lot of teasing involved, teasing and stroking and sudden surprise and tickling and deep pleasure.

A lot of clients tried to get their money's worth of time with me by restraining themselves. A couple of clients even complained that I made them come too fast. "Just go up and down, up and down," they said. But I found that I could sneak in a little fancy rhythm and surprise, in between the ups and downs, and I was still able to get them off pretty quickly. It usually didn't take longer than seven minutes.

I got a lot of rave reviews from clients, and a lot of repeat business, but it was very tiring to perform this way. If I didn't do it every day my tongue got tired, my jaws got tired, my lips got tired. When I went home for some R & R in Atlanta, however, everyone commented about how the structure of my face seemed to have changed. My cheeks seemed leaner, my jawline tighter. I knew it was from giving head.

Another thing the hookers at the Black Angus told me about was biters. On my very first night there, one woman leaned over and said, "That one's a biter." The women told me I shouldn't ever let a Puerto Rican eat my pussy because he would bite.

And Puerto Ricans did. They would bite me everywhere: on the neck, the ankle, the wrist, the breast.

I learned right away how to say in Spanish, "No biting. No biting, and I mean it." They would bite me anyhow. I would have to keep my hands somewhere near their ears, so I could grab them and pull them away from where they were biting. They were like big, strong wood ticks.

Some of the biters were on to my defensive hands-on-his-ears technique, and with them the session was like a seven-minute wrestling match. They would be trying to bite, I would be trying to grab their ears, they would be trying to maneuver out of my reach, and I would be trying to close my legs, to keep them from biting me there.

One guy was a dedicated biter. I warned him in advance: No biting. He nodded in agreement, very solemnly: no biting.

When he bit me, I said, "Didn't I tell you no biting? Didn't you say you weren't going to bite me? Why did you bite me?"

He smiled and said, *"Me gusto."* I like it.

It was a pretty stressful way to work, expecting to be bitten all the time. But other than the biters, I loved the Black Angus. The people who ran the place simply would not tolerate anyone bothering the "girls." That meant that the sheet boys took care of problems upstairs, and the bouncers kept watch over us downstairs. I didn't know what that meant until one night, when a young, drunken French guy started annoying me. It was a few minutes before closing. He came up to me saying that I was beautiful, that he wanted to go upstairs with me. But when I told him how much it would cost, he looked disappointed and said he only had eleven dollars. At 3:30 in the morning, after having seen five clients, I wasn't interested in another trip upstairs, especially for eleven dollars, and I politely told him so. But he was persistent. Some men just don't believe that when a woman says no, she means no.

Meanwhile, there was a nice man from the mainland who came in and sat down beside me, a man I had seen the night before and wouldn't have minded seeing again. But the drunk French guy kept cutting in on our conversation. I again told him politely but firmly to leave me alone.

He took that as an invitation to move in closer. He started pleading with me and rubbing his cock against my knee, thus committing what I considered petty theft. I pushed him away gently and told him in my most civilized angry voice that if he rubbed his cock against my knee again, I was going to smack the shit out of him and take his eleven dollars besides to cover the cheap thrill he was stealing. He retreated a bit behind a structural post but was soon back again, this time pointing a finger at me and slurring, "You're a bad, dirty woman."

That was as far as he got, because now I was really pissed. I shot up off the bar stool, screaming, "Get away from me, you asshole. Don't you touch me and don't you come near me." That's when I caught sight of the bouncer in the background, who, I realized, had been watching the whole thing. He grabbed the guy cartoon-style, by the collar and the back of the pants, and threw him as far as you can throw a person. The guy hit every support post and piece of furniture between the bar and the front door. I hadn't seen so much violence since the civil rights march on Auburn Avenue in Atlanta in 1972. I sat on my stool dumbfounded. I had imagined that what bouncers would do was come over to a guy, kind of lean on him, and say something like, "Hey, buddy, ease off." Now the bouncer was outside the bar with this guy, and a crowd was gathering. I was too shocked to want to know what was happening, and I never asked.

Most of the women at the Black Angus were "migrant workers," either poor women from third world countries—women who would charge ten to fifteen dollars a session, they were so desperate for money—or fairly well educated, black or white Americans or Europeans, who would charge thirty to fifty dollars a trick.

Needless to say, the two groups often divided along class lines, both inside the bar and when socializing.

One member of the fairly well educated group was a hooker named Linda, who looked like a young Katharine Hepburn. Linda was really sharp, graceful, and she had a wholesome beauty that looked a little out of place in the Angus. She made a lot of money there, and she seemed to spend it all, which surprised me. Because of the way I was brought up, I thought nice middle-class girls should save their money. I once asked her what she spent her money on, and she said "I don't know. Clothes, shoes, hotels, plane fares, food, jewelry, stuff like that. I spend about two hundred dollars a day and I just buy whatever I want." It was Linda who taught me how to get a rubber on a man without his knowing it. (A lot of the clients were reluctant to wear rubbers, and the Black Angus management didn't insist.) At first I spent more time arguing with clients about wearing rubbers than I did actually performing sex acts. So a way to get a rubber on a client without his knowing was a valuable thing to learn. She used her thumb to demonstrate:

First, she explained, you put the rubber in your mouth. "Hide it in your cheek like this," Linda said. She opened her mouth to show me she had kept it hidden the whole time we were talking. "Use the unlubricated kind," she said.

"Why?"

"Have you ever tasted a lubricated rubber?" she asked, making a face. "Then, when you're ready, flick it to the front of your mouth with your tongue." She showed me that the rubber was now right behind her lips. "It's important to put it in so that it's ready to roll right down."

"How do you get it on him?"

"You just put your head down like you're going to do a blow job, but just before your lips touch the head of his cock, push the rubber out of your mouth so it lays on the tip of his dick. Then purse your lips against it and just suck. Then all you have to do is inch it down with your tongue."

"That's all?" I was skeptical about it being that easy.

"Well, it helps to touch him somewhere else while you're working it down. That'll distract him." I still looked doubtful.

"It really works," she said. "They never know it's on until you take it off them."

I found it hard to believe, but she sent me upstairs with one of her condoms to try for myself. My first try was a disaster—I tried to put the thing on inside out. But I was lucky in that I had four or five more chances to practice that night. Pretty soon, I was able to put one on without a man having the slightest idea what was going on. Blowing on a rubber became a standard part of my routine. I never even asked a man if he wanted to wear one.

I learned enough about bizarre sex at the Black Angus to write a revised edition of *Psychopathia Sexualis*. The women charged extra for anal sex, and I charged a lot extra. One of my favorite regular clients was a man I called the asshole eater. Unlike most Puerto Ricans, he was very, very tall. He was about thirty-five, balding, with big bulging brown eyes and a little pencil mustache that made him look French, in a cartoonish way. He had a pointy nose, wide thin lips, and a sharp chin.

For asshole eating, I would charge him thirty dollars extra. By the time we would get into the room, he would already have a huge hard-on. I would wash him first, and while I was washing my crotch and anus, he would move the heavy wood furniture around so he could have an unobstructed view of my soon-to-be-revealed ass in the wall mirror.

(These mirrors were about three by four feet and hung about a foot off the floor to provide a view of the single beds. All of the mirrors had cracks in them, from, I suspected, some kind of overly enthusiastic sex or some act of violence.)

When I returned from washing myself, the asshole eater would have me lie down, naked, on the bed. He would position me so my crotch faced the mirror. Then he would place my hand in my pubic hair and indicate that he wanted me to run my fingers through it while he watched. All of his gestures and movements were frantic and comically exaggerated. I would try to lie calmly and to transfer some of my tranquillity to a guy who was, by now, frantically hopping from one socked foot to the other, jerking off like a maniac and fingering his gold crucifix with his other hand. He would purse his lips while nodding in my direction, as if he would be tossing kisses to me if his hands weren't so busy.

He talked too: *"Muy linda, me gusto,"* over and over, on and on, while shaking his head from side to side as if to indicate he had never seen anything like this before. All the while he was hopping and masturbating without interruption.

He occasionally closed his eyes in ecstasy. Then, suddenly, he would make a rotary motion with his hand to indicate that I should turn myself over. He would coax me into the position of a Muslim at prayer by tapping and poking my body with all the finesse of a lion tamer. Once I was properly positioned, so he could see my derriere in the mirror, he would admire it like a newly completed work of art. He would stand back and hold out one hand to the mirror, as if presenting my ass to the audience. He would ooh and ahh and suck air noisily through his teeth and make juicy kissing sounds. Then he would come over to me and touch my butt cheeks in a sneaky way. First he would give me a couple of light pats, then he would start squeezing each cheek like mad. Then, making an *ummmmmm* sound, he would start kissing my behind all over. And finally, with a ravenous groan, he would start licking and sucking my asshole. He would wrap his left arm around the crown of my upturned ass, bury his face in me, and jerk off like mad with his right hand, while his crucifix bobbed against my clitoris. In other words, he made out with my ass.

After about twelve minutes had passed, six of which would have been devoted to sucking and probing my asshole with his tongue, I would tell him his time was almost up. In Spanish he would beg me to let him finish. I would tell him, *"Tres minutos,"* and he would say "OK." After five minutes more of this elapsed, I would say, *"Necesito más dinero, ahora."* He would start whining and pleading, and sneaking little licks at me. In order to make him stop I would reach behind me and put a hand over my asshole, like a shutter closing on a camera. Then he would come up with ten dollars more and I would take my hand away.

He had orgasms just as frantically as he did anything else. He must have jerked off at the rate of 150 strokes a minute for the entire session, and he would increase the rate of stroking just before he came. He would tip his head sideways to catch a glimpse of this whole scene in the wall mirror, and then, with loud groans and gasps, he would come and I would feel warm semen splattering on my upturned feet and ankles.

Afterward, while I was washing my feet, he would thank me as if I had saved his life. He would tell me that he loved me, and that he wanted to marry me, and even as we walked out of the room he would be saying, *"Muy linda, me gusto."*

I saw him at least six times, and each time was exactly as I have described it. I began to think of this kind of asshole worship as a normal sexual appetite. So when another fellow came into the

Black Angus, saying he wanted to do something special with my ass, I thought I knew exactly what I was getting into.

He was a black guy from New York City, clean, dressed in designer jeans and a T-shirt, a civilian who was doing engineering work in Puerto Rico for the United States Navy. He told me he would give me a hundred dollars for an hour, which seemed like a lot of time to me.

First we did all of the usual sucking and fucking. Then he put me in the Muslim prayer position so familiar to me, at the edge of the bed. Then he knelt on the floor and licked my asshole for a while. So far, so good.

Shortly after that he started sticking his tongue in my ass. He stuck it in very deep, so deep I could feel it moving around inside me. This went on for about fifteen minutes, and then he really surprised me. He blew air into my ass and then inhaled deeply as the air came back out. He did it over and over, more times than I could count.

I had heard about guys who wanted to sniff farts, but I had figured they just fed their women lots of kidney beans, or sought out someone who specialized in farting. But I guess that serious fart sniffers have to improvise. It was pretty mind expanding to have an experience I had not even realized was possible. Still, the experience shed no light whatsoever on the expression "He was just blowing smoke up my ass."

I guess I'd like to know if there's any way to tell in advance what strange sex acts will turn a particular person on. It seemed to me that absolutely anyone could be turned on by absolutely anything, and it also seemed to me that part of my job was to respond to these people with understanding and compassion. I had to be willing to put up with anything short of having pain inflicted on me. Some people seemed to be like Pavlov's dogs. They had somehow become conditioned to getting sexual pleasure out of things that seemed weird to me and, I would guess, to most everyone. But if I denied these people their sexual expression, if I made them more frustrated or guilty, they were just going to divert this sexual energy into something else.

Weird experiences, the strange clients, the endless supply of innocent country boys and tourists and sailors, new hookers working at the Black Angus, the red lights in the bar—these became like an addictive drug to me. I felt wide-eyed, innocent, intrigued, titillated, and amused all at the same time. I flew home to Atlanta for Christmas—full of bizarre tales about sex and guns and strange clients—to find that Herman, the irascible old coot who had given me so much trouble over money and who had spent his spare time picking up girls at the bus depot, had been murdered.

Apparently it was one of the girls from the bus depot. He had probably finally pushed someone too far, though of course that didn't necessarily mean she was completely justified in sticking a knife into him. After the stabbing, Herman staggered down the hall, trailing blood all the way. The girl had been arrested, and it was the talk of Atlanta: a nice old man who was stabbed by a runaway girl he had befriended.

All the hookers I knew in Atlanta—and by now there were quite a few—laughed when they heard about what had happened to old Herman. He had been so mean to so many women, they felt there was some justice in his violent end. Somehow the papers figured out that Herman had a long history with prostitutes, and the later editions tried to paint the homeless girl who murdered him as a working girl. But we all knew she was one of Herman's victims.

It was good to be home, and I might have stayed, had I not had the feeling that there was still more for me to learn in the Caribbean. I had already spent a year there, and I thought if I went back for a few more months, over the coming winter, I would have my fill. I didn't know when I headed back that there was so much more to learn it would be another year before I left the Caribbean for good.

6

IF THESE ARE TENS AND TWENTIES, WE MUST STILL BE IN SAN JUAN

The slave has but one master; the ambitious [wo]man has as many as can help in making a fortune.
—JEAN DE LA BRUYÈRE
The Characters, or Manners of the Age, 1688

When I came back to Puerto Rico after Christmas, I decided it was important for me to learn about other whorehouses besides the Black Angus. The Angus, as you may have gathered, was hardly decorous, but it was like the Harvard Club when compared to La Riviera, in Old San Juan. Outside La Riviera, a mechanical band of life-sized female mannequins played Latin music, sort of a Puerto Rican whorehouse version of Disney audio animatronics. The signs at the front door advertised a one-drink minimum, a topless disco, erotic dancing, and, perhaps the greatest draw of all, a giant TV. Another sign suggested that shirt and shoes were required for men. I noted as I went in that it didn't specify pants.

I entered by way of a staircase decorated with black nude silhouettes, past a dripping, leaky fountain and into . . . well, Toto, I don't think we're in Kansas anymore. The main room had a huge circular bar wrapped around a stage, where strippers, completely naked strippers, did the bump and grind—on customers' faces, if that was necessary to get their attention—to a loud and low-down Latin beat. Next to the bar was a huge teddy bear that was sometimes humped by the dancers. And all around there were lights, more lights than I had ever seen before in one place: blue-and-red police car roof-rack lights, men-at-work yellow blinking lights, K mart blue light special lights, strobe lights, spotlights aimed at crystal balls, and, of course, twinkling Christmas lights.

If patrons were getting bored with the psychedelic light-and-sex show in the main bar, there was always the game room, with pinball and video, and the TV room, where there were videotapes showing everything from porn cartoons to magic tricks done with condoms.

On walking into La Riviera I was struck by the thought that I might have been born too late. I wondered what Cuba had been like, thirty years ago. Could it have been any more decadent, any wilder than what was still available here in Puerto Rico?

I was impressed with how much fun both the strippers and the customers seemed to be having. It was Caligula come to life. Sodom and Gomorrah. La Riviera had a reputation as a seedy, grungy, raunchy whorehouse, but to me the sexual-carnival atmosphere was heaven. This was a place where, obviously, anything went. The decor was schlock city, tacky-tacky-tacky, definitely done to Puerto Rican taste. To my way of thinking, Puerto Ricans possess the highest natural sense of kitschy design, and La Riviera was the culmination of Puerto Rican sensibilities.

I introduced myself around, and a woman named María gave me the grand tour and the lowdown. I learned that there were twenty-five to fifty women on hand any night of the week and they charged from twenty to thirty dollars for their services, which wasn't that different from the Black Angus. But at La Riviera, rooms cost seven dollars for forty-five minutes, and a sign boasted NO WAITING.

When I got my first customer, he was a nice little Puerto Rican man, not too drunk, and he readily agreed to thirty-five dollars. We left the main room of the bar and set off to find the Royal Hotel, actually an attached building just down the hall and up a few stairs.

Here that Puerto Rican sense of style was truly evident. The hallway was covered with draped silver lamé material, no doubt chosen to compliment the silver insulation that covered the air-conditioning ducts along the ceiling. The concrete-block walls in the stairwell had been masterfully painted to resemble nothing so much as cheap laminated wood paneling. Michelangelo would have been flabbergasted by the handiwork. (So much talent in pursuit of so little effect, I thought.) Once we reached the hotel we found the actual cheap wood paneling the stairs had been painted to match. What style!

A nice gray-haired old man named Duke, who spoke perfect English, stood at the top of the stairs to take the room money. He explained that the guy had to have seven dollars exactly. Duke didn't give any change. And when the money was handed over, it was slipped through a slot in the wall, into a safe. (The hotel management wasn't taking any chances.) "If you bring a drunk up to the room," Duke said, taking a look at my slightly swaying client, "that's your responsibility. But if you get into any trouble, just yell for help."

Down the hall there was a stack of towels rolled up with a little bar of soap inside each one. The soap was not new, but it had been washed off and dried before being recycled. A box sat next to the stack of towels, for tips. A sign indicated that a dollar would be appropriate, which seemed steep to me.

The rooms were neater and cleaner than those at the Black Angus. Every room had a bathroom with a working shower. I had been told that each room also had a bidet, but I found a bidet as it could only have been designed by a Puerto Rican: a rinse hose that stretched from the water line—cold of course—over to a seat-less toilet. There was another nice touch in the bathrooms, however: a small black wooden box under the sink that could be pulled out so short men could have their cocks washed.

The single bed was soft instead of bouncy like the Black Angus beds, which meant I would have to work harder. And, unlike service at the Black Angus, at La Riviera the sheets weren't changed after every use. Instead a sheet was folded into quarters. After each client the sheet would be refolded, so it could last four times before being removed and replaced. The mattress had a fitted sheet covering it that got changed once a day. I finished quickly with my client, and we went back down to the bar for a postcoital drink: *jugo de China, con hielo, por favor.* Orange juice with ice, please.

One of the nude dancers there was a twenty-four-year-old native, Ryina, the star of the show. Without any particular tricks or shtick, without using the teddy bear, Ryina did an erotic, sensual dance that had all the patrons clapping rhythmically. She gracefully balanced on the balls of her feet and spread her knees to offer the bar patrons a glimpse of what they couldn't otherwise see. There were a hundred or so customers around the bar, and, for a dollar apiece, she would give each one a little private peek. For five dollars a man could lick her pussy as she danced. Between shows, she let it be known, she was available for private performances at the hotel. (Buddy, the fellow who had brought me and Sunny down to the Caribbean in the first place, had once said that hookers don't dance and dancers don't hook. Ryina was actually the first—and only—woman I knew to do both.)

Sitting in the bar I saw an old man who had given me a hundred dollars for a short and easy job at the Black Angus a few months before. He didn't remember me—senility, I guess—but he said he'd be willing to try again, if it *was* again. He ordered some drinks for the two of us, and I excused myself to the ladies' room. When I came out, expecting another quick trip upstairs, La Riviera was in a panic. The old man was gone. Women and customers were running in all directions—those with their bearings toward the door. The screams and the jabbered Spanish made it difficult for me to understand exactly what was going on. I did see men with big sticks and guns, and that was what gave me the idea that La Riviera was under attack by rival gangsters, or perhaps was the focus of a banana republic revolution. Had Puerto Rico finally seceded from the union? To most Puerto Rican men, I reasoned, taking over a whorehouse was the likely first step to seizing power in a country.

I ran back into the ladies' room and found a bilingual hooker. When I explained to her what was going on outside, she said, "Oh, not *that* again. Stay here," she said, "and you'll be safe."

With that she disappeared.

What did she mean, Not that again?

And safe from what?

It sounded like a riot was going on in the bar. Were people being beaten? Would I hear gunshots? Was this just a normal, nightly occurrence at La Riviera?

There was no way out for me. The bar and its accompanying bathroom were on the second floor, so I couldn't crawl out of a window. And the exit was across the bar from the bathroom, so I didn't think a mad dash was the right idea. Shortly a man came in, waving a gun at me. He indicated I was to follow him across the bar to the dancers' dressing room. And then he indicated I was to wait.

Wait for what, I wondered, the firing squad? Puerto Rico was still part of the United States, wasn't it? I mean, they didn't just shoot you, did they? Didn't they have some kind of a trial first?

Eventually someone explained to me in English that the police were looking for nude dancers. Right away I asked for an English-speaking officer. A handsome young Puerto Rican vice squad officer came over and we had a conference. "Are you sure you're not a nude dancer?" he teased. I had no problem declaring that I was definitely not a nude dancer at La Riviera. "What's a nice American lady like you doing here, in this place?"

"I'm a hooker."

He asked one of the dancers. "Is that right? She's a hooker? You ever see her dance?"

She shook her head. "No."

"How about you?"

"No."

"Anybody ever seen that lady dancing?" he asked.

"No! No! No!" they chorused.

The vice officer released me, but only after giving me his phone number at the precinct and inviting me out to dinner. "Say tonight, eleven-thirty?"

It was one of the most educational dinners I have ever had. The vice cop told me, for instance, that the dancers had simply been fined. He explained that there hadn't been a conviction for prostitution in the four years he'd worked on the vice squad. For a conviction, a prostitute had to approach a man and specifically suggest they have sex for money within earshot of someone else. The reason for this is that a Puerto Rican man might feel embarrassed if someone overheard him having to offer money to have sex. So the law was made to protect men from being embarrassed. When they did whorehouse raids, the cop said, they went in with specific names, took everyone to the police station in a school bus, called off this list of names, none of which seemed to be the name of anyone there. When no one answered the roll call, everyone who'd been brought in had to pay an arrest processing fee, about thirty dollars, and all charges were dropped. Then everybody was put back on the bus and returned to the whorehouse. After that, they ran a piece in the paper saying how many people were arrested. Puerto Rico, I thought, was great.

With my newfound information I decided to try out something I had always wanted to do but been afraid to try: out-and-out street prostitution. I had already picked up men in shopping malls, and I had picked up men in Europe, but that had been casual. Now I wanted to try classic streetwalking.

A taxi driver told me the best place was on Ashford Avenue near the La Concha Hotel. So early one evening, I found a table across the street, at the la Consulada Restaurant, an open-air café, and set up observation as if I were Marlin Perkins recording the mating habits of emperor penguins.

The café owner noticed that I was jotting down notes as I watched the women working. My second night there, he sauntered over to the table and asked if I was a writer. "For the moment," I responded, smiling pleasantly.

"You are writing for a story? Maybe for a magazine or newspaper?" he asked slyly.

"For now I'm just observing and making a few notes," I said. "It will be awhile before I write anything. Do you know any of these women?" I asked.

"No, no, but I see them every night," he said, "and my customers get a big kick out of watching them." He told me a story about a table of Japanese and American businessmen who were making bets on which girl would get a customer first.

"Who won?" I asked.

"Oh, the Japanese. And they left me a two-hundred-dollar tip."

"How much did they bet?"

He leaned close and confided to me, "A thousand dollars."

"And which girl did they bet on?"

He pointed across the street to a black hooker. "The one in the green pants," he said. "As soon as the Japanese picked her, I knew they would win. She works every night, and she's very good."

"Oh," I said, "have you . . ."

"No, no, no, no," he said, recoiling. "I've just heard."

"Did the Japanese give *her* a tip?"

He looked at me as if I were mad.

"She makes more money than me, every night of the week," he said.

For several evenings I dropped by la Consulada. The owner was right about the woman wearing green pants. She was out there strictly for business. She always looked sharp and acted alert. She never made any gesture to solicit business. While the other women waved and sometimes walked right up to guys and grabbed them by the arm, the woman in green pants just walked, or stood, or waited. And every night the woman in green pants went off on a date or two while the other, more aggressive women stood around giggling and chitchatting with each other.

When I went over to talk to the woman in green pants, I told her that I had been watching her for a while. I quickly gave her my hooking résumé—El Echo and Raphaelo's on Saint Croix, the Black Angus and La Riviera in San Juan—and told her enough about myself to make her believe that I wasn't a cop, a reporter, or a lunatic.

Streetwalkers, I learned, generally hold themselves apart from whorehouse hookers. They think that women who work in whorehouses have too many restrictions and rules and that the hookers have to give up too much money for the services they get. The street allows for a broader class spectrum than the bordello. There are people working on the street who wouldn't be accepted in a whorehouse because of a drug habit or because they couldn't show up on time, or at all, or because they couldn't get along with other women. The street welcomed everyone democratically. There were people with college degrees and people who had never been to school at all, people who had other jobs on the side and people who were down-and-out junkies just there long enough to get money for a fix.

Some streetwalkers felt they were above call girls because they had more independence. They felt they were like cowboys out on the range, or spies on a dangerous mission. They bragged about how free they were. They didn't seem to have much overhead but shoes, clothes, makeup, and condoms. Some of them kept apartments nearby for customers. They had no one to answer to but themselves.

The woman in green pants, Margueritte, turned out to be an American. She agreed to explain the business to me. In fact, she was flattered and impressed that someone really wanted to know about streetwalking and about her. The first thing Margueritte told me was, "You've got to get you some new shoes, honey." Her arms were folded across her midriff, and she leaned back and shifted her weight to one foot, digging the heel of the other into the concrete sidewalk. She pursed her lips just a little and stared at my feet, waiting for my reaction.

I glanced at my brand-new gold lamé sandal-strap high-heeled sling backs, bought just for this occasion, and said, "Oh . . . these aren't appropriate?"

She shook her head from side to side. "They look good, but you wear those prissy little things out here all night, those skinny straps will cut your feet so you can't work for a week. Can't make no money like that. When you work the street you make your money on your feet; don't forget that."

"What type of shoe is that you're wearing?" I asked. She had on open-toed pumps with four-inch heels.

She gave me a designer name and said, "Hundred-and-eighty-dollar shoes. All leather. Italian leather, see there, 'Made in Italy.' I only buy Italian shoes. Forget bargain basement shoes. Don't pay less than a hundred dollars for a pair of streetwalking shoes. And make sure they fit and feel comfortable when you try 'em on in the store. This ain't no place to be breakin' in shoes. They'll break you in before you break them in."

She told me which hotels to go to, how to separate the good clients from the bad on the street, how much to charge. Obviously men who were alone were better bets, but sometimes it was possible to deal with a pair of guys. Local businessmen were best. Tourists were so-so. Merchant seamen were usually good. Sailors were often a pain in the butt. But beware the Arabs (too rough) and the Japanese (too nervous and judgmental). She made it clear to me that, if I picked up a man on the street, I had to let someone else know where I was going, with whom, and for how long. I could do that by walking the man over to another woman, introducing him, and making all of the arrangements in front of her. "We're going to so-and-so hotel," I was to say, "and if I'm not back in twenty minutes, come looking for me."

It was to be clear to the man that this woman knew who he was and where we were going. That was one form of life insurance on the street.

I had to watch the way a guy dressed as well, if there was anything about him that simply didn't look right—if he wore mismatched clothes, or extreme clothes, if he was too happy or too depressed. She said, "If a guy is belligerent or dirty or looks like a wino you probably wouldn't go with him anyway. But you gotta watch out for those charmers and rich bastards. And guys that are too friendly and too generous."

"How will I know when somebody's being too generous or too friendly?"

"Too friendly is when they want to know all about your business. Not like what you're doing; I mean, personal business—how old your kids are or where you live; which hand you wipe your ass with, that kind of stuff." Then she explained, "The going rate is four hundred dollars or five hundred dollars for the night; if a guy comes over and says right off he's got a thousand dollars for you, you'd best let him go. Nobody gives money away for nothin'. If you take that thousand dollars, you earn it somehow, and it's probably not going to be how you choose."

"By mismatched, do you mean different colored socks?" I asked.

"I mean, use your head, if his socks don't match, is he color-blind or is he a psycho? You find out before you go off with him. What's important is that you be alert to every little thing that's not right and know why. Never assume anything."

I coaxed, "But aren't there some rules you go by based on your experience?"

"Yeah, I won't get in a car if the hubcaps don't match." But at the same time I was to beware of very expensive cars. Marguer-itte said, "In Puerto Rico a guy with enough money for a fancy car can afford to treat every woman on this street to a torture-murder. And if people see it and object to what he's doing, a guy with enough money can buy them off. This is a poor island. People with money here can do anything they want. Lots of people are murdered and dumped into that bay. It's only if the guy is so lazy he doesn't take them out far enough for the fish to eat them that they ever wash up onshore."

Well.

She made it clear that I should ask the other women about clients. Had anyone seen this man before? Was he OK? Most of the men who picked up women on the streets were known, and it was up to me to find out what was known about them.

I started streetwalking, cautiously, as I did everything, and I found that everything Margueritte had told me was true, especially the part about shoes. I was going through a phase of physical fitness at the time: a healthy diet, no alcohol, and plenty of exercise. My weight was down to what it had been in high school, and I ran three to four miles every morning, at 5:00 A.M. Being on the street meant that I could add four to five miles of walking to my daily regimen.

On the street, I found it was important to dress in a way that allowed air to get to my body, but at the same time I needed to dress conservatively enough to go into the casinos and hotels. I started wearing harem pants, with slits up the side to let air in, but with little ties at the ankles to anchor them down. It was too windy for a wraparound skirt.

I developed my own style of streetwalking. The Condado is a very touristy area; it has everything from coffee shops to casinos that are open until four in the morning. It was very well lighted, and there were always people walking from one place to another, pretty much like in the shopping malls back in Atlanta.

Clients sometimes asked me to go to casinos with them, but I never enjoyed doing it. Watching a client gamble away a thousand dollars in ten minutes and then spend only a hundred dollars on me was annoying. It seemed inequitable.

Occasionally I went into the casinos to scout out clients. But Margueritte warned me, "The casinos work hard getting people to come in, and they don't want us taking them out." The casinos didn't mind my being there. I was even considered a draw. But it was a faux pas to approach anyone at a gaming table. Instead I was supposed to do my business in the lounge, where people went to numb their poor nerves after losing heavily or toast their intelligence after winning big. The casino didn't mind if I did business with someone, as long as it was after they had finished their business.

Whether I was on the street, in a casino, or in a whorehouse, I never approached anyone. I let men approach me. I would walk down the street and look into store windows. I would go in and shop. Sometimes I would stop and have coffee. Street vendors—people selling jewelry, clothing, hats, scarves, and tourist items—often referred clients to me. I, in turn, took my clients to my favorite vendors and suggested they buy trinkets to take back home.

But usually men just stopped me on the street. "Where are you going?" That was the classic line asked of any woman walking by herself.

I always answered with something vague: "Up the street," or "To get some coffee." It didn't matter what I said, and the men almost always ignored it. After a few of those, "Where are *you* going? Where are you going?" kinds of conversations, I started automatically asking, "What do you have in mind?"

Then the guy would say, "I want to spend some time with someone," or go into a casino, or have a drink, and I would say, "How much do you want to spend?"

Most men knew the going rate. If not, they might ask me how much I wanted. A lot of them wanted to barter. After we had settled the money—though in Puerto Rico one could rarely say anything was settled—I would suggest we go back to his hotel, or, if it was a local guy, that we go to one of the cheap trick hotels where people knew me. Trick hotels always had police in them, and people patrolling the halls. They were almost as safe as the Black Angus.

I didn't make any more working on the street then I did in the whorehouses, but I enjoyed being outdoors. San Juan is beautiful, or at least parts of it are, and I enjoyed the street scene, the people, the store windows, the casinos, the hotels. I did do some cars, mostly with men I had met before at the Black Angus or La Riviera. Men in cars usually just wanted to drive to a hotel, and I made sure that the women on the street knew which one I was headed for.

I did do one Rolls-Royce, against the advice Margueritte gave me, and it was the worst job I had in the Caribbean. I was walking down the Condado early one evening when this Rolls started following me. A chauffeur got out and asked if I would have a drink at a casino with his boss, a wealthy department store owner, for seventy-five dollars. I was leery of him because of the Rolls. It took his chauffeur a long time to talk me into it. I said, "There are a lot of people out here, pick one of them." I kept walking and the Rolls kept following me. Having a fancy car on my tail was keeping everyone else from approaching me. Finally, because they had made such a spectacle and drawn so much attention to themselves, and because a street vendor told me the guy was OK, I began negotiating a deal.

"No sex?" I asked, "Just a drink? One hour?" I wanted to make sure everything was understood right at the start. The chauffeur nodded, paid me, and off we went.

The boss man in the back was a complete jerk. He was greasy, swarthy, smug, wearing a custom-made $1,500 suit, and he was already drunk. We got to the casino, and people bowed and scraped in his direction. The guy, meanwhile, was making an overt effort to be a total jerk. He was totally obnoxious to the waitresses, grabbing their tits, calling them sluts and whores. He called every busboy who came nearby a faggot. He scratched his ass, blew his nose into the tablecloth. We are talking gross here. It was torture just to sit at the same table with him.

At some point I noticed that his fly was open. It was fairly obvious because the tail of his white silk shirt was sticking out of the open zipper. I leaned toward him and tried to pull his zipper up. He tried to brush me away, as if I were trying to *un*dress him in public. Since he was so drunk, I figured he just didn't know what he was doing. But when I tried again I realized that this man *wanted* his fly open. He wanted his shirttail to stick out.

After the hour was up I stood up and said, "I've got to go." The boss man gestured, and the chauffeur, who was sitting with us, offered me another fifty dollars to stay half an hour.

Nope, I said. Not only was the boss man crude and obnoxious, he hadn't even spoken one word to me since I got in the car.

The boss man gestured and nodded and winked, and this time the chauffeur said, "OK, he wants to pay you a hundred dollars to dance with me."

A hundred dollars. One dance. That seemed worth it. We went out and made a turn around the floor. (My mother's insistence on going to dancing lessons was finally paying off.) When we got back to the table the haggling began again. They ended up paying me five hundred dollars, and I was there for a little under three hours. The chauffeur kept stepping in and saying another fifty dollars, just stay with him. He would hold out his arm to keep me from going.

I finally had had enough. The last hour had been spent solely in arguing. They had offered me some amount like two hundred dollars if I would stay for fifteen more minutes, and I had gotten the attention of somebody in the casino and said, "I want to leave and if I *don't* leave right this minute, we're all going to have a lot of problems here."

The whole experience made me understand there were limits to what I would do for money. There had been times in my life when I had worked hard for two hundred dollars. But I knew that, no matter how easy it sounded, I didn't want to sit in this person's presence for fifteen minutes longer. Not for two hundred dollars.

Sometime later that week I happened to stop by la Consulada, the café from which I had first spied Margueritte. The owner wouldn't let me in. He waved a dish towel at me, as if he was trying to scare away chickens. He said, in an accusing tone, "I've seen you working over there."

"And you've seen me eating over here."

He said, "I don't let any of those people in here. You tricked me."

"I didn't trick you. I ate. I paid my bill. I even left a tip."

"I didn't know you were like them," he said. "I thought you were a nice girl."

I paid taxes like a good American citizen, reporting my income as an "entertainer" accurately but also deducting all the legal business expenses I was allowed: plane fare (to and from work), meals on the job, transportation, apartments kept for work purposes, condoms. Once I got finished doing my deductibles, there wasn't much income left to pay tax on. That was the way a lot of executives lived, I discovered: very well.

Working for three weeks, and then taking a week off—the way Buddy had originally proposed—seemed to be the ideal schedule for me. About three weeks of Caribbean intensity was all I could take at one time. I'm sure Buddy believed that women would want to take a week off when we had our periods, but a hooker at El Echo had showed me how to get around problems with that. You just wore a diaphragm when you had your period and you were fine. She did show me one neat twist on that. If you stuffed a sterilized cosmetic sponge inside you, over the diaphragm, it absorbed any leaks and provided a nice, lifelike feel, even if a guy put his fingers in there.

The only problem in the Caribbean was that men sometimes got carried away with their fishing around. One man actually reached in and pulled out this bloody sponge. He screamed and jumped back, not afraid that he had pulled out one of my organs, oh no, but convinced that I was inhabited by demons.

Caribbean people are sooooo strange.

On one of my tax-deductible business trips, I flew to California to meet Margo St. James, the founder of the first prostitutes' rights organization in the United States, COYOTE—Call Off Your Old Tired Ethics. Margo was interested in what I had to tell her about the Caribbean. I was interested in moving to California to work with COYOTE, perhaps give talks and do research, and maybe hook a little on the side, just to keep up my income.

Margo was a wonder. She introduced me to a number of working women in San Francisco—most of whom lived like well-heeled hippies, wearing designer jeans, high-fashion boots, and leather jackets—and suggested that if I was ever interested in working in the city, she might be able to help me find an apartment. After the full-tilt boogie, quasi-legal style of prostitution I had gotten used to in the Caribbean, it was hard for me to imagine going back to prostitution as an illegal occupation, in which Margo even had to be careful how she phrased her offer, so that she wouldn't be guilty of pandering. I loved Margo and the other women I met, but I realized that San Francisco was a much more expensive place to live than Atlanta, and I wasn't convinced that I would be able to live in the style to which I had become accustomed. Not unless I could save up a lot more money than I had before making a permanent move.

It seemed to me my fate was back in the Caribbean, where I was relatively safe from arrest and where I could earn a decent income.

I love the intimacy, the serenity, the fluidity, and the safety of the whorehouse. In a whorehouse there's an acceptance of everyone's place in the universe. To some people the word *bordello* is the name of a suburb of hell, a scarlet outpost of an alien world. To me, it came to mean sanctuary. Like a convent, a whorehouse operates by its own inner laws. Like pop festivals of the late sixties and early seventies, a whorehouse offers those within shelter from some of the institutionalized irrationalities of society. It's easy for customers to leave their insecurities, their status, their airs at the door; for the prostitute, that's essential. The one unique aspect of this cloistered society is simply that none of the inhabitants is destitute.

It was a world I found myself gravitating back to after I had learned how to work the streets. (Most prostitutes, I was discovering, knew only one kind of prostitution. Elaine had worked only with the personal ads. Margueritte knew about streetwalking. Patty knew everything there was to know about whorehouses. Women tend to stick with whatever form of prostitution they first encounter. I, on the other hand, wanted to know everything about prostitution, all aspects.

In the interest of being thorough, and because I knew that no whorehouse was safe from raids and shutdowns, I decided to scout a number of other whorehouses, both in San Juan and out in the countryside, just in case I might have to make a sudden move. The Caribe Night Club was too far fallen into decay for my taste, the

Prados was too close to the governor's mansion, and therefore too likely to be raided by the police, El Torreón was take-out only, no beds on the premises, and there were too many girls already working there. A little country roadside bar named the Tortuguero Cafeteria was conveniently located right next to the Camp Tortuguero National Guard reservation and was filled with freewheeling women in hot pants and high heels. The Campo Alegre Hotel, right behind the cafeteria, had special *"un corto tiempo"* (short-time) rates of nine dollars. Another place nearby, La Corvette, looked clean and well-kept, but you had to dance to work there and I *knew* I was a hooker and not a dancer.

I did work for one night at La Balanca, and it turned out to be one of my favorite places. La Balanca was on a high bluff, not far from the Atlantic Ocean, and was cooled by ocean breezes. There was no hot water, the bar was too dark and the music too loud, but the clients were more friendly and relaxed than the men back in San Juan, and work was easy. I moved across the street to La Balanca's upscale cousin, El Alcázar, and then I moved to La Revancha, a club in Aguadilla, a small town on the west coast, and finally to Pamela, a club northeast of Ponce. Pamela was a lot like the Black Angus, except that it had a huge shrine of the Virgin Mary as its central focus. Perhaps customers felt better if they could do a quick rosary before and after sex. A bartender claimed the place was used for church services on Sundays. It didn't do anything for me, though, and I headed back to San Juan.

I worked for three weeks straight and then took a week off in Atlanta. On one particular trip home, a young woman, Amanda, came to see me. She was asking my help because she wanted to learn the business of prostitution. I gave her the names of some of the whorehouses I worked in, but I made it clear to her that I wasn't encouraging her to come, because that would constitute illegal trafficking and because I felt she was too young.

But she turned up on Saint Croix anyhow. I stopped by El Echo, for old times' sake, to introduce her to Yolanda. I figured El Echo would be the best place for Amanda, simply because Yolanda had so many rules. People regard prostitution as something dangerous, like riding a motorcycle, but, like riding a motorcycle, it's only dangerous when you crash. Rules, especially for a beginner, minimize the number of crashes. The problem was that Amanda was so thrilled to be on her own, she didn't want to follow rules.

As a result, she had a few crashes. She was kidnapped twice in a week.

Whenever a seasoned prostitute told me something—like let someone else know where you're going, or don't get into a car with mismatched hubcaps—I listened. I figured that there was very little reason for a working woman to tell another working woman something that was false. Even working in one of the houses, I told Amanda, you made sure someone saw who you were going with. If you had any doubts, you asked. I told Amanda that since she was new she should ask about everyone. "Ask if he's OK," I said, and she acted as if I was babying her.

She didn't even listen when I told her what to do with her money. This was something Patty had taught me. When you had a room of your own, as you did at El Echo, you didn't want to worry about anyone stealing your money, so you hung a wet bathing suit in the bathroom, even if you had to wet the bathing suit in the sink. Every bathing suit has a panel inside the crotch that's always open on one or both ends. It was a simple thing to put your excess cash in the crotch of the wet bathing suit. No one was going to look for it there. No one wants to handle a wet, clammy bathing suit. If you kept your money there, I said, you didn't have to go to your safe-deposit box at the bank every day. Amanda didn't want to hear about it.

She was on Saint Croix for two days before she got kidnapped the first time. On Tuesday, she had gone out of El Echo to buy something in a store. A guy asked her to go into one of the ritzier nightclubs, and because he was a white American wearing a lot of jewelry, she thought it was OK to go off with him without telling anybody. The guy didn't beat her up, but he sure took what he wanted from her. He kept her all night at his house, a fortress with high walls and gates, island style, and then he didn't pay her.

After we searched all night for her, she turned up the next day and told us what had happened. She said she wasn't going to report the kidnapping to the police, because she felt so stupid.

I had another talk with Amanda on Wednesday. A whore-house isn't utopia, I told her, it's a business, and she hadn't been a good businesswoman. "People really do disappear all the time," I told her. "This isn't Atlanta, this is the Caribbean. Things are different here. Killing and dying are common, which makes the rules of life very simple. You've got to be careful. You've got to think. You don't want to piss someone off," I said. "Even accidentally. You've got to be nice to clients, and careful about who you let *be* your clients. You don't want to just disappear off the face of the earth.''

You would have thought that was enough for her, but Amanda really wanted to show that she could make it on her own, without any help from me or anyone else.

At El Echo, Amanda had chosen the room farthest from Yolanda's. She knew that Yolanda didn't tolerate drugs or loud music in the rooms, so she figured that, if she took the farthest room, she could smoke a lot of dope and not get thrown out.

My attitude was different. When I was at El Echo, I took the room right next to Yolanda and her husband, Juan. Mine was the biggest room in the place, with a queen-sized bed. I always charged extra in that room, because, I told the clients, "Look at the size of the bed." (Bigger room, bigger bed, any excuse will do.) The reason the room was usually unoccupied was because it was next to Yolanda; it was like living next door to the principal. Yolanda could see you come and go. Because it was an airy, open room, with concrete blocks in an open, geometric design along one wall, Yolanda could also hear what was going on, which was fine with me. I wasn't there to party; I was there to work.

But Amanda was at an age where she wanted to party and break the rules. On Thursday she was working at the house but decided she wanted to take a client, a tall guy from Saint Croix, outside. It was twenty minutes before anyone realized they hadn't seen the new kid from the mainland for a while. At El Echo there was a ten-dollar fee to leave the building with a client. Part of the fee was so that Yolanda could talk with the guy and size him up. If she didn't like the looks of the guy, she would say, "You had better stay here," and that meant "Don't go with him." It was like a security deposit; someone knew what the guy looked like. Amanda didn't see it that way, however. She figured that if the guy didn't pay Yolanda the exit fee, that was ten dollars more for her.

This time Amanda came back in a little worse shape. She decided that the Caribbean was not for her, and she got a ticket to go home to Atlanta on Sunday. Until then, she said, she wasn't going out on the street anymore. She was just going to stay right there at El Echo and be a good girl.

On Friday in came a client none of the other girls would have dreamt of going upstairs with. He was a very, very big black guy from New York City. Just to look at him, you knew he was bad news. For one thing, he was filthy. We saw a lot of Rastafarians in the Caribbean, and they were dirty too, but they were nice people. They tend to be dirty because they live in trees, but they're pot heads and they're gentle, pleasant fellows. This guy was no Rasta. Americans who are dirty, with matted hair that hasn't been washed or combed in several years, you know are problems.

At a distance you could see that this guy was a junkie or a psycho. As a hooker, you don't have to decide which one it is, all you have to do is avoid him. This guy came up to Amanda and offered her a hundred dollars to go upstairs. That should have been a tip-off right there, since the going rate for an hour was sixty to seventy-five dollars. Almost every client started by offering twenty dollars, and you worked them up to sixty. So not only did he look like a psycho, but offering a hundred dollars right off the bat meant he was acting like a psycho.

Amanda skipped upstairs with this guy, went to her room, way at the end of the hall, and ducked inside. All the doors had locks on them, but you were never supposed to lock the door when you had a client inside. The guy told Amanda that he had a joint they could smoke, and she decided the better part of discretion was to lock the door for this treat. (I had told Amanda that if she smoked dope Yolanda would throw her out, but I had also told her that if she locked the door she could be killed.)

The guy gave her a hundred dollars and then watched as she put the money into the drawer next to her bed. (I wonder if that girl had brain damage.) When he saw where she put the money, he grabbed her, took the money out of the drawer, and then started beating her up, because, even though he had just stolen her money, he still wanted to have sex with her. She got frightened and decided the best thing to do was be cooperative. He decided, since he was a crazed junkie, that he was going to beat her up anyway.

Amanda started screaming, but because her room was so far down the hall and because the jukebox was playing, as always, downstairs, no one could hear her. And if it weren't for the fact that one of the security guys had noticed her going upstairs with this weirdo, and felt that, after ten minutes, she had been gone a long time, she might not have lived long enough to take a plane out of the Caribbean.

The security guard climbed the stairs and started down the hall. Then he heard her screaming and broke down the door. That got some other people's attention, and we all started pouring out of our rooms. I had been having a nice time with an island guy, and I really didn't want to come out, but I knew by now that if there was trouble, Amanda was probably at the center of it.

Yolanda's husband heard the commotion and ran to get his gun. The psycho was at least six foot four, and our security guy was only about five eleven, so the psycho, who by now had stripped off his pants, was clearly besting the security guard. Women and johns were screaming and pulling and hitting at the psycho, and then here came Juan with his gun. There was the kind of respectful silence you hear when someone produces a gun, and then someone screamed, "You'd better get out of here."

The psycho started running down the hall, skinny shanks pumping and cock bouncing from side to side, Juan chasing him with the gun. The guy got down the entire flight of stairs in two leaps. He was so big that it wasn't even a great strain. Somewhere between the first bound and the second, Juan fired his gun a couple of times. After seeing all those guns waved around, this was the first time I'd heard one fired. As the gun went off, I noticed one of the other women rolling her eyes, and I wondered what that was all about.

Juan had shot the guy point-blank, and I was surprised that the guy was still running. He flew out the door and was gone.

Everybody was in a big panic. And then Amanda came down the hall with a woman on one side and the security guard on the other, sort of supporting her weight, half dragging her. She was crying, bleeding, her face was beginning to puff up.

I felt sorry for her, but my main feeling was annoyance.

"He didn't get the money," Amanda mumbled through a bleeding and now swelling lip. "He left his pants."

Well, I thought, maybe she wasn't all that dumb.

I was up in arms. "Shouldn't the police go after that guy? He's hurt Amanda and he's going to hurt someone else." I figured it wouldn't be too hard for the police to find him—a tall, black naked American with a bullet wound in his back.

After Amanda was hauled off to her room, for sympathy and medical treatment, Juan took me aside and confided that his gun was loaded with blanks.

"Why?" I said. "Why do you have a gun that's loaded with blanks? Why were you *chasing* someone with a gun that fires blanks?"

That's when Juan explained to me that it was illegal for a whorehouse to have a loaded gun on the premises. One of the reasons El Echo and the other whorehouses had so much security was because they could operate only until there was a "problem," and shooting an American constituted a problem, especially if he lived to complain about it. The police would not become involved—except as customers—until you shot a customer. So no one wanted to shoot a customer.

-There was another purpose to the gun, Juan said. Most people didn't know it had blanks in it, and I was specifically not supposed to tell Amanda. Part of this theatrical production had been for her to feel vindicated, so she wouldn't press charges.

I now understood a lot, even why Amanda shouldn't press charges. And I had witnessed firsthand a perfect example of why prostitution should be regulated under the same ordinances as other personal-service businesses. Otherwise the entire prostitution community is denied protection under the law and whorehouses become feudal zones.

Just before she boarded her flight, I told Amanda about the blanks in the gun, so she wouldn't create any more trouble with tales of men being murdered at El Echo.

There was a woman I'll call Cricket. I had known her in Atlanta, but we had lost touch until she turned up in the Caribbean practically on my doorstep. When Cricket was twenty she looked thirteen, which was the reason, I suppose, for her silly nickname. She was a short, freckled redhead with the face of a child.

When women's magazines talk about supermoms, they must mean someone like Cricket. She could take care of her four-year-old child, work as a secretary, type like a wizard, manage an office, and work as a prostitute in her spare time. When she arrived in the Caribbean I had a chance to find out something about her history.

Cricket and her brother were seriously neglected children. At the age of twelve, Cricket couldn't see any reason to live at home anymore. She got pregnant when she was sixteen. She moved in with some friends, but she kept going to school. She sold loose joints to support herself and disassociated herself totally from the guy who got her pregnant.

The one thing that kept her going was the idea of finishing high school. She told me she carried her baby so inconspicuously, no one even knew she was pregnant until she went into labor. Three days later, she was back in school.

Cricket started working as a prostitute to save her life. She had found an apartment, which she scrimped and saved to furnish. And then one day Cricket came home from work to find that her roommate had not paid the rent for months. Cricket's furniture was on the street, as were all her clothes. She found her daughter with a neighbor. Her front door was padlocked, and half her things had been stolen.

She ended up sitting on a street corner. Cricket was patting her daughter when a man pulled up and said, "What's wrong?" When Cricket told him, he said, "If you really need money, I know some people in the escort business. You can do that for a little while." And that's how she got into it. She needed a lot of money to start all over again. She knew she was never going to make that kind of money working as a typist.

Cricket asked me if I was interested in a roommate. Her daughter was in Atlanta with relatives, and she was now free.

I told her, "Why don't you work with me? We'll run an escort service right here in San Juan. You know how to do it, there are lots of tourists here, and no one's thought of doing that here yet. We'll make a bundle." It was my capitalistic upbringing.

We found a suitable apartment for our business on the eighth floor of a very nice building, right on the Condado, the main drag. It was near the Holiday Inn, had a balcony overlooking the ocean, and—is this too perfect or what?—it already had a phone, which was a hard thing to come by in San Juan and central to running an escort agency. The apartment cost about seven hundred dollars a month. I asked my friend in California to wire me some money right away, a sort of small-business loan to myself. Then Cricket and I wrote up an ad and put it in "Tourist Tips" in the San Juan paper, *El Mundo*: "American Pie Escort Service. English spoken. Blondes and redheads only. Ask for Cynthia. Call XXX-XXXX." If someone called using that name, we would know he was from the ad.

Pretty soon, we had dozens of calls a day. We charged a hundred dollars an hour, and we got so busy we had to go to La Riviera and the Black Angus to recruit some more "blondes and redheads," who were thrilled to work for one hundred dollars an hour.

While I was getting the business off the ground, I continued to work at the Black Angus, and sometimes I would see the same clients at both places. People who found me at the Black Angus would say, "Hey, wait a minute. Here you charge only thirty dollars, and when I call the service it's a hundred." I pointed out that there wasn't much difference between thirty dollars for twenty minutes (especially when it wasn't even twenty minutes) and a hundred dollars for an hour, and that at the escort service I had overhead and they didn't have to pay a room fee, and that at the escort service they could make an appointment to see me, whereas at the Black Angus they just had to hope they caught up with me.

Cricket and I got the usual mix of clients: local businessmen, tourists and sailors, sailors and tourists. One of the strangest clients I had was an airline pilot who wanted me to take a shit on a piece of newspaper. But he paid me $150 for it, and I had to go to the bathroom anyhow, so it all worked out.

It was the ad for the escort service that eventually got us in trouble with our landlord. He recognized the phone number, and he seemed almost apologetic about throwing us out. He said, "Why didn't you get your own phone number?"

Cricket and I found another apartment, but I had to pay a bribe to get a new phone. One of the clients at the Black Angus worked at the phone company. He told us that it usually took two years to get a new phone. If we wanted one sooner, we would have to pay for it.

So Cricket and I calculated just how much of a bribe we would pay. We decided we could go as high as $800. Well, maybe $1,000, but that was absolute tops. A thousand dollars, and not a penny more. We got in touch with our telephone company friend at the Black Angus and asked him to stop by the apartment so we could discuss phone service.

He was acting very important when he walked in the door, and we were treating him like a kingpin. We thought that we had an inside line to this telephone business and that the whole thing had to be hush-hush. He sat down and we gave him a drink. So, after a lot of polite chat, he said, "You can give the money to me. I'll take care of it."

"How much?" we wanted to know.

"Thirty dollars," he said, and we were stunned.

We looked at each other and tried not to gasp in $970-hysterical relief. We were so dumbfounded that neither of us said anything. The telephone guy immediately interpreted this to mean that thirty dollars was too much for us, so he said, "Well, maybe for you kids, we could make it twenty."

"Fine," we both said. We were afraid he was going to say, "No, no, it's too much money for you girls, you shouldn't be doing this."

Before he left with our thirty dollars—it turned out he had hoped to take out ten dollars in trade, but we told him we wanted to keep this businesslike—he told us where *all this money* went. There were about ten people at the San Juan phone company who had to process an application for a new telephone. Someone needed to walk around to all the desks and give each person two dollars to speed things along. And the guy who walked around with the cash took ten dollars.

Nine-tenths of the island was without modern telephone communication, and it was all for lack of a twenty-dollar bribe.

Cricket stayed for a total of four months and left San Juan with a bankroll for a trip to Arizona to open her own boutique. I have no idea if her black cloud of misfortune has started following someone else or still dogs her.

To replace her, a wonderful, beautiful black woman from New York named Yvette moved in. She was one of the few black American women who worked at the Black Angus. One of the most remarkable things about Yvette was that when she was working she had an air of sophistication. The way she walked, the way she held herself, Yvette had more polish than Princess Di.

The following experience, which I shared with Yvette, was so weird that I sat down and wrote out the whole thing right after it happened:

San Juan, Puerto Rico, October 21, 1981. On my way to pick up a pizza for Yvette, I noticed a man carrying a large paper bag. He was crossing the street and coming toward me. Oh, good, I thought, a typical American businessman.

As usual I responded with a kind and courteous nod of my head and a small twitch of a smile, while at the same time never breaking my stride. The man caught up with me and asked, like 75 percent of the men who approached me on the street, "Where are you going?"

"Just up the avenue," I said. I stopped walking. This man looked like he had just found what he was looking for. "How long have you been in Puerto Rico?" he asked.

"About a week," I said. "How long are you in town for?"

"A couple of days."

"Are you staying in a hotel?"

"No, I'm on vacation."

"What's in the bag?"

"My laundry."

Now, politely, I asked, "What is it you have in mind?"

"A little light dominance," he said.

"Do you want to dominate me, or do you want me to dominate you?"

"I want you to dominate me," he said.

"OK," I said. "I charge fifty dollars for a half hour and a hundred for an hour." (People in Puerto Rico don't seem to understand that kinky activities cost more, so I've stopped putting myself through the irritation of arguing about it. Besides, I'd never known much about domination. I needed the practice.)

"I'll take a half hour."

"OK, wait for me here, I've got to go to the bathroom."

"Save it for me."

"I can't wait that long," I told him. "But there's plenty more where this comes from."

"Where shall I wait, mistress?"

I thought, Oh, God, he's starting this stuff already, and I haven't even gotten any money from him yet.

"Anywhere."

"No, tell me where."

"There," I said, pointing to a long bench near a bus stop where several people were sitting.

He must have been about fifty. His hair was half gray, cut stylishly short and combed slightly forward to reveal a hint of baldness in the crown. He had a cheerful but nondescript face. His mannerisms were ever so slightly effeminate. His voice was quietly mischievous until I agreed to do a domination scene; then it became timid and submissive.

When I returned he was not sitting where I had told him to wait but standing nearby. I put a scowl on my face and said, "Why aren't you sitting on the bench?"

"Because those people over there look too weird," he said, pouting like a child who has done something he is about to get in trouble for.

I glanced at him and thought, Oh, brother. You think they're weird!

He followed me to the taxi stand across the street. On the way to the apartment I questioned him on his ability to do household chores.

"Can you do dishes?"

"Yes, mistress."

"Can you do laundry?"

"Yes, mistress."

"Can you fix a TV?"

"No, mistress, I'm sorry. May I be your permanent slave, mistress?"

"I don't know. Probably not."

"You are so beautiful and superior, mistress, I would do anything for you. Anything at all. Just command me."

"Shut up."

"Yes, mistress."

This is what I hate about slaves—all the verbal bullshit. And they all do it. The word *mistress* has never sounded that attractive to me, and I certainly didn't want to hear it every few seconds.

We arrived at the apartment. He paid the cabdriver and then followed me into the building. I let him stand at the back of the elevator, holding his big "laundry" bag and Yvette's pizza.

Yvette was delighted to see that I had brought home a slave to do the chores. I told him to put his bag in my bedroom, then to come into the kitchen. There I gave him cleaning instructions as politely as I might explain housework procedures to a housemaid. Yvette and I ate pizza while he toiled over a week's worth of dirty dishes.

Though I had done a few dominance sessions with Elaine, and there was an occasional client at the Black Angus who wanted to be spanked, I didn't really know much about it. I'd never felt very inspired about spanking anyone, or pissing on them, or verbally abusing them. (Clients kept telling me I was a natural dominatrix; maybe they were just trying to flatter me. On the other hand, I do like submissive men.)

While our gentleman-slave cleaned up the mess we had made with the pizza, Yvette and I went into the bedroom to take a peek into his brown paper bag. We were like a couple of teenagers, giggling hysterically over what might be in the bag.

Yvette thrust her hand under the clothes on top.

"Oh shit! What the fuck is this?" she said, leaping back, recoiling in laughter and disgust, like someone who's had the spring-loaded-peanut-can trick pulled on them. While she was frantically ransacking my room looking for a Kleenex, or anything to wipe her hand on, Yvette explained, "It had Vaseline on it!"

"Ooo, what was it?" I asked.

"I don't know! A dildo or something," she said.

"Here. Here! Yvette, use this." I handed her a clean shirt from the clothes wadded in his bag.

We couldn't contain our curiosity any longer. I lifted the rest of the clothes out and called out the items: "A dildo and harness, a big butt plug, clothespins, a can opener, cat food, a black leather hood. Oh good, a whip [at least I knew what that was probably used for], a dog collar, Vaseline, that's all."

"Cat food?" Yvette said. "What's the cat food for?"

"I don't know, maybe he has a cat."

I was so innocent.

Shortly our slave turned up at the bedroom door. "I'm done with the dishes, mistress. Would you like to come and inspect the kitchen, mistress?"

"In a minute," I snapped. "Would you please bring me a glass of apple juice with two ice cubes in it?"

"Yes, mistress. Shall I crawl, mistress?"

"Oh, sure."

"Would you like me to take my clothes off for you, mistress?"

"Right. I forgot. Crawling wears out the knees of your pants. Put them there," I said, pointing to a chair in my bedroom. He had a big hard-on.

"Shall I lick your feet, mistress?"

"No. Crawl into the kitchen and get my apple juice, you slimy low-life slave. Down on your knees."

"Yes, mistress."

Yvette, lying on my bed, was rolling from side to side, smothering her laughter with both hands, which made my need to laugh almost uncontrollable. Humiliation was what this guy was after, but somehow it didn't seem right to outright laugh at him. I rolled a joint for Yvette and myself. (It takes a long time to crawl to the kitchen and fix a drink, on your knees.)

Yvette took a big drag and said, "Shit, girl. You've done this stuff before." She seemed impressed.

"Oh, yeah," I said, bragging. Then I admitted, "But only a few times. If he wasn't cuing me I wouldn't know what to do. I really want to get better at this, though. This is all good practice, really. I don't understand how it works, but I will eventually."

By then I realized I had to pee again. When he returned with my apple juice, making little rustling sounds as he crawled toward us, I told him it was time for him to go into the bathroom and lie down in the tub. (Luckily people had paid me to piss on them before, so I knew what to do.)

"May I have some rush first, mistress?"

"Oh, you have rush?" I said. (It's a drug similar to amyl nitrate.) "Sure, have some. Do you want some of this?" I asked, holding out the joint for him.

"No thank you, mistress."

Once he had taken his place in the bathtub, I stood over him with one foot planted on each side of the tub. I aimed at his face. There was only a slow drizzle at first; then a heavy stream started splattering into his mouth as he masturbated. He said, "Tell me to drink it, mistress."

"Of course drink it. I thought that went without saying." Apparently with slaves you have to tell them to do everything. "Come on, drink it all." I stopped peeing and then started aiming in different places, so he had to bob his head around like a hungry baby bird. He had to keep his eyes open to see where I was aiming, and certainly some of my piss ended up in his eyes, which had to have burned. He was panting and moaning like someone on the edge of an orgasm. Every time I told him "Drink it all, don't miss a drop," his cock got bigger and pulsated, as though it were sound activated.

I stopped urinating. "Don't come," I commanded.

"I won't. I promise," he said. "Please don't stop. I want to drink your superior piss, mistress."

"Are you sure you're not going to come?"

"No, I promise, mistress. Please let me drink the rest."

"All right, but if you come I'll be really mad."

After the pissing scene, Yvette and I hoped to get this man to separate all our laundry into colors and do a couple of loads of wash for us, but we were out of detergent. Since there weren't any other household chores for him to do, all that was left was sexual abuse and humiliation. I had him take out all his equipment and display it on a table beside my bed, so I could choose which instrument I wanted to use, and perhaps pick up some hints on what to use it for.

"What's the can opener for?" I asked.

"The cat food."

"And what's the cat food for?"

"For you to make me eat when I get hungry."

God help me, I decided to go for the whip. I at least had had some experience with that. I picked up the whip and then said, "I need money."

"How much, mistress?"

"As much as you've got, idiot."

"I've only got fifty dollars," he said. "That and a couple of dollars to get back to the ship, mistress."

That was all I needed to hear to really begin to feel my part.

"What!" I said. "Fifty dollars, you son of a bitch? You've been here in my presence two hours—doing my dishes and being pissed on—and you've only got fifty dollars? You're really in trouble now."

I swatted him across his bare back with the cat-o'-nine-tails, and he whimpered and whined, "Please don't hurt me, mistress."

Welts rose across his back. It was a frightening sight. His cock was so hard it was turning blue at the end. I was naked by now and pacing back and forth, bitching about how little money he had brought. I brushed the whip across his welts, but I didn't dare hit him again. Nonetheless, I had really worked myself into a fury. What was weird was that I was getting wet myself. This man was so sniveling and pathetic, I couldn't help disliking him. I was really enjoying torturing him.

I grabbed the dildo and the harness and thought, This thing is about ten inches long and it's going to hurt going in and this guy is going to love it. I can say every rude, unkind, abusive thing that comes to mind and he'll love it. My clit was throbbing. How bizarre. At the same time I thought how embarrassing it would be if anyone found out how turned on I was about all this. I put the dildo on the dresser behind him so he could imagine that I would use it soon.

How sick it all seemed. But I'd always wondered what people got out of sadomasochism, and now I was going to find out.

"Do you enjoy being fucked in the ass?" I asked him.

"No, mistress."

"Too bad, you're going to get fucked in the ass anyway, and you're going to act like you love it."

I put the harness and pink plastic dildo on and greased the dildo up with Vaseline, all the while telling him how much he was going to love it. His cock was lubricating so much it was dripping on the floor. This no longer seemed like a job to me. My clitoris was bulging between my cunt lips, and I was wet.

He was on his knees on the bed. I knelt behind him and teased him with the tip of the dildo for a short time, rubbing it against his testicles and around his ass. I dipped my fingers into the wet leaking off the end of his penis and made him lick it off my hand while I told him how disgusting he was. Since I didn't want him to be seriously hurt, I refrained from ramming the whole dildo up his ass without warning. Actually, I gently worked it in the way I like to have a cock worked into my own ass. I was surprised, and disappointed, at how easily the dildo slipped into his ass. Obviously he had done this a lot of times before. I asked him if it hurt and he said it did, which really pissed me off. He was being a patronizing slave. It couldn't possibly have hurt.

"Oh, mistress, it hurts," he said in that soft voice.

"No it doesn't, you patronizing bastard." I tried to get my anger at his condescending attitude into each stroke, since that was what he was paying me for.

"Tell me how much you like it," I said.

"I like it, mistress."

"Tell me it feels good."

"It feels good."

"Does it hurt?"

"No, mistress."

"Yes, it does," I said. No point letting him get complacent. "Tell me how much it hurts."

"It hurts a lot."

"But you like it, don't you?"

"Yes, it hurts but I like it."

By now his sweat had worked itself up into a foam. I was soaking wet from the sheer physical workout involved. My clit was still throbbing, and my thighs were now wet with my own come. I warned him not to come and reminded him that I still had the whip and would beat him at the slightest provocation.

"Tell me that you like being fucked in the ass."

"Yes, I do, mistress."

I stopped. "Beg me. I won't do it unless you beg me."

"Please, mistress, please."

"Harder?"

"Yes, harder."

"Say it again."

"Harder."

"Say it again!"

"Harder."

"Say you love it."

"Yes, mistress, I love it."

I gave him a few more hard strokes and then jerked the dildo out of his ass. I lay down on the bed and told him to put a rubber on his still-hard cock and to fuck me. He had such a big cock I was really looking forward to this command performance, but he couldn't stay hard.

"If you spit on me, it'll help," he said.

Oh, great. I was on the bottom, which meant I was going to have to spit upward. Sure enough, each time I spit on him, I could feel his cock grow inside me. But by now there was almost as much spit on me as there was on him, so I didn't like it at all.

"Tell me what a piece of shit I am," he said.

That worked too, but the verbal abuse had to be almost continuous to do any good. It was interesting, however, to see how immediately his cock would respond. A word of abuse and his cock would become more erect, like when you touch a man's cock or balls in exactly the right way.

Keeping up the continuous abuse was too distracting for me to have an orgasm, however. I finally got up from under him and told him to jerk himself off. He pouted and moped until he annoyed me into helping him. I didn't care about his frustrations, but I was frustrated about not having my own orgasm. He wanted to touch my breasts and suck my nipples while I spit on him and degraded him. I bitched and rambled about what a bad fuck he was. He liked that, but clearly he liked being spit on better.

(This is the interesting part.) As soon as he had his orgasm, he began to change. It took about two minutes, and it was an amazing physical process.

He sat back on his heels briefly, first with his head down, then with his head up. His eyes were closed. His facial structure seemed to change: his cheekbones got higher. I swear his nose seemed to get bigger. His hair seemed to grow longer. And in general he seemed to get larger.

He became a totally different person. By the time he got up off the floor, he had a perky personality, and his energy level was rising dramatically.

He looked in the mirror, picked up my comb, and started combing his hair in a superconfident way. Suddenly he was moving with a lot of bounce, like someone who fancied himself Mr. Show Business. He was honestly a pretty sexy-looking guy.

As impressed as I was with his metamorphosis, I was still annoyed about not having an orgasm.

"Hey, babe, don't be mad," he said in a jovial way.

"I'm not mad."

He echoed me, in almost my exact voice: "I'm not mad." It was spooky hearing my own voice thrown back at me.

He started dressing, and then he stopped and said, "You never asked what I do for a living."

"That's right. I don't care what you do."

"Oh, come on," he said. "Guess." He was all but poking me in the ribs, trying to get a grin out of me. He was by now all smiles.

"You're a mob boss laundering money through cabaret clubs," I said.

He looked annoyed and said, "No, guess again." He was by now debonair and childishly freewheeling. "Come on, guess."

"You're the hatcheck girl."

"Now you're being silly." By now he looked adorably cute.

"I give up."

"I'm an entertainer," he said. "I sing, I dance, I do impressions." He whirled around from the mirror and started doing impressions: Walter Brennan, Jimmy Cagney, Ethel Merman, Ronald Reagan, Jimmy Carter.

"Well," I said, "that should give you a lot of opportunity for humiliation."

"Not at all," he said. "People love me. You never asked my name, either. ———— ————. Ever heard of me?"

"Nope."

"I'll bring you a videotape of my act," he said. "You'll love it."

"How did you pick me out tonight?" I asked.

"What do you mean?"

"There were a lot of people on the street. You picked me out of a crowd. I wasn't even dressed for work. How could you tell I would do all this?" I asked.

"I wasn't sure you'd go for it," he said, "but you're obviously a dominant personality."

"How could you tell that?" I insisted.

"I don't know," he said. "Just could. Well, sweets, gotta go." He pulled on his shirt and leaned to kiss me.

"Don't kiss me."

"You don't want me to kiss you?"

"No," I said, suddenly tired and confused.

He buttoned his shirt and looked at me. He said, "You think I'm weird because I pay people to spit on me, humiliate me, and abuse me. But, hey, I'm a normal guy. I've just pinpointed my neuroses, and I can deal with them. I get it out of my system and then go on with my life. I don't have to be dominated every day, day in and day out. It's over for me. I've had enough abuse tonight to get me through another week. But you have that dominant character of yours with you all the time, always just a little suppressed, always ready to run amok. You see, I've worked my problem out in a couple of hours, for fifty dollars. You. You've had to build a whole life-style around your problem, to camouflage it."

He left without further ado.

The next afternoon, he called from Saint Thomas in Ronald Reagan's voice to tell me what a great time he'd had. He asked if I would see him again next week. I told him I couldn't decide about that yet. I'd think about it. . . .

Condomania arrived in San Juan. Yvette and I were gentrified out of our second apartment. We spent a lot of time looking at new places for our escort business. When we eventually found a place, telephone problems struck again. This time a thirty-dollar bribe wouldn't suffice, however. The apartment building didn't have enough junctions for a new phone line. It didn't matter how much money we offered, if there wasn't an available junction, we were out of luck. We tried to bribe someone into accidentally disconnecting someone else's phone and giving us that junction, but it was no go. We had an $850 deposit down on the apartment, plus two months' rent and utilities. We had over $3,000 tied up in an apartment that had no phone, and was therefore useless to us.

By now I was tiring of the way everything worked, or didn't work, in San Juan. You couldn't get normal, everyday American things like Granny Smith apples. And if there were recently released movies playing nearby, so what? They were all dubbed into Spanish. Very few people actually spoke fluent English. I could get the Sunday *New York Times* on Tuesday. The TV reception was terrible. And Puerto Rican politics were not amusing. I missed Atlanta.

Of course my friends from Atlanta came down to visit. It was a great opportunity for people to visit Puerto Rico and stay in an apartment overlooking the ocean. At first I had gone home to Atlanta every three weeks, then five weeks, six weeks. Lately eight to twelve weeks went by before I got home. No wonder it was harder for me to come back each time I left.

The last straw was a kid on a motorcycle on the Condado. I was walking in front of the Dupont Plaza, which has a horseshoe-shaped driveway. I was walking between the two ends of the driveway when a guy on a motorcycle drove up behind me. He had probably been waiting awhile for someone to come by. When I heard the motorcycle behind me, I thought, OK, a motorcycle has come up behind me and someone on it is going to try to snatch my purse and drive away. I pirouetted so the guy couldn't possibly reach my purse and just kept walking. He drove right on by me, and that was that.

I thought, If I accept this as a normal part of life, then I've stayed here too long.

"That's it," I told Yvette. "I'm going home." I packed a bag and went to the airport. I knew I wanted to see my family for Thanksgiving, and be in Atlanta to have a last weekend with some old friends who were heading off to different parts of the world. I thought I'd come back to work in the Caribbean the Sunday after Thanksgiving, just to make a little extra cash before Christmas.

But a group of prostitutes in Atlanta had called Margo St. James, of COYOTE, for some help with organizing. I didn't know any of the women, but they had heard about me and began putting on a campaign to get me to stay. They offered to teach me how they worked. They said they needed me; I was flattered. They told me the clients they had in Atlanta were clean, spoke English, seldom carried guns, and didn't bite. It seemed possible to work in my own milieu again, to unite my political activism with my career. And they knew a great escort agency I could work with.

A new cycle began.

I gave a friend a round-trip ticket to San Juan, two big suitcases, and my keys to the apartment. I said, Go down and bring all my stuff back. Just leave the keys on the kitchen table and close the door behind you. I never went back.

7

I'M FOR HIRE

Nowhere is woman treated according to the merit of her work but rather as a sex. It is therefore almost inevitable that she pay for her right to exist . . . with sex favors. Thus it is merely a question of degree whether she sells herself to one man, in or out of marriage, or to many men.
—EMMA GOLDMAN
  "The Traffic in Women," 1917

I was the ideal candidate to work on prostitutes' rights, the Atlanta prostitutes said. I had worked on political campaigns in Atlanta for ten years—helping elect city council people, judges, the mayor, state senators, and U.S. senators. I had worked for the ERA, I had worked on Julian Bond's presidential campaign. I had contact with at least a dozen political groups, from Gay and Lesbian Rights to the Georgia Civil Liberties Union to the Democratic National Party. I had been a community activist, they said. Now I could be a prostitutes' rights activist too.

    I had thought of going to San Francisco, and Margo wanted me there. San Francisco was a high-competition city. Rents were high, and there were too many women working as prostitutes. As far as I could tell, a woman had to be a hooker to afford to live there. And even then the quality of life wasn't very good. Women lived mostly in small, cramped apartments; and not many could afford fur coats. At the same time, the women I was meeting in Atlanta were living in luxurious apartments, they had fur coats and fine jewelry they'd bought themselves, and they were driving new cars.

Generally in life, I do whatever looks easiest to me, what it looks like someone is willing to help me with. These women were making it very easy for me.

I felt I was being offered a great opportunity. I could earn good money and help other people and stay home in Atlanta—all at the same time. The Atlanta women wanted me, and there are few things more seductive than being wanted . . . or needed. The police in Atlanta were cracking down on call girls. They were calling up hookers, trying to entrap them and, if that failed, harassing them on the street and in hotels. The women had begun to band together to do something about it, but they felt they needed a leader, someone who would speak to neighborhood groups and at community board meetings. They wanted someone who had worked in other cities, someone who could speak to call girls *and* to street-walkers, since they realized that both were equal in the eyes of the law.

The women who approached me had a simple political creed: that a woman has a right to sell sexual services just as much as she has a right to sell her brains to a law firm when she works as a lawyer, or to sell her creative work to a museum when she works as an artist, or to sell her image to a photographer when she works as a model or to sell her body when she works as a ballerina. Since most people can have sex without going to jail, there was no reason except old-fashioned prudery to make sex for money illegal. Therefore they wanted prostitution decriminalized (*not* legalized, which would make it subject to state regulation, like tobacco and alcohol—thus treating women's bodies as another controlled substance); they wanted to assert prostitutes' rightful place within the women's movement; and they wanted to provide an outreach program, to help other prostitutes.

In addition to the attraction of working in Atlanta to decriminalize prostitution, the women offered me something else. They passed along the name of a wonderful agent, Sarah, the owner of

Magnolia Blossoms Modeling Agency. She taught me about the realities of prostitution in Atlanta; she taught me how to work safely and carefully, how to avoid cops, how to screen clients accurately—and she did it all over the telephone. ("It's safer for me that you never see me," she said, "and it's safer for you if you learn to listen on the phone." She was right on both counts.)

While I was in San Juan I had gotten away from screening clients because I felt protected in the whorehouses; on the street I had a chance to see guys before I went anywhere with them, and I could always ask one of the other women about them; and at Elaine's I had been naive—completely naive—about the real dangers we faced. I was older and wiser now and terrified to remember how things had been done at Elaine's. We had often brought men right to Elaine's apartment; we had rarely had the sense to check IDs; and we didn't really know how vulnerable we were to arrest.

Sarah knew the modeling agency business inside out; she had a lot of common sense; she had business sense, she had cop sense, and she had a great voice too. I couldn't tell over the telephone if she was twenty-three or fifty-two. She had a perfectly modulated voice, pleasantly high-pitched. Whatever she told me, her voice inspired me to do. If she said, in that perky voice, "I need you at the hotel in twenty minutes. You have to hurry up and get ready," I hurried up and got ready. On the other hand, if I explained to her that I didn't want to go out on a call—for any reason—she accepted it, without trying to talk me into doing something I didn't feel like doing. She was a good agent, someone I felt was looking out for my career.

Magnolia Blossoms was the cornerstone of Sarah's business, but she ran additional escort agencies and modeling agencies from AAA to ZZZ. (The idea was to run five to twenty ads in the yellow pages, all with different names and promising different specialities—Coeds; Oriental beauties; massage done by blondes, brunettes, redheads; English spoken here. Some of the listed agencies had different phone numbers, but all were answered by the same person. There were about sixty escort and "modeling" agencies listed in the yellow pages in Atlanta, but there were actually only about five different services. That way the agencies got clients coming and going—from A to Z. There was a lot of competition each year to see who could come up with an agency name that would be listed either first or last in the yellow pages.)

Sarah ran her business out of a big house, but I'm sure she never left the telephone room. She worked around the clock. She slept with her phones, seven days a week. She lived that business day and night, which was one reason the women were so loyal to her. She was always there when they needed her.

When a client called one of the escort service's numbers and said "I want an escort for the night," Sarah would say, in her perky voice, "We have several lovely models available." (She had decided that, because the agencies were having trouble getting an escort license, we were to be models.) Usually the caller would understand and say, "Fine, do you have any brunettes? Or red-heads? Or blondes?" But if he started asking questions about, "Do these girls . . . ah, ah . . ." Sarah would explain carefully: "Our models only model, sir—lingerie, topless, bottomless, or all nude." The women who worked with her were all required to sign a contract stating that they were there to model, to do nothing more than model, and that there was no touching allowed. (The idea was deniability: Sarah *thought* the women were there only to model; the women *understood* that they were not being hired to do anything other than model.)

Sarah represented models ranging in age from nineteen to forty-eight. The nineteen-year-old was the daughter of a doctor and a nurse. Another woman, in her early thirties, was divorced, working as a secretary, and the mother of two children. One woman sold business equipment and copiers during the day.

After explaining to a caller that the agency fee was fifty dollars, Sarah would say that the minimum model's fee would at least match the agency fee and might be higher. Then she would ask any of a dozen questions: What city was the gentleman from? What hotel was he staying in? What room number? Did he arrive by plane? Did he have a rental car? What company did he work for? How long was he staying in town? If he lived in town, how long had he lived there? Was this a private house or an apartment building? Did he own or rent? Did he have a driver's license? What other forms of ID did he have? Was he paying cash, or would he be using a credit card?

She would explain to the caller that the model would, upon entering, ask for three forms of identification. She told me not to be impressed with a driver's license or a credit card or an insurance card. Anyone could get those in any name, she said. We were more impressed with hunting licenses and library cards and country club membership cards, because those were offbeat requests, things the police might not think of. Bar association membership cards were too easy for the police to get. Sarah said all ID was useless, really. A careful vice cop would have more ID than anyone would dream of. We were supposed to be looking at the ID to buy time. We were checking photographs, checking addresses, trying to see if there was anything unusual. If a man offered a hunting license, a bar association membership card, a driver's license, and an insurance card as his ID, for instance, we knew there was a good possibility he was a cop. We were also to look at the condition of the ID. Was it too new? Was it complete? Were there any inconsistencies? And did he know what was on it? I was supposed to start off suspicious of everything.

Sarah's rule was that she told the customer on the phone two of the three forms of ID he would be required to show. It was up to the model to decide the third form she wanted to see. (That gave us a lot of free play. If there was anything suspicious about the guy, we would ask for some really obscure form of ID and see what he came up with. People might pull out a McDonald's gift certificate their nephew had given them, and that was always impressive. It was a test of the guy's imagination.)

After the client had agreed to the agency fee and the minimum model's fee, and had passed Sarah's battery of questions, after he had told how he would pay and what form of ID he had, Sarah would tell him that the model would be there in twenty minutes to a half hour. (If she told a caller longer than that, he would call another agency.) Then she would say, "I think Heather is available," or Marlena, Penny, Jasmine, Mimi, Taffy, Veronika, Noelle, Kristin, Suzie, or Bibi.

Everyone else has to live with the names their parents give them, but performers, models, nuns, and hookers get to make up new names—because they want to pick a prettier name, or because they don't want to embarrass their families, for legal reasons, or as a device to keep their working lives and their private lives separate. When I was a young girl I often sat around with my friends and talked about what we'd name our children. For some reason, my favorite names invariably turned out to be hooker names, names that are sweet and sexy: Cheri, Tiffany, Chastity—which is ironically a typical hooker name. If I had twins, I wanted to name them Candy and Brandy.

When I went to the Caribbean I called myself Sylvia Adams.

Sylvia was relatively easy for people to pronounce, but I had a problem. Whenever I had to sign my name, say on a credit card slip, I always started writing a *D*. So I picked a new name—Debra Grant. Debra is easy to pronounce in any language; I used Grant because it is a neighborhood in Atlanta.

When I started working with Sarah, though, Debra seemed too ordinary, so it was time for me to choose a new name. Dolores French is not a bad name for a prostitute, but I wanted to work under a stage name, just like everybody else.

I didn't want to use a typical hooker name, yet I wanted a name that people could remember and that was close to my own. I'm not going to tell you my professional name here, because I still work under that name. Let's just say it was Delilah Fox. Delilah begins with a *D*, and Fox would be a good hooker name. If a client called the agency and wanted to see me again, a name like Fox might help. He might be able to say, "She had red hair and her name was some kind of red animal." Unless the client and the agent were particularly dense and guessed *Red Squirrel* or *Irish Setter*, they would come up with *Fox*.

Delilah Fox has credit cards, by the way; she has a better credit rating than I do.

When hookers and agents meet each other, they often give both their names, as an act of intimacy and professional respect: my real name, my work name. I'm never sure which name to use after that. Some women want to be known only by their work names; some feel vulnerable if you use their work names. One woman mentioned in this book—Sunny—has been called by her real work name: she wanted it that way. In all other cases, however, I have changed women's work names to protect their livelihood, and I have never mentioned any working woman's real name. (By the way, if my real hooker name became known, no escort agency could represent me under that name. Escort agencies have to be careful not to represent "known" prostitutes. Prostitution is, you see, largely a crime of words.)

If Sarah was calling me for a job she would say, "Delilah, I have a client at such-and-such hotel. He wants a lingerie model for one-thirty. Can you be ready in time?"

Getting ready would mean not only getting dressed but finding the right wig (if he wanted a blonde I could be a blonde; if he wanted a redhead, voilà, I was a redhead), finding the right pair of shoes (if he wanted a short girl, I would have to wear flats; if he wanted someone statuesque, out would come the five-inch heels), and getting to the hotel by 1:30. If I said yes, Sarah would have me call the man and make final arrangements. Sarah taught me to tape any phone calls I made to clients—as a way of protecting myself. (It's perfectly legal to tape a phone conversation, as long as one of the parties knows the conversation is on tape.) If I knew I was on tape, I would be particularly careful not to say anything that implied I was offering sex for money. And if it turned out I was talking to a cop, I could later prove that I had not committed an act of prostitution—because I would have everything on tape. It's pretty hard to argue with a tape. Sarah also taught me that, before leaving home, I should write a note giving all the information about the person I was going to see. It was a lot of paperwork, but I was making $50 to $500 a job. It wasn't like I was selling magazine subscriptions for $4 apiece. For $50 to $500 I could afford to take the time to do paperwork.

Many women, after a few years of work as a prostitute, either give up the life for good or accept it for good. At that point a woman realizes how dangerous the work is, when she's seen or heard of prostitutes being robbed, assaulted, or arrested. If it weren't dangerous, she realizes, it wouldn't pay as much. She sees that there is a balance between the risks of the job and the rewards. It's the point at which she either can't live with the fear or can't live without it. For me, there was something exhilarating about feeling that fear. Every job was like a covert mission. I felt like Rambo in rhinestones, a daredevil in diamonds as I set out, late at night, to see a client.

My heartbeat would increase as I spotted the hotel from the interstate. When I made my turn toward the hotel parking garage, I felt there should be a musical score, something written for a suspense thriller, to drown out *The Larry King Show*, which I was listening to on the radio. The front of my white Cadillac would rear up and over the go-slow hump in the middle of the garage drive, and then I would nose down into a deserted parking garage, where amber lighting made everything sepia toned and there was no such thing as a friendly sound, not even my own.

The acoustics would amplify my door slamming, my spiked heels on the concrete, every little scrape and thump. If I saw anyone else in the garage at that hour, I paid attention. After all, I knew why I was there, but, hey buddy, what are you doing here? Parking lots and ramps and garages are dangerous places.

The indoor-outdoor carpeting in front of the elevator was a welcome sign of civilization, as were the fluorescent lamps that silhouetted the dead bodies of little winged creatures. When I reached for the elevator button to go to the lobby, I felt as if my hand rose and pressed the button all by itself.

I wasn't going into a whorehouse, where there were bouncers downstairs and sheet boys upstairs. I was completely alone when I walked into that hotel, except for Sarah. I would call her when I got near the hotel to let her know that I was almost there, and that I would call her again from the room. It was important that she know I was about to go into the hotel and up to the room. If I didn't call back, she could call the room and try to find out what was going on. If after she called the room she thought there was something wrong, then she would call another model who might be in the hotel or, as a last resort, she'd call hotel security and ask them to go to the room or check the parking lot. If she called hotel security, she would probably tell them the truth, that a woman from the agency was there. But she would rather do that than have something awful happen to one of us. And hotel security people would rather have an agent call and ask if there was something wrong than find out later that somebody had been killed in their hotel, or kidnapped.

I went to some hotels, especially the ones at the airport, ten or fifteen times a week. As far as I was concerned, hotel security was there to make sure that the hotel was not damaged and that no people in the hotel were hurt. At friendly hotels, I would go straight to hotel security when I arrived, tell them who I was, tell them were I was going and how long I was staying. There was one hotel where the security guard would walk me to the client's room. He would be discreet about it. He would back down the hall and disappear when the client opened the door. It was a professional courtesy; the security guard treated me like a co-worker.

Then there were the unfriendly hotels. Hotels tend to hire guards from the lower socioeconomic groups, and, for a lot of these people, being a security guard is the most power they have ever had, or will ever have, in life. Keeping a prostitute from reaching her destination can seem a lot more exciting than stopping someone from stealing a towel, so some eager-beaver security guards stopped any unaccompanied woman entering the hotel late at night. (At some hotels, the lobby is considered public space, so the guards would stop unaccompanied women as soon as they step off the elevator on an upper floor.) However, the Civil Rights Act prohibits denial of access to public accommodations if that denial is based upon race, religion or national origin. (Note that it does not cover gender.) Generally, trespassing laws require a person to vacate private or semi-public property upon request. However, a person does not have to leave if he or she is there for a legitimate purpose, such as visiting a guest, provided the person is not violating any rules of the premises or doing something blatantly illegal.

If the woman is not a guest, and not of a racial minority, the security guards can tell her that she has to leave. They often try to intimidate her into coming with them to the security office, where they coerce her to sign a statement and take her photograph. (The signed statement can be used as proof that she has been evicted from the hotel previously, so she can be charged with criminal trespassing if she enters the hotel again.)

My lawyer made it clear to me, however, that no one at a hotel could force me to go to a security office: "If they ask you to go with them to the security office, tell them, 'You can escort me to the nearest exit.' If they try to drag you anyplace, it's kidnapping and you have a wonderful lawsuit on your hands."

Any security guards I met knew enough not to touch me—assault!—as long as I was being cooperative. They knew they couldn't drag me down to the security office or push me out of the hotel. They also knew I couldn't touch them—assault!—so they would keep their distance as they walked me to the door, and at the same time they would keep me surrounded, like a little force field, until I was outside.

When they stopped me the first thing they would say was "Where are you going?" (Apparently, "Where are you going?" is the universally OK thing to ask a woman.)

I'd tell the guard, "I'm going to room thirteen thirteen." And they would ask, "Are you a guest of the hotel?"

When I would say no, they would ask for my ID, and as soon as they asked for ID I would pull out my tape recorder and turn it on. I would say, "I'm visiting a guest," and then they would want to know the guest's name and where he was from. At that point they would call downstairs to reception and check the information I had given them.

One night I was in a hotel and this young security guard stopped me. I pulled out my tape recorder, and he got a funny smile on his face, like, "Gotcha. Caught myself a prostitute."

"What's that, a beeper?" he asked.

I said, "This is a tape recorder."

"What's it for?" he asked, baffled now.

"Wait," I said. "It doesn't work until I turn it on. There. My attorney has informed me that any time there is a conversation that might end up in a lawsuit or litigation, I should make a tape recording of exactly what was said, so there's no possibility of any misunderstanding." The young guard was digesting this information when another security guard showed up.

This guy was a little more sophisticated. "I'll escort her to the room," he told the kid. "Why don't you go down to the lobby and cool out?" When I got to the room, I was concerned about bumping into the kid again when it was time for me to leave. "Will you walk me down to the lobby when I finish?" I asked the older security guard. "Sure," he said, "just call the desk and have them ask for Chip."

When he walked me down to the lobby, Chip told me that the kid had been upset about my turning on the tape recorder. "I never had anybody pull a tape recorder on me before," the kid had said. "Do you think I said something that could get me into trouble?"

As soon as I got inside a hotel room, I would call Sarah again to let her know that I was there. Then I would begin looking at the client, at his room, at his ID. If everything checked out, I would give him my little talk. I had learned that, in pitching a sale, the most important thing is to repeat the prices several times. I would rattle off, in a pleasant voice: "The agent's fee is fifty dollars; that goes entirely to the agent. The models don't get any part of the fifty dollars. All the models determine their own fees depending on the type of session that you have in mind. Normally a model's fee is about a hundred dollars. You can pay for this in cash, or with Visa, MasterCard, American Express, Diners Club, traveler's checks. If you choose to use a credit card, there is an additional service fee. And the models don't get any part of that. My fee is one hundred dollars."

If I said my spiel at the right pace, at the end the client might say, "That's fine." But sometimes he would say, "Would you say that again?" (Which I could do. The same way.) Or he might say, "That's too much" or "What do I get for one hundred dollars?"

Coming from San Juan, where every customer was ready to

argue over $5—where arguing about price took more time and energy than the sex itself—I was amazed to find that most clients in the United States were willing to fork over $50 for Sarah and $100 for the model—no questions asked. I was so amazed, after two weeks I decided to raise my price to $150. I figured the clients would try to argue me down to $120, but usually they didn't. They paid $150.

I figured, OK, they're willing to spend $150, let's try $200. They reacted pretty well to that too. I knew this was outside the regular range of prices, so I always made sure the customer knew there were extra things thrown in for the extra money: a bubble bath, a rub, a complete hour instead of a forty-minute hour. (Sarah counted the time from when I called her to tell her everything was OK to when she called back to say, "Is Delilah ready to go?"— which meant that normally I was in the room for only forty minutes.) For my "full-hour" pitch, I explained to the customers that the other models charged less but were there a shorter time. I was going to be inside the room for sixty minutes, I said. I had a special code for Sarah to let her know I was doing a full sixty minutes. When I said "I'm doing a complete session," she knew I was getting extra money and she wouldn't call back for sixty minutes.

After I had negotiated the price, and called Sarah to let her know that everything was OK, I would start unpacking my work bag. I unpacked that bag so many times, I could have done it blind. Everything went into the bag a certain way, so when I pulled things out I didn't have to fumble around looking for them. I would take things out as if I were a surgeon preparing for an operation, lay my instruments out on the bed or a dresser. Men were fascinated to watch me pull things out of that bag. In it I always carried my credit card printer, a few changes of sexy lingerie, several pairs of stockings, a Panasonic Panabrator II vibrator, some bubble bath, lotions and baby powder (in case the customer wanted a rub and also for myself), a spare washcloth and towel, two pairs of shoes, a wig, some tampons, a diaphragm, a blindfold, my makeup kit, cosmetic sponges, prophylactics, and usually a number of complimentary soaps and shampoos I had picked up from the hotels.

I also carried juggling balls. I used them several times a week, usually when I was going to be there longer than an hour. I'd just pull them out, say "I bet you haven't seen this before," and start juggling. Sometimes I would juggle at the very beginning, while they talked about money. People were fascinated by a juggling hooker. They figured, If she can juggle, who knows what else she can do? It also made whatever else remained in the bag seem that much stranger and more magical.

Some of the men were frightened by the sight of the vibrator. (Note: This was not a vibrating dildo but a vibrator meant for external use. It was good for massaging sore muscles but it was also good for a lot more.) The vibrator was about fourteen inches long, and I always kept a nine-foot extension cord attached to it. Sometimes a man would say, "What the hell is that?" Or "Are you going to use it on me?" I would say, "It's a vibrator, and I wouldn't think of using it on you. Not a chance. Don't you wish I would?" I usually used it on myself while they watched.

I would have them lie down on the bed, and then I would stand up near the bed and do an erotic act with the vibrator for them. Vibrators do make noise, but not as much as a truck or a motorcycle, more like the noise of a big razor. Men seem fascinated by watching women use vibrators. I used it for show and also to get myself off before I had intercourse with them, so that later I could concentrate on their orgasms and not my own.

This did not go over well with Japanese clients. Quite a few Japanese businessmen came to Atlanta, and quite a few called escort services. No matter what I was doing—say hanging up my skirt—a Japanese client would usually ask me *what* I was doing. It wasn't that Japanese clients thought I was doing anything wrong, they just wanted to know everything. If I opened up my purse: "What in there?" If I started unpacking my bag: "What you got in there?" One night an elderly gentleman pointed at my portaprinter as if it were some Oriental torture device. "What else you do with that? What else you got in there? Extra? You charge extra for that? I don't pay extra." I found that seeing Japanese meant taking too much energy to explain everything.

The first work bag I carried was actually just a large shoulder bag. But the shoes and the portaprinter and the vibrator were heavy, and I was wearing all my bags out. I noticed that several pilots I had seen were carrying their flight logs in a big bag that looked just perfect for me. If was called a brief bag; a lawyer might use it to carry legal files. It had straps on the bottom, and even when it got travel weary, it still managed to stay in one piece. So I switched to carrying a brief bag.

After I unpacked the bag I never asked the clients what they wanted to do. Whatever they wanted to do, it was probably illegal to discuss it. Besides, American men are shy about discussing sexual matters and, on top of that, most American men don't want to indicate that they are paying for sex. (Which was fine with me because I didn't want to indicate they were paying me for sex either.)

Sometimes, when I had finished my spiel, taken the money, and started undressing, I found that the client did not want any sexual services at all. He wouldn't want to touch me but only to look at me while I flounced around his hotel room in a black lace teddy. The agency, in fact, preferred that no sexual services take place. Sarah's attitude about clients was "We don't care what you want or what you get. All we want is the money. And we want everyone to be glad to exchange it."

Before I left the hotel room, I would call Sarah again, to let her know that I was OK and to find out if I had any more clients to see that night. I also carried a beeper so Sarah could reach me while I was in the car. That was before the advent of car telephones, which have made prostitutes' lives so much easier.

Then, when I left the hotel, I would call her again, to let her know that I was all right. I once figured out that Sarah and I would talk anywhere from five to fifteen times on every client.

Later that night or the next day I would go to Sarah's office and drop off her money: the agency fees and the credit card slips. Her office was at the back of a little two-story office building, with a breezeway and wrought-iron railings. You could pretty much see everything from there, which was fine with me because I was usually carrying a lot of money and didn't want to be robbed. I didn't want to be watched by the police either. I'd knock on the door and then put my envelope in through a mail slot. Regular pay night was Wednesday, so that's when I went by the office to pick up any money owed me on credit card slips.

Even though Sarah was the clearinghouse for all the money, I did not work for her. If anything Sarah worked for me, since the agency fee was taken out of the money I collected, and earned. You will note that I always say I worked *with* Sarah and not *for* her. If you ask me who I worked *for* I will correct you. I am an independent contractor, and I work for myself.

Sometimes clients would ask to see me again, and would ask for my phone number. I always gave them the agency number. I paid Sarah's agency fee even if I went back and saw the same person on my own. As far as I was concerned that was what I was paying her for, to keep up with my clients and to make sure that I was safe and that I got out in one piece. I knew that if I didn't try to steal any of Sarah's clients, she would trust me and send me out frequently. And she also knew that, since I wasn't running around and seeing people free-lance, if she couldn't get hold of me, there was something wrong.

I would sometimes see other women at the mail slot, turning their money in, and that was the only contact I had with the rest of Sarah's Magnolia Blossoms, unless Sarah suggested I meet someone or scheduled me for a double.

A lot of people believe that most prostitutes are lesbians, but it simply isn't true. What is true is that many men want to see two women together, even though it costs them $300 and up for this sight. Often clients wanted what I call a good whore–bad whore combo—one woman as sweet and innocent as fresh milk and a "hookerish" hooker, in black lace and red fingernail polish. It was fun sometimes to be there with another hooker. One man hired two of us and then said, "Do anything you want to do." The two of us sat down and had a long chat.

It's nice to work with friends—and it's often more interesting, because some of the men are so boring—but I don't like going out as a twosome because the number of possible mistakes is compounded and there is an increased risk of being arrested. I spent a lot of time worrying that the other hooker would say something that would make us both liable to be arrested.

The police had started putting a lot of time, money, and energy into catching call girls right before Christmas 1981. Some nights I couldn't complete a single assignment; all the calls coming in were from cops. I wasn't sure if they had excess budget to burn, or if the cops were trying to get in a lot of overtime before year's end, or if they just liked playing Scrooge. They were certainly ruining my Christmas because I couldn't earn any money; they were certainly ruining other women's Christmases—not to mention the rest of their lives—by arresting them for prostitution.

I was so angry I called my city council representative at 6:30 in the morning to complain about how the police were behaving. I wanted a formal statement of their intentions, I said. Who had ordered this crackdown? Who was paying for it? I didn't want *my* taxes used to entrap prostitutes.

Fifteen working women got together that night to discuss formally turning ourselves into a nonprofit group. The women were all very enthusiastic about the idea of banding together, but there is probably nothing so disorganized on earth as prostitution. It was like trying to organize raw eggs—but then again you can always whip eggs into shape.

The women liked working as prostitutes and wanted to keep on working. But they wanted to stop police harassment. They felt they needed a way to keep up with laws and to change the laws. To do that they needed the power of an organization.

We talked about not only what the police had been doing but also what had been happening in court, what happened when prostitutes went to health clinics and to hotels, and the prices we were charging. I don't want to give anyone the idea that we were involved in price-fixing. We were cooperative about raising prices— we didn't all charge the same price, but when a few women raised their prices, almost everyone decided to go up too. No one wanted to undercut anyone else.

We talked about a name for our group. HOA was offered, standing for Hookers of Atlanta. (The fact that southerners pronounce *whore* "ho-a" was a plus.) We thought about calling ourselves the Atlanta Division of the National Task Force on Prostitution, which was dignified but not very catchy. We finally decided on HIRE—Hooking Is Real Employment. We asked Margo St. James if we could be a sister organization to COYOTE, and she sent us some materials to use in writing up our position paper.

In that position paper we stated that prostitutes provide sexual services and also act as therapists, mother figures, and companions for their clients. We called for decriminalization of prostitution, not legalization. And we published some facts and figures to support our position:

There were approximately 1,300,000 prostitutes in the United States.

In 1981, 100,000 people had been arrested for prostitution: 70 percent of them female prostitutes, 20 percent of them male prostitutes and transvestites, and only 10 percent of them clients.

While only 10 to 15 percent of all prostitutes were street prostitutes, street prostitutes made up 90 percent of those arrested.

About the only way police officers could arrest prostitutes was by entrapping them and invading their privacy.

In 1978 it had cost the San Francisco taxpayer $2,400 to arrest and keep each prostitute in jail for two weeks.

Women arrested for prostitution and jailed often learned criminal activity in jail. (In other words, prison bred rather than deterred criminal activity.)

And in 1973, the National Conference of the National Organization of Women (NOW) had passed a resolution calling for the decriminalization of prostitution.

We made it clear that we were against childhood prostitution and that, of course, we were against anyone being forced into prostitution. The other women elected me president; HIRE got a phone number and answering machine; and as the calls and requests came in, I started speaking as an official representative of HIRE. We hit the streets and started passing out pamphlets to street prostitutes. We wanted to inform as many women as soon as possible.

I went to city council meetings. I spoke with prostitutes who had been arrested, trying to find lawyers for them, trying to make it clear to them that they could go to court with their cases and not just plead guilty. I answered people's questions when they called, and tried to make other prostitutes aware of what their rights and options were. And we began selling and passing out the official T-shirt I designed: I'M FOR HIRE.

Our organization was not universally popular with the working women of Atlanta. One woman, Penny, called and said she wanted to let me know that I was doing the business a terrible disservice. She said, "I'm a call girl and what I do is not prostitution."

I said, "If you're ever busted, you're going to find out that a whore is a whore is a whore. You're going to be charged like any whore on the street." She didn't believe it, and she was busted shortly after that. She had a fabulous apartment, she had a grand piano, fur coats, a nice car, and she had to sell everything to pay her lawyers and her living expenses while she was on trial. She went to trial, but her case set a bad precedent. She was found guilty even though she had never agreed to have sex for money. The verdict went to a higher court, and that court ruled that since Penny had taken off her clothes, jumped under the covers, turned off the lights, and said "Come on, honey, let's go," she had not intended to model but to have sex.

Penny ended up as a street prostitute in Cleveland. She didn't believe that it could happen to her, and when it did and she got treated like anyone else, it blew her mind.

Her whole case taught me how little of what Elaine had said three years before was true: A cop didn't have to hand me money; a cop could undress, he could even have sex with a prostitute; and now, according to a higher court, I didn't even have to agree to have sex to be prosecuted for prostitution. Made bold by Penny's case, the vice cop who arrested her began trying to pick me up: at traffic lights; twice when he saw me loading groceries in my car at around two in the morning. He figured who but a hooker would be dressed like this—high heels, a skirt, an angora sweater, and a black feather boa—in the middle of the night.

So now, by becoming a spokesperson for prostitutes' rights, I became a police target.

I spent Christmas with my family that year, and I bought a lot of Christmas presents for them. They could see that I was in better health than I had ever been. I was thin, taking vitamins, jogging. While I was home, my mom had one of those woman-to-woman talks with me:

"I hope you're all right," she said.

"I'm fine."

"What I mean is, your dad and I don't quite know what you're doing for a living these days. We just want you to be doing something safe and worthwhile."

"Oh, I am," I said. "I'm painting, and I'm doing a lot of speaking on women's rights." (This was true—I just didn't spell out to them which women's rights.)

"And I'm doing a little radio and some writing," I added.

"Well, the next thing you know we're going to see you on TV," she said.

Men must get an erection hearing the music for *The Tonight Show*; at least an awful lot of them call escort agencies from 11:30 to 11:45. By the time I made the appointment and got to the hotel, the Carson show would be over. But there was this other guy who was always on TV. As I was giving a blow job or washing a customer, I kept catching little bits and pieces of his program: weird things for TV—strange guests doing strange things, odd camera angles, juvenile humor. The volume was usually down, so I couldn't really hear what people were saying over the sound of sheets being ruffled, skin slapping, moans, heavy breathing, and sometimes the buzz of a vibrator. But I kept thinking to myself, Who is this guy with a gap between his two front teeth? Sometimes I would stop in the middle of a job and say out loud: "Who is that guy?" He would be doing strange science experiments with the real Mr. Wizard. I began timing my jobs to make sure I would be in the hotel room at 12:30, and I would position myself on the bed so I could see the TV, but I still didn't know who that guy was. He was running over things with a bulldozer. Doing things with a visual impact. Letterman, one client told me. That's David Letterman.

I knew the client was some kind of trouble the minute I walked into the hotel room. There was just something about him that didn't add up. I looked at his ID, and it looked like him, sort of. But he had more hair than the guy in the picture. And the guy in the picture had a cleft chin and he didn't. So I was having this little moment of doubt. I was alone in the room with him, and I felt like I was in a vacuum. I was in a strange place, with a strange person, so I looked at this guy and said to him, in a cute, jocular way, "Have you had cosmetic surgery?" I was actually hoping he would say yes. And then I would have said, "Well it really looks natural."

But he said no.

I asked, "Have you changed your diet?"

I was so innocent.

He said no, but he was starting to get antsy with me. He grabbed for the card. I still wasn't totally suspicious of him, but I wanted to look the card over some more. "No. Wait, wait, wait," I said. "You have more hair now than you had in this picture. And you don't have a cleft chin. You have a cleft chin in this picture."

He just kept saying, "That's me, that's me." And then he was saying, "How about we get it on?"

He kept pressuring me to have sex with him, and I kept saying, "*That* isn't what I told you on the phone." And he said, "Yeah, but we all know what *really* goes on." I decided to call Sarah and give her the signal that I was in trouble. Sarah had told me certain code names that were to be used for cops and crazies—names to use in case a lunatic had a gun to our heads and was telling us, "Go ahead and call the agent and say everything is OK." We tried to use women's names, since they seemed pretty innocuous to a client. "Judy" meant a cop; "Phyllis" meant a crazy. No hooker in the world was called Judy or Phyllis, or at least none in Atlanta.

So I called Sarah and said, "Everything is fine here. By the way, has *Judy* been in the office lately? Well, if *Judy* comes by, tell her I'd like to meet her for coffee."

Sarah said over the phone, "You don't need to use the code, I can tell by the sound of your voice you're in the room with a cop. Your voice goes up two octaves when you're scared."

She asked, "Does he have ID?"

"Uh-huh."

"Did he ask you to have sex?"

"Oh, yes, he's lots of fun."

(Any positive answer I gave meant yes, any negative answer like, "Oh, I think I'm going to be late," meant no. It was amazing how wonderfully this all worked. As soon as Sarah understood there was danger, she was on full alert. It was very dramatic. She knew I was in a bad situation, and she knew it was up to her to help me get out of it. It was a complete, thorough concern—so thick it was almost solid. When Sarah got a call like that, she would put everything else on hold and begin concentrating 100 percent on the woman in trouble. She wasn't going to say, "What a drag. Well, call me later if you get out of there." She was not going to abandon me; she was going to get me out of this mess.)

She said, "Is he between you and the door?"

She was trying to picture how much damage had been done. She was trying to assess whether or not I could get out of there without being arrested. She knew, however, that I couldn't answer many questions.

"Is there anybody else in the room?" she asked. "Was there anybody suspicious in the hallway?"

"Oh, I think I'll be tired later."

"Is there an adjoining room? Can you tell if it's locked?"

"Don't wait for me," I said while looking casually around the room.

"Does he have luggage?" (She was trying to help me figure out whether or not he was a cop. She had a point system. She had told me all about it. She was making little hatch marks on a piece of paper—some in the yes column and some in the no column. Over the phone I could hear her counting under her breath; one, two, three, four, five. One, two, three, four. The sorts of thing she was asking me—Was there a door to another room? Was there anyone suspicious in the hallway?—could be coincidental. But Sarah decided that there's a limit to coincidence; too many coincidences and you have a conspiracy.)

She decided that this guy had more negatives than positives.

"Uh-huh," I said. "You know this guy has some really interesting ID. It's fine, but in his picture he has a cleft chin and he said he outgrew it. Have you ever heard of that happening? And he has more hair, but he says he's eating better. Oh, he wants the ID back.''

"Does he have all of his clothes on?" (He was in his underwear—Jockey shorts and a T-shirt—which was what he'd been wearing when I arrived.)

"Oh, I'm busy on Friday."

"That's it," Sarah said. "Don't take any money and get out of the room."

"Well, everything's fine here. I'll call you back and let you know how long I'm going to stay," I said and hung up the phone.

He was between me and the door, and I knew that I couldn't push him out of the way to get out the door—that would be assaulting an officer. Even if I hadn't done anything except arrive, ask for his ID, and call my agent, I couldn't touch him.

He was maneuvering himself so I didn't see how I could get past him. Now he was saying, "Let's have sex," and I replied, "Oh, I'm just here to model; that's all I'm going to do." I didn't want to take the money he was offering me because he sounded like he was trying to pay for something other than modeling. But he said, "Oh, that's just semantics. I'll pay you for modeling, then." Wink, wink.

I was thinking about how I could get out of the room. There was money stuck under an ashtray, across the room. He was wearing Jockey shorts, so he wasn't likely to chase me down to the lobby. I, meanwhile, was fully dressed. I thought, If I agree to take the money for modeling, he'll have to move to get the money. So I said, "OK, then."

When he stepped over to pull the money out, I pretended to be startled and I backed off. It was a great challenge to act as if everything was OK. This man was trying to ruin the rest of my life. I kept telling myself that the rest of my life was going to be decided in the next few seconds. It was exhilarating, but, like a heart attack, a little too exhilarating. He shoved the money toward me and I said, "Wait a minute, you haven't even decided what you're spending. Just put that down."

I was moving around a little, and he was getting exasperated. Suddenly he gave me my opening. I dashed for the door, whipped it open, and then I turned back to him and gave him a lecture:

"If I were an undercover agent I could arrest you right now for pandering—do you know that? I came here to model and you were trying to solicit me for prostitution." In a joking way I said, "Oh, yeah, and for stealing someone else's ID." I knew it didn't matter what tone of voice I used. If he arrested me, only the words would become court record, not the way I said them.

I had my tape recorder on in my pocket, and I had a record of the whole thing.

I got out of the room, out of the hotel, called Sarah, and went home for the night. I was shaken up, but you do the best you can not to let it destroy your life or even the rest of the night. There would be other times when I would be in the room with a cop and when it would upset me. But not this guy; this wasn't even close.

I liked going to apartments and private homes, but most women didn't. They felt less safe. I liked going because I felt *more* safe. When I went to an apartment or a house, I knew the ID had to be correct if it had a picture and the right address. I also knew that there was little likelihood that a vice cop was using a private home or an apartment to make an arrest. And I wasn't too worried about lunatics, because even lunatics usually didn't want to kill a stranger in their home. Most people were respectful in their homes and didn't want to act up there.

There was one problem with seeing clients in private homes; in Atlanta, drifters would sometimes break into a home and live there for a week or so while the owners were away. One of the first things someone like that would do would be call an escort agency. But there were a few ways to tell whether the person who answered the door actually lived there or not.

First of all, he might have a piece of identification with the right address on it but no picture. (It's pretty easy to look through someone's house and come up with a library card, a credit card, bills, letters, and so on). And I learned pretty quickly to ask for a glass of water. If the guy had to look in more than three cabinets to find a glass, if I asked for a fresh towel and he had no idea where the linen closet was, I might assume he didn't live there. These weren't extraordinary things I was asking for. I wasn't asking where they kept the masking tape. It concerned me that someone breaking into a house wouldn't at least become familiar with the place before inviting someone over. It made me worry that someone so deficient in common sense might also think there would be no problem if he spilled a little blood on the Oriental rug.

I walked out on a lot of clients. I might say anything to get out, from "I don't feel comfortable here," to "I left something in the car," to "I don't think you really live here or even know the people who live here." I usually found that being straight with people was the best policy. Even if somebody is trying to trick you, if you try to trick them back, they can get nasty.

An aging hippie called and asked for someone who would model exotic lingerie, stockings, and garter belts. Sarah always referred to me as the Lingerie Queen, so she decided I was the perfect person to go. I arrived to find someone who lived as if he were in a time warp. He had long hair in a ponytail and a part of a tattoo on his arm, some sort of geometric design that had been only partially filled in.

It was like walking into the past. There were posters on the wall: Jim Morrison and Jimi Hendrix and Janis Joplin. An Indian print bedspread. The guy was wearing a tie-dyed T-shirt, and he was still saying things like *far-out* and *groovy*. He said he worked as a carpenter, and I thought about how carpentry and prostitution are two fields that allow people to freeze in time and isolate themselves from the outside world.

It surprised me that this guy wanted a hooker in fancy lingerie. I would have figured he wanted someone with long natural hair, parted in the middle, someone wearing elephant bell pants. But people do have fantasies about lingerie, and they aren't limited to any kind of man or even limited to men.

As soon as I took my skirt and sweater off and started playing around in my garter belt and stockings, he lit a joint. Then he got the Indian print bedspread and put it on the floor. He wanted a hooker to play Woodstock with him for $150 an hour, plus the agency fee, of course. And he didn't want me to act like a hooker. He wanted to seduce me and kiss me all over. He was terribly concerned about whether or not I was turned on. I thought about getting out my sex toys but decided that this was one customer whose fantasy was the return to innocence: a man, a woman, a bedspread, Jim Morrison on the wall, and a joint.

He was cute, he was fun, he was sweet, and he was just a few years older than me. After we had "made love"—his term—I said to him, "Too bad we didn't meet each other ten years ago, sweetheart." Because ten years before I could really have enjoyed someone like him.

*   *   *

Perhaps 20 percent of the clients calling Sarah's agency were black. (Sarah didn't ask about race or nationality; she could usually tell by his accent if a guy was Afro-American or Spanish or Cajun, or West Indian.) Black clients tended to treat the situation like it was a date. If I seemed to be enjoying the session a black client might say, "Hey, you're having a good time. Why should I pay you?" followed by, "Hold on, baby, you're having *too* good a time. You otta be paying me." Before it was over I would probably be hearing, "Hey, you're a foxy mama. I've been looking for a woman like you—someone to have something go on with." That could mean anything from sex, to dating, to moving in with them, to marriage. I never got away from black clients, even the really old ones, in less than the full amount of time—and that meant sixty minutes of penetration.

Having worked in the Caribbean, I was used to all this nonsense, but most American women thought clients should be businesslike—cool, reserved, and formal, maybe even meek. All this arguing and complimenting and kissing and proposing bothered the local hookers. Black hookers were even less likely to see black clients. Sometimes a hooker who was new to the business would go—once or twice. Then she usually joined in the chorus: "Send someone else."

Everything you've heard about black guys having big dicks is true. Black men were a little rougher—but not in the sense of beating me up, just in the sense of more athletic sex. For a woman looking for that sort of thing, they were better lovers. If I had ever hit it off with one of those guys, it would have been a lot of fun. But I always walked out thinking, "Gee, he was good. Too bad he was so full of shit."

We were having a busy week, which was unusual before Christmas. I had just finished an airport hotel job, and I called Sarah from the lobby to see if there were any other calls in the airport area. Sarah gave me three numbers—and information on three guys—at once. Usually Sarah would screen clients thoroughly and give me a lot of information on each one. This night, because we were so busy, and because she had trained me so well, she hadn't done her usual screening job. (By now I was experienced. Sarah knew that I wasn't likely to make mistakes. That was one of the reasons I was working so much, because Sarah didn't have to worry about me.)

Of the three names she gave me, one client was at the airport and two were in the same hotel downtown. She explained, "Delilah, you have to check these people out." I called the guy at the airport first, but he had already made arrangements to see someone else. (We were so busy, he had been waiting two hours.) Then I called the two guys at the downtown hotel: one guy was coming to consult with Boeing. The other guy said he was from Columbus, Ohio, and said he worked for an airline company.

When he said he was from Columbus, Ohio, I said, "Oh, the home of the child mayor—what's his name? David Snitowitz or something. The one who's twenty-eight?" And as soon as he said, "Yeah, you got it," I remembered out loud that the child mayor lived in Cleveland and not in Columbus. Then I said, "Isn't Columbus the home of Larry Flynt and *Hustler* magazine?" And he said, "Well, I travel all the time. I don't really know what goes on there."

That was all I needed to know about this guy. I said, "OK, I'll see you in twenty minutes." Then I called Sarah and told her, "He's a cop. Nobody's gone so much that he doesn't know *Hustler* magazine's headquarters is in his hometown. And he thinks he's got a child mayor."

I was in a big hurry because I had told the first guy I would be there in twenty minutes. I dashed out to my car, zipped downtown, called Sarah, pulled into the parking lot, and then went straight upstairs to the cop's room. I had gotten my pieces of paper mixed up. I knocked on the door, and as soon as he opened it, I thought, "Oh, no." He looked like an aging hippie drug dealer—in other words, he looked like a vice cop. It's hard to tell the difference between a cop and a drug dealer.

I said to myself, Why didn't you just say "Oops, wrong room." But I went in anyway. I guess it was my sense of adventure, and I wanted him to prove to me he wasn't a cop.

I looked at his ID, and it was pretty new looking. So I asked him why he was staying in this hotel, since he was with the airline. Why wasn't he staying at the airport hotel? He said his secretary made his reservation; it must have been a mistake. I said, "Why don't we get you moved to the right hotel? I know they have room, I was just out there."

No, he said, he was all settled here.

I had told him on the phone that I would want to see two forms of identification: a driver's license and a plane ticket. And that I'd ask for a third ID when I got there. So in my cute, flirtatious voice, I asked for his car rental papers. He said he didn't have a rental car, that he had taken a taxi from the airport, which didn't make any sense at all. I said, still in my cute voice, "Are you doing something else downtown?" I wanted to watch him squirm—trying to figure what a guy from an airline would be doing downtown.

Then I called Sarah to let her know I had made a mistake.

"Hi," I said, "this is Delilah. Tell *Judy* I went to see the guy from the airline."

She said, "Delilah, how could you do that? Does he have a credit card? He said he was going to pay by credit card."

I asked him, and he said, "I forgot it, but I've got cash."

I told Sarah: "He forgot his credit card. Can you imagine that?" I backed toward the door and told him that, because he had already made arrangements to pay by credit card, he would have to call the agent back and make a new appointment to pay by cash. "If you change your means of payment," I told him in all seriousness, "then you have to start over again and reschedule."

I had my purse in one hand and my work bag in the other. He was trying to shove money into my hand, but luckily my hands were full. "Maybe I'll see you later," I said and got out of the room.

Then I went up the elevator to the right client.

There are at least four things I can tell on the phone. I can usually tell whether a client's credit card is good or not by his voice. Guys try to use stolen credit cards all the time with hookers. They figure, As long as I'm dealing with a hooker, no one's going to check. But I can sense if a guy is nervous or lying about his credit card. He'll try to sound carefree about it. He'll agree to a price faster than the usual client. He'll agree to a price as if it has nothing to do with him. I would call Sarah and say, "Credit card's no good. I'm not going." Once in a while Sarah thought I might be wrong and sent someone else; and the credit card usually turned out to be bad.

I can usually tell if a guy's doing coke. I can tell by how fast he talks and a certain kind of rough whisper in his voice and all the sniffling going on. Guys on coke always want a hooker to appear as if by astral projection. Their concept of driving across town is totally out of touch with reality: "You can be here in five minutes." When I agree to see a cocaine user, I try to make him write down what I say, because he can never remember what I've told him on the phone.

Some women like to see a heavy cocaine user, because the

chances are that, by the time they get there, he's going to be so wasted he won't be able to do anything. The woman gets paid, maybe gets high, and goes home. But I'm not eager to do coke heads, because if they aren't wasted they wear you out with talk and paranoia and renegotiation. One coke fiend paid me the most I had ever made in one night—well, let's say I've heard of women making $10,00 for nights like that—and it was the hardest money I had ever earned. He started with the usual price and then, when I was ready to leave, he offered me another $250. I stayed another hour and then I said, "Hey, I really have to go." But he was cranked up and terrified of being alone. He paid me $500 for the next hour, and after that I was really determined to leave. So he paid me more money for the next hour. It went like that all night, and it was mentally and physically exhausting. He didn't really want sexual services, he just wanted me to stay with him. It didn't matter that I made a lot of money, I was so tired I couldn't work again for a week.

I can also tell if a guy's fat. If he's really fat, and he's sitting down, he has trouble breathing. I can hear a noise in the background: uh-uh-uh. It took me a long time to figure out what it was. I thought, this guy is jerking off while I talk to him. You know, uh-uh-uh. Then it dawned on me that the common denominator among all these men was that they were fat, the kind of fat that makes it hard to breathe.

And I can usually tell when a client is old. I often wish I'd taken a course in cardiopulmonary resuscitation. Thank God nobody's died on me yet.

A lot of the clients are old, and not a few of them are ugly, but it never bothers me to be with old and ugly clients. They need entertainment and companionship too. I've never been uncomfortable about the way a client looked. Of course, if a guy looks unsafe—crazy or sick—that's different. But if he is just old and ugly, well, I'm not there to appreciate his looks. If I want to look at something beautiful I go to a museum or take the guy's money and go shopping at Neiman-Marcus.

8

THE MOST PUBLIC PROSTITUTE IN AMERICA

What it comes down to is this: the grocer, the butcher, the baker, the merchant, the landlord, the druggist, the liquor dealer, the policeman, the doctor, the city father and the politician—these are the people who make money out of prostitution.
—POLLY ADLER
A House Is Not a Home, 1953

Political work is much more draining than being a prostitute. When I work as a prostitute I am there because the client wants me to be there. When I speak to someone one-on-one about prostitution, they are usually interested and unembarrassed to talk to me.

But in a crowd, people are embarrassed to be interested in prostitution. I hear the same responses, the same pat questions over and over again, no matter what serious social or political issue I am trying to discuss. I will be talking about the Constitution and someone will raise a hand and say, "What about children who work as prostitutes?" I answer the question briefly—"We are completely against coercive prostitution. I personally don't think anyone should begin working as a prostitute until their midtwenties, until their attitudes about themselves and their own sexuality are fully formed." And then I go back to the Constitution and someone else will raise a hand. "How many times have you had VD?"

"I've never had VD. How many times have you had it? Now about the First Amendment—"

"So how does it *feel* to be a prostitute?"

"I love it. It's the most honest, rewarding work I've ever done. Now about Article—"

"Doesn't it make you feel dirty and degraded?"

It's like working a crowd of hecklers. People often ignore anything positive I say about working as a prostitute.

What's infuriating about these questions is that they are based on false assumptions, assumptions that nearly everyone in the room agrees are true. I feel they might as well have a black person up at the podium and be asking, "Isn't it true that all black people can tap dance? And don't you all smell different?"

It takes a lot of energy to answer these questions without showing my anger and without embarrassing the person asking them. I want to say, "How dare you!" or "Where did you get that idea, from TV movies?" These people are thinking wrong things about not only me but all the other women I have worked with— Cricket and Sunny and Elaine, Margueritte (the streetwalker in San Juan), and even Sarah. But I'm not allowed to be infuriated. I'm a spokesperson, and I have to be polite. I have to keep my good humor. Every time I walk into a meeting or a lecture hall I think, This must be what it's like to go to Johannesburg to talk about civil rights.

I went to Midtown neighborhood meetings, where people wanted to talk about cleaning up the neighborhood, which meant gentrification—planting a few trees and getting rid of the hookers, the poor people, the shelters for the homeless, the drug treatment centers. I went to the Women's Feminist Health Center to talk about dealing with prostitutes who came in for medical care. I wanted the doctors and nurses to deal with these women's needs and not with their status in society. I wanted to make sure that if a woman came in and said she worked as a prostitute, she got all the health checks she needed, from chlamydia to bunions. I went to the rape crisis center at Grady Hospital to talk about the absolute necessity of being sensitive to prostitutes who were rape victims or otherwise assaulted. I wanted people to understand that prostitutes can be assaulted or killed and that they have not brought it on themselves. I wanted people to understand that a prostitute can and should press charges against anyone who commits a crime against her, including a customer. That although prostitutes might not act the way other women do if raped or beaten—even if they are angry or indignant instead of terrified—they still might need understanding and support.

I even went to police officials, to talk to them about prostitutes' rights. Sometimes I got smirks. Usually I got respect.

I spoke to a mental health group, to discuss how, when they are dealing with clients who are prostitutes, they should avoid focusing therapy on the woman's decision to be a prostitute and instead look at some core problems. Prostitutes do have some unique problems, like being arrested, and dealing with fear, and dealing with stigmatization, and worrying that their children might be taken away from them. Women choose to go into prostitution because they need money and they need flexible hours so they can deal with all of life's problems, like taking the kids to first grade and supporting an ailing mother. Prostitution is not the problem, I told these therapists. The problem is that the kids are sick, or flunking math, the washing machine's broken, her father is dying of cancer, they're getting a divorce, or the police are closing in. Those are the real problems.

When I talked to some groups, everyone listened very closely because it was going to make great cocktail party talk: "I heard a prostitute yesterday who felt that, when we treat women who are prostitutes, we should concentrate on their real problems—like that their kids are flunking math."

"Oh, really?"

I would go to meetings at places like the Unitarian church, to talk about prostitutes and prostitutes' rights. I would explain something about the number of women who had been arrested, about what happened to women when they were arrested, what happened to their lives, and I would end my speech by saying, "These women are not fictional people like Moll Flanders. These women are not characters in *Klute*. Prostitutes are not like squirrels or pigeons—urban pests that should be gotten rid of. These are real people. I know them. I am one of them. You people sitting here, the residents of this city, the citizens of this state, have it within your power to change the laws, to decriminalize prostitution. It's a waste of your tax dollars and it's a waste of police power to concentrate on prostitution. Work through the city council. Write to your state legislator. Atlanta has always been a city of change, from the Civil War through the civil rights movement and on up to the present. We in Atlanta can set legal precedent for the whole country. It's up to you." There would be polite applause, and then someone would raise a hand and say, "What about pimps?"

It was at a meeting at the Gay Center, where I was to speak on prostitutes' rights, that I met the lawyer who was to help HIRE with its incorporation papers. Michael Hauptman was an Atlanta defense attorney, originally from New York, who was committed to prostitutes' rights. He had defended a number of prostitutes and was appalled at the way the courts treated them. And, it turned out, he had come to this meeting specifically to meet me.

Our personal relationship didn't begin for another year and a half, but right away I liked Michael. I thought he was smart and funny; just as important, he thought I was smart and funny. (Having someone think I am witty and smart is a complete turn-on for me.) Obviously, he didn't have any problems with the fact that I was a prostitute. (People often do have problems with this idea, but I found that, in general, the men I dated outside my work saw my being a prostitute as interesting and exciting.) And he was immediately interested in the idea of helping HIRE incorporate. I had called several lawyers for such assistance, and they had an assortment of negative responses. One actually said, "If prostitution were decriminalized, what would I do for a living?" When I told Michael this, he was outraged. He said, "How can someone practice law just to make money? How can anyone reject a chance to fix an injustice?" Michael immediately set his hand to HIRE's incorporation.

I, meanwhile, kept campaigning. I went to a city council budget meeting, to discuss just exactly how much of the city budget was going to be allocated to the vice squad. They were talking about mandatory jail sentences for first arrests, and mandatory jail sentences if the prostitutes couldn't pay a fine. It was unconstitutional that some people could buy their way out of jail and other people might be thrown in jail because they couldn't pay a fine; it smacked of the poorhouse, and it certainly didn't seem like due process.

I had gotten an attorney to research the early American essays written in reaction to English common law, pre-Constitutional discussions about how unfair it is to impose jail sentences on people who can't pay a fine. When I stood up, introduced myself as a prostitute, and raised these points, I could see that a few people were somewhat embarrassed and others were merely amused. It was so shocking for a prostitute to turn up at a city council meeting, they didn't know what to do. It may have been the first time most of them had seen a prostitute in public. It was the first time some of them had seen a prostitute ever.

Yes, they had seen me at fund-raisers and on picket lines and in their campaign offices and at their own inaugurations—but that was as Dolores French, community activist. Up until that point, prostitutes were *those* people. Up until that point, prostitution wasn't even an issue. The city council had always felt that they could do whatever they wanted to do to prostitutes because no one was ever going to argue against it. And here I was, and I was announcing not only that I was a prostitute but that I was representing HIRE, and that HIRE's policy was that prostitutes have rights.

The members of the city council were uncomfortable, so they acted as if it were a joke. But they sent their recommendation for mandatory jail sentences back to committee and dropped the idea of pay a fine or go to jail. Lobbying for prostitutes' interests was not quite so amusing. Not anymore.

More and more women were calling Sarah's escort agency for sexual services. These were not lesbians, but normal heterosexual women, usually over forty-five, who didn't know how to—or didn't want to—find a man for sex.

There were gigolos for them to call, but most women were nervous about male prostitutes. One woman worried about getting a disease because "those men might be gay"; in 1982, a few people had begun to be aware of AIDS in the heterosexual community. Some women also worried that men might be violent and rob them. Most of them simply felt uncomfortable having a strange man in their house or hotel room. They were often widows or divorced women; some claimed they had never had sex with anyone except their husbands. Others said they'd tried to have affairs but were disappointed in their lovers. (What I heard from one female client was, "The men are so self-involved, they don't care what I want.")

A few of these women had spent years being sexually frustrated, yet they had no idea where to go for sexual services. Prostitutes, on the other hand, often would not deal with women clients, and a lot of agencies turned them down, either because they didn't believe that women would have enough money or because they had learned that women clients could be difficult. But I enjoyed seeing them. For one thing, almost all of them had crazy stories. (Men clients sometimes had crazy stories too, but if they did, it was almost always a good idea to leave.)

I also liked seeing women because the whole business of calling a prostitute was so new to them. Men generally behaved as though this was an ordinary, everyday activity, whether it was or not. I was usually the first prostitute these women had ever met. It wasn't something any of them had ever discussed with a friend, so they didn't know what to say or how to behave or what to ask for or what to expect. It could be wonderful theater; it could also be time-consuming.

For one thing, women clients never seemed to understand why a prostitute needed to see positive identification. "I *live* here," a woman told me. "Who else could I be?"

I then had to explain that if she used a credit card at a department store, or wanted to write a check, the clerk would ask to see a driver's license. Women clients, who were invariably well-bred and solidly middle class or upper class, didn't seem to understand that prostitutes are cautious about violence, even from another woman. These women didn't see other women as dangerous, so it took some careful verbal dancing to educate them on the dangers without insulting them or giving them the idea that *I* was dangerous.

It often took an hour just to get through the verification. To me that was an hour wasted, because I didn't get paid for explaining why they needed to have an ID, even if they were going to pay cash.

(Women seemed to prefer to pay cash. They were afraid that, someday, their credit card receipt to an escort agency would turn up and they would have to be ashamed. Men, on the other hand, seemed to relish the idea of putting a hooker on a credit card. I'm sure a number of them wrote off expenses at the more ambiguously named agencies as business dinners. Who was to say that "Zebra" wasn't an African restaurant?)

Then there was the problem of language and custom. Most women were too polite or too inhibited to come out and say what they wanted. That's when I would start hearing the long stories: their work, their husbands, men in general. One woman who called the agency for a "rub" was an heiress. She had spent most of her life functioning entirely for her husband. She had lived her whole adult life in the strongly defined role of first lady to her family empire, over which, of course, her husband had reigned. Her lifestyle was perhaps unique to the South: characterized by precise rules of conduct, detailed definitions of responsibility, clear distribution of power, and extensive rituals of behavior. She had an etiquette book for every occasion. She knew how to do every single thing in life, except find an outlet for her sexual needs.

She admitted she had tried going to a male strip club. I prodded her to tell me about it as I started her "rub." As she talked, she realized why she hadn't been able to proposition a man. The bottom line was that she couldn't figure out the proper way to get a man's attention for such an occasion. "Ah yes, of course," I said, "a woman of your status and background would be intimidated under those circumstances. What were you planning to say if you had somehow attracted his attention?" She said, in a deep southern, matronly voice, "That's why I couldn't get up the nerve, for the life of me I couldn't imagine what the appropriate way was to proposition a man. I didn't want him to throw a drink in my face the way girls do to uncouth men on television."

She then told me that she had just gotten back from a trip to Japan. First I heard about the teahouses and the gardens, and then the subways, and then the clothing and the makeup. Finally, about a half an hour into her massage, the woman mentioned that in Japan clitoral manipulation is included in a massage. This woman was very dainty in talking about her Japanese "massage." She raved about how wonderful it was, as if we were two women talking in the beauty parlor about a new hand lotion. Then she said she had never learned how to masturbate, and suggested maybe I could help her.

As I began massaging her clitoris, however, she announced that, in Japan, cunnilingus was used. (Which I doubted, but it seemed to be the only way for this woman to suggest what she wanted.) I thought, No wonder men get so frustrated in trying to please women; they can be so inscrutable.

Women also take a long time to satisfy. The whole process is usually delicate; it's often mysterious. And when it's all over, women cling. While I would be trying to get out the door, the woman would want to make coffee and have a chat. I would say, "I'd be glad to sit and talk, but you'll have to pay me for another hour," which seemed to disappoint her. She thought we were now friends, after what we had shared.

For these women, unlike for my male clients, sex was intimacy. Men want to go to sleep after sex; women want to talk. I usually felt awful when I left a woman client. Often I was tempted to stay and talk, but I also felt it was only fair to treat female clients the same way I treated male clients.

There was a great deal of satisfaction in giving women pleasure and teaching them about their own sexuality. The woman who had been to Japan, for instance, raved about how I had understood exactly what she wanted.

And why shouldn't a woman be able to pay for sex, the same as a man?

I saw Margo St. James in San Francisco at the Hookers' Convention. (Welders have conventions, flight attendants have conventions, even chicken pluckers have conventions, so why not hookers?) About fifty women from all over the country gathered to talk about prostitution: the laws, disease, what to charge, social issues. The women who came to this convention were well educated, better educated than average. These were political women, strong and brave women, women who were oddities in their own communities and who, at a hookers' convention, could be with their own kind.

Just to come to the convention was an act of bravery. A lot of women were afraid to be there because there was a possibility that the police had infiltrated. We were careful in what we said and how we said it so that no one ever said, "Come on out to Atlanta, and I'll help you find work." That would have been pandering or trafficking.

At the convention, when we were making policy, we decided to split into two groups—those who were still working and those who were no longer working as prostitutes. We all agreed that once you stop working, even for a few weeks, your feelings and concerns change and you should not be making policy for women who are still working. Because of the fear and the hardship, women who met at these conventions developed a type of bond—like people who had survived a week on a desert island together.

One of the things that struck me at the convention was the dearth of women who had gone public with their prostitution. Margo, for all her bravery, said she was no longer working as a prostitute. I was the only open prostitute in America, as far as I knew. I asked around at the convention and was told there was no one else. Xaviera Hollander didn't become public until she said she was a *former* prostitute. Even Polly Adler didn't go public until her days of being a madam were over. I, however, was still working. That made me the point woman.

When the Phil Donahue show called Margo in January of 1982, looking for "part-time hookers" for an upcoming show, Margo immediately thought of me. She called to sound me out on the idea. "It's a big step," she said. "You should think about it before you do it."

I was already public as a prostitute. The members of the Atlanta City Council knew I was a prostitute. The women in HIRE knew I was a prostitute. My friends knew I was a prostitute. And anyone who had heard me speak knew I was a prostitute. But that was quite different from going on national television and announcing to the world—and to my parents—that I was a prostitute.

I told Margo that she could have the show's producers call me, and that in the meantime I would think about it.

I was sleeping when the producer called—the sort of thing that any respectable call girl would be doing during the day. A voice said, "This is Darlene Hayes, and I'm calling from the Phil Donahue show. Margo St. James said to get in touch with you. Margo said you might be interested in doing this show on prostitution."

Darlene said they would shoot me behind a screen, of course, and they would use another name and distort my voice. I said, "I have to think it over for a few days," and she said she understood. I told her, "But if I do it, I'm definitely not going to do it behind a screen. You could get anybody to do it behind a screen."

Over the next two days I talked to Margo, my friend Paul Krassner, to Sarah, my friend Berl Boykin, Michael Hauptman, HIRE's attorney, and my personal attorney. Paul said exactly the right thing: "You'll either decide to do it or you won't." Margo said: "It's going to affect the rest of your life. It isn't something that you can take back. Once you do it, it'll be the biggest decision of your life." Berl said, "If you're going to do it, this is the time to do it."

Not only would my parents be finding out what I had been doing with my life but they would have to deal with it publicly. In addition, I was concerned about my future. Despite my speeches and my appearances at city council meetings, I was still at a point where I could have decided, No, I don't want to be an advocate for prostitutes' rights for the rest of my life. But once I did the Donahue show, I would never be able to get a regular job again, ever.

The idea that my parents would find out made me think, No, I can't do this. Then I thought about how so many prostitutes feel—ashamed, alone, frightened, stigmatized. I thought about how, in those fifties movies, there would be a public meeting to decide some critical issue, and there would be a show of hands. The crowd would be silent—all those women in their checkered dresses and tightly rolled hair, all those men in their two-short hair and too-wide ties—and then one brave person would not just raise a hand but stand up. Slowly, one by one, the rest of the crowd would stand. That's what I felt like, deciding to do the Donahue show.

I told Darlene Hayes I would do it, if she paid me. There was some mumbling around about that, but she finally agreed. And, I said, I wanted my real name used and I wanted to be on camera.

Darlene met me at the airport in a limousine, with the three other women who were going to be on the show—one from California, two from New York. Darlene took us to our hotel and let us get acquainted. Because it was a first television appearance for all of us, we were nervous. The other three had decided to sit behind a screen and to have their voices disguised, which I fully understood. Mary, a mother who had traveled there with her daughter, was afraid that one or both of them would be recognized. She specifically asked Darlene if the daughter could watch the show from the dressing room. Another woman was sure her husband's mother would recognize her profile. And the third was nervous just to be seen entering the studio on the day of the show.

We didn't know what to expect from the audience in Chicago, which we assumed would be a pretty conservative group. I had had some preparation for all this because of my public speaking, but I was worried that, if I heard that scornful question about But how does it make you *feel* don't you feel *dirty*? I might not be able to keep a tight rein on my reactions.

It may be hard for people now to understand how big a thing this was, just six years ago, to have four working prostitutes talking about The Life.

At the time I remember thinking, This is going to lift the burden off of everyone. I knew I would be doing it for hundreds of thousands of women. I would be sitting on camera proving that a prostitute does not necessarily wear hot pants or Tammy Faye mascara or have five-inch nails. I wanted to show them that someone could be mature, intelligent, and pretty and still could say, "I'm proud to be a prostitute. I love the work. There are other things I could do, and there are other things I have done, but I would rather be doing this."

I wasn't a twelve-year-old girl who had been tricked or forced into prostitution, I wasn't a junkie. I hadn't been beaten into submission by society. I wasn't going to say, "It's society's fault I ended up this way. I hate prostitution." Instead I was going to say, "It's my choice to do this, and I do a good job and I like doing it."

Right up to the time we went on the air, Darlene kept saying, "If there is any time you decide you don't want to do this, you can back out." She was very up-front and very maternal. She said that I was doing something brave and important, but that it wasn't necessarily essential that I do it, or that I do it right then.

The show would air live in Chicago, but wouldn't be aired for several weeks around the rest of the country, I would have a chance to tell my parents and forewarn them. And I couldn't get into trouble for just standing up and announcing that I was a prostitute. (In 1962, in *Robinson v. California*, the Supreme Court held that no one could be convicted simply because he was a drug addict. A person's status as an alcoholic, a drug addict, a homosexual, or a prostitute is not grounds for being arrested. You can't be arrested for what you *are*, only for what witnesses see you *do*.)

At the same time I knew I had to be careful about what I said on the air, because they would not edit the program. If I said, "This is how much I charge, this is my phone number, we can get together and have a good time," that would be soliciting business. If I said anything hinting that people could get sexual services if they called me, I might have been in trouble for soliciting. If I said at any time, "You too can earn money by becoming a prostitute," I could have been in trouble for pandering. But Sarah and my attorneys had given me great training in watching what I said. I had gotten used to the idea of speaking for the benefit of my tape recorder. Now I would be speaking to a videotape recorder.

I told Darlene, "Women in this business have had to live in the shadows for too long, and I am not going to be one of them."

We walked out and started the show.

* * *

The thing I discovered about doing television is that, in one sense, things never go the way you expect. And, in another way, they always go exactly as you expect. Since I was sitting up front in plain view while the other three women were sitting in shadows, I was the audience's focal point. And indeed I got the question about how did I *feel* being a prostitute, and when I said I felt fine about it, I got the same but-you-can't-really-mean-that-how-do-you-*really*-feel response I had grown accustomed to. One woman asked me if I believed in God, and I simply answered "No," without adding "But I see a priest and a rabbi regularly." I was on my best behavior, trying not to play it for laughs. Nor did I feel compelled to reveal my religious convictions. I didn't make any mistakes of the solicitation-pandering kind, and I thought I controlled my temper pretty well.

You will remember that one of the women in shadow, Mary, had brought her nine-year-old daughter to Chicago with her. She had asked the show's staff that the girl be kept off camera, but somehow the girl ended up in the audience. The woman sitting on the aisle kept asking the girl questions, and saying how horrible these women were. The little girl finally said, "That woman is my mother and she's a wonderful mother. You have no right to talk that way about her." At that, the woman in the audience stood up and announced, on camera, that the little girl sitting next to her was the daughter of one of those prostitutes. The woman addressed a how-could-you kind of question to Mary, and Mary burst into tears.

Her daughter was hustled out of the audience before the next segment began. But during the break the three women and I discussed what had happened. We felt the show had violated something extremely important through carelessness. Mary was distraught.

In the next segment I lambasted that lady in the audience for revealing Mary's daughter's identity. I couldn't keep the anger out of my voice—anger that had been brewing not just during that show but during every speaking engagement I've ever done.

It was anger over the idea that the rules seem to be different when someone is dealing with a prostitute. That, because a woman works as a prostitute instead of as a nurse, anything can be said to her or about her.

The taping finished. All four of us women agreed that the audience was hostile to us, but I felt that there was a kernel of understanding, that maybe something we had said might have penetrated a few minds. Darlene was sympathetic about what had happened with Mary and her daughter and apologized for it, but that couldn't erase what had happened.

Mary cried at lunch. Mary cried that afternoon when we went shopping. When I saw Mary and her daughter off at the airport, Mary was still crying about it. We were all in pain afterward, and not just because of Mary and her daughter, but because it had felt like such a traumatic exposure.

After I put Mary on the airplane, I went to the Art Institute of Chicago. It was snowing, a real Chicago experience. Then I went back to the hotel. The Donahue show had put me up in the nicest hotel I had ever stayed in, the Mayfair Regent. My room had five phones in it. I thought, I could live here.

That evening I wanted to do something special for myself, to make up for the bad day. I got dressed up in a black velvet skirt and a very fitted black top. I put on my gold sequined jacket and very high gold heels. I did my hair and my makeup, put on all my jewelry, and went up to the restaurant.

I wanted to be treated like royalty that night, just because I looked nice, sophisticated. I wanted to sit down at a table by myself and order a wonderful meal. I wanted to be totally left alone, and I even told that to the maître d'. I had been overwhelmed by the number of people who had seen me on TV that day.

Sitting at the table, I felt better. I ordered white asparagus; I got my salad. I ordered a glass of Lacrima-Christi. I was the only woman sitting alone, and there were a lot of men in the room. But it was OK, because I had my own table and I was buying my own food. I was thinking how wonderful it was to be a hooker, because it meant I could afford to eat in a restaurant like that. I was sinking into a pleasant feeling when the waiter came to my table.

"Pardon me," he said. "I know you asked to be alone this evening, but the gentlemen at that table have called me over three times and asked me to ask you to join them." There were eight well-dressed guys sitting together—business executives with angelic faces—and all of them were waving and winking and nodding. It made me laugh.

I told the maître d', "Tell them that I appreciate their offer, but I really do want to be alone tonight. Thank them for me."

About ten minutes later, the maître d' came back apologizing profusely. "The restaurant will pay for your meal, mademoiselle," he said. "I'm sorry those men are bothering you. They have sent you a bottle of champagne. There's a note," he said, discreetly.

I shook my head no and tried to eat my salad. The maître d' came back and said, "Wouldn't it just be easier to go over to their table? I must say, I cannot blame them. You are so beautiful."

As far as I was concerned my meal had been ruined. I had not planned on working that night, but it seemed I already was.

The men asked me to sit down and then asked me what I was doing in Chicago. I wasn't ready to lay that news on them, so I said, "I'll make a deal with you. I'll stay here for a few minutes, but I get to ask the questions. What are *you* all doing here?"

We went around the table and they told me: architect, contractor, banker, manufacturer. They were all trying to impress me, to be charming. There wasn't a sourpuss in the group. They said they were there for a meeting on a big project. They told me which cities they were from. Our food came, and finally one of them said, "Would you mind if we asked you a few questions? Where are you from, what are you doing here?"

I told them about going to the museum, that I used to be an art director.

"Are you here on business or pleasure?"

I said, "It's been pleasant, but I suppose you could say it was business."

Then I said that I had been a guest on the Donahue show.

"What for?" they asked.

"I'm president of HIRE, and I'm a prostitute."

There was a range of reactions. Three guys seemed absolutely delighted. Four guys seemed politely interested. And one man, an investment banker who was quite a bit older than the others, seemed absolutely indignant.

I passed out my business cards and wrote my room number on them. They, in turn, asked me if I wanted to go out for a drink afterward. I said no, that I was going to go up to my room.

So I went back to my room, put on my work lingerie, and waited for the phone to ring. Instead there was a knock on the door.

It was the investment banker. I have since found that when you meet a group of men and the subject of prostitution comes up, it's the killjoy of the group, the prude, who always spends the most money.

Three others from the group called me, or left notes under my door, and I had just enough time to see two of them. Then I caught up on a little of my sleep and made my early plane back to Atlanta.

Writing the letter to my mother was the scariest thing I have ever done. After that, when faced with something difficult, I could tell myself, "You wrote a letter to your mother telling her not only you were a prostitute but also that you were going to appear on national television *saying* you were a prostitute. If you can do that, you can do anything."

"Dear Mom," I wrote.

Do you remember when I was eight and hit that boy (I think his name was Frog) over the head with the baseball bat in our front yard because he was beating up his little sister? In dealing with women's rights, my tactics haven't changed much. Sometimes you have to hit people over the head to make them understand that you're not kidding.

In the past few years, while you and Daddy have been wondering what I was doing, I've been lecturing and learning about women's rights—particularly prostitutes' rights. That's why I've been traveling so much.

For no reason I can understand, the last time I was home you said you were expecting to see me on TV soon. I'm going to be on the Phil Donahue show the twenty-ninth, that's this Friday. It has already been taped. I don't want you to watch it because a lot of things went wrong with the show. Seeing it will give you and everyone else a wrong impression of what I do. I wanted you to know that I was on the show just so that, if some of your friends or customers see it, you won't have to hear about it from them. The makeup artist and the hairdresser did a great job, so I look beautiful. I hope you'll be happy for that.

A short explanation of how all this came about: While working to ratify the ERA in the midseventies it came to my attention that in the South no one was fighting for the repeal of prostitution laws. Moreover, few people were aware of the number of prostitutes arrested and the abuse of prostitutes' rights. As people became aware of my concern I started getting calls from women wanting me to help them, usually to help get them out of jail.

Most of these women weren't strong people like you or me. Their lives were being crushed by these arrests and assaults on their integrity. It broke my heart to see how these women were being treated by the judge, the police, and even their own lawyers. It makes me as mad today to see women being mistreated as it did to see Frog mistreating his sister.

Strong people can get above being treated badly. We can take it and go on. But these women each felt guilty and totally alone. I finally realized that, if I was going to understand these women, I would have to become one with them. You always wanted me to be a missionary. This whole experience has been very much like a missionary entering the jungle to save souls and then going native.

Working with prostitutes has been one of the most rewarding experiences of my life. They are the world's most interesting women. They are tougher, smarter, quicker, and more resilient than other women. Unfortunately, the police department uses them to build arrest statistics with no regard for their lives. I've definitely taken this on as a mission.

By the way, when I am speaking, people often ask me about you. I tell them how much energy you have. I tell them, if you were in charge of passing the Equal Rights Amendment, it would have been done so long ago even the arguing about it would be over by now.

I wish you and Daddy could take some pride in what I'm doing. But I understand that you may not.

I am committed to fighting for prostitutes' rights, and there's no way to go back now. What I'm doing is very difficult. If you feel you cannot be supportive, I understand. If you don't have something supportive to say about what I'm doing, don't say anything at all. This life is tough enough when everyone I love is on my side.

I put "Love" at the bottom, and signed my full name, to show that this was an adult doing it.

In writing the letter, I was trying to explain everything to my mother in a way that was as clear as possible without being shocking. I didn't come right out and say that I was working as a prostitute, but only that I had "become one with them."

I mailed the letter so it would arrive the day before the show was to air in Louisville. My sister was at my mom's store when the letter got there. Yvonne saw the return address and said, "Oh, great, it's a letter from Dolores. Maybe she's coming home." She started reading the letter aloud, while all the customers stood around and listened. My mom had been out, and when she returned, she stood for a moment at the edge of the crowd and listened. Yvonne had just gotten around to reading the part about how I had "become one with them," when my mother said, "That's enough, Yvonne," and took the letter.

My sister thought it was just swell that I was going to be on *Donahue*. She was so excited, she didn't much care what the topic was.

My mom called that afternoon. She was hysterical, which was pretty much as I had expected. She said about everything that every mother has ever said: Where did I go wrong? You weren't raised that way. What will people think? How could you?

She went back and forth between being embarrassed and being proud. I could hear in her voice that most of her struggle was against any tendency to be proud.

"I told your dad," she said, "and you know how he is. He doesn't say much. He just said, 'Well. She's grown. She made her own decision. I didn't think we raised her to do that kind of thing but I guess we did.'"

I explained to her that no one had ever taken these women's side and that I didn't think what prostitutes did was at all bad, in the grand scheme of things. She agreed but pleaded, "I've done everything I know how to do to make a good life for you, an easier life than I had, and now . . ."

I explained that, when I first started doing it, I thought it would be just a few times. But I quickly realized that it was a wonderful occupation. I told her that I had written the letter so that she would have something in her hand when our phone conversation was over. I wanted her to read the letter again, I said. It really did cover all the pertinent points.

She said she and Daddy had been worried about me at Christmas when I was home. "Daddy and me just want you to be safe," she said. "How could you do this to us?" And I said I had given a lot of thought to the fact that, once I had gone public, she and he would have to live with it and perhaps put up with a lot of guff from people.

"You raised me to be tough enough to do what I'm doing," I said, "and I know you and Daddy are tough enough to stand up to it too. I'm sorry I can't make it any easier. But it's tough on these women's lives every day."

She said, "This isn't something that you *have* to do. You could come to us for money." I tried to explain to her that I wasn't doing it for the money. I was doing it because I believed in it, because I didn't think it was dirty or shameful but instead something noble and helpful. I was improving the quality of my clients' lives. I had the opportunity to renew people's self-esteem. I was improving the quality of prostitutes' lives, by fighting for their rights. As long as women were not allowed to voluntarily use our bodies to make a living, we would always, on some level, be denied the right to choose our own destinies. Everyone's body is a commodity, I said. A ballet dancer, a construction worker. All the rest is misplaced puritanism.

Near the end of our conversation, my mom said, "I admire what you're saying, Dolores, and I think you're sincere and honorable and that you've done a wonderful thing. But I don't want you to do it anymore. Will you promise me you won't do it anymore?"

I said, "I just want you to know, Mom, I'm still your daughter, the daughter you raised. I'm dealing with this from the perspective and with the values that you taught me, Mom. But I'm not going to stop."

She ended up by saying , "Well, I guess it isn't the worst thing in the world you could be doing. I'll have to think about it. I don't want to think about it, but I guess I'll have to think about it."

And I said, "Yeah, you probably will think about it whether you want to or not."

She watched the show, and called me afterward. She said that she thought the whole thing was all right, and that I had looked real pretty. "But when you started talking about having sex with a woman, I just thought I'd die," she said. Another proof that mothers are harder to kill off than they claim to be.

We all lived through it, and I, for one, felt we were better off.

My mother never said anything about getting any phone calls from friends who had seen the show. She did say that, when she went to the beauty shop, she knew that everyone there had seen me on *Donahue*. She just knew it.

After the show had aired, I started getting letters and phone calls from women all over the country who said they were glad I had been on. They wrote: I love being a prostitute too, but I've never seen anyone with the guts to stand up and say that in public. Even though it's changed my life, and I'm making a lot of money, I felt like I had to pretend, 'It stinks, I don't like it.' It was a choice for me too, and, at least in my case, it was a good one. A lot of women who had been to college said they were glad I had broken the stereotype of what a prostitute is.

Some women wrote to say they hadn't had a choice the way I did, but they were still glad to see someone who said prostitution is an honest career. The letters and phone calls continued, not for days or weeks but for months.

People in the grocery store, people on the street began to recognize me. On the Donahue show I hadn't worn a wig or something to disguise myself. I was pretty recognizable afterward. My neighbors learned what I really did for a living, and they simply had to accept that Dolores next door was a hooker. They couldn't deny I was the same person as before. I still took out my trash on trash day. I still planted gladiolus and azaleas and daffodils in front of my house.

Some people, however, acted differently after the show. Julian Bond's wife, Alice, had always been pleasant to me when I worked on her husband's campaigns. Once the news was out about me, Alice was both more distant and, I thought, more intrigued.

All the publicity began with the Donahue show and, once it had started, it didn't stop. There were the calls from newspapers and magazines and from radio and TV shows. It got to the point where I could tell when sweeps week was coming up on TV because suddenly my phone would start ringing. Every *Good Morning, Small City USA* program got the idea that, gee, if they could just have a prostitute on, they could get their ratings up. The economics of the situation bothered me, of course. Here were TV and radio stations making money off prostitution, while it was illegal for me to make money off prostitution. I thought that was pretty typical.

The police were arresting people from Magnolia Blossoms, and I told Sarah it would be a wise idea to close down and open another agency. She felt she was safe, however.

About that time, I got a call to go to the Holiday Inn at the airport. Sarah assured me that the guy had good ID, and when I got there I checked him out thoroughly. He was in from Chicago, said he owned a chemical company there, and he was well groomed. I figured he was OK.

He was very nice, polite, pleasant. I called Sarah and said that I was there and that I would call back when we got some things straightened out, meaning my fee. He asked me what my prices were and I began my spiel: "The agent's fee is fifty dollars. The models get no part of the agent's fee. In addition to the fifty dollars agent's fee, the model's fee is normally—"

"Stop right there," he said. "Don't say any more. I don't want you to get yourself into any trouble."

I thought, Pretty weird. He flashed a badge with his picture. He told me he was a federal agent, and I said, "Oh, shit." Then he pulled a really big gun out from under the pillow on the bed and jumped to his feet. When I saw the gun, I picked up my left foot and put it on my right knee and put both of my hands on the arms of the chair, so that he could see that I wasn't going to do anything aggressive, like run for the door. I said, "Do you really believe that gun is necessary? It's rude."

Then he flipped into a John Wayne–type tough-guy act.

"All I want is some information," he said. "We can talk right here, or we can go downtown to talk."

I leaned back in my chair and concentrated on my composure and voice. I calmly articulated, "Whether you're really a federal officer or just a nut, you obviously have excess adrenaline pumping through your brain, and I think I do too. So I'm going to just sit here for a minute, maybe two minutes, and take a few deep breaths to let myself calm down a little bit. In the meantime I suggest you consider putting that gun away, because it's making me nervous. After our deep breathing exercises, we'll see if we feel up to a little chat."

I closed my eyes. In comes the good air; out goes the bad, I chanted to myself as I sucked air in and blew it out. After a couple of repetitions, I opened my eyes to see him staring curiously at me—like It takes all kinds . . . His head was cocked to one side. His left hand was on his hip. His weight had shifted to one foot.

"Come on," I said, "try it with me." (What did I care if he thought I was wacky?) He didn't do it, but he let his gun sink to his side.

"I want to talk about your agent," he said. He showed me a picture of a woman and said, "This is Betty Roth. Have you ever seen this woman before?"

And I said no. As you might remember, I had never seen Sarah at all because we had done everything over the phone, and I had no idea what her real name was. "I've never seen this woman before in my life, and I've never even heard of Betty Roth," I said.

"OK, then," he said. He started asking me very specific questions about work.

He was pretty humorless. "Tell me how much money your agent makes and how many people work for her."

I explained, "I don't work for *her*, she works for *me*. And this time," I added, "she hasn't done a very good job of screening the clients."

About that point, Sarah called back to find out what was going on. He picked up the phone and said, "Oh, we worked it all out. Right, Delilah?" He held the phone up, so I could chirp, "Everything's fine," then he talked to Sarah again and hung up the phone.

He then started asking me more questions I had no answers to, things like where my agent lived, and how long she had been running escort agencies, and who worked *with* her, and did she pay income tax. After saying, "I don't know, I really don't know, I have no idea," about a dozen times I said, "Why don't I give you some answers and you can see if you can find any questions to go with them?"

He seemed to think that was a great idea, and he sat back to hear some really good information. So I told him my life history—starting with my mother and father living in a corncrib when they were first married, and going through first grade and being Little Miss Ferncreek and a Humphrey girl and going to dancing school and art school—and how at art school we saw a lot of *nude models*—and that I had worked on Julian Bond's presidential campaign, and gone to Andrew Young's victory party and worked on the ERA and civil rights. I told him what it was like to work at the radio station and how long it takes to do pointillism and how going to school with some girls I called the Doublemint twins had more of an effect on me than Seurat. I was polite and funny. I told him that I enjoyed working as a model and that I did a really good job. I explained to him that I had signed an agreement that I wasn't to have sex with clients, and that my agent would have no way of knowing if I had. I said, "My agent might assume that we were occasionally engaging in sex—because that kind of thing happens every once in a while—but I never told my agent if I had, and she never asked me. In fact, my agent had told me to leave the hotel room if anyone suggested sex." I said, "You're not going to suggest sex, are you?"

"No," he said, and seemed startled.

"Well, that's all I know," I said.

He tried to give me $150 so I could pay my agent, but I wouldn't take it. He told me not to tell my agent what had happened, and I said, "OK, I'll just tell her that you were a jerk who pulled a gun on me and that she shouldn't send anyone else if you call again."

As soon as I left his room, I drove to a phone booth to call Sarah and tell her what was going on, that these people were serious. These weren't local guys, I said, these were the Feds.

But Sarah refused to be upset. "They're just fishing," she said. "They don't have anything on me."

I have noticed that agents and hookers sometimes spend so much of their lives being paranoid and suspecting everyone and living in fear that they become numb to danger. There have been so many false alarms, so many times they thought they were caught when nothing came of it, so many people they have been suspicious of who didn't turn out to be worthy of suspicion.

If I had been Sarah, I would have packed up and left the city, perhaps even the country. That's a part of this business. As long as the laws are what they are, hookers and agents have to be willing to pick up and leave everything behind.

But Sarah said, "Delilah, don't worry, everything's going to be fine."

It wasn't. The investigation continued, and the Feds talked to other models and other agents. There seemed to be police agents everywhere. And eventually Sarah was arrested. Her house was raided, torn up, but she had already moved her business to an apartment. They tracked her down there and arrested her.

I talked to her when she posted bail, and she said, as perky as ever, "Don't worry, Delilah, I'm going to beat this."

I don't know if she believed that or not, but she talked as if she did.

As you might imagine, I started doing a lot of traveling. I decided, among other things, that it was time I saw the open city of Amsterdam, the commercial sex capital of the Western world.

A conference was being organized in Holland on female sexual slavery, and Margo St. James asked if I'd like to go over with her. Once we got to Rotterdam, however, we were told that no prostitutes were welcome. The leader of the conference, Kathy Barry, the author of *Female Sexual Slavery*, felt that prostitutes were too brainwashed and oppressed to represent themselves, that we were all slaves to our pimps. So, excluded from the conference, we hookers met informally to exchange information. I found out that, although prostitution was not officially legal in Holland, prostitutes had to register and pay a "special" tax. The "special" tax didn't seem to confer any benefits: Women were not given insured medical checkups unless the establishment they were working in provided them. On the other hand, registration as a prostitute was something that was put on a woman's passport, which meant that she was restricted from entering some countries, including the United States, where a record of prostitution automatically denies a person even visiting privileges. (Some Dutch women, therefore, paid an "extra special" tax, a payoff, to avoid being registered.)

We also heard about the problems prostitutes were having in Asia. Young women from throughout the Pacific, for instance, often flocked to Manila to make money in the electronics industry. They worked in sweatshops under low lighting, assembling teeny tiny parts for computers and telephones. After three or four years, having been driven nearly blind, they were no longer able to see well enough to do the work, we were told. Then the women went to the sex-mill whorehouses in Manila. There were so many of them trying to get work as prostitutes, they were among the lowest paid in the world. And there really were places in Asia where women were made sexual slaves.

When it was my turn to talk, I felt embarrassed to be talking about what conditions were like in the United States, where the prostitution laws were way behind those in Europe. I felt like an ugly American, representing a rich society, and talking about how wonderful and quaint things were in Europe.

People around the world still see the United States as a place of golden opportunity. They generally believe that American women can get educations and good jobs if they want them. Therefore, they wonder why American women choose to be prostitutes instead of business executives. They don't believe that women are forced into prostitution in America for lack of other opportunities. Why would a woman in America make the choice to be a prostitute?

I had to explain to them that women in America were still

grossly underpaid for most professions—and that there were a lot of poor people in our country, most of them women. I explained that some women, like myself, chose to be prostitutes for the same reason they did—because we liked the life and because it was the best way for us to make a living.

Then I went into a description of the laws in the United States. Whatever laws they had on the books in Europe, I said, there wasn't the kind of cat-and-mouse game playing with the police and hookers that there was in the United States. There were many countries in Europe where prostitution was illegal but people were allowed to operate as long as they weren't causing a disturbance. As soon as hookers in the United States learned to live within the laws, the authorities changed the laws in order to catch them. It was like living with pretend regulations. In Europe the authorities tended to bend the laws to allow for prostitutes who were perfectly good citizens to keep on working.

"But who is protected by your prostitution laws?" they asked. "Who benefits?"

Well, I said, it wasn't the prostitutes and it wasn't the customers. I said, "I'm sure you remember history, and how a lot of religious fanatics moved to the States in order to be free to practice their own religion. As a result," I said, "the prostitution laws were influenced by a bunch of religious fanatics, trying to preserve monogamy and virginity by not allowing people to be paid for sex."

"But doesn't the American government realize that they could make a lot of money by registering and taxing prostitutes?" one Dutch hooker wanted to know.

"Well, politicians, police officers, bail bondsmen, and attorneys all make money off fighting prostitution or defending prostitutes, and those are the people who make the laws."

People were baffled. America certainly seemed like a strange country. Margo invited everyone to come to the United States and study our laws for themselves. The next Hookers' Convention in San Francisco was scheduled to coincide with the Democratic national convention in the summer of 1984.

I set out to see more of Amsterdam. The earliest tulips were blooming. There were beautiful African flowers in the stalls, flowers I had never seen before.

Jan Visser, the director of the Mr. A. DeGraff Stitching Foundation, a foundation that did research on prostitution and tried to advise the Dutch government on prostitution legislation, offered to take me on a walking tour of the red-light district. I asked to see the famous windows of Amsterdam, and he pointed out Molens Feeg, a street where prostitutes served Arab clients. He explained to me that the Arabs had a lot of money but didn't want to use rubbers, that they were cheap with the prostitutes and had a reputation for roughness. That was enough for me to know to avoid Molens Feeg myself.

The "windows" were tiny storefronts or doorways with windows that opened out onto the street. He walked me through the Dam Straat, where the "better" windows were located, but he discouraged me from working there. "A nice girl like you," he said, "if you want to work, you should go to the Yab Yum."

He explained to me that this was the most elegant, highest-class whorehouse in Holland. He gave me the address and telephone number and suggested I go there that night.

It was near the red-light district but outside of it, about three blocks over from Anne Frank's house. I showed up at 9:30 that evening and found a tastefully conservative brick four-story building with green stained-glass lanterns at each corner. There was a small brass sign that said MEN'S CLUB in small letters and above that YAB YUM. The door was red and so large that the handle was nearly at shoulder level. A video camera was mounted on the building and pointed at the door. Up above the handle was the doorbell. I felt like Dorothy standing at the door to Oz.

A tall, arrogant-looking man answered the bell, looked down at me, and said, "May I help you?" I peered past him into the Yab Yum, to see what it looked like inside. Red and gold, pretty posh. I was wearing red stiletto heels and a Norma Kamali sweat suit, so I decided that a high-class American accent, with a touch of earthiness thrown in, would be the right way to counterbalance the blast of pretentiousness coming out of that door, like heat from my mother's oven.

I hoisted myself up on the doorsill and said, "Yes, I'd like to see the manager."

"Do you have a Dutch passport?" he asked.

"No."

"Well, I'm sorry, but we can only hire Dutch girls. That is the law."

That was a surprise. All I could manage was a weak "Why?"

He explained that the police supervised the "business" and

that they made the rule. Since prostitution wasn't illegal anywhere in Holland, and most everyone agreed it was the best country in the world for a hooker to work in, it made sense to me that the country could restrict prostitution to Dutch women, so that the country wouldn't be overrun with sex workers. But still, Mr. Visser and several other people had recommended the Yab Yum to me; there certainly must be a way for me to work there. And I wanted to find out what it was like to work in a place that was the polar opposite of the Black Angus, so I stood my ground and asked my question another way, "Is the manager in?"

"I am the manager," he said. "Look, it's not that you are not beautiful enough or the right type. But even if you were a Dutch citizen there would be no work here for you. We already have thirty-five women working here. But why don't you come in and look around?"

Another official type, Heuft, appeared, and I began talking to him. We sat down on a velvet sofa, and he ordered some Perrier for me. He seemed to be somehow equal to the guy at the door, so I figured I had another chance. I said, "To be perfectly honest . . ." and then waited to hear what would come out of my mouth next. It was as if I was on automatic pilot, as if I had turned my fate over to that part of my brain that handles reflexive things, like respiration, heartbeats, orgasms, and tap dancing.

"To be perfectly honest," I said, "I've been told that this is the plushest brothel in Holland. We're not sure what we want to do yet, exactly, but—have you heard of cable TV in America? Yes? Good. Well, I want to spend a few days working here and in other places and then we can decide how we want to script the piece. I know it seems like voyeurism, but in the United States, cable is dying for material about sex."

Heuft warmed up right away when I started talking about American television. (I'm sure he had balance of trade in mind, bringing nice, crisp American dollars into Holland.) He immediately started explaining the rules of the house to me.

The first night there I drank Perrier and, since business was slow, I talked to the other women. I learned that a man paid about twenty-five dollars to get in. That covered all his drinks inside except for champagne. The women got 15 percent of any money the men spent on champagne, so champagne was the drink of choice for the women. It cost a man about a hundred dollars to go upstairs for an hour, but that included only one sex act. The regular employees got fifty dollars out of that, plus tips. (It was against the rules to ask for tips, however.) There was closed-circuit TV in each room and a mirrored wall facing the bed. Everything was covered with red carpeting or mirrors, the doors were solid oak, the doorknobs were solid brass, and the lights were adjustable. Each room had a telephone and was designed, as one woman said, to "make a millionaire feel at home."

At midnight a "snack" was set out for the women: asparagus, tiny sandwiches, shrimp salad, an assortment of European cheeses, ham, turkey, and roast beef. It was luxurious, no doubt about that. I was told that a silver Mercedes-Benz was available to take the women home at the end of their workday. A gynecologist and dermatologist came every Tuesday; there were blood tests every six weeks. And music played all night long: everything from Bob Dylan to Brecht-Weill to marimba.

It would have been great if it was a party, but I was there to work and the place was dead. At about three in the morning I was so bored I decided to leave. I met a Chinese guy on the doorstep, and he asked if I would go to his hotel with him for twenty dollars. I figured, what the hell, I hadn't made a cent in this glamorous joint, and I figured I could get him off in ten minutes, and then I could afford the cab fare home. But then I found out he wanted me to spend the night with him for twenty dollars. I explained that we were having a misunderstanding and I went home.

The next night I sipped champagne and did a routine job with a German guy who spoke no English. I gave him a bubble bath and a body rub, blew a rubber on, had intercourse, and that was that. He paid the house with a credit card and, at the end of the night, Heuft handed me forty dollars. Since I didn't speak Japanese, Dutch, German, French, Danish, or Swedish, I was at a distinct disadvantage compared to the other women. At the Yab Yum women were selected for type (the establishment wanted a variety of women to offer customers), for linguistic ability (most women there spoke at least three languages), for ability to engage in conversation, and for ability to be a team player. The women who worked there were as carefully selected and as motivated as executives in Japan.

When a man walked into the Yab Yum he was immediately showered with attention—which I'm sure he attributed to his own irresistible charm. The staff, the furniture, the fixtures, the champagne, and the women all conspired together to seduce and swallow up any man who entered. Although the man would eventually go to a private suite with one woman, all the other women worked along with her—telling the man how beautiful and charming she was and helping the man become comfortable and relax.

It felt like a giant uptown, jet-set party given in honor of each paying guest. There was catered food on hand, an elaborate bar, drugs (Amsterdam was a completely open city as far as marijuana and cocaine were concerned), entertainment. Anything a guy wanted, he could have for $150 at the Yab Yum. For $1,000, he could have had the most fabulous, luxurious night of his life.

The Yab Yum offered everything: perfect hygiene, a regular work schedule (six days a week, eight hours a day), medical services, safety, privacy, no fear of the cops, catered food and, if you worked hard, a living wage. But it bored me to tears. After a couple of days there I was ready to pound the cobblestones and find my own display window in the red-light district.

It rains *a lot* in Holland, and it's cold, and high-heeled shoes get caught in the cobblestones. So streetwalking can be hazardous. To avoid the elements and the cobblestones, women who might otherwise work as streetwalkers rent tiny boutique-sized storefronts. Some of the women had elaborate sets and costumes. One black woman had a Deepest Darkest Africa motif. She wore a skimpy Jane-of-the-Jungle leopard bikini and decorated her space with banana leaves, zebra skins, African masks and carvings. Her window curtain—which would be closed when she was entertaining a customer—was made of an African woodblock print fabric.

I heard that women with themes made the most money, so I immediately began planning my display. I thought an American Wild West theme would work best. I could wear an Indian princess costume, as it might have been made for Buffalo Bill's traveling circus, and I figured I could juggle Indian clubs in the window. I would get a big brass bed and drape it with satin and lace sheets and pillowcases. I'd have a pitcher and a washbasin on an antique table. I thought, Hey, maybe I could get a bucking bronco machine, and let customers have a ride. Or maybe I could set up a stuffed horse and take customers' pictures, standing next to the horse and wearing a cowboy hat and a fringed jacket. Most of the people walking the red-light district were tourists, and American things were hot. A chain of McDonald's restaurants had opened in Europe, and Europeans were flocking to them. I could have an all-American display, sell souvenir pictures, print T-shirts with my picture and THIS WOMAN SUCKED MY DICK on them, sell ashtrays and postcards. There were a lot of female tourists who walked through the red-light district and had nothing, absolutely nothing, to spend their money on. I figured I'd have something for them too: hooker costumes to buy, or at least use to pose for pictures—I'd get a little lamp post and a red-light district background for them to pose against.

I kept my fantasy window in mind, but I settled for something just a little less grand, just a small window with a few shawls and scarves draped around it. I learned that the little snack shops on every corner in the district were operated by the people who ran the windows. The windows ranged from eight to forty dollars for an eight-hour day. I picked one that cost sixteen dollars.

Then I dressed in an Indian blouse and skirt and discovered that I was selling something people wanted. I didn't have to do any sales pitch. All I had to do was sit there, in the window. If someone wanted me, and could afford me, and appreciated me, and needed me—that was it.

(I did learn one interesting thing, however, working on the streets of Amsterdam. I learned just how important high heels are. I would put on my flat moccasins when I was walking the streets, to save my feet and my high-heeled shoes. When I put on my moccasins, no one would stop me. Then I would put on my high heels and men would come right up to me. Then I would switch back to the moccasins and the men would disappear. I realized that taking off my high-heeled shoes was like putting up an out of business sign.)

I loved working in the windows. It was capitalism at its purest, and the street show was amazing. There were several thousand women working in the district. It looked like women had been dumped from the sky. I had never seen such crowds except at Mardi Gras, the Kentucky Derby, and the Vatican on a Sunday. There were people everywhere, and the women outnumbered the men. The rates, as a result, were low, about twenty dollars a guy. I figured, OK, in the States I might make a hundred dollars, but I'd be fretting away eighty of it worrying that he was a cop. Here, no worry.

*   *   *

| 189 |

I was particularly impressed with the women in Holland who were over fifty. Hookers over fifty in the States were few and far between, and I wanted to prove to myself that it was possible to keep working as long as I wanted.

One of the oldest hookers on the street was dressed and made up to look like a working woman: she had on a tube top that was holding up sagging breasts, tight stretch pants that showed off her pudgy thighs, scruffy hot pink high heels that looked as if they were left over from the sixties. She had on horribly chipped red nail polish, and her short, brown-and-red frazzled hair was pulled back with a rhinestone comb. She wasn't blubbery fat, just old and out of shape. She looked like, if she just let go, she would be fat, gray haired, and toothless. She had an expression similar to those of old women who've worked at a fruit stand all their lives—someplace open, rain or shine. After all those years of working, the job interest just wasn't there. This was a woman waiting to retire.

"Who are your clients?" I asked.

"Boys who have fantasies about fucking their grandmothers," she said, half joking.

"Who else?"

"Men who want to have sex with women their own age," she said. "Men who want women with a *lot* of experience. Men who want to be mothered. Everyone wants something different."

"How long have you been doing this?" I asked.

"Since I was sixteen. I was married when I was fifteen, and then my husband got killed and left me with a little baby. I wasn't a virgin anymore, so . . ."

"Have you always worked here?" I asked, meaning the windows.

"Oh, I used to work up there," she said, pointing north toward the train station. "But there were too many kids, you know, smoking dope, bothering customers. No good for business, so I moved here."

I'm sure this woman had answered these same questions for tourists for the last forty years or so, so she was rapidly losing interest in me. "How long do you plan to keep on working?" I asked. "Is there some kind of socialized retirement program for you?"

She gave me a "piss-off" kind of look, but she said, "I'll retire in about two years, when I'm sixty-five."

I quickly explained to her that I was a working woman myself, working in the windows too, but originally working in the States. I told her how great it was that she had kept working, that in the States hookers burned out in four years from the stress of worrying about being arrested. "Do you enjoy working?" I asked.

She got up and folded her chair to go inside. As long as she was talking to me she wasn't making any money. But she stopped and she said, "Ya, the people are nice. It's a good living. It's been good to me. I raised my children."

Before she shut her door I pulled out seven dollars. I don't know why it hadn't occurred to me before to pay her. I thanked her for talking to me and handed her the money. She took it, nodded thanks, and closed the door.

If I'd had the rest of my life to spend in Europe, I certainly would have spent a year or two in Amsterdam. But I was concerned about HIRE, and I needed to see my family and friends; I missed my house and I missed my garden. After a month, I decided to return home.

When I got back there were a zillion messages on my answering machine: a bunch from the media, some from cranks and crazies who had seen me on the Donahue show, some from Elaine's old clients who were still trying to see me (at the old prices, of course), and a whole lot of messages from women in HIRE, telling me that things with cops were even worse in Atlanta than before. Sarah's trial date had been set. Several of us might be called to testify. And the cops had not stopped harassing working women— instead they had stepped up their program of intimidation, trickery, and arrest. So, after a quick trip home to see my mother, father, and sister, and after taking in a few plays in Atlanta and going shopping and visiting my hairdresser, I went to Saint Thomas.

A magazine had asked me to write an article about whorehouses in the Caribbean. What I was to be paid for the article didn't begin to compare with what I could earn as a prostitute, but I had never tried to write an article on this subject before, and I figured that it would be a learning experience and that something good might eventually come of it. (It did, too. The reason I have used the real names of the whorehouses in the Caribbean here is that they have already been made public.)

There was one more reason to go to Saint Thomas. The USS *Nimitz* was about to arrive, which meant that 7,000 horny American sailors were about to hit shore. From what my friends had told me, the impact of a big naval vessel on a small port like Charlotte Amalie was pretty spectacular. Hookers from all over the Caribbean, all over the southern United States, were trying to get to Saint Thomas before the boat docked. I had never worked the fleet before, and I thought, Ah, here's one more thing I should know about.

I felt as if I were about to be initiated into a rite that had long been told of and joked about by men, a situation that was considered the right of all men throughout history—a boatload of men descending on the local (and not-so-local) whores. Yet to my knowledge no prostitute had ever written about it from her perspective.

The *Nimitz* is one of the largest aircraft carriers in the world. The ship was on naval maneuvers for months at a time. When it docked to give shore leave, the sailors were on rotation, with only 2,000 to 3,000 of them in port at any one time. The navy pretends that the fleet's docking dates are top secret (at least one screw holding the hinges of national security together), but a quick phone call to any whorehouse near a port, or a check with the other local merchants, will reveal exactly when a boat is due in and how long it is staying.

Awaiting the boys in white were about 400 hookers. Compare those numbers—7,000 men, even in shifts, and 400 hookers—and you get an idea of what the occasion was like. Considering that I worked practically around the clock for several days, I didn't make a great deal of money. But the experience was golden.

The afternoon my taxi approached town, I was absolutely thrilled at the sight of so many potential customers. I knew that, within a few hours, the negligible number of civilians circulating among the sailors and streetwalkers would be gone. Only thousands of sailors and hundreds of whores would be left to negotiate life in the most historically pure fashion I've ever seen. It was a flesh carnival.

I had the taxi drop me off right in front of the Windward Passage Hotel. A friend had recommended Las Astronautas as the best whorehouse on Saint Thomas, right near where the ship was going to dock. But to my horror, there were MPs stationed in front of Las Astronautas telling sailors they couldn't go in. It was off-limits. Apparently a sailor had been badly beaten up there the last time a ship was in port. (I later found out that the last time a ship was in port, at another whorehouse, a woman's throat had been cut "from here to here," as everyone said, gesturing from ear to ear. The sailor stole all her money too, and she lived to tell about it, although with a scarf permanently draped around her throat. That whorehouse remained open for the *Nimitz*'s visit. Hmmmm.)

The proprietor of Las Astronautas had a long face but, she told me, they had been declared off-limits before and somehow everything had worked out. She said, "Why don't you try the Clarysol?" When I asked if I could leave my backpack with her, she said, No, she didn't want to be responsible, so I walked around town carrying my backpack and looking like a combination hippie-hooker: high heels, red curly hair under a big-brimmed straw hat, long, carefully manicured fingernails, an Indian blouse and skirt, and a backpack. Fortunately, the Clarysol Bar and Pool Room was not too far away, located right between the Tasty Chick fried chicken joint and the Catholic church.

As I walked toward the Clarysol it was clear the party was beginning without me. There were sailors hanging out of hotel windows, hollering and whistling. They started beckoning me, and I held up a "Wait one minute" finger to them, and hoped that they would wait until I found a place to leave my things. Drunk sailors were pouring into the street, and the black and brown island people, the hookers and the bar regulars stared dumbfounded at the rambunctiousness of these well-fed, close-cropped, clean and scrubbed American boys on shore leave. All the white sailors were chugalugging beer, occasionally stopping to crush an aluminum can with their bare hands, playing pool, screaming, singing, and generally celebrating their liberty and the falling-down-drunk good time they planned to have.

A woman named Conchata, originally from Santo Domingo, ran the Clarysol, clearly one of the sleaziest whorehouses I had ever worked in. Conchata had this flowered 1950s-type kitchen wallpaper in her bedroom, which was decorated with vivid tropical-island icons, so the whole place was like a museum. When I went inside to ask for a place to work, I looked so middle class, Conchata stared at me as if to say, Does this woman know what she's talking about?

Then I could see her taking a look at me again and thinking, Well, if she wants to work here, we might be able to use her.

She told me the house rules and showed me a room. Rooms were three dollars for twenty minutes, and the sheets were changed every night.. I asked, very meekly and politely, "Could I have a pillow?" And she rocked back on her heels and said, "No, we don't have no peeellows." I said, OK, fine. Then I asked, "What about air conditioning?" It was hot as hell. And she put one hand on her hip and separated her feet a little bit, and said, "We are not here to be luxooorious, we are here to *make money*."

I laughed, and said, "You're right."

And she did make money. She knew she wasn't the best. But boy, was she making money. I really loved her. She knew what she was selling. I decided to leave my things there and head out to meet the fleet, down at dockside.

Doing the *Nimitz* was like Mardi Gras and a frat party rolled into one. By the time I made it back to the boot camp for women, I was ready to go out there and work, to deal with whatever happened. I headed for a place right on the water. In tourist brochures it advertised that guests could get a 10 percent discount at the while-you-wait film-processing place next door. What it didn't advertise was that people could also get a while-you-wait blow job or hand job.

Next door there was a hotel, crawling with "squids." There was pandemonium in the lobby. Dozens of sailors were competing for the privilege of sleeping in a real bed, in a room that didn't rock, and taking long hot showers. Because I was the only woman in the place, they parted when I entered, as if I were Moses parting the Red Sea. Then the sea closed behind me and the party truly began.

Most of these boys looked like they could have modeled for a Norman Rockwell painting. I was swept upstairs, and for the next twenty-four hours I never made it back down to the lobby. As soon as I would finish in one room and go out into the hall, a line of sailors would be waiting for me. I would pick the next one, like the only girl at a dance, and he would lead me down the hall to his room, and the rest of the guys would follow us and stand there and wait. When I complained that I was hungry and said that I would go with the next guy who brought me some food, I found four guys standing outside the next room with trays. And thank God that the United States Navy gave those boys lectures about condoms. I never would have had enough to last me the time I was in that hotel. Luckily, most of the sailors had brought their own.

*   *   *

I stayed on after the fleet left, trying to avoid Sarah's trial and also to get a little R & R. I worked at the Clarysol, and I saw a few of Conchata's customers, just to get back my Caribbean whorehouse sea legs. I also went back to Las Astronautas and commiserated with Rosa, the woman whose whorehouse had been closed down for the *Nimitz*. And I practiced a little of my streetwalking outside Las Astronautas.

One day, when I was on the street outside, Rosa sent a bar boy out to get me. It seemed that two Hollywood stuntmen were in town and had asked Rosa if she knew any nice American girls, ones who spoke English, for a little fun. That's how I met the Stunt Guys.

Pete and Sam told me all about the stunts they were doing for a TV episode back in the States. They were both good looking, probably in their mid- to late forties, but they had bodies that were better than twenty-year-olds'. I think there's something exceptionally sexy and attractive about older people who have great bodies. If they had had face-lifts, you would have thought they were twenty-five. Pete and Sam were actually looking for two ladies, but since I was the only English-speaking American around, we made a deal that I would do both of them.

We grabbed a cab and headed for their bungalow. We talked for a while and had a glass of wine. They were really fun guys, the kind of guys I would have gone out with on a date. We were having a great time, talking about the States, joking around. Then they noticed that, every once in a while, I would grimace.

"Is there something wrong?" Pete asked.

I had a pain in my back, like someone stabbing me in the right shoulder blade. I had been to a chiropractor, but she had done no good at all. I was trying my best to be a good trouper and to hide how much my shoulder was bothering me.

"Come on," Sam said, "is there something wrong?"

"Yes, it hurts right here." I indicated over my shoulder. "Right in the muscle."

And they said, "OK, that's—" and they mentioned the name of the muscle, which sounded right. Then Pete said, "Sam gets that all the time. We know how to fix that." I was, of course, thrilled.

Then they said, "Lie face down on the floor."

That worried me, because one of the first rules of being a hooker is Never turn your back on a client. And wasn't lying face down on the floor the position bank robbers put you in, before they shot you in the head?

But they seemed like such nice guys, and it made sense that they got a lot of injuries in their line of work. They said they were licensed chiropractors, and I had no reason not to believe them.

I lay face down on the floor and said, "Like this?"

Yeah, they said, with what sounded like a little too much relish. Then one of them grabbed my right leg, the other one put his foot in the middle of my back and grabbed my left arm, and they wrung me out like a dishrag.

I said, "Wait a minute guys—" twist, crunch "—if this is something kinky"—crunch, twist— "I get paid extra for it." All the bones and muscles in my back were creaking and groaning. I was making sounds, too, like *"Arrgh, agggg, ummmpf, aaaaaaa, eeeee."* If someone had been listening at the door, he would have thought it was an orgy. But when the guys stopped and put me down, my back was cured.

Then I had sex with them both, lots of it, and they were both great. They were one and a half of the best lays I had ever had, which is to say that Pete was merely pretty good and Sam was spectacular.

Um guys, by the way, I have that same pain again. But I can assure you, it didn't come back for years.

9

LADIES NEED NOT WEAR TIARAS

A prostitute is a girl who knows how to give as well as take. She knows how to make a man feel good even if he is underendowed, a lousy lover, four feet tall, and has a face only a mother could love.
—XAVIERA HOLLANDER
   The Happy Hooker, 1972

Sarah was convicted of pimping and pandering. They also accused her of mail fraud because, in order to have the credit card slips processed, she had to tell the bank that her business did something other than provide escorts. I'm not sure exactly what she told the bank, but I do know that, at one point, one of my clients put down "airplane parts" on the receipt (you can imagine how large the amount was), and Sarah got in touch with me right away. "Tennis shoes are OK, limo service, equipment rental is OK," she said, "but not airplane parts."

The minute Sarah signed the papers to do business with the bank as whatever company she claimed to be running, she was committing bank fraud. And when she sent credit card slips through the mail, she was committing mail fraud.

Sarah was sentenced to two years in prison, and she served every day of her term. When I went to see her in the Fulton County Jail, I dressed conservatively—a suit jacket, a skirt, and high heels—and wore nice makeup and a few diamonds.

I showed my ID, and I figured the matrons would want to look in my purse or something. When I asked them what to do, they acted like I was giving them a hard time. One took a billy club and hit the bars in front of me and said, in a rude voice, "Step over here!" I had brought some presents for Sarah: books and perfume and little shampoos and mink oil soap—things I thought would cheer her up. I was worried about the books I brought because Sarah had told me on the phone that she had a restricted reading list. Since she had been convicted of a sex crime—pimping—she was not allowed to read books with any sex in them. It's pretty hard to find books with no sex in them, except for books on gardening and cooking—and I didn't see how she would have use for either of those. I was not trying to bring in *The Joy of Sex*, but I did try to bring her a copy of Rosemary Daniell's book, *Fatal Flowers*.

The matrons decided all the books except the one with crossword puzzles had too much sex in them. I brought Sarah a HIRE T-shirt, but that was banned too because it had words on it. The matrons ordered, "Stand here, go there." They searched me. They pawed through the things I'd brought. They showed very bad manners. I was shocked that they didn't have any higher standards about how they dealt with the public. I told them next time I'd bring them an etiquette book, so that they could narrow the cultural gap between themselves and the prisoners.

Finally I was led into the visiting room. There were little booths with a glass wall separating the two sides and phones on each side. Sarah was brought in, and she looked great for someone in jail. She was an exceptionally pretty, tall, thin woman in her mid-thirties, with dark, naturally curly hair going prematurely gray. Even in prison clothes she looked glamorous.

As long as I didn't look through the glass in the little two-way booth, I could pretend that I was sitting at home and that Sarah was still running Magnolia Blossoms and we were just chatting on the phone. She was very cheery, considering her situation, and she immediately began talking about what we were going to do next, no regrets. She felt that the ideal thing would be for me to scout out new cities for us to work in, and that as soon as she was out of jail we could move and set up our own agency. She talked about New York—"There are no good agencies in New York," Sarah said— and I talked about San Francisco. I left the jail figuring that Sarah and I would do just what she said . . . as soon as she finished serving her sentence.

I had been to New York several times. I had visited friends there, I had appeared on some TV shows there, and one of my clients, a Bolivian businessman who said he was in the car alarm business, had taken me shopping there. Ramón had brought with him not only me but his bodyguard, Feliz; his partner, Carlos; and another hooker named Debbie.

A fat, balding Italian man met us at the airport and steered us toward a silver limousine for the ride into the city. The Italian and Ramón soon fell into an intense discussion about . . . something. I don't know what because it was in rapid-fire Newyorickan Spanish, and I sensed it was in code. They seemed to be talking about bananas and air conditioners. I didn't hear them mention anything about cars or car alarms. (I had my suspicions that Ramón sold something other than car alarms, but it wasn't my job to play *Miami Vice.*)

Ramón checked us into the hotel and then said we were going shopping. Both Ramón and Carlos had wives, and they had decided it was time to buy a few diamonds for them. Ramón magically produced $30,000 in cash. He wanted me to carry it, but I had no intention of carrying $30,000 in cash around town. As far as I knew, "buying diamonds for the wives" was code for "buying a few Uzis."

As it turned out, we actually did go shopping for diamonds. The limo dropped us in the diamond district. I was being paid $1,000 a day for this. Life is hard.

Debbie and I were dressed to the teeth. I had on high heels, and I was wearing a beautiful coat over a silk dress and, with it, my signature black feather boa. Debbie was dressed in white boots, yellow hot pants, and a sequined top—with a fur coat thrown over the ensemble. Carlos was tall and thin, dressed in tight jeans and a black leather jacket. He looked like a member of a street gang, with dark, deep-set eyes, a mustache, and a big scar on his face.

Ramón was short, about five foot five. He tried to dress like a preppie—sweaters, corduroy pants, leather loafers, no socks. But with all that he wore more flashy jewelry than a Las Vegas comedian.

Add to that the fact that we had all been doing cocaine for three days straight. We were nervous, jumpy, acting strange, and asking to see trays of very expensive watches. I wasn't surprised when the jewelry store called the cops.

When the men in blue crashed through the door, they apparently expected to see a robbery in progress. When they found nothing unusual except a couple of possible gangsters and two likely hookers, hyped up on cocaine and looking at watches, they moseyed around for a while and then went to chat with the store manager.

Ramón and Carlos continued looking at watches for their wives. Every once in a while one of them would turn to us and say, "Do you think she would like this?" Debbie and I were beginning to get bored. It's boring to stand in a fancy store and help someone buy jewelry for his wife. I was trying my best to be charming and delightful, but Ramón noticed I wasn't really having a good time. "Pick out anything you want," he said, so I picked out the most valuable thing in the store, a beautiful platinum watch, loaded with diamonds and rubies. After he bought me the watch, he started picking out more things for his wife—a set of earrings. He bought his daughter a watch. Again I got bored. I wasn't trying to play a game or be coy with him. I truly was bored, and tired and wired. So Ramón told me to pick a necklace for myself. I pointed to the one with the biggest diamond.

Carlos asked Debbie what she wanted, and she pointed to a necklace with gold coins. She was smart, I thought. She could sell the coins, one by one, when she needed money. The necklace I picked had a huge diamond in it: it's often the one I wear when I'm photographed. But it's too uncomfortable to wear otherwise. At the time I wasn't thinking; I was just going for the thing with the highest value.

We walked out of the jewelry store and immediately went into a department store. In the fur department, Ramón picked up a full-length mink coat and said, "This is for you." The problem was that I hated it. My grandmother would have loved it, but I hated it.

I said, "Why don't we look at some other coats?" Ramón

looked at me sharply. "What's wrong?" he asked. "Don't you like it?"

When I said, "Gee, I'm not sure I really like the style," he said, "We'll find you another one," but he lost interest.

I learned a lesson on that trip: If you don't take what's offered, it's lost. I could have had that coat redone. I could at least have had the pelts. It was a very expensive fur coat. In life maybe it's best not to compromise your standards. But that's not true of fur coats.

(On the other hand, a few months later I went out and bought my own fox coat. If I'd taken that ugly mink I probably would have been stuck with a mink I hated, so it all worked out.)

By the summer of 1983, public appearances, TV and radio talk shows, college lectures, had become part of the routine of my life. It seemed that every magazine and newspaper from *Hustler* to the *Wall Street Journal* had at least mentioned me in type. What Darlene Hayes had told me was true: Appearing on the Donahue show had changed my life. And what was true nationally was especially true in Atlanta, where I began to be considered something between a local landmark and a celebrity.

At first, I found it strange to be recognized. People, in turn, found it strange that I, a prostitute, did ordinary things like have my tires rotated, pick up dry cleaning, and attend openings at art galleries. This was greeted with as much wonder as a talking dog.

The fact was that I lived a pretty ordinary life. I lived in Midtown, a neighborhood of mostly single-family homes, with little front yards and deep backyards. I shared my big Victorian four-bedroom house with several roommates, none of them prostitutes. I drove a 1976 white Cadillac. I shopped at K mart. I went to yard sales. And some of my best friends had straight jobs. A few people seemed puzzled when they found out I didn't live in a penthouse with hot and cold running champagne.

One day a woman stopped by to see me and found me crying. I had just had a terrible fight with my then-boyfriend, Lou. When this woman found out what I was crying about, she was appalled. "I don't believe this," she said. "You—Dolores French, of all people—are having problems handling a *man*?"

I sobbed. "I'm a person, too, you know," which idea seemed to shock her. She threw up her hands and walked out.

To have people stare at me and whisper while I bought Kotex, to have even friends treat me as if I were somebody else, made me feel that, in Atlanta, I was expected to be a celebrity-prostitute at all times. I decided I wanted to go to a place where people had no opinion of me whatsoever.

Since that seemed impossible, I decided to go someplace where everyone had so many opinions—about everything, and everyone—and had opinions that were so far off the wall, that it amounted to being a place where people had no opinions at all: New York City.

I got a room at the Chelsea Hotel, which seemed pretty much like home. The people who hung out in the lobby looked just like the kind of people who hung out in my living room. The walls were hung with art painted by residents, everyone was friendly and reasonable, and the desk actually managed to get messages to me.

On one of my first nights in town I stopped by the Pyramid Club, a punk rock club. Some people came in and sat near me. One of the women seemed agitated and disturbed. She kept saying over and over, "I've got to call Paul. I've got to call Paul."

I leaned closer to her and said, "Paul who?" I had often felt that way myself, and when I said, "I've got to call Paul," I meant Paul Krassner, the editor of *The Realist*.

She said, "Oh, you don't know him. He's a writer in California."

I said, "Yes, I do know him. Paul Krassner, right?"

She introduced herself. Her name was Claudette, and she happened to be a hooker too. We went back to the Chelsea to call Paul and to schmooze about how coincidental life is. Then Claudette and I settled into a business discussion. Paul had told Claudette about me years before, and she had seen me on TV, so I was being treated not as a typical hooker who blew into town from Atlanta to find work, but as a friend and celebrity.

I explained to Claudette that one of the reasons I had come to New York was to get an overview of the working conditions. She gave me a rollicking rundown on all the agencies she had worked with—and most of them sounded pretty bad. "There's this one place, Cachet, that you've got to try," Claudette said. "It's run by this woman named Sheila Devin, who's really more of a friend than an agent. Her real name is Sydney, which I like better, but she wants some anonymity, you know. Her family is real well known in the New England states. She claims they came over on the *May-flower*; well . . . if Sheila says they did, I'm sure they did, but, who cares, you know what I mean? Anyway"—Claudette perked along—"it's the best-run escort service in New York City. They have nice offices, and they're good about keeping records; no one I know has ever had any problems with Sheila. She's fair and honest and she has some pretty good ideas. I want you to meet her. You two seem a lot alike."

Then her voice dropped an octave, she assumed an extremely erect posture, formed an aloof expression, and took on a very serious tone to say, "And Cachet caters to only the 'highest-class clientele.' "

"Really?" I said, with a good bit of skepticism.

"Well . . ." She broke character and laughed and lit a cigarette. "They're a lot like customers anywhere. But Sheila pretends they're more . . . you know."

"No, I don't. They're more sophisticated? More obnoxious? More insane? More wealthy?"

"Yeah, they have more money," she said.

"Well, do they spend more money?"

"No."

"No? What good does it do for them to have more money if they don't part with more of it?" I asked, and she agreed. "Are they more fun?"

"Well, not particularly. They're nice," Claudette said, "but I have to admit that what's really different about Cachet's clients is Sheila. She screens them better than anyone else, and she feels you don't have to service somebody if you don't want to. If there's a dispute or a problem between a worker and a customer, she can be counted on to take your side, which is not always true of other agents in New York." Claudette complained, "It's a big pain in the butt, though, to have to run by Cachet all the time to pick up champagne. You'd think she'd just give us a case at a time, to keep ready."

"Ready for what?" I asked.

"You name it. Every time a client has a birthday or an anniversary, every time the stock market goes up five points or his cat has kittens, the client gets a present—a little bottle of champagne."

I didn't work with Sheila long enough to find out if this was an exaggeration, but the first job I did with that agency I had to pick up a bottle of champagne.

While Claudette and I were having great fun making jokes and carrying on like we'd been best friends for more like ten years than two hours, I was getting disillusioned about working in New York. Claudette explained that although Cachet had the air of being expensive and exclusive, it wasn't a very good place for a hooker to make a lot of money. "Sometimes I think Sheila's too picky about customers. You'll get more work at the other agencies," she said. Claudette said the going rate was still only seventy-five dollars for a full sixty-minute hour in New York and that agents set the prices.

"Why do the agents regulate the women's rates?" I asked.

"Competition," she said.

Several agents had policies about not accepting payment in advance. And most wanted you to bring in their fee after each call. That really ate up a lot of work time. In Atlanta, competition inspired every agency to operate much like Claudette described Cachet. But Atlanta agents would have been out of business in a minute if they'd limited women's income to seventy-five dollars an hour.

Most of the agents I met in New York conducted business about as badly as movies portray. Women were treated like a limitless, unskilled labor pool. So Claudette was right. Sheila, aka Sydney, was different from most agents in the city.

Claudette said there was one thing about Cachet that I should not miss: "The orientation session. It's a real hoot," she said. Claudette offered to give me a recommendation and introduction to Sheila.

Sheila was then running Elan, Cachet, and Finesse. I called her and made an appointment to come in. She told me to dress up for the interview, so I wore a Norma Kamali outfit and carried my new fox coat.

That was the year that Norma Kamali's clothes were all yellow or black or both. On the way to my appointment I stopped by the Kamali shop, to look through the new clothes, and I thought, "My God! Who would wear these colors? Then I went to meet Sheila and found out. There she was, dressed head to toe in yellow and black. I liked her right away.

There were five other women waiting to be interviewed that day. Some of the women who were there had worked before and some hadn't. They looked just about the same as the women at any other escort agency I had worked with. They all seemed to have a pretty good idea of what working with an escort agency in New York meant.

As Sheila explained it, there was relatively little chance of being arrested for being an escort in New York City (unless you shotgunned someone to death in the middle of Broadway).

With Sarah, we had not even been allowed to insinuate we might have sexual contact with the clients. Sheila, so well organized and sensible, nevertheless made it quite clear that sex was part of the service. She talked about giving blow jobs. She said that the escorts shouldn't use prophylactics for blow jobs, that her clients weren't the type to have diseases. And she showed how we could pull our hair down so the clients wouldn't see we weren't swallowing. This was undoubtedly the hoot that Claudette had been talking about: watching this prim and proper woman talking about giving a blow job and then demonstrating in a precise way how to hide spitting out come.

Sheila's seminar was reminiscent of Elaine's tutoring sessions. What amazed me was that here, in Manhattan, Sheila was sitting around actually giving instructions to a room full of strangers on how to work as a prostitute, how to perform oral sex. If any one of those women had been a police officer, we could all have been busted.

Maybe things were done differently in New York. Maybe it was OK to be open about sex; maybe the law really wouldn't bother about escort agencies. Gee, I thought, things are sure different in New York than they were in Atlanta.

We would be paid $75 for each hour with a client, and the agency would take $75. Claudette told me New York agencies commonly kept 60 percent of the money the women earned, so this fifty-fifty split was a relatively good deal for the women. With Sarah I had worked my way up to $200 an hour, plus tips; Sarah had never taken anything like 50 percent of anyone's money. But wherever I worked, I tried to fit in with community standards. If that was the New York split, that was that.

Just as Elaine and Sarah had coached me, Sheila explained that we should read up on culture and current affairs, so we could chat the customers up. "That way, the client might go into a second hour," Sheila said. Sarah and Elaine had also stressed the importance of being able to talk with clients about a broad range of topics. I generally talked to clients about something of interest to them, which usually meant themselves. After all the work I'd done— and I don't mean solely as a prostitute—after all the places I had been, it was pretty hard for me to meet someone I couldn't talk with. I usually tried to focus on something that the client had some pride in—his occupation, his apartment, his appearance, his hobby. Anything I could get a handle on. Once I'd reached them that way, I found they were more pleasant and cooperative. It made them better clients. And I liked doing it anyway. I considered it a major part of my job.

Sheila said the only lies she told clients were "that you girls go out only once a night, that you only work three days a week, and that none of you are professional hookers." She told us, "It's not true, but that's what I tell them. That's so the client will respect you just a little bit more. And that will be very important to you when it comes time to collect your tip."

She talked about panty liners and the need to be delicate and fresh. She said she gave that lecture just in case one of the women there didn't know about feminine hygiene. If someone needed a bath, she said, as Elaine had, we were to suggest that they take a shower, or leave.

I sat through all of her instructions. Then she asked each of us to go into a small room and undress, one by one, so she could look at us, in a mirror. What a rule of etiquette. I wondered if this was something she had learned in her previous career in merchandising—that customers in a dressing room in their underwear, or less, would be less likely to be embarrassed if you looked at them in the mirror. She said she was looking for moles and birthmarks and tattoos. One of her customers, she confided to us, had called after a date with one of her escorts and complained that the girl had a tattoo on her behind. It was so embarrassing, she said. That was not the sort of image she wanted for Cachet and Finesse. No lady has a tattoo on her ass.

She made notes with a pencil as she studied the applicants' nude bodies and said things like, "Is that a birthmark on the right shoulder?" After each woman undressed and then dressed again, Sheila would tell her, "I'll be calling you to let you know when we have a place for you." She was very gracious.

I waited until last because I wanted to talk with Sheila. When it was my turn I said, "I'll undress if you will." I had heard Sheila had had some cosmetic surgery, and I wanted to see what it looked like, which I explained to her. She said, "Oh, sure." It seemed fair to her that if I was going to undress she would too.

Then we sat down for a chat. "Delilah is my professional name. Once I start getting dressed for work I prefer to use that name. The rest of the time you can call me Dolores, if you prefer."

"I feel the same way. My whole name is Sydney Biddle Barrows, but everybody calls me Sydney. But, *please*, only Sheila around the office."

Sydney knew who I was. Prostitutes thought it was great that I was standing up for them, and in turn they tried to help connect me to the best agencies. Agencies were pleased to work with me, and they usually gave me a lot of work because I had established a reputation of being reliable and honest. Some agents felt my notoriety was now a selling point. It was a plus to be able to say to a client, "Oh, she's been on the Phil Donahue show. You've probably seen her on the Playboy Channel."

Sydney told me she admired what I was doing—speaking in public, being identified with prostitution—but, she said, she could never do anything like that. I said, "You may have no choice, if you continue being so open about what you're doing here. You may find yourself in jail, and you won't have the luxury of contemplating whether you want to be identified with prostitution or not."

I explained a little about Sarah's arrest and conviction and how Sarah had always been so careful never even to mention sex. "You're sitting here telling women you hardly know how to perform fellatio when they go out on a job. You're admitting that sex is involved," I said. "What if one of those women had been a cop?"

She just smiled. "Did any of these women *look like* police officers?" she asked.

"They *all* looked like police officers to me," I answered.

Sydney thought I was being paranoid; but to me the situation seemed too dangerous.

"Now about the money," I went on. "I'm used to working for much, much more."

"Well," she said, "I wanted to talk to you about that. You are one of the older women, and I find I don't get much call for older women." (I was thirty-two at the time.)

"I don't know how many calls I would get for someone your age," she said, "but I am looking for someone who would do some specialty work. For that you could charge much more. Do you know anything about domination?"

As a matter of fact, I did.

The last time I had been in New York, it was to do a television show. An interesting couple from the studio audience asked me to go out to dinner. I was planning on having dinner with a boy-friend, I said, and the man replied: "Fine, let's make it a foursome. My treat." Which sounded fine to me.

We went to a place in Chinatown. As soon as we sat down, this man, Herb, and his wife, Sylvia, started talking about their favorite subjects: sadism and masochism. Herb had a very loud voice, a voice that carried, and he was yakking on and on about stringing people up in closets for the weekend, and men who wanted to wear diapers and be given baby bottles, and all the different skin preparations, how Icy Hot is hotter than Ben-Gay. Every once in a while his wife would chime in about scarves and handcuffs and needles and champagne enemas, leather gags and restraints, and this S & M club we should check out. The two of them were carrying on, and the entire restaurant was silent. I'm sure they were the only two people talking; everyone else was digging into their mu shu pork with shocked and curious expressions on their faces.

Herb was talking about golden showers and penis torture, and my former boyfriend, Bob, was kicking me under the table, to the point where, the next day, I had bruises all over my legs. Bob was concerned that these weird people were going to take us home with them and practice some of their specialties on him. He was noticeably uncomfortable, but he was also doing real damage to my legs. I started kicking him back. The table was jumping because we kept bumping it with our knees, but Herb and Sylvia didn't seem to notice.

Bob and I thanked our hosts for dinner and we got out of there that night, but I eventually called Herb and Sylvia for more information. I was getting a lot of requests for S & M, and I knew very little about how to do it. Herb and Sylvia were thrilled that someone wanted to learn about it. They invited me to visit their house, which I did. It was filled from top to bottom with equip-ment. Closets and dressers were packed with restraints and chains and fetish shoes and costumes. They showed me a blow-up first aid restraint that could immobilize an arm or a leg. It looked like a pool toy, but, when it was blown up, it did indeed immobilize a limb. (How strange, I thought, that someone would be turned on by being restrained in a blow-up splint, but I had long since learned, as the aged hooker had said in Amsterdam, "Everyone wants something different.")

Herb and Sylvia also took me to New York's premier S & M club. Although the entrance was on street level, and the building went up four stories, most of the activities seemed to take place in the basement and even in an area underneath the street.

This club was so dirty, so raunchy, and so depraved that I wouldn't be surprised if scientists someday discover that AIDS started there. The patrons were well dressed, but they were all eccentric. On the main floor there were different kinds of restraints, manacles, and stocks. People were waiting by the stocks for someone to come over and lock them in.

It was raining the night I went there and, when we went down in the basement, water was pouring from what looked like a manhole cover in the ceiling. It smelled like a sewer, and I have no doubt it was a sewer. That was where they put the bar and also a boutique that sold expensive whips.

In the basement there was a lot of strange activity going on. Guys were sprawled across pommel horses. There were lots of otherwise naked people wearing socks and shoes and carrying their $500 suits rolled up under their arms. Some people were in their underwear. And all around were little miniature flea market booths with specialties. One booth specialized in hot-wax treatments—and they weren't to remove unsightly hair.

The club was one of the finest examples I had ever seen of people doing everything destructive possible to their bodies: restraints, torture, poppers, alcohol, marijuana, speed, cocaine. The drugs were laid out in one booth, and people seemed to be taking them without regard for which ones they got. (It didn't seem like the right place to do smorgasbord, I thought.) And yet at this perverse freak show, the people I met were extraordinarily ordinary: stockbrokers and supermarket cashiers, teachers, and lawyers, and housewives.

It was frightening when I first walked in. And then it was surprising when I found out that people who were into S & M were everyday people.

The next day Herb and Sylvia took me to an S & M supply store, where I saw adult diapers for the first time. And they introduced me to Lee's Mardi Gras, which specialized in women's lingerie and things for men—high-heeled shoes in 14DDD and exotic costumes. Lee's Mardi Gras sold domination pumps—cartoon stilettos with six-inch heels and severe pointy toes.

I noticed a guy in the store who looked like a regular silver-haired executive wearing an expensive gray suit. I was busy looking at lingerie when the executive came out of a dressing room wearing a yellow-and-pink Bo Peep costume, complete with knee socks and Mary Janes—all in a size to fit a guy about six feet tall and weighing 220 pounds. It all seemed so awfully weird, and I thought, Gosh, if the boys on Wall Street could see you now.

And, to complete my education, Herb and Sylvia took me to a performance club where admission was thirty dollars per person. This was a place where personal slaves acted out the audience's fantasies: spankings, whippings, golden showers. The most interesting performance there was by a transsexual who came out by himself and did a recitation, very poetic, almost like Chaucer, about high heels. And then the people who ran the place did a demonstration in which this guy had his wife tied to a pommel horse and hit her on the butt with a paddle and then he talked to the audience about the ethics of S & M. He asked if the audience wanted him to hit her again, and they shouted, "Yes." And then he asked her and she said, "Yes, please." So he hit her again. This continued until he asked her if she wanted to be hit again and she said, "No." Then he turned to the audience and said, "Should I hit her?"

They yelled, "Yes," and he said, "No, don't you see? She doesn't want to be hit again. If she doesn't want me to do it, I don't do it. Because it has to be for mutual pleasure."

So when Sydney Barrows asked me if I knew anything about specialty work, I felt more than qualified to say yes.

"Good," she said, "I'm sure we'll be able to send you out to see someone."

But as it turned out, the first person she sent me to was a straight call. This guy, she said, was "looking for someone older, someone nearer his own age."

The client was a young blood on Wall Street, an intense bond trader, and all he wanted was a straight job. I didn't see that working in New York was very different from working in Atlanta. If anything, well-off people in New York seemed to have a lower standard of living than people in my hometown.

Sure, they had expensive furniture and they lived in buildings with doormen on Fifth Avenue and Park Avenue. But their apartments were teensy-tinsy things. One place was so small we would have to move the coffee table closer to the entertainment center in order to pull out the sofa bed. I've made love in a Volkswagen Beetle that was more comfortable than some of those apartments. And, I thought, This is where these guys sleep every night—guys who are making a fortune on Wall Street, but living in studio apartments.

Most of the customers I saw were single. They seemed very lonely and isolated, and I doubted many of them would ever marry. They worked, they went out to dinner, they came home, sometimes they called an escort service, they went to bed, and then they got up and went to the office by 8:00 A.M. Once they got past the doorman at night and into the apartment, they acted as if it wasn't safe to go out again. They seemed amazed that I went out at night alone. And indeed, it was different than driving around in Atlanta. The streets were empty. There were no stores open in most neighborhoods. It was like a city of the dead.

I worked with three other agencies while I was in New York. There was plenty of work. The clients I saw were usually businesspeople of some sort—lawyers, stockbrokers—and they often seemed scared of being caught. They were very reserved, and they acted as though having someone come into their apartment was a new experience, almost a violation of their, as they called it, "space." I also saw clients from the New York area I had first met when they were in Atlanta or the Caribbean or San Francisco. I worked nearly every night, and I worked a lot of jobs. But I didn't see that being a call girl in New York was all that lucrative, or safe, or even interesting.

I thought Sydney, like all the other agents I met in New York, could have been arrested at any minute. What frightened me most was her attitude: "We're all nice girls. Our clients are nice. Why would anyone arrest us?" Most of the women I knew who had been arrested were "nice girls." They worked hard for their money, they were honest, they provided a service, and no one was hurt, but they got arrested and some of them, like Sarah, went to prison.

I quoted Sydney some statistics about arrests for prostitution, and she said, "That has nothing to do with businesses like this." Cachet and Finesse worked, Sydney thought, because they were exclusive and classy. I knew from the Black Angus that it wasn't class that made sex sell, or marketing either. Sex sells no matter how it's packaged.

Sydney was such a good businesswoman, she could have made a great deal of money through her agencies. I talked to her a little bit about it, because I could see she had the right ingredients, but she said she wanted to run a business that was exclusive. To her, Finesse and Cachet were like wonderful, elegant restaurants that serve fabulous food, but to no more than ten people a night. When those ten people called for reservations, she would check them out to see if they were worthy of her restaurant: "Sir, where have you eaten before?" If she felt a client could truly appreciate the meal that she was going to make, then she'd let him come to dinner.

Her prices weren't any higher than those of any other good escort service in town. Claudette told me that Sydney was barely making enough money to pay her expenses. But she was worried that, if she served more clients, the quality would go down.

Claudette was right about New York agents' attitude that the customer was always right, whereas elsewhere I had gotten used to the idea that, if there was any disagreement between a customer and a call girl, the customer was always wrong. We weren't supposed to abuse clients, but if there was a conflict, the agency or the madam always took our side. In New York, the women were always wrong.

It was Christmas 1983, and I returned to Atlanta. I missed my friends, I missed my house, and I didn't see New York as a great place for me and Sarah to set up business. And besides, New York was getting very cold. I wanted to go someplace where I didn't have to wear a coat.

There was also one other reason to come back to Atlanta around Christmastime. On New Year's Day, Sandy and Marvin Cohen gave the biggest, most important party of the year. All the politicians would be there, the governor and the state senators and the people on the city council, all the politicos I needed to stay in touch with because of HIRE and all the people I had ever worked with in the civil rights movement and the women's rights movement, all the media people in town, in other words, everyone in Atlanta would be there. I wanted to be there too. Because I had been working so hard, and traveling so much, I didn't get a chance to see people that often. New Year's Day would be my big chance.

I found a new agency in Atlanta I liked, the biggest and oldest agency in town. They had nice offices, with three or four staff people there around the clock, and they put any agency I'd seen in New York to shame. The agency represented thirty to eighty male and female models—from eighteen to fifty years old—at any one time. Some of the models had been with the agency for ten years, which was a sign that it was pretty decent to work with. As it turned out, Sarah had started working as a model with this agency, which is how she'd learned all the things she'd taught me. I find that people who run agencies have usually, at some time in their careers, worked as escorts or models or prostitutes, whether they will admit it or not.

By this point, I had graduated as a prostitute: I knew a lot about the business—both what to do to please clients and how to protect myself from deadbeats, cops, and nuts. As a result, I was able to work more than I had ever worked before. There are a lot of prostitute workaholics, and I was one of them. So much so that I was even working on New Year's Eve, for prostitutes, the biggest night of the year.

That was when I learned that looking around a client's apartment can be a lifesaver. I was seeing a new client in a very expensive apartment, which in Atlanta at that time meant one that cost $1,200 to $1,500 a month. It was a spacious two-bedroom, with big beveled-glass doors between the living room and dining room. The man had given me slightly incorrect directions, which put me on my guard. When he opened the door, I knew something was wrong. The guy had a three-dollar haircut and clearly did not suit this apartment. He looked like he should have been living in a trailer.

He had the sofa bed pulled out when I arrived, which made me suspicious. (After all, there were two bedrooms. Why was he using the sofa bed?) I asked for an ID, and he said he had to go get it. While he was gone I started fingering through the mail sitting on a small table in the living room. This mail looked like my hairdresser's mail or like *my* mail—invitations to the symphony and the museum, copies of the *New Yorker*. None of it fit a guy with a three-dollar haircut.

On the other hand, the apartment was in a nice neighborhood. The guy looked clean-cut. He didn't look like he was going to kill me or mug me. I figured he wasn't a maniac; I didn't think he was a drug dealer. Since there seemed to be basically only four kinds of clients—maniacs, druggies, nice guys, and cops—that meant that he was either a nice guy or a cop. The problem was to figure out which.

I sneaked into the foyer—something I don't usually do when I'm in someone's apartment, because I might be accused of trying to steal the silver-tipped cane. I opened the closet door, and hanging there was a heavy SWAT team jacket. And on the shelf was a SWAT team hat. I tried to shut the door very quietly, and just as I was doing so—Alfred Hitchcock time—I saw him standing there.

It was clear that I had been snooping, so I asked about the jacket. He explained, "My roommate's a cop." He told me the guy was a traffic cop. Sure, a traffic cop with a $1,500 apartment and a SWAT team jacket.

I was trying to be cool, but every cell in my body was screaming, "*Get out!*"

I said, lightly, "Oh, really? What's it *like* to have a cop as a roommate?"

Then he said, "By the way, I didn't give you the right name. I gave you my roommate's name." He explained that he was from Tennessee, which I knew was a state that didn't print pictures on its drivers' licenses. The points were really piling up against him; I thought of how Sarah would have been making her little hatch marks on a piece of paper, all of them in the negative column.

So I told him I had to call my agency, since the name he'd given me wasn't his own. I called my agency and used their code words for cop—every agency had different ones, which meant I had to keep my code words straight. "I'm just checking in with you," I said, "because we don't have the right ID here. By the way, did you ever mail that letter for me?" I knew there had to be other cops in the apartment. I could see tiny lights on in one of the bedrooms down the hall; the door was slightly cracked open. I set up an argument on the phone with Maya, the agent I worked with. I told her, "Oh, but that's such a bother to go back out to the street. No, I'm sure it's OK. What if he walks me out to a phone? OK, all right, I'll walk myself out and call you from there. It won't take me five minutes to get to the phone booth. Then you can straighten this whole thing out." I pretended Maya was still giving me a hard time.

"OK," I said, "if I'm not there in five minutes, you can start looking for me."

I tried to reassure him. "Look," I said, "cops have to live somewhere. And they have roommates. You just happen to be one of them." I eased him back into the living room and convinced him that if he just let me go down to the phone booth at the corner, to check in with my agent (who was just *insisting* that I do this), then I'd come back and be foolish enough to agree to perform some really interesting sex acts with him. (So he could get a really good arrest.) I was eight feet from the door—and it was really Edgar Allan Poe–land: thump, thump, thump—when at the last minute I just lost it. I tried to open the door. It was locked and I tried to go through it anyway.

It was pure slapstick. I kept trying to open the door, and then trying to go through it, even though it was shut. Finally he came over and helped me. "Here, here, here," he said, and unlocked the door and let me out. It was one of the worst work experiences I'd ever had.

I called Maya from a phone booth outside, and she could tell I was pretty upset. She suggested I meet her for a drink at a nearby bar, and she was there in fifteen minutes. By then I was hyperventilating and thirsty, shaken and scared. So I had three Bloody Marys. I'm not much of a drinker, and I was drinking on an empty stomach, so those drinks had a pretty strong effect.

Maya, I should mention, is handicapped. She uses leg braces to get around; so it took her a long time to help me out of that bar, into her car, and up the stairs to my bedroom. You can imagine the scene: One person on a crutch and two bad legs helping another person, staggering drunk, up the stairs. By the time I got into my bed I had the dry heaves. I think that's what broke the blood vessel in my left eye. When I woke up around noon on New Year's Day, I felt only marginally better than I did when I went to bed, and I looked like high holy hell, but I knew I just had to make it to that party.

I looked at myself in the mirror, and I was shocked at what one night of terror and drinking had done to my face. I looked like I had just gone ten rounds with Larry Holmes. One eye was completely red. My face was swollen. My skin had changed color. Something bad had happened to my hair—it looked as if it had just given up and laid down to die. I took a bath and I washed my hair and I did my makeup—the afternoon was getting away from me—and when I looked in the mirror again, I still looked like a ghoul.

I thought, How can I go to the party looking like this? What was in the mirror was so far from beautiful it was laughable.

Finally I realized that I had to go, that I wasn't going to that party to be seen, but to see my friends. They would understand about one bad night, wouldn't they?

I went, and every person I talked to took one look at me and said, "My God, what happened to you?" I explained that it was their tax dollars at work.

I was getting a Perrier from the bartender when Eldrin Bell, a middle-aged black man who was then deputy chief of police, pulled me aside. "You look awful," he said. "You can't go around in public looking like this. You represent your entire industry. You're a damn fine-looking woman, and people take a look at you and they say, 'So that's what a prostitute looks like.' But today, you look terrible, Dolores."

"If it wasn't for people like you, Eldrin, I wouldn't look like this."

"What do you mean?"

"One of your men tried to arrest me last night, Eldrin. Don't you people have enough to do on New Year's Eve, you've got to go trying to arrest me?"

"He was just doing his job, Dolores. If some guy got you, that would be a feather in his cap. Some guys think they could make a career out of sending Dolores French to jail," he said, and walked off to talk to a reporter.

One of the things the new agency offered me was rich clients and celebrities—neither of which were likely to be cops. I particularly liked seeing the managers and promoters of rock bands—they had money to spend.

A lot of celebrities call escort agencies. What they're looking for is anonymity. A rock star or a tennis star or a famous author or politician or athlete wants sexual services but is worried that the person they meet might talk afterward and want more from them, either personally or financially.

There's another reason celebrities want to have sex with call girls. They want things to happen right now. They don't want to have to go out of their way to meet someone, to court them for even ten minutes, and they don't want to take a groupie home. They want to be able to pick up the phone and say, "Send someone here now."

One day my agency called and said they had a client for me. They told me his name and hotel, and I thought, That name sounds familiar. I asked, "What does he do for a living?" and they said,

"Something to do with music." But I still didn't think it was *him*; I thought this might be the guy's nephew or something.

When he opened the door I realized it *was* the guy. It had been ten years since I had seen one of his concerts, but I still considered myself a fan. Still, it was only after I had checked his ID and we'd negotiated a price and he had paid me that I told him how much I liked his music.

"It's nice to provide services for someone who has made the world a better place to live in," I told him. I was a little disappointed that he wanted only a half hour, but, he told me, he had used a lot of call girls in his career, and he knew exactly what he wanted. He was on the road about fifty weeks out of the year. He had a wife and kids at home and he would really rather be with his wife, he said. So his solution was to call in prostitutes and have sex with them but to think of his wife. He didn't want to have any kind of relationship, just sex.

He did know what he wanted: a straight job, a little oral sex and then intercourse, something fast. He had beautiful hands and a huge cock. I thought as the time started running out, Maybe he'll barter something for the extra time. (Clients had often gone over the time they'd paid for. That's how I ended up with new floor mats for my car, twelve sets of steak knives, a telephone, a case of cassette tapes, and four frozen ducks.) I thought, Gee, maybe this guy will play something for me. But he knew what he was doing, and he finished exactly thirty minutes after he started.

We talked a little bit before I left. I told him, "It must be very lonely staying in hotel rooms all the time."

"Yeah," he said. "But this is what I get paid for—staying in hotel rooms. I do the music for free, but they have to pay me to leave home and spend all this time in hotel rooms." I said, "Same thing with me. I don't get paid for the sex. I get paid for spending time in hotel rooms." We both laughed.

He offered me tickets to his concert the next night, but I was busy and I had to turn them down.

This particular celebrity was pleasant and polite. Most celebrities are when they're with call girls. When they call an escort service, it is for private time. At least when I've been called by a celebrity, it's never been for an orgy or a party with a lot of other people around. They want to have someone to talk to; they're lonely, more than most other clients.

*　　*　　*

I usually felt that it was polite to talk to both the man and the woman when I was getting a call to see a couple. Agnes and Bill changed that politesse to a hard-and-fast rule: I would never again see a couple unless I talked to both people first.

I called the number I had been given, and a man picked up the phone. "May I speak to Bill, please?"

A voice inflected with three or four good-time beers responded, "This is him. Hey, darlin', come on over."

"I understand that you and your friend would like to see a model," I said. "What's your friend's name?"

"We sure would. My girlfriend's name is Agnes. This whole thing is for her. She's been pestering me for weeks to get another woman on over here, but hell, I didn't know anyone to call. So I called your service. Is this Delilah?"

"Yes, it is," I said. This guy was speaking in whole sentences. That was a good sign. "I'm going to tell you what I look like, and you can decide if I'm what you had in mind," I said. I told him what I looked like, and he indicated that was just right. He had a good-old-boy attitude that any woman who bathed and had all her front teeth was beautiful.

Then I told him I would like to speak to Agnes, to make sure she thought I was suitable. He said, "Oh, she just went down to the kitchen to get something."

"OK," I said, "describe her to me." I wanted to hear what his attitude was about her, which would explain a lot about how all of us would get along.

"She's a little bit older than you, about thirty-five, but she don't look a day over thirty." He went on to describe her favorably and not dwell too long on her breasts. In other words, he sounded OK to me, and I got directions to drive to their house.

They were way out in the suburbs, so I told him it would take me an hour to get there. When I arrived, he answered the door wearing a bathrobe and slippers. "Come on in," he said. "Agnes is upstairs waiting for you. She's real shy, but believe you me, she's looking forward to this like Christmas morning. I never knew how much this meant to her until I told her you were on your way."

"What do you mean?" I asked.

"Well, she's acting real anxious. She's been wild telling me all the things she wants the two of you to do together. I never knew she had that much of an imagination. Come on up. She's upstairs. I'll carry your bag."

"That's all right," I said. "I'll carry it myself."

I followed him to the bedroom, where a meek-looking woman sat propped up against the headboard of the bed. She had her knees drawn up against her chin. When she saw me she pulled the sheet up around her chin.

"Bill," she whined, "I thought you were kidding me about having a girl come over here."

"Hi, Agnes," I said. "Bill told me a lot of nice things about you. I'm Delilah." Agnes didn't seem too thrilled to make my acquaintance, so I turned my attentions back to Bill.

"I'm going to need the hundred-and-twenty-dollar appointment fee now, and I need to see your driver's license, a business card, and some kind of proof of occupancy." He fumbled his way around in his billfold for a while, and Agnes kept repeating, "I can't believe you did this, Bill."

She was as shocked to hear that the appointment fee was $120 as she was to see me in the bedroom. I gave her an OK sign behind Bill's back, as if to say, I understand you don't want to do this, just leave it to me.

Bill finally had all his papers together, along with the $120. I checked his IDs, took his money, and then said, "As I explained to you on the phone, the hundred and twenty dollars is the agency fee. I get an additional fee. Usually that fee is two hundred dollars, so for the two of you that will be four hundred dollars."

As I expected, he balked, and Agnes agreed that was way too much money to spend. (She obviously hoped he would back out of the whole deal.) But Bill made a counteroffer: "How about three hundred dollars for forty-five minutes?" I decided to confront him.

"I know that four hundred dollars is a lot of money," I said, "but besides being a lot of money, I don't think Agnes really wants to do this, do you, Agnes?"

She was ready to chime in, "No, I don't, especially not for four hundred dollars."

This was Bill's chance to show a little sensitivity, but he didn't even bother to acknowledge what Agnes had said.

"She swore to me this is what she wanted."

"You thought that once I came out here and got my money, I'd go through with it whether she wanted to or not, didn't you?"

Bill looked right at her and said, "Go on, tell her, honey. Tell her how much you've been wanting to do this."

Without waiting for her to respond he turned to me and said, "Here, take the four hundred dollars. Just so Agnes can have sex with a woman once in her life and stop nagging me about it."

He tried to stuff the money down the neck of my sweater. I felt things were deteriorating badly, but I eventually took the four hundred dollars.

"Agnes," I said, "I need to freshen up. Could you show me where the bathroom is?"

It took a little prodding, but I got Agnes to come out from under the sheets and walk me to the bathroom. When we got there we closed the door and I said, "Is he always like this?" She indicated that he wasn't like this all the time and that if he was she wouldn't be with him.

"What would happen if I just left? Would there be a problem?"

She indicated that there wouldn't.

"OK," I said, "I can just leave, and give him back his four hundred dollars. . . . I'll have to keep the agency fee, but I can give him back the rest. . . . *Or* I can split the money with you. You can make a couple hundred, I can make a couple hundred. You don't have to do anything but just lay there. It seems clear to me that this is for him and not for you, and in that case, you should get paid for it too. And that way I won't have wasted a trip out here. And you can take that money and spend it on something really nice, something you can look at, and you can look at it and remember what a jerk he was tonight. What do you think?"

She thought it was a swell idea. A smile blossomed on her unhappy little face.

I added, "I advise that you never, ever tell him that we pulled this." And she said, "No, I won't."

"Is there anything you don't want me to do?"

"I don't know *what* to do," she said.

"Well you just lay back and enjoy making two hundred dollars for twenty minutes, and then help me get out of here in twenty minutes."

When I left that house later that night, I left two satisfied customers behind.

There are a lot of couples who hire me, and who see me over

and over again. There's a reservation about doing this the first time. I think both the man and woman are each afraid that the other one will like me better. But I try to make them understand that I am there to help them enjoy each other more. I'm like a waiter. This is their evening, and I want them both to enjoy it.

When I do couples, they usually want all three of us to be together. They figure that two people don't have enough hands and mouths and orifices. They use me as a sexual device that allows them to do something they have always wanted to do together, but couldn't.

They almost always want massages. Sometimes couples want me to dress up in lingerie, to bring lingerie for one or both of them, to get drinks for them, to get the Jacuzzi ready, to plug in the vibrators. It's a big job, doing couples. Occasionally they don't want me to have sex at all; they just want someone to take care of them while they enjoy each other. You can't call up a temp service and ask them to send someone over to wear lingerie and roll joints and fill in the gaps in the conversation. I can honestly say that every one of these I've done has made the couples' relationship better. It's one of the most rewarding jobs in the business.

I called HIRE's attorney, Michael Hauptman, to see if he had a few minutes to answer some questions I had about legal issues. He was teaching at a law school at the time, but he said he could spare some time if I wanted to meet him for dinner. I met him at his office and he took me to International House of Pancakes. I told him, just as an observation, mind you, that I would never go out with anyone who couldn't afford to take me to a restaurant that was nicer than any restaurant I could afford myself.

I also mentioned to him that I had just broken up with a guy I was dating. I thought Michael was cute, and I knew that he was funny and smart, and that he had legally separated from his wife. The minute he started laughing at my jokes, I let him know that I was available.

Within a week or so, Michael asked me to dinner at the Abbey, one of the fanciest restaurants in town, where a meal takes at least four hours. We ate and we drank. I drank more than I had ever drunk before in my life. I took Michael back to my place, and we made love for hours. He was the best lay I'd ever had until he passed out. Then I got a call from a client, offering me $200 to come over right away. I looked at this comatose man in my bed, considered my checking account, and went out to see the client, locking my house up behind me.

How was I to know that Michael might wake up in the middle of the night, that he might stagger around and discover that all my doors had dead-bolt locks that had been locked from the outside? That he would end up climbing out of the bathroom window and walking home at 3:00 A.M.? When I returned I was very disappointed to find that he had somehow escaped. Before our next date I let him know that I wasn't going to put up with a man passing out, then running out, on me. I made it clear that if I couldn't get a lot more from a personal relationship than I could get from clients who paid me, I didn't want to waste my time and energy doing for free what I could be doing for money. He said that made sense to him.

A forty-five-year-old man who owned a winery was staying in a big suite at one of the most elegant hotels in town. He wanted someone with a college education to spend three hours with him. The agency sent me. His suite had been the scene of a big meeting that day, and it was stocked with champagne and flowers, alcohol and food. I charged him $750 for three hours—$150 for the agent and $600 for me. One of the things I liked about him was that, when I told him the price, he simply said fine. The money was coming out of his own pocket yet, in order to see me, he wasn't going to have to give up on something else. He earned a lot of money, and he decided he wanted to spend a little on me. He thought I was great fun, and we spent most of our time chitchatting.

He told me all about his wife and politics and his feelings about capitalism. He said that he had been a radical hippie but that at one point he'd decided he wanted to make money so he had worked his way up in the wine business. He offered me some dope, and we drank champagne. We talked about different drug habits. He said he didn't do cocaine anymore because it made him too crazy. (Unlike wine, I thought to myself.)

One of the things I like about my job is that clients often tell me all sorts of things about their work and their companies. Most of it I can't relate to. But I could relate to one client who told me that coffee companies make more money decaffeinating coffee and then selling the caffeine to drug companies than they do selling the decaffeinated coffee itself. The vintner told me about hista-mines in wine.

I tried to teach him how to juggle. After he'd had a few glasses of champagne he said, "Hey, I can do that. This is easy." Then he dropped a few balls and said, "Why don't you do it? You do it better than I do." As pleasant as he was, I didn't want to stay more than three hours. With someone I was meeting for the first time, I usually didn't have more than three good hours of conversation in me. We actually had two good hours of conversation and an hour of good sex. That was enough time together so that, when I walked out the door, we were both still happy with each other.

I wasn't bored the whole time I was with him. And while he wasn't the kind of man I would have gone out with on a date, he was the kind of client who makes me love my job.

I had just left one job and I was on the way to another when I got a message on my beeper from a roommate: "This is Sheila. Your house is on fire. There are cops and firemen all over the place." I made one of those illegal Smokey and the Bandit U-turns, and then found a phone and called my friend Maria. By the time I got to my house everything was destroyed, all my clothes, my records, my furniture, all the work I had put into the house. The house was still standing, but it was gutted. The kitchen was gone, the dining room was gone, the back porch was gone. The stairs were barely safe to climb. What wasn't burned in the fire had been dam-aged by smoke and water, including my paintings and drawings, all of my photographs, and many letters. My bedroom upstairs was destroyed. I had on my good jewelry and my fox coat, a tight black skirt with a slit up the back, a lace blouse, and a pair of red high heels. Except for what was on my back and my feet, I had no personal possessions left.

I climbed the stairs to my room and got what money I had saved out of a safe. I was still trying to look at the bright side of things. At least the house was standing. The new carpeting I had put in might have been destroyed, but the woodwork downstairs was still intact. This wasn't as bad as it could be, I said to anyone who would listen.

Then I cried. My friends took care of me and tried to comfort me. My friend Maria helped me board up the house. I was board-ing up my house in a fox coat and high heels, a tight skirt and a see-through blouse. At some point during the night I remembered that I had stood up a client, and I called the agency and apologized.

The fire inspectors arrived the next day and looked through the house. They showed me where the fire had started—on the wall opposite the back windows. The problem was that there were no electrical outlets on that wall, there was no appliance there, no wiring at all; there were not even any matches or candles near the wall. There was no way a fire could have started there of its own accord. The fire inspector looked at the back windows and said, "You don't have any enemies, do you, Miss French?"

No one ever figured out what started the fire, which led me to believe it was arson. But the last thing I wanted to think about was that someone might have firebombed my house.

I got depressed. I got very, very depressed. There were things I had to do and I did them. I had insurance. I had never thought I would need insurance; in fact, I had thought of insurance as extortion. But I had insurance. This is where I learned more about insurance than I ever wanted to know, because I had an old house and the amount of insurance I had covered only 50 percent of what the house was worth. I was only able to collect for things I was able to prove I'd lost and would be able to replace. It was crazy.

Grieving over the ruin of my beautiful house was such a long and painful process. For several days I thought I was going to be all right, but I kept having nightmares. I did my best to keep myself together, but my life took a nosedive. I couldn't work. I kept trying to salvage things from the house, going back again and again and digging through the ruins. I found some of the paintings and drawings I had done, which had been protected because they were in cases. The Atlanta Historical Society took them and spent months lifting water damage and smoke damage from them.

I started gaining weight after the fire. I was eating, I suppose, to console myself. Luckily I found, when I did go back to work, that the weight didn't matter to most of my clients.

I wasn't ready to have someone permanently in my life, but I enjoyed going out with Michael and he helped me during that time. I didn't ask him to do any of my legal work for me, however, because when I saw him I wanted it just to be fun and not about legal problems. I found out later that hurt his feelings.

*   *   *

After the fire, I went to visit Sarah in prison in Macon, Georgia. (She had been transferred from the Fulton County Jail to Macon, which meant that it was that much harder for any of her family and friends to see her.) Since my house was nearly gone, she suggested I look on the bright side. Maybe this was a cosmic excuse for leaving Atlanta. She knew that I hadn't much liked the working conditions in New York City and she knew I was planning on attending the joint Hookers' Convention and Democratic national convention in San Francisco in the summer. So Sarah proposed that the two of us move to San Francisco, as soon as she got out of prison, and start a new agency.

I certainly needed money to fix my house up again. And I couldn't live there in the interim. My roommates found other places to live, and I found myself without a base. I decided that Sarah was right. And maybe someone *had* firebombed my house. Religious lunatics firebomb abortion centers, why shouldn't they take it as the word of God that my house should go too?

I went out to the coast in May, two months ahead of the conventions and a month ahead of Sarah's release from jail. I rented an apartment in Haight-Ashbury and started working.

As soon as Sarah got out of prison, she called me. She said she was staying in a hotel in Atlanta, and she asked me how work was in San Francisco. I said I thought there was money to be made, and Sarah said, "That's just what I was hoping I'd hear. Look, I've got to take care of something before I leave. But how about if I fly out over the weekend? Can I stay with you for a while? And we can start setting up our business."

Sarah and I went as far as discussing which flight she would take. And when she hung up, she said, "I'll see you Sunday."

That was four years ago, and neither I nor anyone else has ever heard from her again. When she didn't show up that Sunday, I called the hotel she said she had been staying at. They said they had no record of her. I thought it was strange that Sarah would willingly disappear, but I've never made any effort to track her down because I felt either she was dead or she absolutely did not want to be found. I would prefer not to know if she's dead. I would prefer to think that, in some city in America, there is a terrific woman running a top-notch agency, and that Sarah is happier than she has ever been before.

*   *   *

San Francisco men seemed pretty ordinary, or maybe I was losing my sense of adventure in being a prostitute. Once I got back from the Caribbean and Europe, American men all seemed to be the same, no matter where I was working. I saw a Jewish guy from New York who was impotent. I saw a zookeeper who kept a giraffe skin in his living room. Most of the clients I saw in San Francisco weren't businessmen traveling through. The clients I saw lived there; they were very nice, they were just a little boring.

That's when someone approached me to ask if I'd like to do telephone sex. This guy, Alex, almost singlehandedly ran a telephone sex business by doing a whole range of women's voices. He could do southern belle and Japanese geisha and high-class English lady and tough-speaking German. He had at least a dozen different voices, plus the efficient woman's voice he used to answer the phone. His problem was that, as a one-man show, he needed some time off. That's where I would come in.

I sat with Alex one day while he worked, and I was amazed. He charged fifteen to twenty-five dollars a call, and most of that went to the telephone company. Once he paid his overhead, he was clearing maybe five dollars a call, with no tips. And it was hard work. He told me that there were telephone sex wars going on, and that if he survived the competition he could later raise his rates.

After I heard him do his voices, I said, "Why don't you just go on the stage and do this? You could make a lot more money that way."

But he seemed stuck in the profession he had chosen. He said, "If I did that, I'd have to have costumes and makeup, I'd have to find an agent, I'd have to go on the road, and even then I probably wouldn't break even. This way, I can run the business out of my apartment. All I need is a telephone, a bank account, some credit card processing companies and enough money to run a few ads in the newspapers and sex magazines. I'm set. As soon as I answer the phone, I'm making money."

Alex was an aging hippie, a man in his forties with wire-rimmed glasses and a fringe of hair around the ears. It was captivating to sit there and watch him do his telephone sex routine. I had to watch his face and his lips move to believe that these voices were coming out of a man's mouth—Heidi, Keiko, Mathilde, Sable, Chastity, Edwina, Hilary, Eva.

The guys who called tended to have fantasies that people would never ask for face-to-face with a prostitute: incest fantasies, rape fantasies, sex with animals—the kinds of things it would be hard for a prostitute to do in person. Alex would answer the phone in his operator's voice, get the callers' credit card numbers, ask them how much time they wanted to spend on the phone, and give them a price breakdown. Then he would tell them that Ginger or Marlene would be calling them back. He would hang up and do some quick checking. He would pull out a book of bad credit card numbers, phone books and cross directories to check addresses— and then he would call back as Ginger or Marlene: "Hi, I hear you have a very interesting fantasy . . ."

Most of the requests that were coming in were raunchier than anything I had ever been asked to do in person, raunchier than anything I had seen in any magazine. (And I've seen some pretty raunchy magazines.) One man wanted Hildegard, the tough-sounding German Alex did, to pretend over the phone to tie him up to a straight-backed chair. This guy wanted to be tied so that he was doubled over, and then he wanted Hildegard to describe how she was going to shove a salami up his ass and then turn her two Dobermans loose—to do what Dobermans would do if they were hungry and smelled salami.

Then there was one guy who wanted to have sex with his daughter. Alex said that it was amazing how many men called up saying they wanted to have sex with their daughters or their sisters or their mothers. I was listening to his conversation, and the guy was acting very nervous about calling, saying that he had been wanting to have sex with his daughter for a long time (she was now *seven*), but that he knew he shouldn't do it and he thought that, if he pretended to do it on the telephone, maybe that would end his obsession. Alex put on his sexy, little girl's voice and said, "Daddy, would you come into my room and read me a story?" And then he had the little girl seduce the caller. The man on the other end of the phone seemed to enjoy the whole thing. I don't know if it helped the guy get over his incest fantasy or not; I do know that he lived in one of the tonier suburbs of San Francisco and that he put the call on his American Express card.

I knew while I was sitting there that this was something I did not want to be involved with myself. I thought it was too weird . . . too much work for too little money. But watching Alex do it was fascinating.

*　　*　　*

The women in San Francisco were very helpful in setting me up with clients. There were a lot of limousine services that worked with the prostitutes. In San Francisco, apparently, if someone wanted drugs or girls (or anything else, one chauffeur told me), all he had to do was call certain limo companies.

One of the limo services I worked with called on a Saturday morning to ask me to do a job in L.A. There had been a request for champagne, Quaaludes, cocaine, and girls to be delivered to a visiting football team (which one was never even mentioned). Seven other women and I were picked up and driven to the airport, where we boarded a private jet. The chauffeur hopped right on the plane with us. As soon as we were airborne, Stanley passed out five crisp one-hundred-dollar bills to each of us, as routinely as a train conductor punches tickets.

When we arrived at an airport in L.A, another limousine was waiting only a few yards from the plane. We stepped off the plane and were off again, with the same chauffeur. This was *really* door-to-door service. We were driven forty miles to an enormous house with an olympic-sized swimming pool and indoor and outdoor Jacuzzis. We had been hired for the whole day. It was fun, sort of. The football players were big and stupid, but the house was great. The guys on the team were doing a *lot* of coke and booze. I personally don't find people who have been doing a lot of coke and booze to be a lot of fun; no one does unless they've been doing a lot of coke and booze too. The combination of cocaine and booze makes people talk nonsense, jabber and slur, get paranoid and absentminded, fall down and stand up all in rapid succession.

The guys would say, "Let's go swimming." We'd get undressed and then the guys would realize their coordination was not very good and they were about to drown, so it would be "Everyone out of the pool."

One of them wanted me to get in the Jacuzzi in my garter belt and stockings. I said sure. I had done it before. What were $8 stockings when I was being paid $500? But about the time I got wet in the Jacuzzi he had changed his mind and wanted a massage. Meanwhile I was standing there in wet stockings. I thought, *Puh-leez.* But one of the reasons we got paid this kind of money was because these weren't things a woman would do willingly on a date. It was tiring and irritating—about $500 worth of tiring and irritating.

People were screwing all over the house. By the time I got paid for doing a double and got my tip for the night, I had made $1,000. We didn't land in San Francisco until long after midnight. On the way back to my apartment, the limo driver showed me where he kept his stash of drugs to be delivered. Between the front seats was a trapdoor that led directly to the street. If a cop tried to stop the limo, the driver would drop the drugs through the trap-door.

The limo driver, Stanley, took my telephone number and said he would be calling me again soon for another evening. By that point, it didn't sound very appealing.

Then the Democrats blew into town and with them seventy or so prostitutes for Margo's convention. I knew that 30,000 people were expected—delegates, press, and hangers-on—so I expected to make at least a little money.

All the hookers in town had theories about why the Democratic convention was a blowout. One woman said it was because Democrats had less disposable income than Republicans. Another thought the problem was that half the delegates were women. Some women said, "Hey, they're too busy going to parties and drinking," which I thought was closer to the truth. I mean, when you're struggling for the right to run a country, it seems to me that you might not set aside a whole lot of time for sex. Sex is something you can do *after* you're running the country. And then, too, any guy who came there and wanted sex probably brought his own partner with him, either a wife or a woman hired from home. How much does it cost to bring a hooker to the convention? When you're scheming to control the fate of a nation, what's a couple of thousand dollars?

It was such a high-intensity convention, there were so many people, there was so much power being wielded, there were so many meetings, so many things being bought and sold, that people didn't have much time for extracurricular activities. But I was determined to Do the Democrats.

Since delegates weren't calling any of the services I worked with, I decided to cruise the hotels. That was the first time I felt that I was becoming too well-known to be able to work effectively. Everywhere I went either I met friends who were there as delegates or working behind the scenes or I met people I knew from the media. It's one thing to walk into a bar, sidle up to some expensively dressed man, and tell him your name is Delilah. It was another to walk into a bar and have half the room turn around and scream, "Dolores!" Not good for business.

Finally an anchorman I knew from Houston asked if I'd like to do some cocaine with him. I said, "Well, why not? But you'll have to pay me." And he promised he would. I thought we were going to go up to his room, but instead we headed out to the street and hailed a taxi. It turned out that this guy didn't actually have any cocaine on him. (He may even have thought that I had some, but I have never supplied drugs to a client.)

We spent two hours driving around, while he alternately tried to score and tried to get me to come by putting his hand up my skirt. Eventually I said, "It's very nice of you to ask me to share this cosmic experience, but I'm tired. Could you just drop me off at my place?" It was 2:00 A.M., and San Francisco closes up at midnight. When we got to my place, the guy invited himself in and then paid me a hundred dollars for the whole evening. That was the only money I made that was remotely connected to the convention.

After a while I returned to Atlanta, to begin picking up the pieces of my life. I heard about Sydney Biddle Barrows's getting busted from Claudette, who called me late at night with the news. A number of women had been picked up, but Claudette had lucked out. She hadn't been working that night. Claudette said the police were looking for Sydney and anyone who had ever had anything to do with her.

Sometimes it scares me more when I'm right than when I'm wrong. I had told the people in New York that something like this was sure to happen, but they thought they knew everything and didn't need to listen to someone from Atlanta, Georgia. They had been living like ostriches—ignorant of most of the law and believing that they were unaffected by what little bit of law they knew. Yet I didn't get any pleasure out of thinking, I was right—they got busted. I just felt it was too bad that Sydney had to learn the hard way.

I liked Sydney, and I was sorry she and the other women had been arrested. Claudette kept me posted on what was happening. I was amazed when Sydney turned herself in and then thought she could bluff her way through, saying Cachet was just an escort agency, with no sex involved. Sydney acted as though, if she said it enough times, the courts would begin to believe her. I told her that was ridiculous, she couldn't just keep on saying that escort services didn't have anything to do with sex.

In many ways I felt that year that my life and Sydney's life were on parallel tracks. She was arrested for pimping; my house burned. Something had happened to both of us that neither of us had ever considered would happen.

My invitation to Sydney's party came in the mail:

The Friends of Sydney Biddle Barrows
request the pleasure of your company
at
The Mayflower Defense Fund Ball
on Tuesday Evening, April 30
at The Limelight

Black Tie optional,
Uniform for serving officers,
Ladies need not wear tiaras.

Donation is $40 per person, with invitation.
Please arrive at the Ball by 10:30 to insure entry.

I then got a phone call from New York, saying that I had been sent the invitation out of friendship and professional courtesy but that Sydney did not want me to attend the ball, because by now I was too closely associated with prostitution. Sydney was trying to keep up appearances.

Sydney didn't take my advice; I didn't go to her ball. But Sydney came out of it all right, considering what the consequences might have been.

10

BETTER SAFE THAN SORRY

The disease [AIDS] appears to have entered the
Philippines, in many cases through prostitutes who
have had contact with servicemen near two large
American bases, the doctors said.
—*The New York Times*
November 25, 1987

I would like you to reread that quote. Do you find anything wrong with it?

The doctors blamed prostitutes in the Philippines for introducing AIDS into the country; they did not blame the American servicemen who actually brought it there. That casual misstatement is an example of how the media misrepresents prostitution and AIDS. Those Philippine prostitutes did not bring AIDS to the Philippines; they are the *victims* of AIDS.

In about 1984, stories started emerging about GIs stationed abroad contracting AIDS from prostitutes. What the press rarely bothered to mention was that most of those cases turned out to be the result of exposure to the virus through intravenous drug use or homosexuality. (The soldiers tended to tell military medical authorities that their only risky behavior had been contact with a hooker. Since both homosexuality and intravenous drug abuse are offenses against the code of military justice, admitting to either could have earned a dishonorable discharge, imprisonment, stigmatization, or loss of pensions and benefits. A GI claiming that he caught AIDS from a hooker faced none of those disadvantages.)

The press has not been very rigorous about reporting the relationships between soldiers, AIDS, and homosexuality, or soldiers, AIDS, and IV drug use, but then again the military isn't any too eager to publicize those relationships either. And so, in the good-old-boy network of doctors, the military, and male journalists, hookers get blamed for heterosexually transmitted AIDS.

Before I say any more about AIDS, let's go back three or four years to the day I got a call from the Omni International Hotel, which is a fairly fancy Atlanta hotel, with doormen dressed in top hats. Mr. Suave opened the hotel room door. A handsome man who could have stepped out of the pages of *GQ*, he was dressed in an expensive-looking tweed suit, a crisply starched shirt open at the collar, and soft, leather slip-on shoes. And when he saw me, he acted thrilled, as if I were his oldest and best friend, perhaps his fiancée.

He took my fur coat and laid it on a chair where I could see it. I noticed there was classical music on the radio. He offered me a glass of champagne, and the scene was complete.

After all the talk about champagne in this book, I have to admit right here that I don't like it very much. To me it tastes sweet and bitter and sour all at once, like medicine that has been sweetened to hide a bad taste, or like something that should be put in my car, antifreeze perhaps. It doesn't taste like something people should drink willingly.

I took a couple of sips, because it would be ungracious not to have any. The fellow introduced himself as Peter, a business consultant from Chicago who was in town to make a deal. He had a smooth voice, and he was gracious and polished and, even on closer inspection, good looking. The lights were low and the room seemed very atmospheric.

Peter had all his identification ready. Once I had looked it over, we made a deal: $200 plus the agent's fee of $65, plus the 18 percent service charge for putting it on his credit card. (The 18 percent was a laundering cost; agencies often made deals with established businesses—restaurants or equipment rental businesses—that ran escort agency credit card receipts through their accounts in exchange for a hefty cut.)

I called my agent to get an approval code on the card. (I didn't even have to tell her how long the session would be; she could tell by the amount, $312.70, that I would be there for forty minutes.) And while I was waiting for the code, Peter began telling me what he had in mind.

It had been his fantasy that a beautiful woman he had long lusted after would drop by to visit him in his suite. They would have a glass of champagne, and then he would tell her that he had been admiring her beautiful breasts and had fantasized about touching them. Contrary to being offended, the woman would look into his eyes and say, "Do you want to touch them now?"

He would say, "Yes, may I?" and she would stand up and walk toward him until she was right in front of him. Then he would reach up and caress one of her breasts through her sweater. She would grab his hand as if to shove it away, and then, instead, she would push his hand under her sweater and place it on her bare breast. "Then I'll start undressing you and finally seduce you," he said.

I had the phone to my ear while I listened to all this. "Code twenty-four," I said into the receiver. "I'll call you when I'm ready to leave. Bye." Then I turned to him and said, "Peter, I'm so glad you invited me in for a glass of champagne." I smiled seductively at him, to signal that his fantasy had begun. I was pretty sure he wasn't a cop, because I had never met a cop with such good manners. But there was something about this guy that bothered me. He was handsome and charming and I was liking the whole business too much. Listening to his fantasy while I was on the phone with my agent had actually turned me on just a little bit.

I found myself thinking, This is so nice, why should I get paid for it? And that's a very bad sign. Men hire prostitutes for a reason. As far as I could tell, this guy could have gone down to the bar and gotten almost any woman to come upstairs with him and play his scenario, for free. It was true that some guys didn't want to bother, or risk rejection, or take the chance of getting involved. But I was still suspicious.

As casually as I could, I looked around the room, to see if

there was something I was missing. I didn't see anything out of the ordinary. He started undressing me, and we went over to the bed. I moved the pillow up as if to lean against it, but what I was really doing was checking underneath for weapons, or hypodermic needles, or something that would justify my uneasiness about this erotic interlude. There was nothing.

I got up to fetch a washcloth and towel from the bathroom. I noticed that it was still a little steamy in there, as if he had just taken a shower. That made me suspicious too, because he was dressed as if he had just gotten back from work. If he had just taken a shower, why hadn't he put on casual clothes?

He smelled wonderful. He had shaved sometime in the last hour. He was clean, he even had wonderful breath. He was a damned wonderful guy, and I was getting more nervous by the minute. The lights were really low. He was still dressed, and as he leaned over to touch me I seemed to be doing a lot of passionate touching and feeling myself. But I was frisking him, something I'm quite good at. I was checking his clothes for a microphone, a gun, a knife. Nothing.

I reached for the washcloth, and he said, "Do you have to do that? It spoils the mood." He was modest as he undressed, as if he was trying to hide his penis. I honestly explained, "I know you just showered, but this is something I do with everyone, no matter how clean they are. That's so I won't feel uncomfortable, or out of practice, when I see someone who really needs to be washed. This way I don't have to pass judgment about what's hygienically acceptable."

While I was wringing out the washcloth, he started trying to kiss me. I had a hard time trying to wash him and at the same time keep my mouth away from him. I'd slipped a condom in my cheek while I was in the bathroom, so I could put it on him without his knowing—my usual procedure—and I didn't want any deep kissing. Besides, a mouth is often much dirtier than a penis.

I didn't get a chance to do my usually thorough wash job. He was insistent that we go immediately into penetration. I still had the washcloth in my hand, and he was trying to stick his penis inside me and I hadn't even gotten the rubber on him. I was trying to act passionate and at the same time to squirm away from him and not to let his penis touch me anywhere and to get my mouth down to it; he was trying to pin me down and to get his dick inside me. It really was like a scene at a drive-in movie, so I supposed the whole thing was pretty close to his fantasy of passionate seduction.

Finally I worked my head down to his crotch and sneaked the rubber on him. As soon as I did, I let him penetrate me. He was no sexual athlete, nothing like the stunt guys on Saint Thomas, but he was a passionate and seemingly sensitive lover.

Afterward, he lay on top of me and we talked. I didn't have the control I usually have when I'm on top, when I can reach down between my legs as I lift myself off of a softening penis, retrieve the condom while distracting the man's attention, and then safely dispose of it in a towel I keep near the bed.

When Peter leaped up to get a cigarette I tried to snatch the rubber, but I missed. I could see it was still dangling from his penis; he, on the other hand, seemed unaware of it.

I flipped on the little light beside the bed and reached for the wet washcloth and then motioned for him to come near me. When he sat down on the bed, I slapped the washcloth on his penis and pulled the rubber off. As soon as I did that, I could see that he had herpes lesions.

At that moment I thought, Thank God I learned how to get a rubber on a man. I immediately started interrogating myself: Did I ever touch his penis with my bare hands? With my lips? Had I touched myself with the washcloth after I touched him?

I looked at him and said, "I think you should see a doctor about that."

He looked down and said, casually, "Oh, I have."

"Do you know how contagious this is?"

Peter shrugged and said, "Well, it's in remission."

I was really pissed off. It was clearly not in remission. I could see that this whole romantic production number had been a way for him to trick me into having unprotected sex. "You knew and you didn't even suggest we use a rubber," I said. "You made every effort to make sure that we would have sex without a prophylactic."

He tried to laugh it off, as if he had put one over on me, even though he had seen me pull the rubber off of him.

I said, "Do you realize that you could put me out of work for the rest of my life, if you've infected me?" Peter, who had once been so charming, turned into a cad. "Well," he said nonchalantly, "I guess those are the risks of being in a business like yours."

"No, those are not," I said. I was so mad, I didn't say another word to him. I stood up, picked up my clothes and my fur coat, my purse and my work bag, and went straight into the bathroom. I took a new guest soap out of its wrapper, ran very hot water, and washed and scrubbed my whole body. Then I washed some more. And douched. And washed. Like someone would do after exposure to radiation.

I got dressed in the bathroom and went straight to the door, afraid to even look at him for fear of what I might do. It took every ounce of control I had not to slam the door off its hinges when I left. I felt that, if I let go, if I said another word to him or even looked at him, I would fly into a homicidal rage.

There was absolutely no doubt in my mind that he had intended to infect me, perhaps not me particularly, but to infect some woman. Ever since I had started working, I had been concerned that somebody would have a disease and be pissed off at women, perhaps blame a prostitute, and try to take it out on me.

Some people don't think of prostitutes as citizens who pay taxes, who have rights, and who deserve or will get protection under the law, much less a little consideration. Nearly all men convicted of serially murdering women confess that they practiced first on prostitutes because "I knew I could get away with it."

I immediately started thinking about filing a lawsuit against this guy if I came down with herpes. Whether I won the suit or not, I wasn't going to let him get away with it. I kept photocopies of Peter's credit card slip and his business card, in case I needed them as evidence. I had also taken down the home address on his driver's license, his driver's license number, and the name of the airline he came in on; I kept those as well.

When I got home I washed and douched some more: Betadine, vinegar, Massengill Medicated, hydrogen peroxide, even Listerine. I then injected some of a lubricant containing nonoxynol-9 that was distributed at the 1984 Hookers' Convention. I didn't know which, if any, of these chemicals would kill the herpes virus, but I knew I didn't want to take any chances. Next I went to the library and got every bit of literature I could find on herpes and sat down to read. Each article, each chapter, each passage seemed more horrifying than the last. I plotted my lawsuit against this guy, in case I came down with the disease. And I cried.

The next day I went to see my attorney and my gynecologist. My attorney said I had a good enough personal injury suit that he'd be willing to try it on contingency. He agreed that, if I'd caught herpes, I would have a shot at a sizable settlement for lost income for the rest of my life, if the jury was as outraged by my story as he was.

My doctor did a herpes test and told me that he was almost sure I had not been infected. He showed me some eight-by-ten-inch color glossy photos of herpes sores in early stages, and he listed some symptoms I could occupy my time watching for. Of course, I went back two more times to be tested, just to make sure I was negative. I certainly spent more on doctor's bills and lab tests than I made on Peter. And herpes now pales in comparison to the threat of catching AIDS.

Women made up less than 10 percent of the people in the United States who have died from AIDS as of 1987. Street prostitutes, who have a higher rate of IV drug use, have a much higher rate of infection than do call girls or women who work in the reputable brothels. A study at the University of Miami in 1987 found no positive tests for HIV infection in twenty-five female escorts studied but a 41 percent infection rate in street prostitutes.

The point of these figures is that prostitutes apparently do not catch AIDS because of multiple sexual contacts. Prostitutes seem to be positive for the HIV antibodies as a result of IV drug use or perhaps from unprotected sexual encounters with boyfriends who are IV drug users, or perhaps even from unprotected sexual encounters with clients. (Generally, the lower the socioeconomic level of the prostitute, the better the chance that she will not practice safe sex. Safe sex requires money for condoms, the time to bother insisting that clients use condoms, and some sense of a future. If a woman feels she has no future, if she instead is focusing on her next drug buy, or on getting enough money for her next meal, the threat of a disease which may strike three or more years down the road does not seem terribly important.)

If prostitutes were a source of AIDS infection in heterosexual men, there would have been a much larger increase by now in the number of cases of heterosexual AIDS not related to IV drug use or transfusion. However, the explosion of AIDS into the heterosexual community has not happened, except among IV drug users. That has not stopped people from trying to blame prostitutes for spreading AIDS.

*   *   *

| 238 |

We had talked about AIDS at the 1984 Hookers' Convention in San Francisco, and Priscilla Alexander had presented an important paper on prostitutes and AIDS. We had been talking about AIDS at these conventions long before the Centers for Disease Control started worrying about the heterosexual transmission of AIDS. We knew that, as soon as the heterosexual community became concerned about AIDS, prostitutes would be blamed. We knew that we needed to do something. Several of the women shared information about nonoxynol-9, a spermicide ingredient that some laboratories believed kills or neutralizes the AIDS virus. Hookers were talking about using nonoxynol-9 at least three years before the CDC made public the fact that it is effective against the AIDS virus.

We talked about how we women could protect ourselves and our customers. Of course, by protecting ourselves we *were* protecting our customers. We considered ways to get the word about safe sex out to as many working women as possible because, if a man frequents prostitutes, he usually frequents a lot of prostitutes. It was imperative, therefore, that we protect ourselves by doing everything in our power to see to it that AIDS did not enter the client population. And the best way to do that was to protect ourselves from people with AIDS.

One of our primary concerns at the 1984 convention was that— when faced with the threat of heterosexually transmitted AIDS— the government might try to legalize prostitution. That way prostitutes could be controlled and tested and "made safe" for clients. What worried us was that the government would end up treating prostitutes like a commodity. Certainly what we had seen of legalized prostitution in this country—the rural counties in Nevada— did not impress many of us working women as ideal. At that time, women in Nevada whorehouses were not *allowed* to use condoms. Now, with the fear of AIDS, however, prostitutes in Nevada are *required* to use condoms and have an AIDS antibody test every six weeks. That sounds all well and good. It protects the women and it protects the men, no? But I worry that the government's real concern is not protecting prostitutes at all. Why do I say that? Because if a woman is found to be AIDS antibody positive, she isn't given another kind of employment or offered worker's compensation. She is simply kicked out of the state of Nevada. And the men, meanwhile, can go to the brothels assured that the remaining women are "clean."

We had heard from women who had worked in the legal

whorehouses, and they told us that the women were treated like slaves. They had to live in a restricted area. They were not allowed to travel to Las Vegas. And they were not that well paid. They were treated more like performing circus animals than people. Which is why most politically active prostitutes are for the decriminalization of prostitution and not its legalization.

At the 1984 convention we realized that, as working prostitutes, we faced an almost insurmountable challenge. Historically, society has blamed prostitutes for spreading all kinds of disease. Syphilis was blamed on prostitutes. The plague was blamed on prostitutes. During World War I the government locked up prostitutes to protect enlisted men from VD. (The men got it anyway, apparently from amateurs or from each other.)

In this country, by some quirk, AIDS struck the gay community first. In 1984 heterosexuals were still going on their merry way, not caring or even knowing about safe sex, thinking of AIDS as something that happened to *those people*. But we prostitutes knew that, sooner or later, AIDS would spread into the heterosexual community and that when it did not only would we be blamed but, if history was any guide, we would also be arrested, quarantined, and worse.

No one could be more interested in the possibility of the heterosexual transmission of AIDS than a prostitute. So we who were active in prostitutes' rights decided to find out everything we could about the disease. Priscilla Alexander, cochair of the National Task Force on Prostitution, seemed to be the point woman.

Prostitutes' organizations started cooperating with the CDC and with private and public health agencies to get a clearer picture of how AIDS affected working women. And we traded medical papers like we had once traded Beatles bubble-gum cards.

We had a few basic questions: (1) How many prostitutes in the United States had AIDS? (2) Where had they gotten it from? (3) Did condoms provide protection from the disease? (4) What would happen to a prostitute if it was discovered that she was positive for the HIV antibodies?

The first question—a question that seemed very straightforward—in fact was not. Most of the prostitutes who were being tested for AIDS had been arrested and convicted and were in jail. They made up a very good sampling of prostitutes who had been arrested and convicted and sent to jail. They did not make up a very good sampling of prostitutes, period.

New York City claims every ten years that its actual population is being undercounted in the U.S. census, since there are so many homeless people and illegal residents—people at the bottom of the economic scale—the census takers never find. With prostitutes, there was the opposite problem. Almost the only ones who are ever studied are the ones at the bottom, the ones who end up in jail, most of them streetwalkers. We knew, according to estimates by the National Task Force on Prostitution, that the world of prostitution consisted 90 percent of women who worked at escort agencies and massage parlors, courtesans like Elaine, and women who worked in elegant bordellos, and 10 percent of streetwalkers. So when the first data came out about prostitution and AIDS, we were skeptical. As far as we could tell, the prostitutes tested had been mostly streetwalkers, and of them, virtually all those who had AIDS were IV drug users. Most of us felt that these women weren't getting AIDS in the course of their work. They were getting it from dirty needles. Even the CDC eventually chimed in with the opinion that "Seroprevalence [for HIV antibodies] among prostitutes . . . has been largely attributed to a coincidental history of IV drug abuse."

So that began to answer the second question: Where were prostitutes getting AIDS? As to the third question, well, it seemed clear that condoms provide some protection against the disease—so much so that male homosexuals were warned to begin immediately to practice safe sex. Since the HIV virus seemed so much more common among homosexual men, many of us felt, "Well, if it's good enough to protect gay men, it's good enough for us."

We had heard that it was wise to avoid lambskin condoms, as any condoms made out of a natural membrane might be permeable by the virus. And some women began using two condoms, for fear that one might break. Prostitutes all over the country, much to the dismay of some of their clients, began requiring condoms for oral sex.

We may have to wait some time for the answer to the fourth question: What will be done with prostitutes who have AIDS? Four states—Nevada, Illinois, Florida, and Georgia—immediately passed laws that required prostitutes to submit to AIDS tests. Some cities proposed the quarantine of any AIDS-infected prostitute. Seattle,

Washington, decided to force-test all women arrested for prostitution to see if they have AIDS. Several cities have proposed statutes that would require AIDS testing for anyone convicted of prostitution. The city statutes would not require AIDS testing for convicted IV drug users, rapists, child molesters, or Haitians, or for prisoners with a history of homosexuality—people who might be considered "at risk" for AIDS infection.

If a woman was tested for AIDS antibodies and found positive, some cities planned to prosecute her for endangering the lives of others if she was later caught working as a prostitute. Now that may sound like a good idea to you, but consider, for a moment, what that law means. The main effect of such a law would be to encourage an HIV-positive prostitute to move elsewhere, thus making these cities' problems someone else's problems. Does that sound like a good solution?

Let's take a worst-case scenario on those first three questions, for you moralistic doubting Thomases out there. Say that AIDS widely affected the population of female prostitutes. Say that it turned out that AIDS *was* being transmitted from client to prostitute and from prostitute to client. Say that condoms were *not* effective. That's about as bad as it can get. OK, now, what do you do about it?

Do you think that such a scenario would be the end of prostitution? Remember that prostitution has endured despite the threat of pregnancy, syphilis, and herpes, despite laws against it in every state of the union, and despite stigmatization.

What would the law do with prostitutes who tested positive for the AIDS antibody? Put them in jail for life? (Aside from the fact that it is a gross violation of human rights, just think of the impracticality of that idea. Think of the expense. And remember also that, in some states, inmates with AIDS are released into the community on humanitarian grounds, possibly to go out and infect others.) Would you quarantine prostitutes for life? Make them promise not to have sex again, for life? And if so, how?

The legal system will never be able to cope with the threat of AIDS. The only ways to deal with it are to inform people about safe sex, to provide an alternate form of employment for infected prostitutes (and I don't mean employment that pays $4.25 an hour), to provide free medical care and support for prostitutes who are AIDS sufferers, so they won't have to go out and sell sexual services to pay for medical care, and to find a vaccine for the disease and, eventually, a cure.

When people really are trying to frighten me with the possibility that I, as a prostitute, might catch AIDS, they haul up the figures on the male-to-female transmission of AIDS in Africa. Priscilla Alexander's paper on prostitution and AIDS dealt with the situation of female prostitutes in Africa quite effectively. According to Priscilla, in Africa rubbers are expensive and sex is cheap. Few prostitutes can afford to practice safe sex. There is also a male aversion to condoms in Africa, and many men refuse to frequent a prostitute who insists on condoms. The Catholic church in Africa frowns on the use of "birth control devices," including condoms. Then there is bad nutrition, low levels of medical care, and the high rate of VD infections in Africa, all of which seem to be cofactors in reducing immune response and making someone more susceptible to the disease. And last, it is my understanding that, in Africa, anal sex is often used as a form of birth control. Anal sex, most authorities agree, is the most dangerous form in terms of transmission of the AIDS virus.

I personally don't know many prostitutes in America with AIDS; I don't know any prostitutes in America with AIDS who weren't also IV drug users.

Prostitutes for the most part insist on the use of rubbers. Prostitutes, especially street prostitutes, also spend a lot of time doing oral sex, which leaves them more likely to catch the disease from a client—if no rubber is used—than to give the disease to a client. Enough said?

Because of the fear of AIDS, I get more calls for fantasy play than ever before. In fantasy play there's little or no sexual contact. Sometimes a client simply wants me to prance around in sexy lingerie or he wants to suck the toe or heel of my shoe. Sometimes he wants to be degraded or spit on. Sometimes he wants someone to talk "dirty" with him. Other times, the scenarios a man lays out would require me to be a combination of Meryl Streep, Laurie Anderson, and Nadia Comaneci.

The more obsessive and organized a client is, the better the chance that he will hand me a script when I walk in the door. This is a script I just happen to have saved. It is no more bizarre or interesting than a dozen other ones I've been given, but it is a fair sample.

"Ma'am," it started in blue ink on lined spiral-notebook paper.

"You walk into the living room fully dressed. I'll be sitting at the table completely naked. When you walk in, look around the living room, then look over and smile at me. Continue looking around the room. Walk over to the front door, and when you turn around pretend you have just noticed that I am naked. Start giggling and make a point of leaning around to look at my dick. Stand there a few minutes making a point of looking at my dick and looking at me while giggling and asking over and over, 'What do you think you're doing, boy?' Also while you giggling [sic], point at my dick and say, 'I can see your dick, stupid.' "

The script instructed me to call him a wimp and a pansy, then to grab his dick, squeeze it, and walk over to the couch and sit down. Then there was a numbered list of things I was to say to him: (1) "I've heard of pussy whipped boys, but your [sic] ridiculous." (2) "I bet you'd like to rub your big dick and your big balls against my feet and legs, wouldn't you, stupid?" (3) "Whooo-weee! Look at that dick. Do you always get a hard-on in front of girls, wimp?" I got to say twenty lines like that, more than most actresses get in five commercials.

On the third page was a list of ten things for me to do, headed "Please do the following:

"1. Prop your feet up on the table where I'm sitting and make me rub my dick and balls against your legs and feet.

"2. Also, while your feet are propped up, make me lick and kiss your feet and legs."

The list went on in this vein. Number 8 was "Make me kneel in front of you while you rub your feet against my dick and balls and then make me suck your toes and lick your feet." Number 9 was "Act like you are amused by all this. Act like you think it's terribly funny having a naked wimp at your mercy." And number 10, the all-purpose "Grap [sic] and slap and squeeze my dick while your [sic] talking to me."

Guys will sometimes say, "I can't tell my wife what I really like to do in bed," and in most cases, they're right. Wives should be grateful there are prostitutes around to take care of clients like this one, or the next.

* * *

I had been told by my agent that this would be a "fantasy" job. He was a local fellow from the suburbs who had discreetly checked into a moderately priced hotel.

When I knocked on the door, the guy opened it and looked relieved to see me, like someone grateful that the plumber has arrived because he has a bad leak. Once inside I hoisted my fantasy case up onto the bed closest to the door. I noticed that the fellow had hung a jacket over a vent near the ceiling. I noticed it for three reasons. First, it was bright blue. Second, I wondered how in the world he got high enough to have a jacket over a vent nine feet off the ground. And third, I figured it meant he was not a cop, because he was opting for secrecy and privacy. This guy was paranoid.

I asked to see his ID, and then, satisfied that he was who he said he was, I explained the fee structure to him: $65 to the agent, $200 for me. He was surprised; he had figured that $200 would cover the whole thing. "Maybe before we discuss the fee," he said, "I should explain what I want."

He had searched for a long time for this hotel room, he said. In fact, he had visited about five other hotels first, saying he wanted to see rooms because his daughter was getting married and he was looking for a place to put up wedding guests. What he had actually been looking for, he said, was a hotel that had rooms with high ceilings and a ceiling beam.

I looked up, and he was right. There, across the ceiling, was a wooden beam.

"Have you ever executed anyone?" he asked.

"What do you mean?"

He reached under the bed and pulled out a noose on the end of a long piece of rope and another, shorter, rope. Then he plopped down on the bed and looked at me, as if to say, What do you think of this?

"I have a very unusual fantasy," he said. "Have you ever hanged anyone?"

"No, I haven't," I said, "but it isn't an unusual fantasy. In fact, insurance companies pay off several times a year when someone tries it and messes up and actually kills himself. It's a pretty good idea to call someone to come in and help you," I said.

"I don't want any rope burns," he said, which struck me as pretty funny. The guy wanted to simulate an execution, but he was concerned about a little skin abrasion.

He pointed now to a hook in the ceiling. "I put that up before you got here," he said. He had gone to the hardware store and bought himself an industrial-strength eye hook.

He explained how he wanted it done.

I was to be the executioner. He told me it was common, hundreds of years ago, for the family of a condemned man to pay the executioner to make sure that the execution was done well—i.e., that the person was hanged efficiently and died quickly. Otherwise the condemned might die of strangulation and not a broken neck.

He wanted to be a spy, to be hanged for selling secrets to a foreign government. The deal was that he would pay me all the money he had—$225. But he wouldn't pay me all at once. He got up on a chair and threaded the rope through the hook in the ceiling and tested it with his weight. Then he pulled a second chair up for me. He wanted me to use the short piece of rope to tie his hands behind his back.

"I'll pay you a hundred dollars now and fifty dollars more after you put the noose around my neck," he said. "And then I'll pay you more as we go along."

This was a bit out of the ordinary, but by now you know that I'm the adventurous type. So I tied his hands behind his back and escorted him to the gallows.

"Do you want me to be a kind executioner? Or a mean executioner?"

"Oh, a mean one, who ultimately becomes kind." When I got enough money, apparently.

He wanted me to make him beg for mercy, plead for a quick and painless end. He wanted me to describe to him in detail how awful it would be if I let him strangle slowly.

What really got him off was my manipulating the rope on his neck. Switching it from one side—where it would merely strangle him—to another, where his end would be sudden and painless. He never did step off the chair, but he had a spontaneous ejaculation after I told him, near the end of my hour, and at the end of his money, "This is it. Prepare to die."

Foot fetishists, people who want me to wear costumes, people who want hand jobs, people who want me to sit with them while they watch dirty movies and jerk off, people who want to be tied up, blindfolded, spanked, people who want to wear diapers and be given a bottle—those are the kinds of calls that really picked up after AIDS came into the news, jobs with very little sexual contact and almost no genital or anal contact.

I sometimes think that these fetishes are not something a guy comes up with on his own, but something he reads about and thinks, That's so kinky, I want to try it. After *Mommie Dearest*, suddenly there were guys who wanted to be hit with wire coat hangers. If one of the sex magazines publishes a story about some strange obsession, sure enough, four or five guys will call me right away and ask for it. I wonder if anyone has an original obsession, something he arrived at on his own and not something he read about or saw in a movie.

Will AIDS be the end of prostitution? Let's put it this way: Prostitution had its leanest time in recent history in the early 1970s, when there was an explosion in dirty movies, dirty books, and nude bars. Plato's Retreat was open in New York City. Open marriage was in. Swingers were in. People practiced free love. Who needed to pay prostitutes? People were giving sex away.

There were prostitutes working then, of course, because there are always people who prefer sex with prostitutes or who can't get sex any other way.

Now, with the fear of AIDS, film companies are censoring themselves so that little or no "casual" sex takes place in stories. TV shows are cutting back on "gratuitous" sex. Some sex magazines are being withdrawn from some retail stores. Women's magazines trumpet the idea that the best sex outside marriage is no sex at all. Casual sex is much less prevalent, and the demand for prostitutes is increasing. As James Laver said in *Taste and Fashion from the French Revolution until Today*, "An epoch which is not an age of promiscuity is necessarily an age of prostitution."

When people have no other way to find sexual expression, when they can't go to a peep show or buy a dirty book, when they can't go to a bar and pick someone up for a one-night stand, they are going to turn to prostitutes. AIDS is not going to stop prostitution; on the contrary, AIDS may lead to even more prostitution.

In 1985 Mayor Andrew Young decided that the city of Atlanta needed a task force on prostitution, to help formulate laws and policy. Obviously he wanted law enforcement people on the task force, and people from the city council, and people from Midtown, an area where prostitutes worked openly. He surprised everyone, however, when he announced that he wanted me to serve on the task force too.

The task force consisted of Jackie Bowles, a sociologist who had helped us in founding HIRE; Gale Mull, an attorney I knew on the board of directors of the Georgia Civil Liberties Union; the police chief commander for Midtown, whom I also knew; my city council representative, Mary Davis; and a number of other people I had a nodding acquaintance with. I felt I was among friends, or at least colleagues, and I was warmly welcomed.

Of course, the media latched on to my involvement in the task force and made a big deal of it. Andy Young took something of a drubbing for putting me on that committee, but I think it was an honorable and brave thing to do.

Once upon a time, if I suggested using a rubber with a client, or if a client noticed that I sneaked a rubber onto him—which maybe one guy out of twenty did—he was likely to say, "We don't need to use that. You look fine to me," or "I'm sure you're the kind of person who would get herself checked," or, worst of all, "I'm sure you use rubbers with everyone else, so you don't need to use one with me."

Then AIDS hit the headlines in connection with heterosexuals. All across the country school boards started discussing teaching safe, or as it began to be called, in a bow to the abstinence lobby, "safer" sex. AIDS was in the headlines of every newspaper, certainly every women's magazine, and everyone in the whole world agreed that the only way to have casual sex was with a rubber.

Ha. At the height of the AIDS frenzy, a man noticed I had slipped a condom on his cock; he ripped it right off. He was indignant that I thought he wasn't "clean." I got indignant right back at him.

"You might know someone who has AIDS," I said, hoping to play on the flurry of paranoia.

"Nope," he said, "not a chance."

"Well I do," I said. I didn't bother to tell him I hadn't had sex with any of those people.

He put another rubber on, all by himself.

Just as I treat every customer as if he might be a cop, I treat every customer as if he might have AIDS or God knows what else. I was worried about AIDS before anyone had a name for it. It seemed to me that, if you could catch a disease just by shaking hands with someone, it stood to reason that you could get some very exotic diseases through sexual contact. There are a lot of crazy, hostile people out there. If there are people so wacky they will put cyanide into Tylenol capsules, there are people so crazy they will try to infect someone through intercourse with a serious, perhaps fatal, disease.

I have practiced a very rigorous form of safe sex for the last seven years. I always, but always, make sure each of my clients wears a prophylactic. I never touch his penis with my lips, and I never put a finger in my mouth after I have touched his penis. I never even let semen touch my cuticles; hands have a lot of cuts and abrasions and could be a possible entry point for viruses and bacteria.

I have never had a venereal disease, and considering I've worked in as many countries and under as many circumstances as I have, I'd say I'm living proof that prophylactics work.

Are men afraid of AIDS? They are now. It's gotten to the point where every session I have with a new client is an AIDS lecture. I think some men call prostitutes just so they can ask questions about AIDS.

"What do you think about this AIDS?" they'll ask. "Have you ever gotten any diseases? Have you been tested for AIDS? Do you worry about it?" If a man expresses fear of AIDS, he'll usually say, "That's why I'm paying a professional instead of picking up some girl in a bar." Men almost always wonder if *I'm* worried about catching AIDS. When I say I'm not, they act surprised. I tell them, "It's not that I'm not *concerned,* but I take all the precautions that are known to be effective." I usually explain to them that my sister is a hospice nurse in Kentucky and that she works with dying AIDS patients every day.

"My mom's a lot more worried about her coming down with AIDS than me. I am too. Being a prostitute is a lot more sanitary and less dangerous than being a nurse."

I was asked to help the Centers for Disease Control reach prostitutes in Atlanta to be tested for AIDS. (The study was to include San Francisco; Miami–Dade County; Jersey City, Newark, and Patterson in New Jersey; Los Angeles; Colorado Springs; San Juan; and Boston.) There was quite a bit of discussion about the politics of such testing. Was the CDC going to go about it honorably? Or were they looking for high percentages by testing the prostitutes most likely to be positive—street prostitutes who were ex-junkies? We decided that the only way the CDC would reach a broad spectrum of women who were working as prostitutes was if we helped them.

HIRE prepared flyers and circulars: "Free AIDS Testing for Women Only! If you are currently working as a prostitute or have exchanged any sexual services for money since 1980, you are eligible for the free AIDS testing program. You need not be working now as a prostitute to be eligible. No name, no address, no social security number. Confidential test results. The test can be done at the time and place of your choice."

One hundred and twenty women volunteered to be tested. As part of the study I took the first test. I have to admit it was scary for me, even though I had vigilantly practiced safe sex while working. (I had, however, had an affair with a bisexual, some years before.) I spent quite a bit of time thinking about what I would do if I were positive. I thought about my life, mostly, how I would spend it. I thought about Michael, my boyfriend. And last, I thought about whether I would work or not if I turned out to be positive.

Most of those questions were never answered. The answers I have now might be different from the answers I had then. The answers I will have in the future might be different from the answers I have now. I think it's one of those situations where you can't imagine what if? At least I couldn't.

Several weeks later, the results of my test came back: negative.

Only one female prostitute in Atlanta tested positive for AIDS in the survey, and that woman was an admitted IV drug user.

11

COPS AND ROBBERS

Prostitution gives her a chance to meet people. It provides fresh air and wholesome exercise and it keeps her out of trouble.
—JOSEPH HELLER
  Catch-22, 1961

No one could understand how I kept working without being arrested. My picture had been in the paper often enough—in connection with the task force, in connection with the AIDS study—that everyone in town knew who I was. Certainly, the fellows on the vice squad knew me on sight; I, in turn, had seen vice cops testify at prostitutes' trials and knew most of them on sight.

One vice cop, a guy named Ernie Hughie, called me so often that I began to recognize his voice. Ernie's quest was to get me to testify against one of my agents. This had been going on all the way back to Sarah. "Agents are just pimps," he said. "She's ripping you off, taking your money. She's just using you."

Ernie was the kind of guy who just couldn't take no for an answer. Every six months or so I would get a call from him, and the calls didn't stop when I was on the Mayor's Task Force on Prostitution.

Jimmy Webb, the Fulton County solicitor, and Daryl Adams, special agent in charge of Metro Drug and Vice, came to a meeting of the task force one day in early March. I didn't want to aggravate any hostilities, so I didn't ask any questions. But the others asked plenty. The task force wanted to know how they decided to concentrate on vice in Atlanta. Did they respond to citizen complaints? No, they said, they had never received a complaint. Why, then, someone wanted to know, did they arrest prostitutes?

Webb and Adams said: "Because prostitution is against the law." Adams seemed a little resentful that citizens were asking questions about how Drug and Vice did their job.

Before they left I thanked them for taking the time to come.

On March 27, 1985, I was called to go to the Piedmont Inn to see a dentist from Florida. I was late starting out for the appointment because I had been talking on the phone with an old friend, Rosemary Daniell, the author of *Fatal Flowers*. She called to check on me, because she had seen me on the news lately. The first words out of her mouth were, "Have you been arrested yet?"

"Not yet, but I think soon." I had reserved a rental car that day—the first time I had taken that precaution—because I had a hunch that I was going to be busted soon, and I wanted to be driving a rental car when it happened. I didn't want to go through the bother of having my own car impounded. I can't say that I knew for sure the police were closing in that night, but I felt they were going to pretty soon.

But with the call from Rosemary, I was way behind schedule. The dentist from Florida sounded ordinary enough for me not to worry about him, and I went to the appointment in my own car. I figured I'd have plenty of time to pick up the rental car after I finished with the dentist.

I got to his hotel room and everything looked OK. I said, "I understand you're a dentist," and with that I launched into a description of a concept I had, a sort of frontiers-of-dentistry idea. "You know it used to be that women only got their nails done twice in their lives, when they went to the senior prom and when they got married, but now middle-class women think nothing of getting their nails done once a week, and I see no reason why dentistry can't go the same direction," I said, and then continued, "So I think dentists need to popularize dentistry the same way nail clinics have popularized the idea of getting your nails done, by making their offices more attractive, making them easier to get into, sort of walk-in places, with soft lighting and posh decor, and people could have a standing monthly appointment to get their teeth cleaned, and while there they could get a facial and maybe a massage, and maybe even their legs waxed, make it a total-care kind of place."

I went on in this vein for about five minutes. I was really interested in this idea and had been wanting to talk to a dentist about it. I was about up to the idea of a sideline in breast implants and eyelid lifts when there was a knock on the door.

And another woman came in.

She had a fit when she saw me. She really came in swinging: "We had a deal on the phone," she said to the dentist. "A hundred and fifty-seven dollars and you never told me there was going to be someone else here."

I was pissed at him too. It was true I had been late, but I didn't like his attitude. Plus, I had been there for a while, and he had never even mentioned calling another agency.

I decided there had to be something really wrong with this guy. I said, "Just give me a cancellation fee, and I'll leave."

"I don't have any more money," he said.

"That's fine, we can put in on a credit card."

"I didn't bring any credit cards."

"You say you're in town for a dentists' convention, and now you're saying you don't have a credit card? You're lying. You haven't been honorable with either of us. I know I was late, but you could have called my agent to find out why. Besides, you didn't make a point of the time. And once you made an appointment with somebody else, don't you think you should have called my agent and canceled?"

Now the guy was playing dumb. Or at least I thought he was playing dumb. That's before I found out what he was really up to.

The other woman was still being pissy about it while I was reading him the riot act. So I picked up my bag and said to her, "Time is money, so I'm leaving. I think you ought to leave too.

There's something seriously wrong with this man. Anybody who can pull what he pulled will do anything. If you decide to stay here, you be careful, because this man is not honorable."

It didn't occur to me that he was a cop. I thought he was just a misogynistic asshole. One of the great things about being a prostitute is that, if I decide someone is being an asshole, or unpleasant or disrespectful, I don't have to put up with it. So I was feeling pretty pleased with myself when I walked out of the hotel and down the breezeway.

I was halfway to my car when two vice cops, walking stiff and trying to be cool, like second-rate Blues Brothers, came toward me and then pivoted, so that they had me surrounded: one was on one side, one on the other. I knew they were Bailey and Bartlett. I also figured I was safe. I hadn't done anything upstairs. I hadn't even discussed modeling with the dentist. I wasn't guilty of anything and I knew it; I figured they knew it too.

They asked me where I was going. (There was that question again.) I said, "To my car." Then they asked if I had seen the man in Room 331.

"Well, not in the biblical sense," I said.

"OK," Bartlett said, "we'd like to see some ID."

I laughed and said, "Sure. I'd like to see yours too, Dave."

I handed my driver's license to Bartlett and said to his partner, "We've never been formally introduced, but I believe you're Jim Bailey." He acknowledged that he was.

I said, "I'm glad we're finally meeting face to face. I've heard good things about you." He leaned back just a little and got a wary look on his face, as if I was about to claim that he fixed parking tickets. I assured him, "I just heard that your testimony is usually good. You can be counted on to tell the truth in court. So what can I do for you fellows?"

They said they just wanted to ask me a few questions, and I said, "OK, fine, but I need to call my attorney first. You want to make an appointment to see him with me?"

"No," they said.

"Well then, got to go," I said. "I'm running late. If you need me, I'm sure you've got my number."

"Wait," Jim said, hurrying now. He whipped out a card and read aloud, "You have the right to remain silent; anything you say will be used against you in a court of law. You have the right to talk to a lawyer and have him present with you while you're being questioned. If you can't afford to hire a lawyer, one will be appointed to represent you before any questioning. If you wish, you can decide at any time to exercise these rights and not answer any questions or make any statement. Do you understand each of these rights I have explained to you?"

"Are you saying I'm under arrest?" I asked. They seemed to think I was under arrest, but they didn't know for what.

I had all but forgotten about the dentist until Jim Bailey and Dave Bartlett escorted me back up to Room 331. The other woman, Sylvia, was still there, and she had mascara running down her face. I felt sorry for her. Ray Collins, the field commander of Metro Drugs and Vice, joined us at that point. I was pretty sure he was the man who had said he was from Columbus, Ohio, the man I had walked out on a couple of years before. I had seen all these Metro Drug and Vice guys before: Collins, Bailey, Bartlett . . . and Ernie Hughie. I was kicking myself for not recognizing his voice and not recognizing him. He had shaved off his beard, it was true, but I still should have known what Ernie Hughie looked like.

Ernie, the man who had called me who knew how many times and tried to get me to turn against Sarah and other agents, Ernie was the dentist from Florida.

It was like *This Is Your Life*—all these people who had been intimately involved in my life for so many years. And now we were together in one room. Swell.

Ernie was already foaming at the mouth. It was "Aha, ha, ha—I got her." He had been going to law school in his spare time, but he had failed the bar exam. Ernie was a frustrated lawyer; no wonder the other cops were leaving it up to him to find something to charge me with.

I asked if I could use the phone to call Michael, and they said no. Then I asked if I could use the phone to call my lawyer, not mentioning that my lawyer and my boyfriend were one and the same. Jim said, "You'll get a chance to call your lawyer when you're taken to Fulton County Jail."

They had already told Sylvia that she was under arrest for prostitution. They had still not figured out what to charge me with. I had only been in the room for a few minutes. I had not negotiated a fee with the dentist; I had not even discussed modeling with him. I had discussed dental clinics.

From the moment they read me my Miranda rights, I did

everything the way I was supposed to. I asked to call my lawyer and they said no. They asked me to answer questions and I told them I wanted my attorney present. There was nothing I could do to stop them.

"We need your car keys," Jim said.

"I'm sorry," I said. "You know I can't cooperate with you until I talk to my lawyer." (I knew that giving them my keys would be granting them permission to search and seize my car. I had no intention of doing that.)

"Dump out your bag," Ernie said.

"I can't do that either."

"Dump it out!"

Without saying a word, I leaned back in the chair and crossed my legs. What a little Nazi, I thought. Things were just getting better and better. I knew they were violating my rights all over the place. I wasn't trying to trick them, but I was trying to protect myself—to ask for lawyers, not to volunteer anything—and they were getting themselves in deeper and deeper. They went into a huddle about what to do next. Keep in mind that I hadn't actually been charged with anything yet.

"I thought you couldn't do that," I said, as they went through the contents of my bag. I was glad there were so many witnesses in the room.

They found some car keys in the bag and threw them down to some agents below, who tried them on my car. No good.

"You must have some other car keys," Jim said.

"Could I call my attorney now?"

"No. Give us your car keys."

"Since you won't let me call my attorney, I have no one to advise me or explain the situation to me."

They decided that my car keys must be in my pants pocket, but none of them wanted to take them from me. "Turn your pants pockets out," they said.

"I'm sorry," I said, "but I don't think I can do that."

That one really seemed to stump them, as though no one had ever refused to turn out his or her pants pockets before. Finally one of them worked up the nerve to touch my pants and slowly, inch by inch, to turn my pockets inside out without touching anything other than the cloth. The keys fell out onto the bed, and now these guys were really excited. The keys were thrown down to some officers below, and soon someone arrived at the door triumphantly carrying my big work bag.

Ernie seemed pretty pleased with this turn of events. Evidence! He dumped my bag out on the floor, to see if there was anything in it that he could charge me with. (Aha, I thought, cheering up. Another illegal search.) But when I saw all my clothes and equipment hit the floor, I was really upset. I had put everything into plastic bags, to keep it clean. I am fanatical about germs on my equipment, and here it was dumped on a hotel room floor. Ernie was down on his hands and knees on that filthy floor picking up my equipment with a towel, as if it was dirty, and I was thinking, I'll have to sterilize everything again.

Ernie was having a great time pawing through things, ripping open plastic bags, and holding things up like a kid who has never had a Christmas present. He announced each item—stockings! vibrator! earrings! dress! dildo! black shoes! pro-phy-lac-tics!—and Jim wrote it down on a list. I turned to Jim, who seemed like a nice, decent guy, and said, "Isn't it embarrassing to work with a man like that?" indicating Ernie.

"Yes, sometimes it is," he said.

Ray Collins, who seemed to be heading things up, came back into the room and stepped over Ernie like a parent walking over a kid who is putting together a toy train. He asked the very question I had been asking: "What are you going to charge her with?"

Ernie said, "I think we can charge her with contraband," indicating the things in my bag. Ray sort of sighed and said, "You can't charge somebody with possession of contraband." Ernie looked disappointed, but not for long. He yelled to someone outside the room—there must have been eight cops involved in this whole thing—"Go look up some laws. There must be *something* we can charge her with."

They must have ruffled a lot of pages in the municipal code book before they decided to charge me with "escorting without a license." They added "distribution of obscene materials" because of the dildo. And, at the last minute, someone suggested, "Go ahead and write her up for possession of marijuana and cocaine too." Those were the always popular, multifunctional state misdemeanor and felony charges. They might make a prosecutor think this was a serious offense, not something that would be thrown out of court because the charge was ridiculous ("escorting without a license").

Let me explain the bit about "distribution of obscene materials." In many places, if you are in possession of anything that has been declared obscene, from a girlie magazine to a dildo, you can be charged with distribution of obscene materials. *Distribution* in this sense meant "display." *Display* meant not only that it could be seen, but simply that it could be found. When laws like this are passed, citizens are told they will put racketeers and gangsters and child pornographers in jail. But the laws end up being used against the citizens themselves. It was apparently one of Ernie's favorite charges; he had been the cop who prosecuted *Penthouse* magazine in Georgia and tried to have them charged with the distribution of obscene materials for the Vanessa Williams pictures. (A case that he, incidentally, lost.)

A person is permitted under the First Amendment to possess obscene materials like books and magazines and videotapes, as long as they are for private use. So if I had been carrying girlie magazines, I would have been protected under First Amendment rights. But there is no First Amendment right to a dildo. Of course I had a right to privacy. It was legal to possess things like a dildo, but in Georgia a person couldn't sell a dildo or "distribute" one. I didn't think there was any chance that I could be convicted of "distributing" a dildo—which had been inside a suitcase locked in the trunk of a legally parked car—to a dentist way up in Room 331.

They took me in to the station to be "processed." There I called Michael and asked him to reach a bail bondsman. Then I called some friends and told them to strip my house. I knew what the police had done when they'd arrested Sarah. They had torn up the walls, the carpet, and even the floorboards of her house looking for things. It seemed to me that having the police search my house would be worse than the fire. So I asked my friends to get all my notes and journals and letters and literature, all my appointment books and address books, out of the house.

While destroying my house and everything in it would have been way out of line, considering the charges against me, the police had already conducted two illegal searches, made an illegal arrest, and illegally impounded my car. So I was convinced that neither the law nor my constitutional rights would stand in the way of their ripping my house apart.

The police knew that my arrest would make headlines. I was an official member of the Mayor's Task Force on Prostitution. My picture had been in the papers for weeks in connection with my work on the task force. So, from the moment I was arrested, I was not treated like a typical prostitute. And I found I had support in surprising places.

On arriving at the Fulton County Jail, the cops took me into one of those little conference booths, and soon police officers were filing in to talk to me: "Oh, I've seen you on TV. I sure am glad to meet you." One lieutenant confided, "I'll say one thing, you sure got guts. I admire you for that."

The matron who took my fingerprints and pictures, a nice black woman who reminded me of Conchata on Saint Thomas, said that, as far as she was concerned, I was a celebrity. She said, "I think what you're doing with these prostitutes' rights is the right thing. What you're saying is what every woman ought to know. There comes a time in every woman's life when she needs to know the things you're talking about." She loaned me some lipstick and a comb so I could look good for my mug shots, she let me see the pictures to make sure that I liked them, and she offered me a little jar of cream, so I could get the fingerprint ink off my hands. She said, "You try to get that off any other way, you'll just take the skin off your hands."

A clerk told me that an attorney and a bail bondsman had come for me. Bail was set at $6,500. I was out of jail before Ernie had finished processing the paperwork. They didn't search my house. All in all, it wasn't the worst experience in my life.

The day after I was arrested, I went to Michael's apartment. It was one of the few places in Atlanta where I could hide from everyone who wanted to interview me.

The *Atlanta Constitution* printed my picture with the headline "Prostitution Panel Member Arrested." Their story claimed I was charged with running an escort service as well as possessing cocaine and marijuana and distributing obscene material. My picture was on all the noon and evening news programs. I was the biggest criminal to hit Atlanta since Wayne Williams. But I was safe at Michael's apartment because almost everyone else in his building was a Vietnamese refugee. They had their own problems and didn't care about mine.

The next morning Michael and I got busy choosing my attorney. While Michael is one of the best attorneys in town, he was also my boyfriend. Attorneys rarely represent their spouses or lovers, so, although Michael agreed to supervise my case, I needed another lawyer.

Everyone in town wanted to represent me, and why not? It was a case any competent lawyer was almost sure to win; it was a case guaranteed to get a lot of publicity. A number of important political people immediately came out and declared themselves on my side. Gale Mull, the chairperson of the task force, declared that he hoped I wouldn't be removed from my position. "I'd hate to see her position jeopardized," he said, and then he went on to say how articulate and knowledgeable I was, and how valuable to the task force. Mayor Young had been contacted after the arrest, of course. He had been the one to appoint me to the task force. He was the mayor, a former congressman, a former ambassador to the UN, and an ordained minister. Anything he had to say about a prostitute would sell papers and raise ratings.

I watched him on the news, being pursued by reporters as he headed for his car. Was Dolores French going to be removed from the task force? someone asked. And Andy said, No, he wasn't going to remove me. "Why not?" the reporter persisted. Andy said, "What we need is some expert knowledge. Nobody else has come forward and admitted they have expert knowledge."

He stated the obvious, that I was innocent until proven guilty, and when someone pressed him for an opinion on my arrest he snapped, "She was just doing her job." It was hot copy.

Michael and I decided that Bruce Morris was the best defense lawyer in Atlanta, besides Michael, of course. Bruce made a motion to postpone my court appearance until he could familiarize himself with the case. The prosecutor agreed to the continuance and told the judge so in court. But the calendar had already been called, and a "failure to appear" warrant was issued for my arrest. At that point reporters ran out of the building to write their headline stories: "Dolores French, Fugitive."

The papers and the evening news blared the story about my being a fugitive from justice. It was a frightening experience for me to be lying in bed, thinking that I had handled everything pretty well, and then see a news bulletin flash on the screen with my picture and the word *Fugitive*.

I decided the only reasonable way to cope with all the journalists trying to interview me was to hold a press conference.

I looked forward to going to my own media event about as much as someone looks forward to a long and tedious dinner with a rich aunt whose hobby is cutting her in and out of her will. It wasn't as bad as being, say, electrocuted, but it wasn't the way I would have chosen to spend my time either. But it was important that I not disappear or give the appearance of retreating from my stand on prostitutes' rights. I figured that if I stood up and said, publicly, "I've been arrested, but so what? I'm still alive," some women out there wouldn't feel their lives were over because some person who'd flashed a badge had read them their Miranda rights.

Between arraignment and my hearing I saw clients. After all, I had to raise money to pay for all this. I wasn't too concerned about being arrested again because the vice squad either believed they had a solid case against me or didn't. If they realized what a bad arrest they'd made, they probably wouldn't want to stir up more publicity.

The "escorting without a license" case was heard in city court. The drug and distributing obscene materials charges were being tried separately, since they were misdemeanor and felony charges and were to be handled by the state. And, since the issue of illegal search was based on whether the city could get a conviction on their charges, the prosecutor, Christina Craddock, didn't want to proceed on the state charges until the city case was over.

Before the hearing could begin, we had to move to a larger courtroom because we had so many spectators. On April 11, 1985, Ernie Hughie, Dave Bartlett, and a guy from the city licensing bureau showed up in the Municipal Court for the City of Atlanta.

Ernie originally stated that he had called an escort agency, "Adventurous Coeds"; that the agency had said they would send him an "escort"; and that I had introduced myself as his "date." After my lawyers "refreshed" Ernie's memory with the tape I had made when he called me and scheduled the appointment, Ernie admitted that my agent and I had described me as a model and not as an escort or date.

Then Bruce Morris questioned Ernie closely on why Dave Bartlett and Jim Bailey had arrested me when I left the hotel room. I had only been there ten minutes. Was there a signal Ernie was supposed to use, to indicate that something illegal had happened in the room?

The answer was no.

Bruce asked if it had been prearranged, then, that when I left the hotel I was to be detained and arrested, regardless of what was said (or done) in the room.

"She would be arrested if the circumstances warranted it," Ernie said.

"What were those circumstances?" Bruce asked.

"Just certain different things," Ernie said, displaying his usual flair.

Bruce went a few more rounds with Ernie on the business of

why I was arrested. He asked Ernie on the stand, "You said if circumstances warranted it and if the crime were committed. Could you tell me what you mean by that?"

"No, sir, I can't."

"You don't know?" Bruce asked.

"Well, there are various things that can occur that would be a crime," Ernie said. "If Miss French had propositioned me for sex or money, then, of course, she would have been arrested for prostitution."

"That did not occur, is that correct?" Bruce asked.

"That's correct."

Ernie may have been dumb, but he wasn't stupid. He could see that Bruce was getting around to the very interesting point that, if I had been arrested outside the hotel, the officers couldn't have known that I had committed a crime. So Ernie now amended his testimony to say that the officers had agreed to "detain" me when I left the hotel room and to bring me back to the room, where they could "go over the code section" before they actually advised me that I was under arrest.

Then Bruce led Ernie through the search and seizure part of his testimony. Did Ernie know what was in my work bag, or had I told him or offered to show him what was in it before he opened it? Did he know what was in my purse before he examined the contents? Did he have a search warrant to go through my bag or my purse? Did I give him permission to go through my bag or my purse? Did they have my permission to search my car?

No, no, no, no, and no.

Bruce asked him if I had ever touched any of his private parts and explained that he was using that term as expansively as Ernie would like it to be used. Ernie said no. Bruce asked if we had ever discussed money, or exchanged money, or if I had asked Ernie to accompany me anywhere, and again Ernie answered no, no, and no.

And then Bruce got Ernie to admit that he had never before, in a long career with the vice squad, arrested anyone for being an escort without a license.

When Detective W. M. Frederick took the stand, he explained that, as a license investigator for the License and Permit Section of the Bureau of Police Services, he had not issued a license for an escort in 1985, nor had there been any licenses issued in 1984, and there had been only one application for an escort's license, in

1983, which was turned down. He also answered that there had been no prosecutions for escorting without a license as far back as he could recall, at least to 1982.

In closing, Bruce argued that there had been no discussion of sex, that there had been no discussion of money except for a cancellation fee, that Ernie and I had never touched during those few minutes I was in the room nor was any form of the word *escort* ever used, that Detective Fredericks had testified that no escorting licenses were being issued, and that it was not illegal to "model" without a license. Michael argued that Ernie and the other officers were not city of Atlanta police officers and were therefore not allowed to arrest anyone for a violation of a city ordinance. The prosecutor made a batch of motions. My lawyers made a batch of motions, including that the judge give a directed verdict of acquittal, which she turned down.

The judge said she was not going to make any immediate rulings on the other motions, and she adjourned court.

Michael and Bruce and I walked out of the courtroom and sort of sagged against the stairway railing. So much had been at stake, so much had happened, and then again, nothing had happened. It was obvious to me, at least, that the city couldn't win their case, but it also seemed that they were perfectly willing to pursue it for as long as Georgia was a sovereign state, and that I would have to pay huge lawyers' fees if this thing went on to a trial and a state case. We had to figure some way to keep the prosecutor from pursuing the case to the point where it would put me in the poorhouse. We knew that the city had itself in a bind, but that the prosecutor wouldn't just drop the charges, which would (a) be embarrassing in a case that had gotten so much publicity, and (b) give me a chance to sue everyone involved. The city had no intention of letting that happen.

"What do we do now?" I asked.

"Well," Michael joked, "we could always file a petition for interlocutory writ of certiorari."

"What's that?"

Bruce said, "Dolores, there's no such thing."

"Come on, guys, what is it?"

"It's an appeal, but it only applies in state and superior court cases," Michael said.

"What does it appeal for?"

Michael and Bruce gave the kind of arguments that through-out my life have been a sure sign of victory: "It won't work." "It's never been done." "You'll be laughed out of the courtroom."

"That's what they said to Columbus," I said.

"And he died in jail," Bruce answered.

"Better prison than the poorhouse," I said. "Now tell me how this writ of whatever-it-is works."

Michael and Bruce explained that even though there was no such thing, this was the way it would work if it existed: It would be an appeal for a nonfinal judgment from a lower court to a superior court. The judge on my case would have to authorize the writ. A judge from the superior court would have to approve the filing of the writ. A third judge would have to rule on the merits of the writ. Anything that involved three judges and two courts was bound to take up a lot of time, create a lot of paperwork and stress, and just might ball things up enough to entangle the case forever, a sort of *Bleak House* maneuver.

"Let's do it," I said.

One of the things I try to make clear to prostitutes is that, when they hire an attorney, the attorney works for them. People often pay their lawyers huge amounts of money and then do whatever the lawyers say. But when you're paying a lawyer, you're paying for advice and service. The lawyer isn't going to go to jail for you if you lose, or continue to represent you after your money is gone. So I said, "I really mean it. Let's do the writ. And if there's no such thing, all the better. That will really confuse them. Which one of you is going to write it up?"

Michael researched and wrote up the writ and presented it to our judge, who then authorized it. The presiding judge in Fulton County approved it for filing, and then Michael filed the petition that said that our judge and the city had thirty days to answer the writ, for which there could be no response. We think the prosecutor on my case spent those thirty days digging through law books trying to figure out what these two hotshot lawyers were pulling.

If there was no response in thirty days, the writ-which-dare-not-speak-its-name could be dismissed. Neither the city nor the judge responded. The writ came up to the presiding superior court judge, and he ordered the city and our judge to respond within thirty more days. Twenty days after that, sometime in November, Michael got a letter from the judge on our case, directing him to remand the case back to her court so she could dismiss it. (We assume that the judge reviewed my case and the law, after which she decided we were right. We also assume that our writ gave her the time to do that.)

When Michael got the message, he called our judge and said, "Is this a joke?"

"Certainly not," she answered.

Michael said, "Well, I'll have to dismiss the interlocutory writ of certiorari, so we can get the case back to your courtroom." The judge apparently sounded relieved about that. Michael called the state prosecutor's office, and they said that they weren't going to proceed on the cocaine and marijuana and distribution of obscene materials charges if the city case was dismissed. (The state had apparently decided on its own that this was a dog of a case.)

Michael dismissed the "Defendant's Petition for Interlocutory Writ of Certiorari," and the judge dismissed my case.

I was asked if I would sign an agreement stating that I wouldn't sue anybody for what had happened—the arresting officers or their subordinates or their superiors. In exchange for my signing that piece of paper, I got my bags and their contents back. The state agreed not to prosecute me for any charges arising out of these arrests.

Between the hearing and the judge's dismissing my case, I married my lawyer. Michael and I were headed for San Francisco for a hookers' convention. On the way there our plane made an unscheduled stop in Las Vegas. "Let's get married," we said. Unfortunately our plane took off again before we could schedule an appointment at one of those rented-veil wedding parlors.

As it turned out, Gloria Lockett, a COYOTE member, was also a minister. She offered to marry us, and we took her up on the offer. Michael and I made up a list of things we would try to do within the marriage. I thought Michael gave himself an impossibly long list, and I told him so. The main request I had of him was that he not take on the defense of rapists. His main request for me was that I not behave rudely with waiters. We were married at Coit Tower, which meant we could buy a lot of postcards to tell all of our friends.

The first time I said I was Michael's wife was when I was called for jury duty in Atlanta. When I was questioned by the assistant prosecutor, he glossed over the fact that I had put down "prostitute" on my juror's questionnaire, but he was worried about my being married to a defense lawyer. Carole Wall, the lead prosecutor, had it on good faith that I was inclined in a purse snatching case toward the prosecution. (As far as I was concerned the defendants had purse snatchers written all over them.) But Carole's assistant was naive enough to think that the wife of a defense attorney would side with the defense. I was excused.

Michael and I often end up in social situations with prosecutors and cops. I sometimes have to be careful not to be seen fraternizing too much with the prosecutors, because their superiors think it looks improper.

Sometimes people don't know that Michael is married to me. The second month into a seven-month drug trial, Michael happened to mention to one of his co-counselors, Mark Spix, that his wife had once been arrested.

"For what?" Spix asked.

Michael told him, and he said, "You've got to be kidding."

Then he told Spix my name, and Spix was surprised. (Mark Spix has since become one of Michael's closest friends.)

In general Michael hasn't had any negative reaction from the bench or the bar as a consequence of being married to me, except for the occasional expression of surprise. Otherwise, being married to a prostitute has done him more good than harm. Though I'm notorious in Atlanta, I'm respected.

Michael was elected vice-president of the Georgia Civil Liberties Union in 1987, and that organization is one of the last places anyone would act offended by what I do for a living. When he was hired as general counsel for AID Atlanta, a service agency for people with AIDS, however, some people there expressed shock that he was married to me. He lives with it, and I live with him being a defense attorney. In fact, as he says, our jobs are quite similar: We both free-lance, we both get paid in advance, we both try to get our clients off.

Michael understands my job. He understands that I am not emotionally involved with my clients.

There are things about my job, however, that trouble him. He worries every time I leave the house because I might not be coming back. He worries about lunatics more than I do.

Gina, my new agent, called me about one-thirty in the morning and asked if I minded driving all the way out to a suburb to see a client. "That depends," I said. "What have you got?"

She told me, "He's looking for someone tall, with a pretty face."

"That's me," I said.

"That's why I called you," she said. She told me his name and said that he had given his father's address in a small town outside Atlanta. "He sounds real young and nice," she said. "Call me back and let me know what happens."

I called him and said, "My agent told me you were looking for a tall model with a pretty face."

"Is your face pretty?"

"My face is beautiful, but I'm worried that I might not be tall enough. I'm only five five and a half, maybe five six at best. But when I wear heels I can appear much taller. So if that's OK, I can finish telling you what I look like, and then we can discuss where you're located."

"Fine," he said.

"I've got reddish-blonde hair, curly, about shoulder length. My measurements are about thirty-eight–twenty-eight–thirty-nine. I'm very light complected, with green eyes, and I'm twenty-eight years old." (This description of myself was not completely accurate. But I had found that this was the way most clients perceived me, so it was best to fudge things. My bust, for instance, is really about 40 inches, but I have a broad back and if I say 40-28-39, they expect someone more voluptuous. And I was really thirty-five years old, but I looked twenty-eight. Besides, if I'd said I was thirty-five, people would have expected me to actually be forty-five. Once you say you're any age over thirty, a lot of clients believe you're much, much older and are trying to shave a decade or so off, so I couldn't win by being accurate about my age. Other than that, the description was true.)

"I understand you live in ———," I said, and I named the town his parents lived in. "Yeah, but I go to college in Michigan," he said. "It's school break and they're real religious. It's important for them to have family together for Easter."

"But it's not Easter," I said.

"Well, no, but I can't be here for Easter, so I came home now."

"Why did you check into a hotel?" I asked.

"So I could do this," he said.

I didn't have any trouble finding the hotel because I had been there once before, with Tyler, my second client. It was a cheap hotel, the kind of place where I'd heard of women being robbed, so I was cautious when I pulled into the parking lot. I considered taking off all my jewelry and locking it in the glove compartment, but then I decided this was the kind of place where the car might be broken into, so I decided I was better off wearing it.

Before I got out of the car, I gave a quick look all around at the outside of the building, to make sure there weren't any undesirables lurking about. An exceptionally clean-cut young blond guy was standing on the hotel balcony, wearing no jacket, just in his shirtsleeves, and it seemed likely to me that he was my client.

As I got closer to him I noticed his nervous smile and his glittering eyes and thought he had been doing cocaine. "Delilah?" he said, "I thought you weren't coming. You do have a pretty face. Just what I had in mind."

He stopped in front of an open door, which had the room number I had been given on it. He indicated that I should go in. As soon as I stood at the threshold I felt afraid. The room was completely dark, which was unusual. The bed covers were slightly messed up, but not the way they would look if someone had slept on them or even sat on them. Nothing that belonged to him was in the room. People usually lay something on the dresser or the nightstand as soon as they go into a rented room: a pack of cigarettes, a set of keys, spare change, something to mark the space as their own. There was a towel on the air conditioner and another one, refolded, on the dresser. The TV wasn't on, and the bathroom light wasn't on either. The whole thing was strange.

Since he was still standing outside, between me and the stairs, I decided to step inside and then get out of there the minute he turned his back.

"Sorry I kept you waiting," I said. "It must have been cold out there."

"Nah, it's not bad," he said, and turned toward the bathroom. I figured that was my chance. I reached for the doorknob with my right hand and turned toward the door, so I could slip out of the smallest space possible when I pulled the door open. Then I glanced back to see what he was doing and stood, face to face, with the barrel of a shotgun.

In a vicious voice he said, "Get away from the door."

I jumped back, but there was a chair in the way that I almost fell over. Things cascaded through my mind: Why hadn't I left my jewelry in the car? Why did I think a blond, young kid wouldn't rob me? Why hadn't I just told the agent that I wanted to go to sleep tonight? What does this guy want? Why did I have to wear so many diamonds? Out loud I said, "Jesus Christ, I've heard about this sort of thing happening, and I never wanted to find out what it felt like." I thought, What'll he do if he can't get my ring off? Surely he's not going to kill me.

My foremost thought was, What am I going to do to get out of this alive? He was leaning against the door now, and the door was my only way out.

I inched closer to the door, which meant inching closer to him. "Get back," he said, and I backed up maybe three inches. I still had my car keys in my hand, and I could hear them jingling, my hand was shaking so hard.

"What's in your hand?" he asked.

"My keys, see? I'm sorry they're making so much noise. I'm shaking. I don't know how to stop."

He was shaking too. I didn't want him to get carried away and accidentally pull the trigger, so I dropped my keys into my bag, held up my empty hands, and said, "See, they're in my purse."

I kept my hands up until he said, "OK, put them down." I immediately grabbed the doorknob and tested the door to see if it was locked. As soon as I found out he hadn't locked the door, I determined that the one thing I would not do was let go of the doorknob.

"Get across the room!" he said.

"No, I think I'd better leave now," I answered, keeping my voice as natural as I could.

"You're not going anywhere. Get across the room."

"Why should I do that?"

"Because I said so."

"No," I said. "I'm not going to do that. I've got to go." I knew he was too small to physically force me across the room. I think it stumped him that I wasn't doing what he said. "Please don't shoot me," I said, to fill a pause of several seconds. I didn't want him having any time to think.

"I don't want to hurt you," he answered. "I'm not going to hurt you if you just get across the room."

Was this a Mexican standoff or what? I had no intention of letting go of that door and, since going across the room would mean letting go of the door, I had no intention of going across the room.

I tried a new tack. I didn't think he was planning to rape me, and he hadn't said anything about me giving him my cash and my jewelry. Since he didn't say what he was doing, I decided to ask: "What do you want from me?"

"I want you to get across the room," he said.

The circularity of all this was scaring me. I was terrified that this kid was going to pull the trigger by accident and that I'd have a shotgun going off in my face. At best I would be maimed for life and out of work. At worst I'd be dead. I told him, "I've never been so scared in my life."

"You should be. Now get over there so I don't have to hurt you."

I thought, I'm too scared to keep this up. "Why don't you call someone else who has more experience with this?" I mean, after all, what do you say to a potential psychotic killer?

"Come on now," he said, "you're really pissing me off. I'm getting mad now, and I might have to hurt you. So do what I say."

"Why are you doing this?" I asked. "Why all of this? Why the gun? Why do you want me to go over there?"

"This is just a fantasy of mine," he whined. "I just want to have some fun with you. Please go over there so we can get on with it."

"This is *fun*?" I said. "I'm not having any fun." I tried to pull my voice together, and then I said, "Let me explain something. This cannot work. I will never go across the room or do anything else you tell me, is that clear? You planned this badly. So just let me get out of here and let's forget the whole thing." That sounded pretty good to me, and I half expected him to open the door and say, "OK."

"No," he said, "you'll call the police."

"I will not call the police. I just want to leave."

He said, "You're going to do what I say," but he was beginning to sound panicked. "I'll pay you your fee," he said.

"When?"

"When you get over there."

"If you're going to pay me, pay me now," I said. "Then we can talk about what you have in mind."

"If I go get my money, you'll leave," he said.

No shit, I thought. "You can't get away with this," I said. "My agent will be looking for me soon, and if she can't find me, she'll send someone to look for me." That was a lie. Because I was tired, I had not called my agent before I arrived. It would be at least half an hour before anyone missed me. I knew I couldn't hold this maniac off for that long. This guy really did seem crazy enough to kill me.

I took a deep breath and determined some goals: (1) to get out of the room; (2) not to get killed; (3) not to be seriously hurt; (4) to do all that without killing the kid; and (5) to do all that without tearing my clothes or getting them dirty.

I took a good look at his face, which I knew Michael would want me to do in case I lived long enough to get a chance to identify this guy in a police lineup, and I studied the way he was holding the gun, so that if I got the gun away from him, I would know how to hold it.

"I'll be finished long before anyone even misses you," he said, and I knew I had to act right away. I gave the door a good, hard yank, hoping that the jolt wouldn't make the gun go off. He slammed the door shut again and reached for the chain lock.

The minute his right hand left the shotgun I grabbed the barrel and pushed it up toward the ceiling and grabbed the stock with my other hand, while screaming, "Give me that gun, you little son of a bitch!"

I shoved him off balance, then jerked the gun out of his hands. Now, with the gun on him, I backed up about five feet, until I was in front of the air conditioner. "Get away from the window," he said. "Someone might see you."

What a great idea. I flipped the light on and pulled the curtains back with my elbow, hoping someone in this godforsaken place might notice a woman at the window holding a shotgun. "Now get away from the door," I said. "Move over there."

"You'll call the police," he whined. Nuts are so single-minded. When he reached for the door, I figured he was going to pull it open and run out. No such luck. He finished the job of locking the door.

"Considering that I've got the gun, I think the police are the least of your problems," I said. I was so scared, I started screaming, "Get away from the door. Get away from the door or I'll kill you, you stupid little bastard." He started to move, and I braced the shotgun against my shoulder, the way I'd seen my father do when he was shooting rabbits.

The guy started backing up, and I started inching toward the door. I braced the gun with my knee, while I tried now to get the door unlocked. He came toward me, and I screamed, "Get back!"

He went to the bed and sat down, and the next thing I knew he was coming at me with a butterfly knife with a three-inch blade. "Give me the gun," he said.

"Are you nuts? I'm holding a gun on you," I said.

"It's not loaded," he answered, with a smile. "Do you think I'd let you take a loaded gun away from me." He started sauntering around the room, in a nya-nya-nya-nya-nya way. "Now I've got a knife and you've got an unloaded shotgun. What do you think of that?"

I thought he might be telling the truth. I just wanted out of that room. I turned to the door and started struggling with the lock again. He lunged across the room and grabbed the gun out of my hands. "You're pretty interested in a gun that isn't loaded," I said.

"I'd be crazy not to have a loaded gun," he snarled. "Now get over there, where I told you."

We were at square one again. But if I had gotten the gun away from him once, I was sure I could get it again.

This time I wasn't so careful or calculating. "This is ridiculous," I screamed. "I've had enough." I grabbed the barrel and then the stock. We wrestled around for a while, and I kept up a scream of "Who do you think you are, you blankety-blank so-and-so?" I think he tripped over the chair near the door. In any case, I suddenly had the gun again.

"If you pull one more stunt, I'll kill you right where you stand," I said. "Now get out of my way."

He stood up, but he was still between me and the door.

"Don't just stand there to see whether or not I pull the trigger," I said. "Because I will. It's over."

He slumped his shoulders and walked away from the door. "Go on, get out of here," he said.

I went to the door and got it open even though I still felt totally out of control. I then turned around, and holding the gun on him, backed out of the room. I stumbled halfway out and dropped my lingerie bag, which I was surprised to realize was still over my shoulder. When I knelt down to pick up my things I noticed that he was standing at the dresser, doing a line of cocaine. I started backing away from the open door, then stopped and put the gun down for fear I'd be charged with stealing it. Then I ran down the balcony, down the stairs, and to my car.

My hands were shaking so hard I could barely get the key in the lock. Finally I opened the door, threw my things and myself in, slammed the door, and just sat there for a few moments. Then I started the car and backed up to where I could see his room.

In a few seconds he came running out of the open door and down the stairwell. I moved the car forward now, to see where he would go. He dashed from the stairwell to a small light blue car, opened the trunk and threw something in, then got in the car and roared off. I got the last four digits of the license number as he went by me.

He drove up and over a hill about a hundred yards away, and I decided to let him go. I sat and shook for a few minutes, then drove to the motel office to use the pay telephone.

I called Gina at the agency to let her know what had happened and to tell her that I was going to report it to the police. Then I called Michael. I knew he was asleep, so when he answered, after about the twentieth ring, I said, "Michael, wake up and be alert."

He said, "OK, what's going on?"

I told him what had happened and said I was going to call the police. And then I called the police. I told them what happened and gave the dispatcher a description of the car. I told them where I was, who I was, what room I had been in, and she said a patrol car would come out.

Right away, a "seasoned" cop arrived, and he wouldn't even get out of the car. He said, "Well, little lady, if you're going to be out at this time of night alone, you gotta expect this sort of thing will happen to you once in a while."

Some younger cops, who had obviously been through some kind of sensitivity training, arrived then and went to the room with me. They found cocaine residue on the table. They took fingerprints, and my statement, and they found two pairs of handcuffs, one at the head of the bed and the other at the foot. Who knew what that guy had planned for me?

I did suggest that, if they thought the guy might have broken some law, they might want to radio a description of his car so that somebody might detain him. They said they'd get around to it.

The next day I went in to swear out a warrant. I felt it was important that I follow through, so the police could get used to the idea of a prostitute pressing charges. I told them that I worked with an escort service and that this guy had asked for someone with a pretty face. The police treated me like a criminal. The detective kept implying that I'd had sex with my assailant. I said, "You know who I am. You know I'm a prostitute. If I'd had sex with the guy, why do you think I would come down here?"

"Well," the cop said, "it could be for publicity."

When that guy pulled the shotgun on me, I knew I had to deal with it. It was a far cry from the way I felt six years before in the Caribbean, when Buddy offered me a pistol and I turned him down.

Six years ago I couldn't have taken that gun away from that kid. I suppose that means that in some sense I've gotten stronger as a result of being a prostitute, but it also means I've gotten smarter and more capable and less afraid of a lot of things. Nobody was going to jump out of the woodwork to save me in that motel room. I had no backup team ready to kick in the door. I had to take care of myself and I did.

After all, I was fighting for my life, and all the coke freak was fighting for was a good time.

Now that it's happened, I know what I have to do if there's a next time. And I know I can do what I have to do next time.

Most people could not cope with being a prostitute. Not because it's degrading or dirty but because it's hard work. It's a business that can be frightening and dangerous. It's especially hard on your friends and your mother and your husband, if you're open about your work.

My friends have had to come up with a lot of answers, both for themselves and for the rest of the world. Most of them, however, have stuck with me through my earliest days, through the fire, through the arrest, through writing this book and everything else.

My family supported me all along, after they recovered from their first surprise. My father is ill now, with cancer; he's not the same old Dad. And yet, and yet, he is still proud of his little girl. I suppose I will always be, in some way, Little Miss Ferncreek to him.

Michael and I are still renovating my house, trying to cope with the aftereffects of the fire. I still speak at community meetings and mental health groups and hospitals and universities. I am often asked, in these days of safer sex lectures, to demonstrate how to blow a rubber onto a banana—how's that for a party trick?

I still work with agents wherever I am, and I'm sure the cops are still trying to arrest me. They may even make a real case next time. But I want to keep working, and I want to find out about new places. Sometimes I wonder what it would be like to work at one of the legal brothels in Nevada. I've never worked in Alaska. And I wonder about Hong Kong and Bangkok too. If the police start closing in on me again, I may just find out. As Mae West said, "Between two evils, I always pick the one I've never tried before."

When I don't work I miss the life. I miss the camaraderie of the women I work with. I miss the work itself. I miss the solitude of the drive in my car to a new client. I miss meeting people from all over the world and finding out what they think about things.

There are people who seek me out simply because I am a well-known prostitute, and they include other prostitutes as well as clients and fans. I have a terrible time with housekeepers, however. Once they get the hang of what I do for a living, they quit cleaning houses and begin working as prostitutes, at which occupation they can earn more money.

Sunny works with me here in Atlanta on AIDS research. Elaine disappeared. Margo St. James has moved to France, which she feels is a friendlier country for prostitutes. Ernie is now a carpet salesman. I still wonder what happened to Sarah, and if that girl Amanda, who came down to the Caribbean, ever got any more sense. I look forward to meeting more women like them, even more women like Amanda—although not too many. And I expect I will meet these women at COYOTE conventions and at International World Whores' Congresses like the one held two years ago in the European Parliament Building in Brussels.

Most people are fascinated by the idea of becoming a prostitute; even if it's only a fleeting fantasy, a lot of people have thought about doing it. But unless a person has been a prostitute, it's a choice of career that is difficult to understand.

Some people do criticize me. But then again anyone in a public position—a weather forecaster, for instance, or a professional football player—gets criticism. The key to being happy and successful in any career is having a job you are suited to. Football players are suited to playing football. Meteorologists are suited to being weather forecasters. I am suited to being a prostitute.

I am not inhibited about sex, but that's a very small part of the job. Most of the job involves dealing with people: the other women, my agents, my clients, the police.

Even when I'm bored or when I have other things on my mind, I still feel spiritually uplifted by the work. I am improving the quality of my clients' lives, and the lives of the people around them. I am good at this job. So good that even when I can't give 100 percent, I still have a positive effect on my clients. I'm not selling magazine subscriptions to people who can't read; I'm not selling miracle cures to people who are desperately ill. I'm doing more than people pay me to do.

I am often recognized on the street in Atlanta, but oddly enough people rarely recognize me when I'm working. Sometimes a client will tell me, "You know, you look familiar," and I usually just smile.

A few people, of course, try to call me up after they see my name in the paper. Sometimes clients track me down through the media, or even through city hall. I explain to anyone who calls me under those circumstances that I will see them, if their IDs and credit cards check out, but that I will only model. There's too much of a risk that they will turn out to be cops, you see. I make it clear, so that they will understand: There will be a $60 appointment fee, and then $200 for an hour of my time, but all I will do is model. No sexual contact.

I often get calls from retired men, who have been sitting around and watching morning talk shows on TV. Widowed, older men make lovely clients. One man who contacted me is a retired journalist. One of his hobbies is photography—capturing prize blossoms and fruit at their peak—so he always wants a photo session. During the hour I usually make several lingerie changes and strike dozens of poses while he shoots my picture and gives me gardening tips. No sex takes place, he has some company and some titillation, and I hope that, with his good advice, my bearded irises will bloom next spring. I provide an important service for him, and we both benefit. It's a fine way to make a living.

Recently I got a call from my agent, Diana, to see a client at one of the airport hotels. When I called him, he seemed like a really happy-go-lucky guy, a good old boy, the kind of guy who might do magic tricks at parties. He told me he was a traveling salesman, a parts salesman, and that he was in town from Raleigh, North Carolina.

When I told him that I would be there in twenty minutes, he acted thrilled that I'd be arriving so soon. When he opened the door, he did a double take, his eyes kind of crinkled up and flashed, and he said, "I know you! I've seen your picture. I can't believe this. Don't tell me your name. I've seen you! You're that . . . don't tell me your name. Oh, my God, I'm embarrassed. I can't believe it's you. You're beautiful, and you look just like your pictures. Oh, wow!"

I was still standing in the hall, and I said, "OK, great! Can I come in now?" He was about five foot eight and Scotch-Irish looking, with blond-brown hair, a real cute pudgy guy, about what you'd expect of a parts salesman. The kind of fellow who makes you want to reach up and squeeze his cheeks.

I set my bag down and he was still carrying on.

"This is the most amazing thing that's ever happened to me," he said. "Oh, wow! I know your name. I really do."

"While you're trying to think of who I am, I'm going to call my agent, OK?" I called Diana and told her everything seemed fine and then I turned back to this fellow, Ralph, and said, "You know I need to see some ID."

"Yeah, yeah, yeah." He was hopping around the room, looking for his wallet, fumbling around. "Your name's on the tip of my tongue. Just hold on. I'll think of it. It's an old-fashioned name."

"It's really nice to run into a fan," I said. "You know, I just picked up some copies of a photo of me that appeared in a magazine. Do you want to see them?" I pulled out twenty prints. "You can see them if you want, but I've got to warn you, they have my name on them. Do you want to see them, or do you want to keep guessing?"

"Oh, let me see. Gee, this is so exciting. Who would ever think a thing like this would happen to me? Dolores! Dolores French! I knew it! They're great pictures. They look just like you," he said. "Can I have one? Will you autograph it?"

I said, "Sure," and I got my pen. "Dear Ralph," I wrote, "You were great. Thanks for the memories. Call me anytime." And I signed it, "Dolores." He took it and was looking at it like a kid who has just gotten an autographed baseball card from Mickey Mantle.

"Wow, look at this!"

I said, looking at my watch, "You know I need to get my agency fee."

"Right, right, right," he said. "I can't believe I'm really going to do this, and not with just any hooker, but with you." He said, "You know I've never called an escort service before in my life. It's like the lottery. I've hit the jackpot. I've really hit the jackpot."

"Well," I said, "hitting the jackpot is going to cost you sixty dollars for the agent's fee. The model gets no part of the agent's fee. The model's fee varies according to the type of session you have in mind. The model's fee is usually two hundred dollars, but since you're such a fan . . . how about three hundred dollars?"

He said, "Fine," with no hesitation.

I said, "Well, if that's fine, and if you're so enthusiastic, how about five hundred dollars?"

"I wish I had that much, because you're worth it. I don't, but here's three hundred dollars," he said and handed me cash.

Gee, what a pleasant client, I thought. I got a washcloth and towel from the bathroom, and some soap and hot water, and all the time he was watching me like a Japanese businessman, but at least he wasn't asking, "What's there? Why you do that?" Instead he was watching raptly, like someone watching a tightrope walker, someone who just can't believe someone could do that.

I unpacked my bag and juggled a little for him, and that seemed to impress him even more. "You can juggle!" he said. "You never mentioned that on TV." Eventually I put the juggling balls down and said, "Well, is that what you want to wear?"

I couldn't suggest that he take off his clothes, or even that he "make himself more comfortable," because that might imply that I wanted to have sex with him.

He said, "Oh, oh! I know what you mean!" He started unbuttoning his shirt. He got down to his T-shirt, and then he said, suddenly, "I can't have sex with you."

"OK," I said.

"It's not that I don't want to have sex with you," he said, "but I'm too nervous." He gestured with one pudgy hand toward his crotch.

"Why don't you sit down and take a few deep breaths? Just relax a little."

He tried to sit down, but he kept bouncing out of the chair. "Well, you're here," he said. "I might as well give it a shot. You said on TV that you charge by the time, and I know our time is running out. I guess we'd better do it.''

Ralph got all undressed and he lay down on the bed. He started getting an erection, and I started undressing myself, but then he looked at me and said, "I can't go through with this," and it went down. "Wait till I tell someone that I saw Dolores French," he said. "Who can I tell? *I* know. I can tell the guy in Raleigh who told me to call your agency. That's who I'll tell. He'll be so impressed." He thought for a few minutes, and I did what I could to assist his erection, which wasn't much.

"Wait, wait, wait," he said. "I can't tell him, because he'll blab it all over town. What a secret!" he said. "At least I've got the picture."

Then he said, "Wait a minute. I can't keep the picture." He got a real sad, puppy-dog look on his face. "I can't let anyone see this," he said. "I'm married."

I was nearly naked by now, wearing nothing but stockings, garter belt, and high heels, and I started doing a little erotic show for him, and he said, "No, this is too much. And my time is running out. I just can't believe that you're here!"

I said, "Look, I've only been here for fifteen minutes. I've got a half an hour left. Maybe you'd like to just chat for the rest of the time."

"That would be swell," he said. He seemed so relieved. "Could I get dressed?" he asked.

"Sure," I said. "Do you want me to get dressed?"

"No!"

"Oh," I teased, "you want to get dressed but you don't want *me* to get dressed."

"I'm cold," he said. "Maybe I'll just put on my T-shirt."

"Sure," I said, and that was the session. He put on his T-shirt and I lay on the bed, nearly nude, and we talked. He wanted to know how I got started in the business.

"That's a long story," I said. "Basically, I was interested in women's rights, and in prostitutes' rights, and I met some women who were working as prostitutes and I liked them. One of the women offered to let me see one of her clients, so I tried it. I thought I'd only do it a few times, just to see what it was like, but I enjoyed it and I've been doing it ever since."

"Did you always want to be a prostitute?" he asked.

| 279 |

"Well, I saw this TV show when I was a little kid . . ." I said.

"And do you enjoy it?" he asked.

"I love it."

We talked until my agent called to tell me his time was up. I got dressed and all ready to leave. I told him that he should hang on to the picture, and maybe he could think of a way to keep it.

"Oh, could I?" he said. "I'd like that."

"You can at least enjoy it for the rest of the evening," I said. "Maybe later, when you calm down, you could enjoy it more. You might even be able to enjoy it again in the morning. Then you can either take it with you, or you can put it in the drawer beside the bed. Look, I'll put my telephone number on it, and if you decide to leave it in the drawer, maybe somebody else will call me."

APPENDIX

In my opinion, a government that cannot provide full employment for women who don't have degrees, and even those who do, has a pretty big nerve making the most lucrative occupation a crime.
—FLO KENNEDY
  Color Me Flo: My Hard Life and Good Times,
  1976

I helped Michael draft an informational pamphlet for the National Task Force on Prostitution. This has been widely distributed. I only wish I had been able to read something like it when I first started working.

PROSTITUTION AND THE LAW

All prostitution is illegal in all fifty states, with the exception of some counties in Nevada, where licensed brothels are legal. If you make the decision to work as a prostitute, you must realize that you will be acting outside the law, and that sooner or later you are likely to be arrested.

State laws vary drastically, as do county and city ordinances. Therefore, anyone working as a prostitute in a large metropolitan area must get to know the ordinances of several municipalities and counties, to be able to tell whether or not their activity is illegal.

This pamphlet is an overview of the laws regarding prostitution and the legal rights of prostitutes. It is not designed to replace legal counsel, however. We urge you to contact an attorney in your area for more precise information.

WHAT IS PROSTITUTION?

The legal definition of prostitution is the exchange of sexual services for anything of value. The term *value* is defined by each state. For instance, some states limit the term only to money, while others broaden it to include anything of any worth. Sexual services include sexual intercourse, oral sex, anal sex, and masturbation.

The laws vary from state to state. In some states, it is illegal to solicit or engage in an act of prostitution, in others it is only illegal to agree to engage in an act of prostitution. In a few states, including New York, it is illegal to patronize a prostitute.

WHO ARE PROSTITUTES?

Any person who offers or, in some states, agrees to exchange, sexual services for anything of value is a prostitute. It is not necessary to accept money, or to actually engage in sexual activity; the mere offer or agreement to do so is the criminal act. Each act of prostitution is a separate criminal offense. You can be arrested on your first time.

The laws against prostitution apply to both men and women—straights, lesbians, and gays—and to people of all ages. In addition, most states' laws apply equally to prostitute and customer, although only about 10 to 15 percent of the people arrested are customers.

WHAT ABOUT TAXES?

If you earn income as a prostitute, you must pay federal and, where applicable, state and local income tax on that income. The tax collectors do not care how you make your money, they just want their share. Failure to pay tax is a sure way to go to jail.

It is a good idea to work with a skilled, professional tax consultant to make sure that you take the proper deductions and pay the appropriate taxes.

WHAT ARE PROSTITUTES ARRESTED FOR?

The most common charge is soliciting or engaging, or, in some states, agreeing to engage in prostitution. In addition, if you work in hotels or bars, you can also be arrested for trespassing. Street prostitutes are arrested for such crimes as loitering, jaywalking, and littering.

Police often stack charges in order to get the individual to plead guilty. For example, if you touch the prospective client, and the client is a vice officer, you can be charged with simple battery. In addition, most communities have ordinances against carrying a concealed weapon, and carrying one, or carrying any illegal drugs, can result in much more serious charges.

If you work with another person, both of you can be charged with pimping or pandering, both of which are often felonies. Finally, any activity that includes crossing state lines to commit prostitution could result in federal charges. This includes traveling with another woman across state lines, or even using the telephone.

WHAT IS ENTRAPMENT?

When a police officer convinces or persuades another person to violate the law, that is entrapment. However, the courts have held that the convincing or persuasion must be so great that it overcomes the person's will not to violate the law. Merely offering money for sex is not considered to be entrapment, even if the police officer names the specific sex act and the price.

Many people believe that if you ask an officer if he is a cop and the officer denies it, that is entrapment. This is a myth. Undercover officers do not have to identify themselves as police officers if asked. In fact, if you ask a prospective client if he is a cop, and he happens to be a police officer, you can be sure that the conversation will be introduced as evidence at the trial to show that you were attempting to avoid detection.

Some escort and modeling agencies require clients to sign statements that they are not police officers. Signing such a statement does not mean that the client is not a police officer, and signing such a statement has not been held to be entrapment.

WHAT SHOULD I DO BEFORE I AM ARRESTED?

Plan ahead. Before beginning to work as a prostitute, consult with an attorney in your area. Find out what acts are legal or illegal in the area where you plan to work. Check back with your lawyer periodically, to find out if there have been any changes in the law.

Find out the cost of a legal defense, and set that money aside.

Go to court and watch what happens. Become familiar with the judicial system, so that when you have to go to court, you will know what is going on.

Find a bail bonding company that will make bonds on prostitution cases. Determine their fees, and give those funds to a trusted friend to hold, along with the name and phone number of the bail bondsperson you spoke with. When you are arrested, your friend can go to the bonding company and get you out of jail. Some jurisdictions allow property bonds or signature bonds (also known as OR, or being let out on one's own recognizance). Find out what is available in your community.

HOW DO I SELECT AN ATTORNEY?

Speak with friends about attorneys they have used. You may also contact the National Task Force on Prostitution, or one of the member organizations, such as COYOTE or HIRE, if there is one in your area. In addition the American Civil Liberties Union (ACLU), National Lawyers Guild, criminal defense lawyers' associations, and state and local bar associations often provide referrals to local attorneys.

Look for a lawyer you can trust and are comfortable speaking with. Since most prostitution arrests are at night, it is a good idea to have an attorney who can be reached at night.

Be honest with your attorney; the attorney cannot help you unless he or she is aware of all the facts.

When you talk with your lawyer, find out what each step in the judicial process entails, and find out what the possible penalties are. Does your community offer pretrial diversion to prostitutes? What are your chances for acquittal if you plead not guilty? What is the mandatory sentence, if any, for a prostitution conviction?

Remember, if you are arrested, it is your case, not your lawyer's. Whatever happens in court, your lawyer will go home afterward. Understand your lawyer's advice and strategy, then decide, together, on your plea and defense.

WHAT DO I DO AFTER I AM ARRESTED?

Cooperate with the arresting officer(s). Do not attempt to escape, fight with, or insult the officer(s). Doing so will get you more serious charges, a higher bond, and a very real possibility of serious bodily injury.

Do not give the police a false name. If you do, it may result in additional charges and a delay in making bond.

Other than general identification information, such as name, address, and birth date, do not speak to the police officers at all. Anything you say, even in a general conversation, can be used against you in court.

Do not sign anything, even if the police tell you that you must, until your lawyer tells you to do so.

Do not give the police permission to search you, your automobile, anything you are carrying, or anything else. Helping the police gather evidence against you will not help you.

Tell the police you want to call your lawyer immediately, and call your lawyer at the first opportunity.

WHAT IS PROBATION?

Basically, probation allows you to serve part or all of a jail sentence outside the confines of a prison. While on probation, you may be required to report to a probation officer and/or attend counseling sessions.

If you are arrested for anything while on probation, no matter how minor the charge, the probation may be revoked, and you will have to spend some time in actual jail. This is true even if you are not guilty of the new charge.

Probation can also be revoked for failing to pay a fine, violating the terms of probation, or failing to report to the probation officer.

Prosecutors often recommend probation as a sentence when they know they could not obtain a conviction in a trial, because they know that any arrest during probation will send the person to jail. Moreover, police officers often go out of their way to arrest people on probation as a way to send them to prison.

Some jurisdictions have what is known as first offender treatment or pretrial diversion. If you are offered this option, and you complete the terms of the diversion without being arrested again, your record will not reflect a conviction, or even, in some cases, an arrest. However, should you fail to complete the terms of the probation, or should you get arrested again before the diversion is completed, you can be given up to the maximum allowable sentence.

It is very risky and difficult to continue to work as a prostitute while on probation. If you intend to keep working, tell your lawyer before the probated sentence is entered.

WHAT ABOUT MANDATORY OR INCENTIVE AIDS/STD TESTING?

Some courts are now allowing for reduced sentences on prostitution convictions if the defendant submits to a test for antibodies to the AIDS virus or for other sexually transmitted diseases. In the short run, this may seem like a good idea. However, be warned that a positive test result could be used as aggravating evidence in a later conviction, and could be used to justify the maximum sentence the next time you are arrested, or even a lifelong quarantine.

It is a good idea to be tested periodically, for AIDS and other sexually transmitted diseases, but only on a voluntary basis, and only where your anonymity and confidentiality will be protected.

WHAT IF I AM A VICTIM OF A CRIME?

It is illegal to rape, rob, or assault a prostitute. If you are a victim of a crime, report it to the police.

If a police officer solicits a bribe, whether sex or money, or beats you during an arrest, report this to the police department's internal affairs division.

Even though you may have a hard time getting your complaint acted on, you have a duty to other prostitutes to stop those who prey on prostitutes. If you fail to report crimes against prostitutes, you give in to the victimization of all prostitutes, including yourself.

HOW WILL MY WORKING AS A PROSTITUTE AFFECT FUTURE EMPLOYMENT?

If you are never arrested or convicted of prostitution or related offenses, your future employment will probably not be affected, and ex-prostitutes work in every occupation.

If you are arrested and convicted, some employers will not hire you because prostitution is considered a sex crime. Even if you are sentenced as a first offender, many jobs, including working with children, may not be available to you. However, some ex-prostitutes have successfully fought such discrimination, including women whose admission to the bar to practice law had been challenged.

WHAT ABOUT IMMIGRATION STATUS?

The Immigration and Naturalization Service (INS) takes a very dim view of prostitution. If you were convicted of prostitution, or even worked legally as a prostitute, prior to coming to this country, they can bar you from entry. If you fail to disclose that you worked as a prostitute, or if you begin working as a prostitute after you immigrate, even if legally, and they find out about it, you could be deported.

If you are arrested and you are not a U.S. citizen, you should contact an immigration attorney immediately.

HOW DOES WORKING AS A PROSTITUTE AFFECT CHILD CUSTODY?

Most courts view prostitutes as people with bad morals, and therefore as bad mothers. If a noncustodial parent, a grandparent, a social worker, or any other interested party wants to challenge your right to custody, the court may change custody solely on the ground that you are a prostitute.

If you are a parent, never work in the place where your children live. Always provide adequate child care for your children, including making provisions in case you are arrested. If you are arrested and your children are not cared for, you could be charged with child neglect and your children could be placed, either temporarily or permanently, in the custody of the state.

If your right to custody is challenged, you should seek an attorney who has successfully represented other women with unconventional sexual lives, such as lawyers who have been successful in lesbian custody cases.

WHAT IS THE NATIONAL TASK FORCE ON PROSTITUTION?

The National Task Force on Prostitution is a coalition of prostitutes' rights organizations. We seek the decriminalization of adult prostitution and other consensual adult commercial sex acts, and full civil and human rights for prostitutes and other sex workers, and their clients.

For more information, or to volunteer, become a member, or make a donation, you may contact the National Task Force on Prostitution, P.O. Box 26354, San Francisco, CA 94126, or P.O. Box 892, Atlanta, GA 30301, or any one of its local affiliates.

HQ 144 .F65 1988

French, Dolores.

Working

STATE LIBRARY OF OHIO
SEO Regional Library
Caldwell, Ohio 43724